THE DOLLMAKERS

THE DOLLMAKERS

A NOVEL FROM THE FALLEN PEAKS

LYNN BUCHANAN

HARPER Voyager
An Imprint of HarperCollins*Publishers*

This is a work of fiction. Names, characters, places, and incidents are products of the author's imagination or are used fictitiously and are not to be construed as real. Any resemblance to actual events, locales, organizations, or persons, living or dead, is entirely coincidental.

HarperCollins books may be purchased for educational, business, or sales promotional use. For information, please email the Special Markets Department at SPsales@harpercollins.com.

FIRST EDITION

Breath Mark symbol, title page illustration, and back matter illustration by Deandra Scicluna
Interior illustrations by Conor Nolan
Map by Isaac Stewart
Designed by Jennifer Chung
Leaf art © andin/stock.adobe.com

Library of Congress Cataloging-in-Publication Data has been applied for.

ISBN 978-0-06-330826-8

24 25 26 27 28 LBC 6 5 4 3 2

For my parents,
who never told me I couldn't be a writer.

THE FIRST DOLLMAKER'S EDICTS

Edict One: Dolls are to serve their masters and perform their purpose of protecting human lives without hesitation from doll *or* dollmaker. The misuse of dolls—especially when such results in the harm or loss of life—is an offense deserving of the highest, and severest, form of punishment.

Edict Two: Dollmakers shall be buried with their dolls. Vigils for the fallen dollmaker are to be held in their last place of residence—no mourners are permitted in the graveyards of those who have dedicated their lives to the fight against the Shod. As reward for their sacrifice, in peace they rest, free of all mortal matters.

Edict Three: Dolls are to be of the finest caliber, crafted to a state as near to perfection as possible before the Breath Mark is placed upon them. To prevail against the Shod, exacting standards in the area of craftsmanship must be kept.

Edict Four: The Shod are stronger than fortresses and can withstand more damage than any living creature before falling. Guard dolls must be made to match such strength.

Edict Five: Artisan dolls are to serve their purchasers as they would their masters. Any dolls deemed incapable of such are to be retained by their creators, or retired from work.

Edict Six: Apprentice dollmakers must adhere to their master's wishes in all matters. Upon passing the Breath Mark exams, an apprentice's education must last at least two years. An apprentice may only study for fifteen years; if at the end of this time they have failed to obtain a license, they must retire from dollmaking.

Edict Seven: The licensing of dollmakers is to be performed only by authorized members of the Licensing Guild. The decision of a licensor is final. Dollmakers may only practice dollmaking under the authority of an officially granted license.

Edict Eight: The Shod are drawn to fine craftsmanship. While anything shaped by the hands of humankind may attract them, most keenly they are enticed by well-made items, using our greatest creations to build themselves into stronger, deadlier forms. As such, be wary of ornateness. And while we must not deny the country called One of art and thus precipitate the death of our souls, know that such will bring the Shod to our doorsteps time and time again. Seek restraint in beauty.

Edict Nine: Dolls are tools, crafted for the protection and comfort of the citizens of One. Do not mistake them for creatures of soul or feeling. A doll's purpose in creation is sacrifice for the well-being of those who created it, be that in fighting the Shod or serving its owners as companion or household servant. Dolls have no other purpose. To think otherwise is true, and fatal, folly.

THE COUNTRY CALLED ONE
THE DESERT CALLED WAVE
THE DOLLMAKER'S GRAVEYARD
THE TOWN CALLED BOG
THE CITY CALLED SHOAL
THE VEIL
THE VILLAGE CALLED WEB
THE FOREST CALLED DEEP
THE CITY CALLED DRIFT
THE CITY CALLED SWAMP
THE CITY CALLED HILLS
THE TOWN CALLED MARSH
THE CITY CALLED CARVED
THE VILLAGE CALLED CREST
THE SEA CALLED CLEAR
THE VILLAGE CALLED TWIG
THE CITY CALLED BOUND
THE CITY CALLED GLASS
THE ROAD CALLED WIDE
THE CITY CALLED RESTED
THE CITY CALLED HIGH
THE HILLS CALLED GREEN
THE CITY CALLED COLORS
THE CITY CALLED SHORE
THE FIELDS CALLED GRAZED
THE CITY CALLED PORTS
THE CITY CALLED PEARL
THE CITY CALLED CRAG
THE OCEAN CALLED WEPT

THE DOLLMAKERS

LICENSOR MATON CONSIDERED HERSELF A PATIENT WOMAN—A LICENSOR HAD to be. Dealing with apprentice dollmakers was an endeavor of headaches; Maton had handled many trying situations in the past, including, but not limited to, extreme outbursts of emotion, fainting spells, and, once, an astonishing bout of spontaneous, unprecedented shrieking.

She had never, however, been ignored for this long. It was hard to tell, given the room she sat in had no windows and thus no view of the sun, but judging solely by the soreness of her legs and the increasing stiffness in the small of her back, Maton guessed she'd been sitting for at least an hour, waiting for her latest client to arrive.

"I'm sure she'll be here soon," Master Nock said. The man sat across the room, cross-legged on a mat identical to Maton's. She wondered if he, too, felt the wood of the floor more keenly than he felt the feathers of his cushion. If he did, such discomfort seemed the least of his concerns; he glanced over his shoulder, neck craning with anxiety. Some time ago he'd sent one of his dolls to collect his apprentice, reassuring Maton as he did that she'd be along right away.

"Perhaps she's taken a wrong turn," Maton said wryly, shifting on aching knees. She touched a hand to the tool belt lying in a heap next to her, missing its familiar weight around her waist. Sorely tempted to put it back on. And leave.

Master Nock turned back toward her, wrinkled face sagging with distress. His eyes gleamed damply in the light of the lanterns held by the dolls standing in the corners of the room.

“Forgive us,” he said.

Maton suppressed a sigh, removing her hand from her belt and smiling, a spike of pity for the man, and an even sharper prick of shame at having worsened his embarrassment, keeping her glued in place. It was hard to maintain irritation when half the source of her upset was so distressingly contrite. “Of course,” she said, waving a dismissive hand. “Don’t trouble yourself.”

Master Nock gave her an appreciative smile, mopping his brow with a handkerchief already limp with sweat. “Shean is a good child, truly. Very confident and hardworking. And talented—she’s by far the most talented of all my apprentices.”

Maton’s eyebrows arched. “All of them?”

Master Nock nodded, the worry on his face easing into a more natural smile. “Yes. Her work is exquisite—I’m excited for you to see it.”

“And I greatly anticipate laying eyes upon it as well,” Maton said, and for all the dryness of her tone she meant it. For Master Nock, with his fifty years’ worth of experience as dollmaker and teacher, to speak of a student so highly, she must be extraordinary. Though, in all fairness, Maton had yet to meet a dollmaker who *didn’t* lavish praises upon their final apprentice.

“You say she comes from a family of dollmakers?” Maton asked, relenting to the burn of her knees and moving her legs out from under her, crossing them to mirror Master Nock’s pose. She rubbed at the numb lumps of her anklebones.

Maton wasn’t in the habit of asking questions about those she was to license—knowing too much about an apprentice was a dangerous thing, as excess knowledge might influence a licensing decision. But she was fed up with sitting here in silence, studying the polished red stone of the walls, pretending to be overly interested in the decorative rug spread across the floor. Even gazing at Master Nock's dolls had grown tiresome—one could only marvel at the legendary, faceless figures for so long before their broad shoulders, sturdy legs, and root-thick arms (perfectly suited for crushing the Shod) began to bore.

"Yes," Master Nock said. He relaxed a fraction, hands clasping in front of him and lowering to rest in his lap. "Shean's parents and elder brother were comrades of mine. When they were swept away in the Red Tide, I didn't hesitate to take her as my final apprentice."

Maton's hands stilled in their massage of her ankles. She spoke quietly, and with proper reverence. "The Red Tide?"

Master Nock sighed, head hanging and eyes closing. "Yes. I often regret that I wasn't the one taken by the Shod that day, rather than her family. So many young dollmakers killed. So much wasted talent and potential. Shean's parents were themselves a tragedy, but her brother . . . that poor boy. He was practically still a child. He'd just vowed with another young dollmaker, a beautiful crafter who also failed to survive the Tide."

Maton regretted breaking her rule about questions. Her irritation was ebbing, giving way to pity and unearned leniency. Having the status of an orphan was no excuse for being late to a licensing. No excuse for making a kind old master like Master Nock sit here steeped in embarrassment, reliving bad memories, taking the brunt of his apprentice's rudeness toward Maton and her guild.

But still. An orphan of the Red Tide, the greatest tragedy to befall the city called Pearl—to befall the entire country called One, for that matter. That couldn't be easy.

"How old was she?" Maton asked.

"Barely six years of age. She doesn't remember her family outside of snatches of voices, dreams of faces. Even her memories of the Shod are hazy; she struggles to describe what she saw in the Tide, and, outside of the occasional nightmare, has lived untouched by the terror of that day. Truly, in many ways Shean is a miracle child—to have survived the Tide when so young, and to not suffer from the trauma experienced by the other children of the city who lived! I've done my best in the past fifteen years to make certain she grew up free of her past." Master Nock lifted his clasped hands in front of him, head bowed. "For me, her strength and happiness are the one scrap of good to come from my own survival."

"I see," Maton said. Her hands came together in her lap, fingers lacing and squeezing. "I understand."

And she did. Why this Shean was special, why Master Nock was willing to tolerate her tardiness.

Why Maton herself would continue to wait.

Survivors of the Red Tide, especially the young ones, were to be handled with the utmost care. That was an unspoken and universal rule amongst dollmakers, and a rule that applied especially to someone like Maton, who'd been too far away from the city called Pearl to help fight the Shod that day. Her only part in the Tide had come later, when she'd traveled to the city to aid in rebuilding. And to help gather, count, and identify corpses.

"I'm sure she'll be here soon," Master Nock said again, voice thin. Maton smiled.

"Yes."

An awkward silence fell then, Master Nock gazing down at his hands and Maton quiet, at a loss for what more could be said. Long minutes trickled by, the only sound to be heard the faint drip of melting candles in lanterns.

When Maton was starting to feel sore again from sitting too long,

Master Nock cleared his throat, pushing himself to his feet with an audible pop of stiff joints.

"Perhaps I'll go and—"

The door opened, cutting Master Nock off with a whoosh of fresh air and the clatter of doorframes colliding. The candles guttered, reacting to the breeze that entered the room alongside a young woman.

"Shean!" Master Nock exclaimed, the relief in his voice giving his words a tremor. He stepped toward the young woman, taking her shoulders in his hands. "What's taken you so long?"

Curious, Maton rocked to the side, peering around Master Nock for a better look. She watched Shean give her master an unapologetic smile.

She looked to be around the age Maton had been during the Red Tide—early into her twenties. Her hair was done in the latest style, the left side braided back while the right fell in a silken mass down past her shoulder and neck, so long the midnight strands brushed her waist. From her left ear dangled a spiderweb-thin strand of silver, on the end of which hung one of the large black pearls this city was known for.

Maton was shocked by the earring—such a masculine accessory contrasted starkly with Shean's looks, as well as the dress she wore: a gown with a high collar, fitted bodice, and a skirt that fell past her ankles. Long, tight sleeves swirled down her arms in alternating patterns of silver and transparent gauze, an intricate design of skin and silk. Over her shoulders draped a shawl the same rich blue as the highlights on her dress.

It was the most overdressed Maton had ever seen an apprentice be for their licensing. With all that silk and silver, even in the muted light of the room Shean glinted. She shimmered like cut diamond when she moved, stepping forward and tugging a wheeled doll case into the room before turning and closing the door behind her. Maton eyed the case: hawthorn wood, decorated with metal ornamentations that depicted a golden carp being plucked from a river of copper by the tungsten talons of a kestrel. The box was tall enough to contain a medium-sized child.

"I apologize for my tardiness," Shean said. Her voice was lilting and surprisingly deep. There was a rhythm to her speech similar to poetry, as if she'd rehearsed what she was saying. "I was on my way here when I was overtaken by the most powerful creative urge. The spirit of genius overwhelmed me, and I had no choice but to rush back to my room and realize the inspiration, which guided me to alter the doll I'll present today. When I show you my work, you'll understand why I couldn't resist this call. You'll appreciate that I didn't." She looked past Master Nock, aiming her smile at Maton. "Surely you understand?"

Maton returned the smile, hoping she didn't look as ingenuine as she felt. "Of course. Inspiration is often a dollmaker's greatest tool."

"A tool that comes only to the best of dollmakers," Shean amended. The edge of Maton's lips twitched.

What a mouth this one had.

"Very well, Shean," Master Nock said, mopping his forehead with his soggy handkerchief. He urged her forward. "Now that you're here, let's not make Licensor Maton wait any longer."

Shean yielded to her master's herding, pushing her doll case across the room and following along behind it, moving past Master Nock and stopping in front of Maton. She nudged the case aside and knelt with an elegant billow of shawl, hair falling forward across her face and hiding one dark eye. With a bit of a shuffle she settled, folding her hands in her lap.

Finally, Maton thought. "Master Nock," she said, looking up at the man. "If you would please wait outside."

"Of course," Master Nock said, lowering his head in respect before exiting. Eager to be done with this assignment, Maton wasted no time—before the door had fully shut behind him she began the licensing.

"Apprentice Shean," she said. "My name is—"

"Licensor Maton," Shean interrupted. "I know." She had the same smile on her face that she'd been wearing since arriving. The sight of her teeth was beginning to irritate.

"Of course," Maton said. Willing herself to be calm, she skipped past the traditional introduction between licensor and apprentice, forgoing speaking words that'd been recited for a hundred years, a ritual retained even when so many others had fallen out of use and been forgotten—she'd already spent far too much time here, and while she felt compassion for Master Nock, her patience with his apprentice was wafer thin. And growing thinner. So instead of reciting the speech all apprentice dollmakers worked tirelessly to have recited to them one day, Maton simply said, "Allow me to congratulate you on completing your training with Master Nock. What you've accomplished is—"

"Thank you," Shean said. She was staring at Maton's tool belt.

"Excuse me?" Maton said, voice flat.

Shean looked up, eyes gleaming. "Thank you. I appreciate the compliment." She cocked her head to the side, eyebrows raised expectantly, as if to say, *Get on with it.*

To think Maton had been excited to have the honor of being the licensor for the final apprentice of the great Master Nock. If she'd known said apprentice was going to be so late for the appointment, and turn out to be . . . well, *this*, she would've insisted one of the junior licensors come. Let someone younger spend ten days traveling to the city called Pearl and then sit in this stuffy room waiting for hours, compelled to patience by Master Nock's reputation. Let someone else be interrupted and looked down upon by this young woman who was, clearly, still very much a child.

Maton's hand returned to her tool belt, grip tight. She had half a mind to stand up and leave.

She'd had half that mind for half an hour, though. Taking a deep, steadying breath, she recalled the apprentice from some ten years ago who'd been so nervous he'd vomited all over her tools. It was much better, she reminded herself, to have a rude apprentice to license than a nauseated one. Maton looked back at Shean and did what licensors did best—handled her.

"I see you're very eager, Shean," she said. "You must be excited to receive your license."

Shean nodded, beaming, leaning forward. Her cheeks flushed with anticipation.

"Well, seeing as you've been kept from your license a few more hours than intended already, let's go straight to the assessment, shall we?" Maton sat up straight, palms pressed flat to her knees. "Please present the doll you've selected as your licensing piece."

"As you wish, Licensor Maton," Shean intoned, only now deigning to exchange traditional words. She stood on her knees and turned, pulling the doll box toward her and undoing the latch of the case. The front swung forward, toward Maton, hiding her view of what lay within the container until the doll stepped out, and Shean pushed the case back and away. Maton caught her breath.

The doll was beautiful. At least four feet tall (putting it on the larger side for dolls) and, like most dolls, possessing the general proportions and shape of an adult human. Unlike most dolls, though, great care had been taken to give this doll a very realistic, human face: slightly parted lips painted the shade of pink found inside seashells, a thin and delicate nose, a set of low-lidded eyes made with opal and onyx and a blue stone for the irises that Maton had no name for. The features were perfectly proportioned, complemented by the sweep of painted eyebrows and the presence of long white hair made from horse mane imported from the country called Fields. The doll was even wearing clothing—a hand-stitched ensemble of silk and cotton, a jacket embroidered with leaping cats buttoned over a plain black shirt that fell to the doll's knees, its legs clad in fitted trousers and its feet left bare. Meticulous work, from head to toe.

Maton had seen dolls like this before, but never up close—only in the windows of luxury toy shops she passed on the street. Gorgeous mannequins intended as companions for lonely children or servants for large, wealthy families. Dolls more lifelike than any used as guards for cities and towns and travelers; dolls made to be as close to human as possible.

There were laws in place concerning the treatment of dolls like this one. Such were deemed artistic masterpieces and were accordingly expected to be handled with great care. An expectation Maton kept in mind as she lifted herself up on her knees, shuffling off her kneeling cushion. With reverence she picked up the doll's hand, inspecting long, delicate fingers, each one complete with an artificial fingernail buffed to a realistic sheen. The doll's palms were carved with lines so lifelike, Maton found herself surprised when she pressed her hand to the doll's and felt wood instead of skin. She slid her fingers up the doll's arm, pushing back the sleeve of its jacket to inspect the elbow joint. Long minutes of careful study passed before she found the line that indicated where two pieces of wood had been fastened together.

Letting go of the doll's arm, Maton next inspected its legs, rolling up its pants and urging its knee to bend. Then she pushed the white hair off its shoulders to study its neck, amazed to find that everything from its head down to its waist was carved from one piece of wood. And yet the doll could tilt its head to the side in a very natural way—it was rare that a dollmaker was able to achieve that effect without separate pieces for the head and neck. This doll was truly quality work.

"The Breath Mark?" Maton asked, fingers smoothing flat the collar of the doll's jacket, straightening it from where her inspection had knocked it askew.

"On his back," Shean said.

Maton nodded. She picked the doll up, grunting softly to find it heavier than it looked; a solid creature, to be sure. Once she'd turned the doll to stand with its back to her, she pulled up its jacket and shirt, exposing the pearly slope of its shoulders. Along the curve where its spine would be, in the small of the doll's back, a single black symbol was drawn in nine smooth, clean lines.

The Breath Mark had no meaning—it wasn't part of a language. Not a language anyone knew or could read in the way words written in books were known and read, that is; its function was known through the knowledge of past dollmakers, passed down five generations of craftworkers in a direct line from the First Dollmaker himself. From this heritage, combined with personal experience, every dollmaker knew that a properly drawn Breath Mark made a doll stir and sit up, lifting itself to its feet to obey the commands of its creator. And so, though it didn't resemble any word in the language of the country called One, this symbol was the Breath Mark—that which inspired movement.

It was subtle. At first Maton thought she was imagining it. But the longer she stared at the Mark on the back of Shean's doll, the more she was certain; though the Mark was the familiar, nonsensical arrangement Maton knew, the lines had been tweaked, ever so slightly, to all bend upward, to spread out a bit to the left and the right. The longer one looked at this Mark, the more it resembled a mouth, open to take a breath.

A stylized Breath Mark. That was a clever thing to do, creating a picture out of the symbol without compromising its fundamental shape and rendering it useless. A risky move. But one that had, for Shean, paid off—Maton had never met a dollmaker, apprentice *or* master, who could tweak the Breath Mark and have a doll that still animated. Despite herself, she was impressed.

Maton sat back, allowing the doll's clothing to drop back into place. She lifted and turned the doll to face her. Staring into its jeweled eyes, she saw her own reflection in a patina of blue and black and white.

The doll blinked. A small gesture, but so natural and intelligent Maton shivered.

This doll . . . one could almost believe it was alive.

Maton closed her eyes, shaking her head to clear it of foolish thoughts. No matter what they looked like, dolls weren't people. They didn't think or feel or get offended when a stranger ran her fingers over their body. Dolls were tools, the creations of dollmakers, meant to either keep the Shod at bay or look pretty in a shop window. That was basic dollmaker knowledge; one of the edicts of the trade to never forget, lest one make the mistake of falling in love with one's own creations, or growing infatuated with the masterpieces of others.

Respect dolls, yes. Acknowledge their importance as the only weapon effective against the Shod, treat them well for their services, and trust them to perform their duties. But never view them as human. For dollmakers, this was one of the first tenets apprentices learned.

Feeling silly for having to remind herself of such basic truth, Maton shuffled away from the doll, settling back on her cushion and meeting Shean's eager gaze. It took her a moment to recall what came next in the licensing process, head hazy from the beauty of the doll, the effort it took to resist the urge to just sit and gaze at it for hours.

"You have your designs?" she asked.

"Yes," Shean said, reaching into the case her doll had stepped out from and producing a design book, which she flipped open and handed to Maton. For a moment Maton studied the diagrams drawn on the offered pages, unsurprised to find Shean's design work meticulous, detailed, and thorough—everything from the doll's face to its clothing was depicted and planned out with exactness, extensive notes written alongside turnaround sketches and material lists and piece-by-piece drafts of every limb and joint and feature. Looking at the plans, Maton could imagine the effort that'd gone into making this doll; hours and hours of extremely painstaking, difficult work.

Closing the book, Maton handed it back to Shean with an approving nod. She gestured to the doll. "Please make it move," she said.

Shean bobbed her head, turning to her doll with a brisk "Walk."

The doll obeyed, spinning on a heel and pacing back and forth in front of Maton. Its movements were elegant, with none of the jerk and wobble lesser dolls exhibited. Maton wasn't surprised that this doll mimicked a human's mannerisms more closely than any doll she'd ever assessed.

"That's enough," she said.

"Stop," Shean said, and the doll moved back to its original spot in front of Maton.

"Are all of your dolls this large?" Maton asked, arms folding across her chest. To her relief, her awe was wearing off, her thoughts settling into the familiar procedures that came with awarding a license to an apprentice.

Shean shook her head. "Silver is the largest doll I've ever made. Most are smaller."

Silver was the doll's name. *That suits it*, Maton thought. Aloud she said, "How much smaller?"

Shean lifted her hands, holding them roughly a foot apart. "This big," she said. She pushed her hands together until they were only a few inches from touching. "To this small." Her hands dropped. "I'm confident that I can create more of this size, however."

"How long do your smaller dolls take to make?"

"I can make four to five in two weeks. At least two a week."

"And how long did this one take?" Maton asked, indicating Silver.

"A month."

That was reasonable. A month for something this exquisite . . . that timing might even be astonishing.

Maton gazed at Silver. Then she said, "If I may ask, what was the addition to this doll that contributed to your tardiness?"

If Shean caught the edge of ice in the words, she didn't show it. Which was no great shock; Maton had a feeling Shean didn't hear anything she didn't want to. Smiling pleasantly, she reached out, tapping Silver's cheek. The doll turned its head, allowing Shean to pull the hair back from its face, tucking the white strands behind its ear. Shean pointed.

"That," she said.

Studded in the doll's ear was a large black pearl. Painted along the ridge of the ear were intricate black lines, swoops and swirls of ornamentation that weren't quite dry, still wet and glossy in places.

"It seemed a shame, not giving him a pearl to wear," Shean said, drawing Maton's attention. The young woman flicked a finger against her own earring, making the jewelry sway back and forth like a pendulum. "I had to work slowly while I was drilling a hole for the earring, though, or risk cracking the wood."

A detail that won't be noticed unless pointed out, Maton thought. That *is why you had me waiting here for so long? How frivolous. Even if it* does *suit him.*

Aloud she said, "I see." As she spoke she reached for her tool belt, pulling it out in front of herself. She smoothed a hand over the belt, fingers moving across the bulging pouches, tracing the shapes of her tools while she went over what she'd done so far: the inspection of the doll and its Breath Mark, a study of the apprentice's designs, the request to watch the doll move, questions of size and construction time. Inquiry concerning ornamentation.

In terms of the lengths Maton went to put on a convincing show, each apprentice was different. For Shean, she'd drawn out the inspection part of this licensing because the young woman seemed that type—the type to want to talk about her work, and to have her work admired. Had Maton admired enough, though, to make it seem the licensing depended on that admiration? She glanced up at Shean and found the young woman's attention locked on the tool belt, expression eager. Confident.

Cocky, even.

Yes, Maton decided. *That's enough*. She straightened, cleared her throat, and moved to the very last, most important, part of the licensing assessment. "We're almost finished here, Apprentice Shean. All that's left is for Silver and myself to have a moment alone."

"Of course," Shean said, standing and bowing and excusing herself in one, unprotesting movement. Of course she didn't protest; no dollmaker in her right mind would resist a tradition passed down from the First Dollmaker himself.

She *would* have protested, though, if she knew what Maton was about to do. Any apprentice would. Protest, or devise some way to manipulate the outcome of the private conference between their licensor and their doll.

The members of the Licensing Guild were the secret-keepers of the dollmakers. The truth hoarders and knowledge monitors, the safeguards of all research conducted on the Shod. Maton knew *everything*—even what the Research Guild, the only private, invitation-only guild in all of One, knew. And yet, despite all the privileged information she was given—and notwithstanding the realities she'd been taught that kept her up at night, agonizing over impossibilities and frustrating veracities—the licensing ceremony was the greatest of all secrets. A secret that protected the very structure of dollmaker society and, thus, the very core of the systems in place to maintain and protect the country called One. A secret no licensor would ever surrender, even at the cost of her life.

Which was why, per her oath as a licensor, Maton had never, and would never, tell anyone, not even her own family, what the last step of a licensing assessment was.

The door to the room closed behind Shean. Maton stood and checked that no crack in the door had been left, no peepholes to sneak a look or press an ear against present in any of the room's walls. When she was satisfied she returned to Silver, sitting down in front of him.

"All right," Maton said, voice hushed. She gestured for Silver to sit, which he did, mirroring her cross-legged pose and posture, his face adopting a look she suspected was similar to her own expression. She smiled at his imitation, feeling herself relax. This was the part of the licensing process Maton enjoyed, the part that made dealing with high-maintenance apprentices and fretful masters worth it. She folded her hands in her lap, voice gentling.

"I have a question for you."

Silver smiled and nodded. His lack of surprise was no shock—most dolls knew about this part of the licensing. As if they were made, in part, for this moment.

Maton leaned forward, and, though she was sure none but the doll could hear her, spoke the question she'd been taught to ask in a whisper: "Are you made to fight the Shod?"

Silver's smile grew. And then, to Maton's surprise, he winked.

She'd never seen a doll wink before—nor lift a finger to its lips as Silver did now, as if to shush her. Such human gestures, lifelike to a degree that took her aback, a prickle of emotion caught between unease and delight brushing her. Half of her—the silly half—expected him to answer her aloud, speaking even though she knew full well dolls didn't have the ability to speak. So, of course, he didn't; he responded the way all dolls did when she asked them this question—mutely. And, in this specific case, with a single, firm, and negating shake of the head.

And that was that. Pushing aside the distraction of Silver's strange mannerisms, Maton refocused, nodding her understanding. She stood, walking to the door and opening it to find Shean and Nock speaking to one another.

"—going well?" Nock said in hushed tones.

Shean nodded, answering in a normal voice. "Of course." She noticed Maton and turned, smiling. "Finished already, Licensor?"

"Yes," Maton said, gesturing for Shean to return to the room. She nodded to Nock as she closed the door behind his apprentice, and he returned the favor, a relieved look on his face.

Shean took up her position kneeling on the ground, Silver moving to sit at her side. Maton sat across from them.

"Apprentice Shean," she said, "I commend you—what you've shown me today is very good work."

Maton almost said something more complimentary than "good," such as "impressive" or "breathtaking." Then she felt a twinge in her back, recalled just how long she'd been sitting in this room, and decided to forgo unnecessary compliments.

"I'll now award you your license."

Shean lifted her hands, fingers clasped in front of her. "Thank you, Licensor Maton!"

Maton inclined her head in acknowledgment of the appreciation, reaching for her tool belt. She pulled out the needed materials: a palm-sized, flat piece of rectangular wood, two of her branding pipes, and her box of tobacco and matches.

When it came to license making, there was no rushing things. Maton picked up her licensing pipe, the skinniest of her pipes and light in her hand despite the metal brand welded to its end. She loaded and lit the pipe, lifting it to her lips. She puffed her cheeks out like billows as she inhaled, holding the smoke in her mouth and blowing it back out into the pipe with a burn and rush that made her eyes water. It took three more strong, steady puffs before the brand on the end of the pipe flared a malevolent red.

Once she saw that glow, Maton lowered the pipe, picking up the blank wooden card in front of her. With practiced precision she pressed the glowing end of the licensing pipe to the bottom right corner of the card, producing a white-gray smoke and filling the air with a sweet, scorched scent. After counting three heartbeats she lifted the pipe, setting the smoldering license on a knee. She picked up the second pipe, which was thicker and heavier, displaying a dollmaker brand on its end. She repeated the process, lighting and puffing and searing, adding a master-status symbol to Shean's license.

Careful not to tip any ashes or embers onto the floor, Maton placed her pipes next to her tool belt, lifting the completed license and checking that the brands were legible. She brushed her fingers over the markings, touching the symbol in the center of the card, flicking bits of ash off the thin lines of the stylized spider lily that spread out in burned black across the red wood. Then she tidied her licensor seal, making sure the shape of the faceless doll holding a leaf over its head—which she'd taken on as her personal crest years ago, at her own licensing—was unmistakable.

When Maton was satisfied, she held the completed license out. "Congratulations, Master Shean," she said.

Shean beamed as she took the offering. "Thank y—"

She cut off, smile dropping. A crease appeared between her eyebrows, a furrow to match the sudden, tight press of her lips.

"This is wrong," she said.

"Is it?" Maton said, and she had to suppress a sigh. What was the young woman fussing about *now*?

"This is an artisan's license," Shean said, voice flat.

"Correct."

Shean looked up, a smile on her face. An angry smile. "I'm a *guard* dollmaker."

Maton's eyebrows lifted in surprise. "With a doll like that?" She gestured to Silver, and Shean's eyes darkened with offense.

"Yes. With a doll like that."

This was unexpected. Maton had assumed a dollmaker capable of making something as beautiful as Silver would already know what her license would be—he was art, after all, and, thus, the work of an artisan.

Evidently, she'd been mistaken. Maton studied Shean for a moment, trying to decide what to do. Of course, she couldn't tell Shean that Silver himself had chosen this license for her—if word got out that dolls chose licenses for their creators, all sorts of underhanded schemes would break out. With some (rare) exceptions, dolls did as they were told; if an apprentice was frightened they'd be given a license they didn't want, all they'd have to do was order whatever doll they were presenting to answer their licensor's question one way or another. The way Shean would've, Maton suspected, had she any idea of the Licensing Guild's great secret.

Ah, well. Maton was used to bluffing. In this case, doing so wasn't even difficult. She shook her head and spoke kindly. "Your work is far too delicate for guard work, Master Shean. Your dolls wouldn't last a moment against the Shod."

Shean's hands twisted on her license, fingers arching lines against the wood. "Delicate doesn't mean weak."

"I didn't say that," Maton said, frowning.

"Yes, you did." Shean's voice raised a fraction, lifted a pitch. "You said my dolls are too fragile to be guards."

"From what I can see," Maton said, glancing at Silver, "your work isn't built in a manner conducive to fending off the Shod. That doesn't mean they're weak. I'm sure your dolls will hold up just fine in the presence of children who wish to play with them, and, based on how well this one obeys you, I'm confident they'll complete housework duties set to them by owners efficiently. That's why—"

"I *know* my work doesn't resemble the traditional guard doll," Shean said. "But just because they don't *look* like guard dolls—"

"This is not simply about how your dolls look," Maton interrupted, patience flagging and, with it, her good sense.

Shean glared. "Then what *is* this about?"

Maton had made a mistake. She blamed it on her exhaustion, her impatience, how finished she was with this drawn-out licensing. She set her jaw.

"This is about the fact that I am a licensor," she said, deploying her best excuse when it came to covering up such slips: her title. "My word is final."

But, of course, this declaration wasn't enough for Shean of Pearl.

"My dolls are meant to face the Shod," Shean said. Her eyes burned. "That's why I created them."

"I'm telling you, your work can't—"

"And how would you know that?" Shean snapped, throwing the license she held to the floor. She scowled, voice an accusation. "Have you seen my dolls face a Shod?"

Maton's patience cracked down the middle. Such belligerence. Such arrogance. In all the years, of all the spoiled, selfish apprentices . . . !

Before she could stop herself, Maton spoke her mind. "No. I haven't. And I hope to never see such a thing—*especially* if one of your dolls is meant to be protecting *me* from the Shod."

Shean leapt to her feet, flushed. "How *dare* you!"

Maton stood as well, temper rising. She flung a hand out to indicate the dolls standing in the corners of the room, still as statues and just as forgettable until now. She pointed at their large statures, their thick and sturdy limbs.

"Look at your master's work," she said, biting back the urge to shout. "Can you not see the difference between these dolls, *guard* dolls, and your own?"

"Not all dolls must be faceless and ugly to be effective!"

"I agree. But dolls used as guards against the Shod must be strong enough to protect the cities they patrol." *And they must tell me they're meant to fight*, she added, silently.

"My dolls *are* strong enough—I made them intelligent enough to outwit the Shod!"

"Outwit?" Maton echoed, amazed. "The Shod are mindless; they feel nothing but rage and have enough strength to act on that rage to deadly effect. There's no spark of intelligence *to* outwit!"

Maton may have said more, but before she could the door to the room opened, Master Nock rushing in with a worried look on his face. "I heard shouting! What's the matter?"

Shean spun to him, voice a snarl. "Master, tell her! Tell her she's mistaken!"

"Mistaken?" Master Nock looked from Shean to Maton and back again. "Mistaken how?" The color drained from his face. "Don't tell me you've failed your licensing—"

"Of course not!" Shean interrupted. She jabbed a finger at Maton, the motion making the shawl on her shoulders slip, falling down to dangle from her arms. "This half-wit licensor gave me an *artisan* license!"

Master Nock stared at Shean. "Is that . . . is that a problem?"

Shean's mouth opened, but no sound came out. Her arm lowered, hand dropping to hang slack at her side. "A problem?" she echoed, whispering. The dumbfounded look on her face cleared, and she shouted. "I'm not an artisan! I'm your apprentice! You, who are the greatest of all the guard dollmakers of Pearl! I make dolls like you—dolls that will save people from the Shod!"

Master Nock looked dismayed. Maton didn't blame him—she'd be upset, too, if she'd failed to impress on one of her students the realities of their talent.

"We're finished here," Maton said, kneeling to gather her things. She did so quickly, emptying the ashes of her pipes into a small container and replacing her tools in her belt, which she then clipped secure around her waist. She stood.

"Reconsider," Shean said, turning away from Master Nock. It wasn't a plea—her voice was ice, her glare burning flame.

When Maton looked at the young woman she felt mixed emotions. Annoyance. But also pity. She stepped forward, resting her hand on Shean's shoulder.

"There's no shame in being an artisan," she said. "Toymakers give their clients happiness and provide dutiful servants for those in need of them. You'll be able to continue to develop your craft and skill by making such dolls, and I'm confident that in doing so you'll become a dollmaker known not only in your own time, but in the times of dollmakers to come. After all, many beautiful pieces of art have been made by artisan dollmakers; art that far outlives guard dolls in the stories of history." She smiled. "And, besides—we are in a time of peace, with the Shod causing so few problems in recent years. Now is the best time for beautiful, artful dolls to be made. Now is *your* time."

Shean slapped Maton's hand away, words a sneer and face twisted with disdain. "I care nothing for children's bobbles and frivolous aesthetic pieces. My aspirations transcend such a petty employ of dollmaking. I intend to dedicate my life to protecting the people of the country called One from a threat that, no matter how quiet it's been of late, will never cease to terrorize. I'll accept nothing less!"

"You must accept it," Maton said, smile dropping. She walked past Shean, toward where Master Nock still stood in the doorway, looking paler by the second. "Your work is suited for nothing else."

Shean's hand clamped on Maton's wrist, yanking her to a stop.

"*No.*"

"Release me."

"Not until you reconsider."

"I will not."

"You will."

"No, I *won't*."

"Say you'll give me a guard license," Shean said. Her fingers clenched hard enough to bruise.

"*No.*" Maton yanked her arm from Shean, stepping back and speaking firmly. "I strongly encourage you, Master Shean, to stop this. Give up on being a guard—it will *not* happen. Accept your place in this world and learn to do the best that you can with the skills you possess. Don't chase after impossible dreams. To do so would be a waste of your talents."

Shean's face slackened. It blanked, like a design sketch erased from a chalkboard. For a moment Maton thought she'd finally reached the young woman, that her words had, at last, struck a chord.

Then Shean grabbed Maton's wrist, yanking her forward. Shean's arm wound back. Master Nock cried out, and Maton realized what was about to happen a moment before Shean punched her in the face.

MASTER NOCK KNELT IN FRONT OF THE GATES TO HIS SCHOOL, BENT DOUBLE ON THE dirty cobbles of the street in a posture that made his old back injury flare. Night had fallen, the sun replaced by stars and street lanterns that cast an egg-yolk haze upon the world, a diffused light barely enough to see by. In front of him stood Licensor Maton, her travel elk standing at the ready beside her, saddled and prepared for departure. For what felt the hundredth time, he said, "Please forgive me."

"I forgive you for nothing, as I blame you for nothing," Maton said, voice thick and strained. Master Nock lifted his eyes to her and immediately dropped them, incapable of looking at the swelling and bruising around the woman's nose and left eye without his own eyes filling with tears. "Your apprentice should be the one apologizing."

"She can't be reasoned with right now," Master Nock said. In confirmation of his words, at that moment Shean's voice rose from the school in a distant shriek, followed by a crash and an ominous shattering noise. Nock closed his eyes, a nauseating mixture of disappointment, embarrassment, and sorrow overwhelming him. He planted his hands on the ground and lowered his face until he was inhaling dirt.

"Accept my apologies on her behalf!"

"I refuse. She'll be forgiven, or not, when *she* apologizes." A pause. A sigh. "Please, Master Nock. Stand up."

Conceding defeat to both the licensor and his apprentice, Nock took Maton's offered hand, allowing her to help him to his feet. Standing was an endeavor almost as difficult as kneeling had been, the joints of his body burning and aching as he rose, his back popping and sending a sharp spark of pain through his spine.

Ignoring this discomfort, as well as the distressing smear of dirt and dust upon his clothing, Nock forced himself to look at Maton. The damage to her face was even worse up close—the red of her skin putrid, her nose starting to purple, her eye swelled shut and oozing a trickle of thick, milky tears. To Nock, Maton had always been youthful; close to middle-aged, but clear-faced enough to still look a young woman. Now, though, her damaged face showed its age, its weariness apparent in its injury. She looked tired.

"Your mind can't be changed?" he asked, miserable.

Maton shook her head. "No dollmaker is deserving of a license when they conduct themselves in such a manner." She rested a hand on her tool belt, on the pouch into which she'd shoved Shean's license. "And, besides—would she want this license back, the license of an artisan, even if I offered it?"

Nock lifted a hand to cover his eyes. "I don't understand," he said, voice wretched. "I never told her that I was training her to be a guard. I thought I made it clear to her, what manner of work her dolls were meant for."

"Did you ever expressly tell her that she would be an artisan? Did you ever look at her dolls, turn to her, and tell her what you thought they were suited for, that they would best serve the world as companions rather than protectors?"

Nock dropped his hand, eyes on the ground. "No. I . . . Shean's so clever. It never even *occurred* to me . . ."

Nock trailed off. He had to, because what he was saying, if not a lie, was a shameful truth. A terrible admittance, because he *should've* known. After all these years spent raising Shean, teaching Shean, fostering her talent, he knew her as well as he'd know his own child. He should've guessed her thoughts. He should've seen this coming.

But he, like a blind fool, truly and painfully hadn't.

Maton waited for Nock to go on. When he didn't, wallowing in his own miserable silence, she said, "It would've been wise to discuss this with her. But I'm afraid it's too late for that—I have no choice but to report this incident to the Licensor Head."

Nock's heart sank. "What will happen to her?" he asked.

"In the worst case, she'll be marked as unfit for work and denied a second licensing. She's young, so I doubt that'll happen. But it *is* a possibility—assaulting a licensor is no small offense." Behind Maton her elk stirred, spooked by some small noise and sidestepping, cloven hooves tapping the street cobbles. She lifted a hand, patting the animal's neck and stroking its blond fur as she continued. "More likely she'll be suspended from a second licensing for a set amount of time."

"How long?"

"I've heard of cases as short as a week and as long as five years. It'll depend on what the Head decides is best, after hearing my report."

Nock nodded. He saw no point in arguing—of all the guilds of dollmakers in One, licensors were the least tolerant of having their ways questioned. But he did say one last thing, making one final effort to impress upon Maton how desperately he wished Shean spared from the harshest judgment.

"She's my last apprentice. The most talented of any child I've trained. I truly believe she's destined for greatness as a dollmaker."

Maton turned, reaching up to grip the pommel of her elk's saddle. She spoke over her shoulder.

"Perhaps that's something you *shouldn't* have told her."

Maton pulled herself onto her elk. She clicked her tongue to urge the steed forward, and the elk obeyed the request without hesitation, taking off at a leaping run down the street. Nock watched Maton bound down the hill on which his school had stood for the past fifty years. He watched her go with hands clasped before him, fingers twisted together with an anguish he didn't know how to quell. When the sound of elk hooves on stone faded, and he could no longer see even the faintest outline of Maton moving through the winding streets of Pearl, Nock turned and reentered his school.

HE FOUND SHEAN IN THE PROCESS OF DESTROYING HER ROOM.

Wall hangings ripped down and torn apart, lying in sad, curling strips across the ground. The stand Nock had made for Shean's twelfth birthday was tipped over, the books and scrolls she'd collected over the years scattered everywhere, covers bent, half unrolled and boasting crumpled edges where angry heels had stomped them. A decorative urn from the city called Colors had been removed from its display stand and dropped, its neck broken from its wide, glazed torso.

The only exceptions to the destruction were the potted plants and flower vases Shean kept on every flat surface of the room (her "garden")—those had, with great care and deliberation, been set on a table shoved into the far left corner of the room, over a dozen pots arranged in close quarters, with several more spread out along the windowsill next to the table. Lacy leaves of turquoise blue and rich, deep purples, crimson stems and airy, yellow choke blossoms, all placed out of range of her ire and untouched. Which was a relief; if any of the delicate glass containers she kept those plants in shattered, she'd run the risk of cutting herself to ribbons.

But there was no threat of that. Shean loved her plants. She said they were living beauty, and that she couldn't decide what pleased her more: their aesthetic appeal or their enduring heartiness.

An odd thing to say, maybe. But not for Shean. For many years, now, Nock had noticed she had a certain . . . fixation on life. Ever since the Red Tide, when she'd been surrounded by so much death over the course of just one night, she'd exhibited an aversion to killing. She refused to even squash an errant spider when it came into her room, an insistence that'd many times gotten her bitten and, once, poisoned.

It wasn't that she hated all things dead. She still ate the meat imported from the fields called Grazed and the fish caught on the lower docks of Pearl, and she'd never demonstrated any qualms over the death of the plants she consumed from the school garden. But when it came to senseless killing—pointless, mindless killing simply to get rid of some living thing that wasn't convenient or appreciated in any given situation—Shean disdained. Vocally.

Nock supposed, in a dismal way, that was one virtue to her credit, one admirable mark of maturity. She valued life, fiercely. And she truly, genuinely wished to protect it against the Shod.

Witnessing the results of her rampage, though, he found it hard to feel that was enough to excuse, let alone justify, her current behavior.

And quite the behavior it was. Shean had changed out of her licensing dress, throwing the decadent garment into the corner of the room to lay in a crumpled heap. In nothing but a simple sleeping dress, white and silken and flapping around her legs, she ran from one end of the room to the other, hands out and fingers curled like claws to sink into whatever unlucky thing stood in her way. Nock stood in the doorway and watched her, wincing when, having finished with all the obviously breakable things, she leapt upon her bed with a shriek, falling to her knees and snatching up one of her many pillows. She first tried to tear it apart with her bare hands. Upon finding that impossible, she proceeded to bite the pillow, yanking at it with aggressive—manic—jerks of her head.

Bracing himself, Nock forced himself forward. "Shean—" he started, cutting off when a great ripping noise sounded, announcing a prevail against the pillow. Shean was engulfed in a cloud of feathers, her voice lifting in triumph. As the down settled about her, sticking to her cheeks and nestling in her hair, she reached for another pillow.

"Shean," Nock said, trying to take a step forward only to have his foot catch on some piece of debris. He winced, stumbling. At the motion Shean startled, dropping the pillow she held and looking up. She pushed herself to her feet, face bright.

"Master! Did you come to give me my guard license?"

"No, Shean, we need to—"

"Then go away," Shean said, words flat and final. Scowling, she bent, snatching up a fresh pillow.

"Shean," Nock said, pleading. "We need to talk."

"About what?"

"Apologizing."

Shean pulled herself to her full height, tossing her head so her hair flared around her. Feathers scattered in all directions, lazily floating to the ground as she let out a loud, condescending sniff. "When Licensor Maton is prepared to apologize, I'll gladly forgive her."

"Shean, be reasonable. You know full well that *you* must apologize."

"For *what*?"

"For what?" Nock felt his face growing warm, his sadness and fear welling up and turning into a hotter, redder emotion. "Shean, I understand that you're disappointed. But you must accept—"

"I won't!" Shean interrupted. "I won't accept this! Me, an artisan?" She laughed, a loud, barking noise. "Ridiculous! *Insulting!*"

Nock took a calming breath, reminding himself that this was the girl—the young *woman*—who'd dedicated herself to dollmaking from the day they'd met. The young woman who esteemed life and hated death and just wanted her dolls to be of use, to help people. She meant well. He knew that.

He needed to remember that Shean meant well.

"Shean," he said, "what just happened—"

"That pompous woman—telling me to accept my fate, to be content with being nothing but an *artist*!" Shean punctuated her shout by throwing her pillow across the room. It struck the far wall and folded, falling to the ground in a deflated, dejected slump that Nock felt far too much kinship with.

"Please, Shean, calm—"

"After all the work I put in! Getting up before sunrise for the past *fifteen years*, designing at least three dolls a day, sometimes four! Painting lessons since I was eleven, perfecting joint mechanics until my dolls could move as swiftly and precisely as humans! Spending all those hours in Carpenter Parm's shop picking out the best, sturdiest wood to make dolls with. My dolls are *just* as solid as yours, Master, maybe even *more* solid, and infinitely smarter! And for her to say all that work was wasted? That I should make *toys*?" Shean broke off in a wordless shout, whirling and kicking the wall so hard the room rattled.

A soft noise sounded over Nock's head. A hiccup. A giggle. He looked up to find Silver the doll perched on a display shelf mounted on the wall, high up and out of reach of Shean. The doll was miming her, imitating his mistress's distress with mirrored movements as he paced along the shelf. When Nock stared, Silver lifted a finger to his smiling lips. And winked.

That doll was uncanny. And growing more so by the minute. In all his years, Nock had never met a doll with such subtle intelligence, let alone one who could make noises so close to those of a human. And what manner of doll would mimic his creator's fussing with a pleased, amused look on his face, a look that made one think he knew something no one else did?

Before Nock could grow too uneasy, though, his attention was drawn back to Shean, who'd resumed her raging. Putting Silver from his mind for the moment, Nock struggled to think of a way to get through to his apprentice. He was at a loss, though—watching such a childish display from someone who hadn't been a child for half a decade drained him of all hope for a reasonable, adult conversation.

Who was this shouting, furious young woman stomping around in front of him, throwing tables and tearing hangings from the walls? Who was this child who looked an adult, yelling curses because something hadn't gone her way? What had this ungrateful, disrespectful creature done with his dear, hardworking, ambitious, composed apprentice Shean?

It wasn't that Nock hadn't seen such behavior before; she'd had outbursts like this in the early days after the Red Tide, when she couldn't contain her pain, the loss of her family manifest in abrupt screams and thrashing fists. She'd grown out of such conduct, though, the fire of agony giving way in her and making room for demure, cold disdain—Nock was much more familiar with *that* Shean, the Shean who, when upset, locked herself in her room and fumed, or simply stood and stared at you until you felt ashamed, even when you *knew* you were in the right. Never had he imagined her capable of reverting like this, unleashing her frustrations the way she had years ago.

This was . . .

This was *ridiculous.*

The hot, crimson emotion pricking at Nock swelled. His hands clenched into fists, and his face burned. He sucked in as much breath as he could hold, and released it in a bellow.

"Stop!"

It was the loudest Nock had yelled since Shean had come to be his final apprentice. She froze, shock stark on her face when she turned to him.

Panting, Nock lifted a shaking finger, pointing at Shean. "You will be quiet. *Now.* You will sit down, and you will listen to me."

"But—"

"Be quiet and sit down!"

Shean knelt with a thump, fists wadded on the tops of her knees. She ducked her head and scowled at the floor. Her slender shoulders hunched.

"Good," Nock said, lowering his hand. He took a shaky breath, using his feet to clear a space for himself on the ground before sitting down, cross-legged. He rested his hands on his knees and, before she could dare say another word, launched into the only manner of lecture one could give to Shean—a short and blunt one.

"Shean, your behavior has been appalling. In physically attacking a licensor, you've brought great shame to the Nock School."

Shean opened her mouth, inhaling in preparation of argument. Nock pressed on, speaking over her budding protests.

"What's more, your temper has cost you your license. Do you realize what you've done? Licensor Maton is going to report you to the Licensor Head. He may decide to deny you a second assessment. If that happens, you'll be forbidden from making dolls entirely."

Shean didn't lift her head. But her alarm at this information was betrayed by her eyes, which flicked up with a startled flutter of lashes.

"*Now* do you understand?" Nock asked. "Do you see how unwise you've been?"

Shean's eyes lowered, her scowl deepening. "But what she said to me, it was—"

"It was honest."

Now Shean's head jerked up, lips pressed together in a hard line. For a silent moment she stared at Nock. When she spoke, her voice was an accusation.

"You agree with her."

"Yes. I do. Your dolls aren't suited for the work of a guard."

"What are you saying?" Shean's voice was softer. Wounded. And that almost made Nock regret his words. Almost made him take them back.

Instead he swallowed, forcing himself to press on. "You know what I'm saying."

The hurt left Shean's voice, replaced with malice. "Where is this coming from? When have you *ever* said I didn't have what it takes to be a proper dollmaker—"

"Never!" Nock said, lifting a negating hand. "And I won't now. You're the most talented student I've ever trained."

"You say that, yet you agree with that *licensor*?" Shean seethed the last word, lips twisting.

"I do. Your work isn't that of a guard dollmaker."

"It's because my dolls are pretty, isn't it? That's why you're saying this!" The words were spat poison, insult bright in Shean's eyes. "Why can't you, that damn licensor, *anyone* see—we can't go on like this!"

"Like what?" Nock asked, bewildered.

Shean sliced a hand through the air in a sharp, negating gesture. "Using dolls like yours! Like all the guard dolls in use right now, for that matter. Brute strength *clearly* isn't effective! If it was, the

Shod would've been beaten into extinction long ago. We need dolls that're more than just sturdy and fast; we need clever dolls, smart dolls—dolls like *my* dolls, intelligent enough to not just outmatch the Shod's strength, but *outthink* them." Shean leaned forward, eyes wide with conviction. "And concerning the beauty of my dolls—has it ever occurred to you that their designs are *purposeful*? Everyone knows the Shod are attracted to beautiful, well-made things! And my dolls are both! The Shod will be drawn to them like plants to light, giving my dolls and I a chance to trick and trap them!"

Nock had heard Shean present such philosophies before; at many a drinking party she'd cornered a dollmaker or two and subjected them to her theories on doll intelligence and aesthetics. But until now Nock had always assumed such musings to be just that—concepts Shean enjoyed waxing poetic over, but never taken too seriously by her audience or herself.

Clearly he'd been wrong. He'd been wrong about *so many* things regarding Shean.

A dismaying revelation.

"Shean, that's not how the Shod work," Nock said. "You know this; the Shod are, as Licensor Maton said, mindless. They don't think, and therefore cannot be outwitted—there's no wit to work against. Yes, you may be able to attract Shod with your work, but even the most intelligent doll in the world can't hope to stand against a Shod unless that doll is also the monster's equal in strength. Which your dolls will never be."

Shean's eyes filled with heat. "My own master. My own *master* wants to see me wasting my talents on toys and trinkets!"

"How is it a waste? As Maton said, there's no shame in—"

Shean pounded a fist against the ground, cutting him off. "There *is* shame! There's shame because I don't wish to be an artisan! My dream has always been, and remains, to be a certified guard. To aid our people by protecting them from the Shod. To make sure my family didn't die protecting me for nothing! Now you tell me I must slave with the carving knife and the paintbrush, not to thwart the evil that threatens our existence, but to please the sticky hands of children? To flatter the wealthy with demure slaves that obey their every whim?"

Nock shook his head, the anger and upset draining from him and leaving him hollow. He rested his head in his hands. "You don't understand," he said. "In the years since the Red Tide, Pearl has been untouched. The number of Shod attacks has diminished so greatly that you have no experience with the Shod. You don't realize just how terrible they are—how *could* you understand that your dolls wouldn't stand a chance against them?"

"I *have* seen the Shod!" Shean protested. "How have you forgotten?"

Nock lifted his head. "I haven't. But—"

Shean stood, one hand flattening to her chest, the other balled into a fist at her side. "I, a survivor of the Red Tide, one who's experienced the terror of the Shod firsthand, say my dolls can face them—that's why my dolls were created in the first place!"

Frustration warred with sympathy in Nock, coming out as a suffering edge to his voice when he said, "You may've *seen* the Shod, you may've been caught up in the Red Tide, but you've never been a dollmaker *facing* them, Shean. They aren't as easy to thwart as you believe."

Shean took a step toward Nock, the conviction in her voice giving way to begging. "If I could just *show* you that my dolls are smart enough, if I could just prove to you—"

"You can't," Nock said.

"Why not?"

"Because I would have to see your dolls face, and conquer, the Shod to believe them strong enough to do so. And without a guard license, that'll never happen."

Shean folded her arms, glaring. "That's unfair. How am I to prove myself?"

"You aren't," Nock said. "More, you don't *need* to—Licensor Maton has seen more dolls than you can imagine. She knows which are suited for what roles with one look. Her judgment is enough to tell you, and myself, that your dolls shouldn't face the Shod." He sighed, closing his eyes. "That's why we *have* licensors."

"I'll go look for the Shod myself, then," Shean said.

Nock opened his eyes, rising to his feet so quickly the room spun. "Look for the *Shod*?" He half-raised his hands, fingers stretching out to Shean. "Surely, you don't mean to lure one to you?"

"If that's what it takes for you to believe me, then yes!"

Nock took a step back, mouth dry. Memories overwhelmed him: a swarm of compact, many-legged, and squirming shapes writhing over the tops of the iridescent walls of Pearl. Deformed shapes scaling the cliffs, rising from the sea so thickly they looked like some sort of wide, flat animal, shaking and shivering up and up into the city. The many eyes, glowing white and blank and sightless. The sounds, the clacking of stolen bones and the wailing of inhuman voices, a dull roar like crashing waves punctured by *very* human cries of panic, pain, and fear.

That little boy. The one Nock spotted at the start of the Red Tide, close to the city walls, too far away to reach and incapable of fleeing quickly enough on his own. The sound of his scream over the clicking and hissing, a shriek cut short as, with the crack of a Shod's whiplike tail, he was sliced into two halves, two little boys with one eye apiece and half a gaping mouth, falling down in opposite directions. Caught by a swell of monsters as they fell on and further dismantled him, splitting his bones and organs amongst themselves.

Nock could still taste the bile that'd filled his mouth as he'd watched that little boy fall, the child's blood shining on the backs of the stampeding Shod like war paint, crimson as sunset.

The Red Tide indeed.

Nock's knees weakened. Under the weight of Shean's defiant gaze he sat, flinching as his leg landed on something hard and sharp—part of a broken vase.

"Foolish child," he said, voice hoarse. His teeth gritted together, hands curling into fists. "Stupid child! Go *looking* for the Shod? You would kill us all!"

Shean rammed her fists onto her hips. "*Listen* to me, Master! No one would die—my dolls and I would make sure of that!"

Nock's lips parted in amazement. Shean was an ambitious apprentice. Hardworking and determined. Respectful of life, and willing to do whatever it took to achieve the dreams she held close and dear to her heart.

But to suggest drawing the Shod's attention to herself, and to so flippantly brush off the sheer idiocy of such a plan . . .

With sudden, depressing clarity, Nock understood. He realized there was no getting through to Shean. She was blinded, by the desire to prove herself capable of fighting the Shod, and by what injury to her pride she imagined Maton had inflicted upon her. So much so, she was prepared to do something reckless.

But if he *couldn't* get through to her, if he couldn't convince her to go and grovel at Licensor Maton's feet, to beg for forgiveness with all the earnest wish of her heart, Master Nock's last apprentice would be his only apprentice to fail to become a dollmaker. In her desperation for validation, she might even end up getting herself, and others, killed.

Such a waste. In so many ways, such a waste.

"What am I to do with you?" Nock said, voice thin. He closed his eyes and clutched his head. "What am I to *do*?"

"Go to the licensors and argue for my becoming a guard. Believe me, Master—trust me, and—"

Nock stopped listening. There had to be something. Something he could do to make Shean *see*, something to undo the harm he'd unintentionally inflicted by allowing her to think she was something she wasn't. Something, somehow . . .

Someone?

Nock lowered his hands. He stared at Shean's feet, her voice still chattering at him.

"—and then everything will be fine, and we can all go back to our lives." A pause. "Master?" Another, longer pause, followed by an irritated hiss. "Master, are you listening to me?"

Nock spoke slowly, each word careful. "There . . . there is someone you should meet."

"What? Who?"

"A dollmaker. Someone who can help you understand what it means to find one's place in the world."

Shean's face puckered, eyes rolling. "I've no desire to be sent to talk shop with an artisan!"

Nock shook his head, pushing himself to his feet. "Ikiisa maintains a guard license."

That gave Shean pause. "A guard?" she said.

Nock nodded. "Yes. Three days before the Red Tide, I met a young dollmaker. She'd come to the city called Pearl looking for work; she was recently licensed but was having trouble finding employment. She'd already been to the cities called Shore and Crag but had no luck. She'd come to Pearl to speak to me, as her master is a friend of mine."

"Which friend?" Shean asked.

"Master Coen."

Shean frowned. "Coen?"

"From the city called Glass. He died before you came to live with me. Ikiisa was his final apprentice." Nock sighed. "Ikiisa hoped I could find work for her here in Pearl, but I must admit, when I first saw her dolls, I had my doubts."

"What do you mean?"

"Her dolls are very . . . odd. Disquieting, even. That's why she'd been having trouble finding work."

"Disquieting?" Shean echoed.

"Yes. It's hard to describe." Nock glanced up at Silver. The doll was now sitting on his perch, legs swinging, watching Shean with twinkling eyes. *Well*, Nock thought, *maybe not* so *hard*. Then he shook his head, waving a dismissive hand. "But that isn't important. For Coen's sake, I agreed to help Ikiisa find work. Before we could make headway with any of the employment agencies, however, the Red Tide came.

"Ikiisa was swept up in it, as we all were. I lost track of her in the confusion. For days I worried that my dear friend's apprentice had come to me for help only to suffer an untimely death, though I admit that was the least of my worries at the time. Still, when the Tide began to recede, Ikiisa was one of the first I looked for. I searched all over the city, but so few knew her, and describing her and her dolls was difficult. I was beginning to give up all hope when I heard rumors of a young dollmaker who'd not only survived the Tide, but was responsible for saving a large part of Pearl from the Shod, and was busy at work holding off the final cluster of the beasts left in the city. It was said she had very peculiar dolls. When I inquired as to the name of this dollmaker, I discovered it was none other than Ikiisa.

"I rushed to where she was fighting and arrived in time to see her drive the last of the Shod out of Pearl. She was forcing them back with only seven dolls.

"The sight was amazing—I stopped in my tracks, and I couldn't look away from the young woman holding back a sea of nightmares with so little aid. It was then that I realized Ikiisa was the strongest dollmaker I'd ever met. The strongest guard alive.

"Afterward I did my best to get Ikiisa work in Pearl. I managed to secure her a small patrol job with an employment office on the fringes of the city, making dolls to guard the coastline, but there were so many complaints about her dolls Ikiisa was relieved of duty after just three days. After that I couldn't convince another employment office to risk taking her, afraid of tainting their reputations by associating their names with such a dollmaker. The situation was appalling—someone of such talent, a dollmaker responsible for saving so many lives in the city called Pearl, scorned for such petty reasons! In the end I offered to allow Ikiisa to stay with you and myself, to work as your tutor. She declined, saying that she became a dollmaker to work as a dollmaker, not a teacher. She left Pearl, and some years later I received word that she had, at last, secured a contracted job with the village called Web in the forest called Deep."

"I've never heard of that village," Shean said.

"Few have. Web is very small, and known only for its silk—spider silk, to be exact. An unusual commodity that's sparked outlandish stories about the people of Web—that they give their young men to spiders for grooms, or that their young women allow spiders to crawl upon their bodies and weave gauzy garments that they then dance in under half-moons. I've also heard that those of Web are jealous of their privacy, and cold to outsiders—that might have some truth to it, as the forest called Deep is the only place in the country where spiders that produce the proper silk for cloth-weaving can be found. Only those trained to handle such spiders live there, but tailor shops across the country use the cloth woven in Web to make luxury items, embroidered handkerchiefs and the like—you may have even seen a few such pieces in the textile district here in Pearl . . ."

Nock trailed off, belatedly realizing he was rambling. He got like this, sometimes, when his anxiety was particularly high—going on and on about things that didn't really matter. Shean was staring at him with an unreadable expression. She took a breath to speak, and he braced himself for a biting, irked request for him to get to his point.

To his surprise, her voice was merely curious when she asked, "Is this spider silk expensive?"

"Oh, yes," he said, relief making him smile. "Very."

"Is the village called Web wealthy, then?"

"I would suppose so."

"Couldn't they afford to hire any dollmaker they wanted?"

Nock shrugged. "Most likely. But the forest called Deep is remote—the nearest town to Web is a four-day journey. Given that, the village called Web has two historical problems: consistent assault from the Shod, and trouble finding a dollmaker willing to live so far away from the large cities. A perfect place for Ikiisa, whose true desire is to protect others, and who doesn't mind living without other dollmakers. Since beginning her employment there, she's written me several times to say she's very happy. She's found her place in the world."

Nock stepped toward Shean, taking her shoulders. "I want you to meet Ikiisa," he said. "She, like you, had different ideas of what her life would be. And she's learned to adapt, to embrace where she's needed in the world. What's more, she's found a way to flourish. And she's very wise, wise beyond her years, which are not so many more than yours—if you speak to her, if you tell her of your frustrations, I believe she'll be able to help you decide what to do next."

Shean was quiet, staring at Nock with unreadable eyes. He waited for her to speak. When she didn't, he did.

"I'll write you a letter to take to her. An introduction, and an explanation. She'll be surprised to hear from me after so long, but she'll remember me. She may even remember you—you met her when she was in Pearl, in the aftermath of the Tide, though I doubt you remember. You were so very small, and still recovering from the loss of your family."

"And why should I do as you say?" Shean asked, voice quiet.

Nock removed his hands from her shoulders. He knew what to say, though it took him a moment to force the words out.

"If you go to Ikiisa, if you show her your dolls and she believes they're suitable for facing the Shod, then I'll go to the village called Twig. I'll speak to the Licensor Head myself, and insist you be reassessed for a guard license."

Shean's eyes brightened. "Truly?"

"Yes," Nock said. Over his head, he swore he heard Silver giggle.

Shean smiled a wide, pleased smile. "I'll go."

SHEAN STOOD IN THE SCHOOL STABLE WITH HER BACK PRESSED AGAINST A POST of Lintok's stall, fiddling with the seal on Nock's letter. It was a round piece of wood, much like a button, but lacking the proper holes. Nock's insignia was burned into it, a sea urchin's spindly shape outlined in black. And it was stubborn.

She swore as her fingers slipped for the third time, jarring on the round edges of the seal. She scowled, fastening her grip around the button and pulling with all her might. A moment later her hand flew back again, this time slamming into the post she leaned against with a thump.

Shean hissed, pressing a throbbing set of knuckles to her chest and stomping her foot. The sole of her boot made a whumping noise against the compact floor, her frustrated kick causing bits of stray straw to spray out in front of her. When her hand stopped pulsing and she managed to pry her jaw from a clench of pain, Shean held the letter out in front of her, glaring.

"Here," she said to Silver, who was saddling Lintok. The doll paused in the process of passing her, turning to look at the letter she held out to him. He peered over the top of the tack piled high in his arms. Then he looked up at Shean, eyes a question.

"It's a dollmaker's lock. Can you break it?" she asked. Silver cocked his head to the side, as if to ask, *Why*? "I want to see what Nock wrote to Ikiisa." Shean's lips pressed together. "I want to see what he has to say to her about me."

Silver wiggled an arm free from the tack, causing the end of a rein to fall to the ground with a *fwap*, and tapped the top of the lock. At his touch the button shifted a bit. Shean felt a spike of excitement. When she tugged at the seal, though, she found it as secure as ever. She frowned at Silver.

"I thought you were good with locks. You had no trouble breaking into my treasure drawer and rearranging Giko and Father's jewelry by color and size and . . . what *was* the other category? Luster?"

Silver shrugged, turning and carrying his load to Lintok, fallen rein dragging across the floor behind him and leaving a line in the dirt. Shean watched him go, eyes narrowed. Proud as she was of him, she had to admit he was a peculiar doll. She'd given him his Breath Mark a week ago, and in that short time she'd yet to figure out just what was going on in his head—one moment he seemed cheerful and playful, as full of energy as a child; the next he was demure and obedient like the rest of her dolls, doing whatever she asked of him without protest or cheeky evasion. Give him another minute, though, and he'd be rigid and stone-faced, standing still and quiet like the logs he was made from, eyes reverted to lifeless marbles.

For all his peculiarities, Shean had already grown attached to Silver. Part of this, she knew, was because he was the best work she'd ever done. But there was more to the affection she felt; never before had she created a doll with such personality, such life. He was more like a person than a doll. At least, that's what Shean thought sometimes—a dangerous thought, she knew, something that went against the nine edicts of the First Dollmaker, who was wise and knew the perils of mistaking a creation for a creature.

Of course, the First Dollmaker had also been the one to give licensors the authority to decide what manner of dollmaker an apprentice could become. A choice that—after her encounter with Maton—was making Shean seriously question the First Dollmaker's "wisdom."

Whatever the case, Shean couldn't help treating Silver like a friend. Doll or not, right now he was the only ally she had.

Turning her attention away from Silver, Shean tried to pry the seal from the letter one more time. When the effort resulted in failure, she gave up. Fanning herself with the letter to cool the sweat beading on her neck, she considered tossing the note aside, burying it under a pile of dried grass or using a shovel to poke it into Lintok's waste trough. Then she reconsidered, thinking that having the letter might be useful in some way, despite the fact that she was *not* going to use it as Master Nock instructed.

Learn from another master. Hear this Ikiisa's life story and decide a lifelong dream was worth giving up on. Even Nock's promise was ridiculous—as if Shean could believe that anyone he trusted enough to send her to would be inclined to disagree with his and Maton's errant opinion of her dolls.

What sort of coward did Nock take Shean to be? Did he think she'd quit that easily, give up on what she'd spent her *whole life* working toward? Shean gritted her teeth, shoving the letter deep down in the pocket of her travel jacket.

No. No, she wasn't going to travel across the country so she could be brainwashed into thinking being an artisan was a valid way of wasting her life. She wasn't going to *talk* to Ikiisa—she was going to *confront* her. She would go to this village called Web in the forest called Deep and challenge Ikiisa for her position as dollmaker. Once Shean replaced Ikiisa—the strongest guard dollmaker alive, apparently—as the dollmaker of Web, that idiot Maton would *have* to give her a proper license. Even Nock would admit he'd been wrong then.

He'd see. They'd all see. Just like they'd all seen at the last school competition, when Shean had taken the top prize for Excellence in Dollmaking, surpassing all the other apprentices in Pearl. Just like they'd all seen when she'd won the last design contest run by Master Jhoe's employment shop, her design plans for Silver outperforming sketches from the licensed masters of five cities. Just like all the masters who'd ever visited Nock had seen, praising her craftwork with lavish words she'd copied into her diary, lest she forget a single, delicious morsel of flattery.

They'd see: Shean would do what Shean did best, and use her beautiful, clever dolls to prove them all wrong.

Soft lips with an edge of teeth plucked at the back of Shean's head, pulled at her hair before moving to her shoulder to tug at the fabric of her travel jacket. She turned her head and bumped her nose on Lintok's muzzle, sneezing when she took a breath and inhaled fur.

"Too close, Lintok!" she said, the words tempered by a chuckle as she used her arm to gently shove the elk's head away from her, rubbing at her nose and blinking through the itch in her eyes. "You need to be brushed."

The elk snorted, bumping his cheek against the side of Shean's skull before backing away. She turned, resting her arms on the front of his stall and looking up at him, smiling. Night was reaching its zenith and the stable was dark, lit by the single glow lantern Shean had brought with her from the house. She'd chosen a glow lantern, rather than a fire lantern, because the smoke from flame made both Lintok and Silver nervous. Silver disliked fire because all dolls did—though a doll could only be killed by two things (complete obliteration or a Shod), they could be damaged by all the regular, harmful things: water, knives, fire. And there was nothing quite as pathetic as a damaged doll, limping and staggering about with jerking, wooden movements. Even after restoration from a dollmaker, a doll that'd been kissed by flame would never move the way it used to.

There was no way of knowing for sure, but Shean imagined the reason Lintok was spooked by smoke was because it reminded him of the Red Tide, when the Shod had broken into the metal forges and started fires across the city. Shean's brother, Giko, had been riding

Lintok that night, back when the elk was barely old enough to be ridden. From what Shean had been told, Giko had been killed while riding Lintok.

With Giko gone, Lintok had been passed down to Shean, and now he was one of her few remaining ties to her family. A memento like her mother's bracelets and her father's earrings. But Lintok was more significant than scraps of metal and gemstone; much of Shean's childhood had been spent riding him, passing through the gates of Pearl on days when the breeze coming off the ocean was lukewarm and pleasant, growing accustomed to the chafing of her legs against the saddle, the thrill of riding an elk at full sprint through the grassy hills ringing the bottom of the rise upon which Pearl gleamed. It'd been a while, though, since Shean had spent time with him—she'd been forced to hire an animal-keeping apprentice to come and exercise him every week, caught up as she'd been in preparations for her licensing this past year.

Caught up in a farce, she now, bitterly, realized.

Looking up at her elk's long, intelligent face, admiring the antlers that rose like spiraling, bone-colored horn-seashells from his midnight forehead, she regretted neglecting him. She pushed open the gate of his stall, walking to him and wrapping her arms around his neck. Resting her forehead against him, she remembered being a little girl, walking him by his lead around the foothills, stopping to let him pull up grass and wildflowers while she talked about her training and her dolls, asking him questions about Giko that he answered with shakes of his head, little stamps of his hooves that had, at the time, felt full of meaning.

Today had been a terrible day. Tonight was an angry night. But, holding on to Lintok, Shean relaxed. In the presence of her oldest friend she felt, for a moment, that everything would be all right.

Shean lifted her head, stepping back and rubbing the back of her knuckles down Lintok's soft cheek. Silver was standing under the elk's belly, adjusting the straps of the saddle.

"Where's the bridle?" she asked him.

Silver pointed, and she picked the reins and headpiece up from their heap on the floor. She fastened the bridle over Lintok's head, buckling straps over his muzzle and cheeks. When she finished, she draped the reins over his neck. Silver ducked out from under the elk.

"The packs?" Shean asked. Silver walked to the corner of Lintok's stall, bending and dragging a saddle bag into the aquamarine glow of the lantern. When he picked the pack up and lifted it above his head Shean took it, staggering a bit under the weight before turning to Lintok. *My dolls aren't strong, are they*? she thought, scowling as she heaved the pack up, wedging a shoulder under it to keep it in place while she tied it to the saddle, finishing just in time to take the second pack from Silver, fixing this bag to the other side of the saddle. When she finished, she double-checked her work.

The first pack held essentials—changes of clothing, money from recent contest winnings, and her dollmaking tools. The second pack held dolls. For Lintok's sake she could only take so many, and since she'd opted for Silver to be one of them, the number was smaller than she would've liked: five of her best-crafted, foot-tall dolls, secured in a tight bundle and ordered to sleep until she called for them. Silver was large enough to ride with her on Lintok, so he alone would remain conscious for the journey. Which was good—it was wise to have one doll awake and at hand, in case she ran into Shod on her way to Web. A possibility that both thrilled and worried her.

The rest of her dolls would remain here at the school, tending to things she cared about while she was away: watering her plants, cleaning up the—admittedly embarrassing, rash, and juvenile—destruction in her room, guarding her few treasured belongings, and making sure Nock was safe. Not that her master *deserved* her compassion or help after all this, but . . . still. He was Nock. The man who'd raised her.

Even if he didn't deserve it, her dolls would protect him in her absence.

For good measure, Shean added extra knots to the cords of the pack containing her dolls, securing the bag as firmly as she could to Lintok's saddle—it would be a disaster if any of her dolls were to fall out on the road and be crushed by some fellow traveler's cart wheels. When she was satisfied, she turned to Silver, who stood watching her with his hands behind his back, eyes catching the light of the lantern in flashes of reflective blue.

"All right," she said. "Before we go, I need you to borrow Nock's—"

She cut off as Silver lifted his hand to her, brandishing something flat and rectangular. She bent and took the offering, straightening and holding the card toward the soft light of the glow lantern, though she recognized what it was before the light betrayed the symbols burned across its surface.

"License," she finished, amazed. She lowered the card, staring at Silver. "How . . . *When* did you . . . ?"

Silver winked at her, holding a finger to his lips. Shean felt a wave of affection for the doll, a thrill to realize she'd created something that thought so much like her, he obeyed orders before she even gave them. A doll smart enough to outwit the Shod, whatever Maton said. Returning Silver's smile, she decided she didn't care how or when he'd secured Nock's license, content to just admire his success. Which she did, lifting the card close to the glow lantern's light.

Despite being over fifty years old, Nock's license was pristine. No wear on its polished edges, no scratches or stains or accidental burns—a testament to the tight-buttoned, rule-abiding life he lived. In the corner of the license was the brand of Great Licensor Limpi: two overlapping circles with a tiny, delicate flower bloom in the space created by the overlap. Great Licensor Limpi was, of course, long dead. Even so, her authority stood, her brand making this license an active and valid one.

Any competent employment agency that Shean tried to present this license to would notice the outdated brand, feel compelled to check their records, and discover at once that this was the license of Master Nock, not Master Shean. If Web was as small as Nock said, though, she doubted they'd have any sort of official records to check against. All she needed was a license to present to them, proof that she was a professional dollmaker and had the right to challenge their current one for employment in their village.

Which she was. And did. Whatever Licensor Maton thought.

Shean tilted the license, gazing at the design sprawled above Great Licensor Limpi's brand: the silhouette of a boar in profile, head and tusks raised, feet placed as if taking a step forward. The brand of a guard, outlined in sharp lines.

As always, Shean's heart skipped at the sight of the symbol, the crest of not just the First Dollmaker himself, but of the dollmaker who'd saved her life in the Red Tide. Even now she clearly remembered this boar stamped into the leather of the bracers on her rescuer's arms, wrapping around her and lifting her and carrying her from the wreckage of Pearl. She remembered clinging to this symbol, weeping over it because she knew it meant she was safe. Knew it meant *life*.

And what, after finding out her family was dead and Nock was going to take her in, was more noble to dedicate herself to than life itself?

Her fingers squeezed the edges of Nock's license, a pang of longing lancing through her. *This*—this was the manner of license she was meant to hold. Not one decorated with flowers that gave her the paltry authority to make trinkets and toys, a mockery of the hours she'd spent slaving over her craft and becoming a better dollmaker than anyone in Pearl. Better than anyone in any city, for that matter.

Shean was suited to carrying a mighty, majestic boar with her. A license that'd tell everyone who saw it, everyone she served, that they were safe. Just as her savior had been, she was destined to be known by the symbol of the First Dollmaker, that great man who struck the first, most devastating blow against the Shod. It was in *his* footsteps, and not those of nameless, insignificant artisans, that she'd follow.

She knew that. She felt that, down to her bones. No one, not even her own master, was going to tell her otherwise.

"Good work," she said to Silver, tucking the license into the pocket of her travel jacket, next to Nock's letter. She cinched the string of the pocket shut and tied a knot to make sure the card wouldn't slip out. Silver bobbed a bow, one arm sweeping out in grand acknowledgment of her praise.

Smiling at his antics, Shean pushed open the gate of Lintok's stall, picking up her glow lantern. It swung with a creak as she lifted it, the polished seafoam marbles within clicking against one another, their light growing an increment in response to the collisions. She fastened the handle of the lantern on the hook that jutted from the side of Lintok's saddle, tying double knots to make sure the lamp wouldn't be tossed when the elk ran. She took ahold of Lintok's reins.

And then, despite herself, she looked toward the stable door. There it was, wide open, the glow of two moons, both waning, lighting a half-circle of the floor. Bits of straw lay in the light, casting shadows the size of inchworms. The only silhouettes to be seen. Disappointment, sudden and breathtaking, pierced her.

A touch on her fingertips. Shean looked down to see Silver curling his hand around hers, watching her with serious eyes that, if she didn't know better, were full of concern. She squeezed Lintok's reins, the leather creaking in her grip.

What was she expecting? For Nock to be waiting in front of the stable, ready with final words of encouragement? Ridiculous—she knew he wasn't going to see her off. After handing over his letter for Ikiisa he'd closed the doors to his room. And bolted them.

Seclusion and silence; those were Nock's ways of demonstrating how disappointed he was in her.

Well, fine. Let him be disappointed. She was disappointed in *him*—quite a master he'd turned out to be, turning his back on her the moment she stood up for herself, doing her best to live up to the expectations he'd put on her from the moment she'd made her first doll, his praises of that initial effort enough to promise her she was on the right path. One that led to helping people, just like he did.

Yes, she could admit that her reaction to Maton's licensing had been a *tad* overwrought, beneath her, and, frankly, childish. But *not* without merit—how else was she expected to act when it felt like the whole world was against her for some reason, actively working to stop her from becoming who she was destined to be despite her efforts, her talent, her undeniable skill?

Do whatever it takes to help people. Use your dolls to protect everyone in the country called One. Nock had taught Shean that. And to protect everyone, Shean's dolls *had* to be guard dolls.

Given that, how *else* had Nock expected her to react to the events of today? How did he *want* her to act, when the one person she trusted more than anyone sided with her enemies?

Shean's jaw set. If this was what Nock wanted, fine. If this was how he'd decided their parting would be, fine. Let him sulk in his room like a wounded martyr.

Let him rot there.

"Let's go," Shean said to Silver. The doll nodded, releasing her hand but walking close to her side as she led Lintok out of his stall. Despite his massive size and antlers suited for goring, the elk was quietly obedient, following Shean out of the stable and into the main courtyard of the school.

Nock's school sat on a cliff at the far edge of Pearl, overlooking the sea. Shean intended to move quickly once out of the stables, passing the familiar landscape of her home with as much disdain as she could muster. But she stopped at the ancient wall that edged the school's cliff, taking in the view of the nighttime sea for what felt a final time. Water calm and quiet, reflecting the brightest stars overhead. Hand resting on the worn stone of the wall, she breathed in the scent of brine and salt deeply, then turned to look at the moonlight-frosted school.

Nock had told her that, long before he'd taken her as an apprentice, the school had housed as many as a hundred students at a time. Other teachers beside Nock had worked here, specialists in painting and carving who conducted lessons like the ones she'd received by traveling to Master Kol and Master Opwe's workshops. She tried to imagine that as her gaze swept the cluster of shadowy buildings: young people her age all about, children she grew up with and trained with, the sound of their voices in the rooms of the main house, the click and clack of their tools in the workshop.

She was aware, of course, that other apprentices at other schools *did* train with people their age. When she'd been very little, and very concerned with inconsequential things, she'd envied apprentices like that, feeling a hot, sad sort of pain when she passed clusters of children on the street and caught a snippet of laughter from their joking. How she'd begrudged their delight. How she'd wondered, what would growing up with someone be like? What would her life be like if Giko hadn't been so much older than her and hadn't died in the Red Tide, but had come to live with her and Nock?

Lintok let out a huffing breath, a breeze that stirred her hair against her neck in a tickle. Shean shook her head, looking away from the school. "Stupid," she muttered. She might as well consent to being an artisan if she was going to stand around wasting time on sentimental drivel. Putting useless thoughts from her head, she bent and lifted Silver, setting him in the saddle and taking the hand he offered. Together they hoisted her onto Lintok's back.

"Thank you," she said, reaching around Silver and picking up the reins while Lintok shifted, adjusting to her weight. Silver nodded, hands curling around the pommel of the saddle. "Ready?" Shean asked. Another nod.

Shean clicked her tongue, flicking the reins against Lintok's neck while pressing her left heel into his side. He trotted forward, needing no guidance along the path to reach the front of the school. The gate was already open. Waiting.

That's how Nock says goodbye, Shean thought as Lintok bent his head to avoid catching his antlers on the top of the gate. *Leaving the path for my departure wide open*. She felt the back of her throat close a little, eyes pricking. Then she set her jaw.

No. No tears. They'd be wasted on someone who didn't even believe in her.

The stores along the main street of Pearl were closed for the night, windows shuttered and doors clamped shut. No sign of life or light, and a deep hush blanketed the city, broken only by the occasional breeze stirring the occasional wind chime. Pearl would remain this quiet for some hours yet and that was fine—Shean didn't need anyone she knew seeing her, calling out to ask how her licensing had gone or where she was going. In the peace experienced from being one of the only conscious creatures for miles, unnoticed by the many slumbering eyes of her city, Shean slipped away, Lintok's hooves creating sparks on cobbles, the faint light of her glow lantern illuminating her path through, and then out of, Pearl.

She didn't look back.

IT WOULD TAKE OVER TWO WEEKS TO REACH THE VILLAGE CALLED WEB. THE journey was straightforward enough—Shean would travel up the far shore of the country called One, passing through the nine great coast cities before taking the inland road leading from the city called Shoal to the forest called Deep. Once at the edge of Deep, it would take half a day to reach Web.

Before that, though, there was a matter of extreme importance that needed tending to—obtaining proper attire.

What to wear while traveling was simple: rough clothes, travel trousers and a jacket that could endure dust and rain and saddle abrasion without falling to bits. What to wear for her arrival at Web, however, was another matter. First impressions were paramount—the process of Shean winning over the villagers of Web would start the moment they saw her. Which meant she needed something memorable to wear when she presented herself to them, something as beautiful as the dress she'd selected for her licensing.

That dress was, of course, out of the question, ruined the moment Maton had failed to give her a proper license. She'd need something new, something better, to wear in Web. A fresh start.

And there was no place better to find fresh starts than in the city called Ports.

Ports was Pearl's neighbor and, as its name suggested, it was a city of traders local and foreign, composed of a busy assortment of stilted houses and boat-shops that waved flags of every nation and creed upon dipping balconies, a constant flapping that ringed an azure bay on the coastline of the ocean called Wept. Shean arrived in the city at midday, the peak time for trade transactions, and marveled at the sight.

Merchants crowded the narrow streets, bickering and laughing in unknown languages, accompanied by demure dolls carrying crates of wares. Gray-skinned strangers from the country called Shale peered at Shean with lantern eyes that glowed from inside the folds of baggy hoods, speaking in their marble-rolling language to the small-statured citizens of the country called Sway. Ethereal, the tall and slender shapes of people from the country called Fell moved past her in rustles and disinterested bell chimes, the golden ornaments they wore plaited through their long, pale hair winking in the sunlight when they bent to inspect the goods displayed at the fronts of trade stalls.

Shean inspected alongside them, leading Lintok by the reins and ordering Silver to stay astride the elk, lest he get lost amid the crowd pressing in on them. Even on its busiest days Pearl wasn't half as packed as Ports, and Shean found herself creeping through the city, forced to plod along at the same tortoise speed as the people around her while being periodically jostled by stray elbows. At one point a group of middle-aged men and women dressed in the distinct charcoal robes and crimson sashes that served as the uniform for members of the Research Guild—the specific sect of academia in the country called One dedicated to research surrounding dollmaking—spotted and began tailing her, ogling Silver and murmuring among themselves. Shean ignored this attention, making sure to stay far enough ahead of the scholars to avoid a direct interaction; she held little respect for those who chose to simply *study* dolls, rather than becoming dollmakers themselves. Eventually the researchers yielded to her pointed indifference and, some looking crestfallen and some looking irked, left.

Even after that relief, though, Shean's agitation failed to diminish. She'd hoped to find a suitable outfit within an hour, with enough time left in the day to go on to the next city along the shore. As she made her incremental way down the crammed shopping streets, however, midday swung toward evening, the heat of the day cooling with a warning of imminent night. And still nothing caught her eye, only mundane shifts of silk or taffeta gracing the displays she eased past. Shean began to despair of finding anything satisfactory.

And then she saw the dress.

It stood out among the other goods displayed along the trade stalls, a fitted bodice with elbow-length sleeves and a four-tiered layer of skirts hanging from mid-rib to ankle. Primarily maroon and purple (colors that complemented Shean's complexion), the dress had precise white stitching that decorated the hems of its skirts and low neckline in deliberate, sharp lines. Every inch of fabric was covered in gems, diamonds and emeralds beaded in a swirling pattern that resembled a river of shimmer, or the starry sky on a night without clouds. In the country called One, it was impossible to find such elaborate decorations on a piece of women's clothing.

Which explained the foreign nature of the merchant selling the dress—a tall woman who, rather than sit behind her stall's display rack, stood beside the dress like a guard, arms folded across her chest, gaze piercing over the heads of the crowd. She was broad. Firm. And made from jewels.

Shean had heard stories of the people from the country called Gleam. But this was the first time she'd *seen* such a person and, consequently, the first time she realized the rumors weren't just fanciful poetry penned by travelers looking back on their time abroad with blinding fondness. The woman really *did* have skin like cut diamond, sharp edges and ridges protruding from every inch of her like armor. Her eyes were many facets of flashing sapphire, and her lips were powdered in crushed emerald. The hair that swayed about her face was made from strings of diamond crystals that clicked together to produce melodic notes, and the only clothing she wore was her own crystalline skin, milky shades of aquamarine and opaque gray that caught the light of the sun and refracted rainbow lights in all directions.

With some struggle Shean approached the Gleam woman, tugging Lintok through the current of the crowd and ignoring the glares and curses she gathered from those displaced in the process. When she arrived, the Gleam woman eyed her in a swirl of sunlight reflected in blue, looking from her to Lintok to Silver. Her gaze lingered on Silver, and she spoke in a voice that sounded like polished stone struck with a mallet, ringing notes with syllables nestled within them.

Shean didn't understand a word. "Do you speak One?" she asked. The Gleam woman shook her head, waving her hand at Silver and repeating herself, this time slowly, her voice a series of clicks and *thwongs* that formed a short, resonate melody. Shean shot a despairing look at the dress, realizing buying it would prove difficult.

"She asks if your companion is a doll."

The voice had a burring accent and was polite and pleasant, soft but audible above the hubbub of Ports. Shean turned to find a man standing behind her, watching her struggles with a kind smile.

In a word, he was stunning. Dark bronze skin and shoulder-length hair the color and luster of copper, angular features and a stature slender enough to be called delicate, but far too lean to be mistaken for weak. The clothing he wore was of a design she'd never seen in One, coral-pink circles and teal diamonds sewn in an intricate motif along the bottom of his tunic and into the cuff of his right trouser leg, a travel pack tied secure to his back by a strap that cut across his chest, the bag cylindrical in shape with ends dyed pale blue.

What made the man truly arresting, however, were the white marks running along his jaw, twisting up and around the edges of his face in a symmetrical pattern, a design of triangles and lines that reminded Shean of the chalk fractals children drew on the alley walls of Pearl. As his tunic lacked sleeves, she could see that his arms, too, boasted white markings, jagged lines that went all the way down to his hands and curled around his fingertips like silk ribbons—an amount of body art beyond anything she'd ever seen, even on travelers from the country called Drawn.

The man stared at her with silver eyes that penetrated like lances of light, expression expectant. Shean stared back and couldn't make sense of him. For one bewildered moment, she was convinced he was a doll—only dolls had eyes so pale and features so comely. No real person had hair that metallic. The strange white marks adorning him further convinced her that he was a creation. And a decorative one at that.

"A doll," the man said.

Shean startled. "What?"

The man nodded at Silver. "Is he?"

Shean looked up at Silver, who was leaning over the edge of Lintok's saddle, staring at the man with obvious delight. "Oh," she said. "Yes. He is."

The man's eyebrows rose at the confirmation, but he merely turned to the Gleam woman, speaking to her in a warble that sent chills down Shean's spine. His voice was clean and clear, like rain falling in sunlight. As he spoke, the Gleam woman's eyes swirled, two miniature vistas of purple blue. She answered him with a harmonizing note.

"Yours?" the man asked Shean, translating.

"Yes," Shean said, looking from him to the Gleam woman, unsure which to address. She settled on the latter, directing her next words to crystalline features. "I'm a dollmaker."

The man sang her words and the Gleam woman rested her hands on her hips, singing back two long notes, the short phrase tapered like a sigh.

"He's beautiful," the man said.

"So is your dress," Shean said, pointing at the garment.

The Gleam woman looked at the dress, then back at Shean. Her emerald lips lifted in a smile that revealed mother-of-pearl teeth. She lifted the dress from the hook at the top of the stall, the gesture causing the garment to sway, sparkling resplendent. The resulting flash caught in Shean's eyes, blinding her.

The woman of Gleam spoke again, her crystal-shard voice singing tones of a sweet pitch.

"She says it suits you," the man said.

"It does," Shean said, reaching out and running her fingers down the jeweled front of the dress. She imagined arriving in Web wearing this, sweeping into the village with every inch of her sparkling. She looked up at the Gleam woman. "How much?"

Paying for the dress took almost half of her travel funds, but the moment the dress was folded and placed in Shean's hands, when she felt its weight and pressed its glimmer against her, she knew the expense was worth it. Never in her life had she owned something more beautiful than her dolls. Never in her life had she found something that could make *her* so beautiful. In this dress, she'd be a dollmaker impossible to forget.

Tucking the dress into Lintok's saddle bag, Shean told herself she'd be fine—by cutting back on other expenses (such as settling for tolerable inns rather than nice ones, effective meals over edible ones), she'd manage to get to Web. And with this dress acting as her exquisite armor, triumph was surely awaiting her there.

A swapping of melodic lines behind her, then the man was standing next to Shean, leaning close to be heard over the chaos of the street.

"She thanks you for your business," he said.

"Oh," Shean said, glancing back at the Gleam woman. "Will you thank her for me?"

The man smiled. "I already have."

"Thank *you*, then. For the help."

"My pleasure," he said, inclining his head. He turned to go, taking a step around Lintok and toward the stream of people walking down the street. Watching him, Shean felt an unexpected, frantic squeeze in her chest.

"Wait!"

The man paused, half-turning to look at her. "Was there something else you needed help with?" he asked.

The words weren't unkind, but Shean's face grew hot. What *was* she doing, yelling after a stranger like that? But she didn't want him to go. Not yet—he was too strange, too attractive, to let slip away so soon.

So she said, "No, I . . ." Her eyes lifted to the sky as she searched for an excuse, and she saw the sun cresting toward the horizon, retreating as night approached. It was too late, now, for her to go on to the next city. She'd have to find an inn to stay in for the night here in Ports.

At that realization an idea struck her. She looked at the man, smiling, and said, "Please, allow me to thank you for your help."

The man lifted a negating hand. "That's not necessary—"

"I insist," Shean interrupted. "Join me for a meal. I was going to go and find an inn for the night presently anyway." She laughed, a sweet titter accompanied by her hand sliding back through her hair, pushing it off her shoulder with a flick. "Though, I admit, this is my first time in the city—I'm not sure where we can go *to* eat."

The man hesitated a moment longer, then relented, turning to fully face her. "I've never been one to turn away a meal—I accept your gracious offer. And, as luck would have it, I'm *not* new to this city. If you're willing to trust my word, I know of a fine place to both rent a room for the night and eat."

"I'll trust your word, then."

The man turned, gesturing down the street. "Shall we?"

Shean smiled, the idea of being stuck in Ports for the night no longer unappealing.

"Yes," she said. "Let's."

THE INN THE MAN TOOK SHEAN TO WAS CALLED THE STILTS. TRUE TO ITS NAME, it sat atop thick wooden poles on the edge of Ports, next to the harbor and strongly resembling a pier. The bottom floor of the building was a restaurant, the top two floors full of rentable rooms. Shean paid for a room, surrendering Lintok to a stable girl and ordering Silver to take her bags up to her accommodations before joining the man for dinner. At his suggestion they took kneeling cushions to a table in an outdoor eating area, close to a railing past which stretched a view of the ocean. The water turned indigo as the sky purpled with sunset.

A young man waited on them, neatly dressed in a sea glass–green uniform with long sleeves and a high collar. "Your orders?" he asked.

"Chef's choice," Shean said.

"My usual," the man said.

The waiter nodded, turning and striding off with brisk, sure steps. Shean eyed her companion.

"Your usual?" she said.

The man nodded. "Steamed lotus root," he said.

"You come here often?" Shean asked.

The man nodded again, untying the strap across his chest and setting his travel bag on the floor beside him. He kept a hand resting atop the bag, a protective gesture. "I've come to Ports for many years. I've found it to be the best place to begin when traveling through One."

"And you come to One often?"

"On occasion."

"A merchant, then?"

The edge of the man's mouth lifted. "No. I'm a traveling linguist and translator."

A language studier. No wonder he'd spoken the complicated language of Gleam with such grace and confidence. Shean wondered what'd led him to that path, but she decided not to press, reluctant to overstep and inject any awkwardness into a conversation more enjoyable than any she'd had in years. The men her age in Pearl, at least the ones who ran in the circles she frequented, were pompous peacocks, arrogant trolls who fancied themselves the next great talent of their generation, be they painters or dollmakers or tailors. This man was nothing like them—so quiet and polite, deferential and eloquent without condescension. Shean found herself smiling, resting her elbow on the table and her cheek in her palm, head cocked in a way she knew caused her hair to fall in a becoming wave down the side of her face.

"If I may ask, where are you from?" the man asked.

"The city called Pearl."

"Close by. On a shopping trip?"

"No. I'm headed up the far shore."

"I see. Business?"

"Yes. I'm seeking employment in a village up that way."

"You're quite young for a licensed dollmaker. Your first assignment?"

"Of sorts." Shean straightened, resting her arms on the table. "And you? Where are you headed?"

"I have business in Ports for another day, and then I think I'll head west."

When he spoke, he had a habit of tipping his head to the side. A quizzical gesture that he caught and corrected every few words, straightening only to end up tilting again. It was charming, and

Shean had to repress a smile as she continued their conversation. "I see. And where are *you* from?"

"The country called Steep."

Shean wasn't expecting the joke, laughing more out of startlement than mirth. "You don't have to tell me, if you'd rather not."

"It's the truth—I come from the country called Steep."

"But Steep's been at war with itself for over a hundred years! I thought no one was allowed to leave the country. Or go into it, for that matter, outside of permissioned merchants."

"All truth."

"Then how are you here?"

"I decided to leave. So I did."

"That simple?"

"No. But true."

Their conversation was interrupted by the arrival of food. A platter of roasted pebble fish drizzled in honey sauce and surrounded by thin strips of baked kelp for Shean, and a dish of fragrant steamed lotus root on a bed of wheat noodles for her companion. She eyed the flower-shaped arrangement on his plate, inhaling its earthy aroma, and regretted her choice for a moment. The next, though, she took a mouthful of fish sweet as apples and decided her choice was sound enough.

They ate for a few moments in silence, the only noise the click of their utensils and the distant caw of gulls sweeping over foam-capped waves. Shean broke first, finishing a final mouthful of chewy, slightly spicy kelp and clearing her throat.

"I've never been out of the country called One. Would you mind telling me about Steep?"

The man looked out over the water of the ocean called Wept, toward the distant horizon. For a moment Shean worried she'd offended him. Then he said, "It's a beautiful place. Hundreds of mountains wreathed in mantles of cloud, valleys lush and green and wooded. Lakes so still they're as mirrors, and rivers that chatter into waterfalls that sing songs of a beauty human voice can only envy. With its own dangers, of course, its rockslides and earthquakes and predators. But, nonetheless, an enchanting place." The man sighed, turning back to face Shean but looking down at his half-empty plate. "Or, at least that's how it was. Before the fighting."

Shean wondered how he would know that, young as he was. Stories, she supposed, from parents or grandparents—the same way she knew the First Dollmaker had been wise, strong, kind. And, of course, handsome. Picking up an eating hook, she prodded the remains of her meal, wondering how much prying was polite. Curiosity won over decorum, and she looked up.

"No one I've ever asked knows the cause of the war in Steep," she said. "Not even the merchants who've been there; they know rumors, but nothing concrete."

The man smiled, humor in his eyes. "I can tell you. But if I do, you'll never know if I'm being truthful—you'll have nothing to compare my story to."

Shean shrugged, smiling. "I'm good at telling when someone's lying."

"I've no doubt you are," he said, returning her smile. As he spoke a waiter walked swiftly by, glow lanterns in hand that she hung on the tops of poles near their table. As the lanterns' light washed over them, Shean realized the sky had darkened toward the black of night, the waves vanishing in gloom, invisible but for the sounds of rush and withdrawal from the beach below.

The man considered Shean, eyes reflecting lantern light and metallic hair gleaming, then said, "Very well. I'll tell you.

"In the country called Steep, we have dozens of monarchs. One for each mountain, and all of them wanting more and *more* mountains. That is, in simplistic terms, the root of our conflict." He sighed. "We aren't unique. The country called Gleam is in similar straits, though to a lesser, more hushed, degree—their uniting sovereign, the one who held their land together under one name, recently died. Now her children bicker over who's to next lead, tearing down their mother's decades-won prosperity like pieces of tissue.

"In Steep, our troubles don't stem from quarreling successors—no blood remains from the line of *our* great unifier. It'd be simpler if that was the case. Rather than heirs, every mountain royal with half a wit barks of 'spiritual' succession, of assuming the mantle left by the Mountain Queen through the right of kindred souls."

"The Mountain Queen?"

"Yes," the man said, face and voice subdued. "The Mountain Queen. Once, long ago, all the mountains were united under her, she who banished the Mountain Lords from the high peaks and drove them into wastelands from which none returned. Her power knew no limit, and under her guidance we were one range, each mountain a part of a greater whole. For however brief a time, there was peace." His head bowed, eyes closing. "Then she died. All she left behind was her king, and he didn't possess even a sliver of her power." He dragged a hand down his face, looking tired. "So men and women claimed each mountain for their own sects, declaring themselves rulers and beginning to war for additional peaks to add to their kingdoms."

"What happened to the Mountain Queen's king?" Shean asked.

"He . . . left."

"He died?"

The man looked down at his hands, clasped in front of him upon the tabletop. "Some say he's the one who killed the Mountain Queen, that he was banished and damned for her murder." He chuckled, a strained noise. "Others say the opposite; that he's the one true champion of his Queen and will return. That he alone can identify the Mountain Queen's destined heir and unite the peaks again."

"This was a hundred years ago?" Shean asked.

"Three hundred, soon."

"Then there's no way he can return; he's dead. He must be!" Shean said.

The man gave her a thin-lipped smile. "He must be," he echoed.

Shean eyed him, suspicious of his tone. "You think he's alive? You believe he'll return to unite your country?"

"Oh, no. I don't believe anyone will ever unite the mountains again." His gaze grew wistful. "It's a lovely dream, though."

She pursed her lips. "I don't understand."

The man cocked his head. "You don't think unity is a lovely dream?"

"I don't understand why it need be a dream—*why* does Steep fight?"

"As I said, the mountain monarchs—"

"But why don't they make peace? For the sake of their people, as One did?" Shean failed to keep a note of pride from her voice as she referenced the Great Alliance that'd united One some hundred years ago. An effort spearheaded by the First Dollmaker himself. "It's foolishness, to quarrel over dominance while clinging to rumors of a long-dead man who'll return to pick the next great queen—that sounds like nothing but an excuse to keep fighting."

The man gave her a pained look. "You don't realize how blessed you are."

"Excuse me?"

The man shook his head. "I mean no offense—it's less that *you* are blessed, so much as your entire country is."

"In what way?"

"You have the Shod."

"The *Shod?*" Shean frowned. "You think those monsters a blessing?"

"In disguise, yes, though I beg you to not misunderstand—I harbor no love for the Shod, and wish, as most do, that they didn't exist."

Shean tapped her fingers on the tabletop, one part irritated, three parts curious to see where he was going with this talk of Shod. "I see," she said. "What *do* you mean, then?"

The man leaned over the table, eyes steady on hers. "The Shod: the demons who torment One, terrify its citizens, tear down its great cities, and, over the decades, have threatened to destroy you entirely." His lips twisted, expression wry. "That description alone questions just how peaceful One is. But it's true enough that this land functions socially in a way I envy and wish could be achieved in Steep. But without the Shod, or some equivalent of the Shod, such civil peace is impossible." He lifted a hand toward Shean, an imploring gesture, like a beggar raising his cup. "You compare Steep to One, and that's unfair. Because, unlike you, we have no common enemy. We lack a universal threat to make all other quarrels and ambitions moot. We did, once, in the form of the Mountain Lords, who were just as terrifying to us as the Shod are to you. But those beasts have long been sealed away—we no longer have our equivalent of the Shod to fight. So we fight one another instead."

"But why fight at all?" Shean said, disliking the suggestion that One's peace thrived only because they hadn't the time to spare to tear one another to pieces. Uncomfortable that a part of her understood such logic. "Why fight when you don't need to in order to survive?"

"A friend of mine used to say we can't help it. That fighting is a part of people's bones."

"That's foolish."

"Oh, yes. Very." He smiled. "But isn't human nature something of a fool?"

Shean felt she should protest, but before she could speak the man stood, pulling his travel pack onto his shoulder. "I apologize, but it's time I be going."

"Oh," Shean said, pushing herself to her feet, a twinge of disappointment smarting between her ribs. "Do you have a place to stay for the night? I'd be more than happy to—"

"That's very kind," the man interrupted, "but I've already made arrangements." He smiled. "The offer is greatly appreciated, though."

Something in the way he said the words, polite as they were, made Shean realize that further protests, no matter how persuasive, would fail. "Well, thank you for sharing this meal with me. And thank you for your help earlier."

He bowed. "My pleasure. One of the joys of traveling is meeting kind strangers. I'm fortunate to have met you today."

Shean had been called many things, some titles more colorful than others. But she'd never been called kind. She was surprised by how flustered the compliment made her, heat rising to her face and her tongue tangling in her mouth, rendering her dumb. It was all she could manage to return the man's bow and stammer a final thanks. Then he was off, walking away, disappearing into The Stilts with a gleam of copper, out of sight before Shean caught her breath. By the time she rushed after him (to do what, she hadn't a clue) he was gone, the only person in sight a waiter who asked, politely, if she was finished with her meal.

Feeling listless, Shean paid the bill and went upstairs to her room. She found Silver jumping on the bed, freezing when she entered the room like a child caught doing something forbidden, but also giving her a broad grin, in no way contrite. She ignored him, changing from her travel clothing to the Gleam dress, which fit as wonderfully as expected. Seeing the jeweled skirts swish around her legs wasn't nearly as satisfying as she'd imagined the sight would be, though, and she swapped them for a sleeping shift, packing the dress away to be saved for Web. She pulled Silver with her into bed, holding him against her chest despite his squirming protests and curling on her side upon a lumpy mattress, under a blanket that made her itch.

She barely noticed her discomfort, though, lying awake late into the night with the traveling man's soft voice and strange words keeping sleep at bay. The Shod, a blessing? A saving grace? If that was true, what would happen if the Shod were, at long last, thwarted? What were the implications of achieving the sacred goal of every dollmaker who'd ever lived, destroying the Shod and leaving One a country free of monsters?

Would One be free if the Shod were gone? Or would they end up like Steep and Gleam, tearing one another to pieces over frail claims to power?

Shean shook her head, squeezing her eyes shut and holding Silver tighter. No. That couldn't be. That man didn't understand. He *couldn't*—he wasn't from the country called One, and—thanks to the efforts of dollmakers—the Shod didn't exist anywhere *but* One, the borders of the country strictly protected to prevent any of the monsters from slipping out and terrorizing the larger world. He meant well, but the fact remained that he was an outsider; he hadn't been in the Red Tide. He hadn't experienced the carnage and heard the screams. He hadn't lost his family to the Shod. He didn't know the horror of living in the haunted world Shean lived in every day of her life, and therefore would never understand the importance of her dolls being the guard dolls she'd made them to be, contributing to the efforts being made to rid One of its demons.

The Shod being destroyed was a good thing. The *best* of things. Something Shean yearned to witness in her lifetime.

Shean's eyelids began to droop, her body relaxing and her thoughts losing cohesion. *I'll never see that man again*, she thought, eyes shutting. Blearily, she felt a pang of sadness at the realization, a regret soon lost amidst the hazy dark settling in her, the warm and comfortable numb of sleep curling around her.

Her last clear thought was that she'd forgotten to tell the man her name.

Or ask him for his.

SEVERAL DAYS LATER, SHEAN CAME UPON THE AFTERMATH OF A SHOD ATTACK. It was on the road called Wide, just past the hills called Green and halfway between the far shore cities called High and Bound. Despite its name the road was a narrow path, flanked on one side by the sea called Clear and on the other by a nameless slope spotted with several leafy bushes. A merchant was the obvious victim, a cart of pottery splintered and crushed across the entire width of the road in many pieces of colorful glaze, like an incomplete mosaic. The destruction was fresh, and indicated as such by the dolls milling about the wreckage, some cleaning up the broken pottery, others rooting about at the back of the destruction, doing something Shean, when she pulled Lintok to a stop and watched, couldn't quite see.

They were clumsy, inelegant dolls. Big and loutish, with hunching shoulders and arms so long they almost brushed the ground, thin, triangle-shaped necks supporting domed heads far too small for their bodies. Their feet were nothing but flat platforms, lacking the distinction of toes, and they only had four fingers on each equally flat hand. A dollmaker was present, overseeing the dolls, and he was the obvious holder of a guard license in every conceivable way, from his tacky leather clothing—the prevailing fashion among younger, provincial dollmakers—to the slicing scar on his right cheek that could only have come from a Shod, a slight white line that must've originated from such a minor wound, Shean wagered the cut had been preserved with care so as to remain as prominent a mark as it was. His ears were studded with rings, plain metal loops that shone in the midday sunlight.

Several minutes passed before the dollmaker noticed Shean. She had to dismount Lintok, come closer, *and* clear her throat to get him to stop scowling at the scene in front of him, his head jerking up at the noise.

"Who are you?" he asked. His eyes flicked over Shean, then moved to Silver, who smiled and waved from where he sat in Lintok's saddle. "You and your son should turn back and go to the city called High, ma'am. There's been a Shod attack."

"I can see that," Shean said, planting a hand on her hip and fighting the urge to roll her eyes. "He's not my son. He's my doll."

"Doll?"

"Yes," Shean said. She reached into the pocket of her travel jacket, pulling and holding out Nock's license, only for a moment—just long enough for the man to see the boar that marked her his equal. If not superior.

"Oh. You're a dollmaker," the man said, voice less than enthused.

"You have a gift for stating the obvious," Shean said, pocketing Nock's license. She looked at the destroyed pottery cart. "What happened here?"

"Shod," the man said, brusque. One of his dolls stumbled as he spoke, dropping half of a large pot that rolled into another doll, who was subsequently knocked off-balance, falling forward and dropping an armful of pottery shards. "Watch it!" the man said, eyes snapping from Shean to his creations. In response his dolls picked up their pace, rushing about in their cumbersome, thumping way.

Shean huffed a sigh, scowling. "There's no need to be difficult. How *many* Shod? When did they attack? How many people died?"

"What's it to you?" the man asked, guarded.

Shean stood tall, lifting her chin and leveling a stern gaze at him. "I am a licensed dollmaker. As such, it's well within my rights to ask for the damage report of a Shod attack," she said. Then, letting go of Lintok's lead, she folded her arms, set her jaw, and waited.

The man scowled, though Shean couldn't tell if the glower was for her or the answer he, after a surly moment of silence, gave her. "Same as what always happens. A merchant thinks he's safe because Shod attacks have decreased since the Red Tide, decides not to 'waste' the coin required to hire a dollmaker to escort him along the far shore cities. Gets attacked, blows an alarm, but before the nearest dollmaker can reach him, it's over."

"You're local?" Shean guessed.

The man dipped his head in a nod, offering his name. "Kerr, of the village called Crest. I've been assigned this stretch of road all the way back to the city called Rested." He pointed as he spoke, gesturing away from the shore, into a smudge of woodland in the distance. Shean's eyebrows rose.

"That's a lot of land for one dollmaker to monitor," she said.

Kerr snorted. "Don't have to tell me that. Merchants aren't the only ones who think we should worry less about the Shod these days."

Shean's lips pursed with displeasure. The craft of dollmaking would never become obsolete—not so long as the Shod existed, and the Shod would always exist, until a dollmaker came along who was clever enough to find a way to put a permanent end to them. Or, to be more specific, until a dollmaker came along who could either drive them to total extinction in one spectacular display, or who could figure out how they were born and cut them off at their source. That said, it was no secret that, since the Red Tide, Shod attacks—and even sightings—had indeed been decreasing in number. It was like the Red Tide had been the Shod's final push, their last attempt to wipe out as many humans as possible. And when they failed to kill everyone in Pearl, when Shean's parents and brother had died to save her and every other broken survivor, the monsters had gone into hiding. To lick their wounds, some said. To die off, others—oh so optimistically—suggested.

But Shean had a different theory. That the Shod had gone into hiding not to lick their wounds or wither to nothing, but to *regather*. They were out there, somewhere. Hiding, yes. But also preparing. Getting ready to strike again.

And this time, Shean would be ready for them.

"You haven't said your name," Kerr said, intruding on Shean's thoughts. She pushed her annoyance at the interruption down and flicked the hair back from her shoulder, fixing him in a cool look.

"I am Dollmaker Shean of Pearl. This is my doll, Silver," she added as Lintok drifted to the leafy side of the road, Silver clambering down from the elk's saddle and trotting to her side.

"You name your dolls?" Kerr said, and he didn't try to mask the sneer in his voice.

"You don't?" Shean asked with a sniff, using her best you-are-an-uncultured-bumpkin voice. Kerr reddened.

"What's the point? They're just dolls."

A common sentiment among dollmakers. Hence why most dolls looked as lovely as toads squatting in mud puddles.

"Right," Shean said. "Would you like my assistance?"

"With what? The Shod are already taken care of," Kerr said, chest puffing out as he spoke, swelling with pride.

"And the pottery merchant? Where is he?"

Kerr's chest deflated. A little. "Dead."

"Show me."

Kerr muttered something under his breath, but turned and led the way, past the dolls cleaning up pottery to the back of what had once been the unfortunate merchant's wares cart. Kerr's dolls looked up at their approach, and as the dolls straightened, Shean could see what they were huddled around.

Shod.

Dead Shod. There were half a dozen of them, and they were scattered around the fringes of the wreckage, necks snapped and long bodies tangled, pounded beyond repair, and the white, glowing light of their eyes vanished like extinguished candles. But even without that searing look they were unmistakable: horrible, twisted creatures cobbled together with pieces of stone and wood and *organic* material, human bones dangling from twisted cords made from an unidentifiable substance and tufts of fur from animals Shean couldn't name wedged in cracks along many, spindly limbs that could be called neither arms nor legs, tipped in stubs and pincers that were neither hands nor feet. Blood streaked the uneven sides of each Shod, and several strands of fresh, fleshy material were wound around the uneven teeth exposed in their slack-jawed mouths.

No two Shod looked exactly alike, but all tended to have generally similar shapes—wedge-like heads, too many limbs, tails made from materials that ran the gamut from stone to rotting berries to stolen human parts. These particular monsters were made unique by the pieces of pottery clutched in their few-digited claws, shoved through their eyes and impaling their stubby limbs. To an untrained eye, it might look like the Shod had been killed by the pottery, but Shean knew better. Kerr's dolls hadn't turned the broken pottery on the Shod, hadn't used the polished pieces of clay to slay the monsters; the monsters had thrust those fragments into themselves on purpose.

Shean hadn't noticed stopping, but she had, feet stuck in place. As she gazed across the carnage, Silver trotted past her, joining Kerr's dolls and crouching next to one of the Shod. Tipping close, he reached out a quizzical hand, rummaging about in the dead monster, poking and prodding and tugging, quick fingers pulling out bits of pottery and lifting limp limbs, holding them up before dropping them and crab-walking over to the next Shod, which received similar treatment.

The sight of hands she'd carved herself digging through the Shod upset Shean—she wanted to tell Silver to stop, but she was aware of Kerr staring at her. The thought of admitting she hadn't told Silver to act as he was acting—implying she had no control over her own doll—was enough to ignite a flame of stubbornness and pride within her, the blaze keeping her from scolding Silver. Right now.

Instead she feigned intention and followed Silver's lead, taking a firm step forward and studying the Shod in as much detail as her stomach could handle, noting shapes and materials, internalizing size and features as she took advantage of an admittedly rare opportunity to have a close look. Little was known about the Shod outside of the fact that only dolls could slay them, but the scholars of the Research Guild speculated that the monsters were always building themselves. That was how they grew—by stealing materials from whatever was around them, using said materials to construct more limbs or longer bodies or tails or teeth. It was scientific fact that the Shod were attracted to well-made, manufactured items, in particular drawn to artistic objects such as tapestries, jewelry, and, yes, pottery. Such fine-crafted things seemed to be their favorite construction materials, second only to the flesh of human bodies.

That was why, as Shean had tried to explain to Nock, it made sense to make beautiful dolls. Dolls that could not only kill the Shod, but would, by the nature of their very appearances and craftsmanship, attract the monsters right to them, straight into carefully plotted traps set to spring far away from populated areas.

Dolls were the only effective weapons the country called One had against Shod. And they should be the most intelligent, beautiful, and elegant weapons conceivable.

Staring at the Shod before her now, Shean felt a hot, twisted anger, potent enough to make her teeth clench. Arms dropping, she balled her hands into fists and wished she'd gotten here sooner. If she'd only arrived in time, she could've fought these creatures herself, proving the merit of her dolls without having to continue on to the village called Web.

One of Kerr's dolls bumped into Shean, and she huffed in annoyance, shoving the thing away with her leg and a glare. Then something tugged on the back of her skirt; she turned, ready to kick out again, but stopped when she found Silver. Evidently finished with his perusal of the Shod, he had one hand anchored on her, the other lifted and pointing just past the dead monsters and the dolls attending them. At dead people.

People.

Shean stared for a long moment, then turned to Kerr. "You didn't say the merchant had a family."

"You have eyes, don't you?" Kerr said, but the snapped words were a bluff. He looked away from Shean as he spoke, a dark red painting his ear tips, the tops of his cheeks gaining a distressed flush.

Shean stared at him, then forced herself to look back at the bodies. They were laid out in a row along the side of the road, with enough care to suggest respect for the dead, but not yet covered by burial sheets. One man, presumably the pottery merchant, with dark black hair in a queue and scored-out eyes, his chest torn open and hollowed out, organs stolen away and leaving gore in their wake. Three children. One teenage girl with a broken neck and a missing arm. Two identical boys who couldn't be older than ten. Both of their throats slit.

Shean didn't know them. And she did. She'd seen them before and never in her life. They were here on a road in the middle of nowhere, and they were also in the city called Pearl, lined up with dozens of other corpses, just four more tortured faces lost in a crowd of death. They were her family and strangers.

They were someone Shean should've protected.

Too much. She turned on a heel, walking to the edge of the road, her back to the bodies and the wreckage and the not-dead-enough Shod. She folded her arms, staring into the undergrowth in front of her until her eyes stung, but not blinking. Not blinking because she knew, if she closed her eyes now, she'd be back there. In the city called Pearl. The night of the Red Tide. Blood in the air. Blood in her mouth. Smoke. Glowing white eyes. Her family in a row, cold to the touch, eyes not seeing her even when she bent over them, said their names, whispered pleas for them to look at her. Say something. Breathe.

A shuddering breath of her own. A long exhale.

The Shod had to be stopped. They had to be stopped, and Shean had to be a part of that. She *had* to—for the sake of her family, for Master Nock, for all the children who hadn't been as lucky as her, who hadn't been saved from the Red Tide and were now nothing but bones under earth, lives and potentials cut short while Shean flourished. For the sake of all of One, for the debt she owed to the dollmaker who'd saved her life, Shean would become a guard dollmaker. And she, along with her beautiful, enticing dolls, would be the Shod's utter ruin.

Cool, small fingers touched Shean's arm, sought out the clench of her own fingers in the crook of her elbow. Silver was beside her, standing on tiptoe and smiling when she looked down at him. Holding a finger to his lips, he winked at her.

"Are you just going to stand there?" Kerr asked from behind her, voice sullen.

"No," Shean said. Unfolding her arms, she took Silver's hand. Then she whirled on a heel. "I'm leaving."

Pulling Silver along with her, she strode past Kerr, past the dead merchant and his family, past the dead Shod and the dolls cleaning up broken pottery, all the way back to Lintok, who'd taken to grazing along the road while she was occupied. It took a firm tug on his lead, and a gentle pat on his neck, to get him to stop snacking, his muzzle nuzzling her shoulder and his soft lips plucking at her hair in passing when she hoisted herself into his saddle, bending to give Silver a hand up when he lifted his arms toward her, imploring. She set him in front of her, containing him within her arms and forcing him to sit against her, just in case he got one of his mischievous ideas and tried to jump from the saddle without permission.

"Leaving?" Kerr said, trailing after her and coming to a stop a pace back from Lintok. He lifted his arms in a protesting jerk. "I thought you said you were going to help me clean up this mess!"

Shean fixed him in a severe look, pleased when he took an involuntary step back from her before catching himself and stopping. "Believe me," she said. "I am."

Then she urged Lintok forward, around and away from the dead merchant and his shattered pottery, away from a handful of thwarted Shod and on to the hundreds, thousands of living monsters awaiting her in the future.

THE REMAINDER OF SHEAN'S JOURNEY TO WEB WAS UNEVENTFUL. TWO STEADY weeks of passing through the remaining cities of the far shore, and then two tedious days of guiding Lintok down ill-kempt roads that grew all the more cracked and overgrown the closer they got to the forest called Deep. They met no one once they left the city called Shoal, veering from the coastline and heading into the hinterlands of One, and not a single Shod appeared to disturb their progress. Each day was the dull golden child of late summer: tepid weather with warm breezes, parched clouds dotting the sky, long hours of light and short nights loud with the sawing of crickets, the drone of cicadas.

Not even the slight excitement of losing one's way colored the days—the last time Shean had been this far from Pearl had been when she and Nock took her family to be buried, the way to the Dollmaker's Graveyard passing by the forest called Deep. As Shean traveled, memories of that journey fifteen years ago returned to her, random road markers striking her as familiar, a cluster of trees catching her attention, autumn copper the last time she'd seen them; soft guides that ensured she took the right turns and followed the correct paths, eliminating the need to loop back from a dead end or turn away from a town she didn't mean to visit.

The closer she came to Deep, the stronger her memories of the funeral grew. On the final days of her journey she found herself thinking constantly of the memorial cart, how its left wheel had squeaked and the paint on the decorative reliefs carved next to the cushioned seat on the front of the wagon had peeled in flecks of black, stripping away from traditional, hand-carved peony flowers and Death Elk motifs. The two white elks Nock had rented to pull the cart were always shaking their heads to discourage late year mosquitos from flocking to their eyes, and when Shean tried to pet them they'd rear and jerk up their horns, a warning to leave them be. Lying curled on the side of the road to Web with her travel pack cushioning her head, Shean found it hard to fall asleep at night, kept awake with the remembrance of how Nock had insisted they not speak while they traveled, fasting from speech as a sign of respect to the three corpses wrapped in linens in the bed of the cart, who'd never speak again.

Nock had insisted on many things concerning that funeral. Shean hadn't even wanted to help with the ceremony, but Nock said she'd regret it if she didn't. *Don't you want to say goodbye to them?* he'd said, eyes red-rimmed from all the weeping he'd done in the days following the Red Tide. *Once they're buried, you won't be allowed to visit them—it's against the First Dollmaker's edicts to return and disturb the peace of a dollmaker's grave. This is your last chance.* And then, almost pleadingly:

Don't you want to put them to rest with the hands of the daughter and sister they loved?

So Shean had gone with Nock to bury her family of corpses in the Dollmaker's Graveyard, a plateau of soft stone just past the forest called Deep, on the edge of the desert called Wave. A sacred place far away from any city or town, the Graveyard was where the First Dollmaker himself was buried, an honored place for the most honored dollmakers. They'd arrived to find prearranged grave slots waiting for them, rectangular holes carved in the stone of the plateau that were deep enough for a body and up to forty dolls.

Not that so much space was needed. Only one of Giko's dolls had survived the Red Tide. All of her parents' dolls were smashed to splinters by the Shod.

By custom, no dolls made by the living were allowed in the Dollmaker's Graveyard, human hands required to lower the dead into their final resting places. A reality that had caused Shean no small amount of anxiety on the trip, her longing to beg Nock to use the guard dolls he'd brought along with them squashed by how cowardly the plea made her feel. It'd been an immense relief when Nock had, unprompted, taken it upon himself to handle the corpses. Fifteen years ago he'd been a middle-aged man who was, if not in his prime, not too far past it, and he'd lifted the bodies from the cart with ease, Shean not wanting to look but unable to tear her gaze from the gilded embroidery on the cloths secured around her family's faces.

Once the bodies were in place it'd fallen to Shean to give them their final companions. She'd placed Giko's remaining doll on his linen-wrapped chest, arranging the figurine with reluctant care.

The doll had been a gift from her brother for her recent birthday, and since the Red Tide the doll, lifeless as it was without Giko, had become her most precious belonging, a memento of a time in her life that was slipping away from her. She'd gazed at the simplistic features of the doll's face, touched the streak of blue painted down its androgynous chest and felt the waning memories of childhood in the grain of the wood. Then, at Nock's urgings, she'd forced herself to move on and place small mannequins in Manma and Father's graves, tucking them under the corpses' arms before scrambling out of the burials.

As she'd worked she'd breathed through her mouth so as not to smell the sickly-sweet of the incense Nock burned on the journey to keep the fragrance of rotting flesh at bay. But breathing through her mouth had been, in some ways, worse—when she inhaled she could taste the incense. And the rot beneath it. So she'd tried not to breathe at all, and was lightheaded by the time she yanked herself out of the final grave, scrambling onto the plateau so quickly she scraped her knees on the rock while taking gasping, desperate breaths of fresh air.

Nock then said the parting words ("You made well your work, and now deserve well rest—may the First Dollmaker welcome you with a feast for your service and sacrifice.") and together they'd lifted and placed stone slabs over the tombs. That'd been the most difficult part, an aging man rushing toward his elder years and a girl not even a decade old struggling to arrange the stones over the corpses of their lost comrades and family. Shean's arms had hurt so badly from the effort, she'd wept.

For days, Shean relived those events, the funeral rising and falling in her mind as she rode toward the forest called Deep, inevitable like the tides of the ocean and combining with the fresher, frustrating memories of the Shod attack she'd witnessed on the road behind her. It was a sleep-deprived and emotionally spent Shean who arrived in Web, feeling each day of the past two weeks in the ache of her back and legs, the heaviness of her eyelids. Her weariness sapped her of any triumph or joy she might've felt when she at last reached the end of the road through Deep and caught her first glimpse of her destination.

Web was the only village she'd ever seen without a wall, sitting exposed in a clearing at the very heart of the forest called Deep with houses built in a tight cluster, like elk huddled in a pasture during winter, shoulder to shoulder for warmth. From the edge of the clearing those houses looked odd, hazy around the edges and tilted. As Shean rode Lintok up to the village, saddle rash burning along her inner thighs, the structures increasingly brought to mind bird nests.

It was past midday, the sun large and close overhead. Sunlight glanced off the jeweled facets of Shean's Gleam dress, which she'd dug from her packs that morning after scrubbing herself in a roadside stream. She still smelled more like Lintok than she would've liked, but no matter—Shean on a bad day was a queen compared to what these backwater villagers would be used to. With that in mind, and as intended, she arrived in Web with (admittedly weary) confidence, clad in splendor and at a time of day when lives would be in full swing, work to be done and voices to be heard. A time that guaranteed an audience.

But there was none of that from Web. All Shean heard as she approached was the soft *thunk* of Lintok's hooves on the dirt path leading to the village. Nothing human disturbed the quiet, Web still as the ocean the day before a typhoon. Shean grew taut from straining to hear signs of life, jumping when Lintok stepped from the dirt road to a stone path, his steps turning from clomps to clicks, a hard noise that sliced the silence to ribbons.

They'd reached the edge of the village. Looking up at the houses they passed, Shean understood why she'd thought of bird nests when she'd seen them from a distance—long, supple tree branches had been woven into curled shapes around each structure, above which peeked roofs of plated tile. Fascinated, she pulled Lintok to a stop and dismounted, helping Silver do the same when he latched onto her wrist and gave her an imploring look. She walked to the nearest house and reached out, running a finger down the slope of a single curved branch.

"Is this why they don't have a wall? Do the branches keep the Shod out?" she wondered, voice loud in the quiet. She looked at her companions as she spoke. Lintok had his head down, grazing on the few clusters of grass poking up at the edges of the house. In response to her question he flicked an ear.

Silver was chasing a giant white-and-yellow butterfly, hands up and waving in attempts to snag the milky wings beating the air just out of his reach. As Shean watched, he tripped over his own feet and fell.

Shean lowered her hand and sighed. It said an uncomfortable amount about her, that she'd taken to talking to these two like they possessed the ability to answer. Though, to be fair, she'd been driven to attempting communication by the sheer tedium of her journey, a drudgery exacerbated by the days that'd passed since they'd left the far shore and, with it, any semblance of civilization. There hadn't been much to do *but* talk to the elk and doll as she'd trudged down a road that increasingly resembled a deer trail, sleeping curled up on the uneven ground beneath trees and bathing in streams that smelled strongly of moss. Pretending to have conversations with them had helped pass time.

She'd expected such remedies to boredom to be unnecessary once she reached Web. Of course, she'd also expected a town with marked signs of life.

As if on cue, a peal of laughter split the air, quickly shushed by several voices. Then the sound of something being dragged across stone, a clatter followed by strange thunks and a birdlike whistle. Shean's attention snapped toward the noises with relief and, grabbing Lintok's reins, she followed a babble of giggles and whispers out into a town square, the irregular stones under her feet replaced by an open stretch of uniform cobbles encircled by the houses of Web. In the center of the square sat a statue of dun stone, polished to catch sunlight in a glazed glare.

In her travels, Shean had seen many statues that depicted many things: local gods, war heroes, famous leaders, even memorials for those lost in the Red Tide and similar tragedies, great stone people atop pedestals inscribed with names and dates and the occasional quote. Of all things, though, the statue of Web was a giant spider, clinging to an intricately woven web with one hairy leg lifted out as if reaching for something, giant pincers parted and a multitude of bulbous, crystalline eyes glaring in all directions. The cobbles spread out around the statue were decorated with stylized spider silhouettes, the entire square a celebration of what were, back in Pearl, venomous, eight-legged vermin. Taking in these decorative spiders along with the houses ringing the square, Shean realized the buildings' woven exteriors were closer to spiderwebs than bird nests.

Nock had said Web was known for its spiders. Shean hadn't realized that meant they were also *obsessed* with spiders.

Next to the spider statue stood a group of children. Six in total, and the source of the giggling and the occasional, stifled laugh. All of them wore tunics and work trousers of gray or brown, necklines and sleeves decorated with stitching that spread to form meshes of overlapping lines. Five children were gathered in a tight circle around something they were teasing—the biggest two, a tall boy and a gangly girl, had sticks they used to poke the thing while three little boys threw twigs and stones at their victim. The sixth child, a girl who looked eight or nine, stood a pace back from the activity, bunching up the bottom of her faded tunic with pale hands and watching with an anxious expression.

At first Shean couldn't make out what the children's prey was. Some animal, from the glimpses she caught of its staggering legs, its movements of a skittering, non-human nature. Too large to be a woodland squirrel, but too small to be a feral boar—a moon badger? Then one of the children turned and ran a few paces to pick up a fresh stone, and Shean had a clear view of what stood in the center of the circle.

Her next breath hitched, catching in her throat as she took in a lopsided, gourd-shaped body, four spindly legs of varying lengths, a crooked and low-set head with a square nub dead-center in its face, above which sat a single hollowed, sunken eye. A spike rose above this hole, stubby like a toenail. The creature emitted a whistling noise as it tried to scamper out of reach of the sticks thwacking it, the stones pitched at it cracking against its thin legs.

The alarmed sound was something Shean had heard before, and in a multitude, a ringing, a terrible shrill that bled into a howl, a scream, a wail echoing down the streets of Pearl, cresting the city's rooftops and penetrating the windows of houses, coming through every crack and nook and jolting Shean awake, making her sit up with bleary eyes that she knuckled, looking toward her window and the outside world for only a moment before Giko came, bursting into her room with their parents close behind, all three barely woken themselves but already wearing armor on their chests and necks and joints, faces grim, voices too loud for nighttime as Giko rushed to Shean's window and closed it, bolted it, as Manma and Father knelt at her bedside, each taking one of her arms in leather-gloved hands and telling her to stay in the house, to not open the doors or the windows, to not go outside no matter what. Then they were gone and Giko was helping her dress, cupping her face and kissing her forehead and telling her to hide under her bed until he came back for her. And then he was gone, too. Gone when the house started to burn, when she was forced to crawl out from her hiding place lest she suffocate on smoke or sear in the flames coming ever closer, running downstairs and opening the door even though she wasn't supposed to, stepping out into the street even though she wasn't supposed to. Seeing the shapes of the creatures filling Pearl with their Cry, lopsided shapes with strange bodies and heads, spikes and juts and jumbles, spindly legs clinging to roofs and people who screamed, screams cut into abrupt silences and spurts of red, sprays that hit her face hot and fragrant, that covered the stones under her feet and made her slip when she tried to run, run, run, screaming for Giko and pursued by the whistling, the baying, the Shod.

The children in front of her had captured a Shod.

Shean stepped forward, dizzy with memories, mouth open to cry a warning. Before she could, the gangly girl leapt forward, aiming a kick at the Shod. Her heel struck the creature's side with a crack, knocking it off-balance. Down it went, legs a frantic wave, whistles turning to hollow, pleading hoots. Watching, Shean hesitated, warnings wilting like a neglected houseplant in her mouth.

Something wasn't right. If that thing was a Shod, how was it being contained, let alone wounded, by a group of children? The Shod held no fear of humans—quite the opposite. And Shod didn't bumble around like this one, heaving itself to its feet and swaying, disoriented and confused. A child threw a rock, hitting the thing above its hollow eye. It spun and Shean saw black lines spread on the back of its head, a familiar sweep of nine strokes. She understood.

The thing had a Breath Mark.

It was a *doll*.

The two children with sticks shared a look and, together, leapt forward, tackling the doll. It whistled in alarm as it was pinned to the ground, unforgiving fists pounding its back before the children flipped it on its side, exposing its belly for the littler children to kick. The girl on the edge of the group made a protesting noise, stepping forward but stopping before coming close enough to intervene, flinching back when the tall boy glared at her. Her face scrunched with distress, spots of red appearing in the center of her pale cheeks.

There was a splintering noise. The girl winced. The doll wheezed.

Shean had seen enough. She marched forward, Lintok and Silver in tow, raising the voice she used when she wanted her audience to know she meant business.

"Stop that! What do you think you're doing?"

The children jumped, more than one dropping their makeshift weapons as they spun to face her. The doll took the pause in its torment as an opportunity, springing into the air and jumping over the children's heads, scampering across the square, one broken leg dragging behind it, clattering against the cobbles. It leapt onto a house and, with many rustles and snaps, climbed out of reach.

The tall boy gave chase, running a few paces after the doll, but stopping when it reached the house. He stomped a foot with anger, whirling to glare at Shean.

"Why did you do that?" he shout-whispered, voice hoarse, furious, and quiet. But not quiet enough; the gangly girl—his sister, if their matching noses and manes of blocky brown hair were anything to go by—shushed him, hurrying up to grab his arm. He glared at her too, shaking her off, but when he looked back at Shean, he continued in even softer tones. "It took us *hours* to catch it!"

"Catch it?" Shean said at a normal volume that made all six children flinch. She scowled back at the tall boy. "What do you think you're doing, treating a doll like that? It's beyond disrespectful, acting in such a way toward something that protects you from the Shod!"

The tall boy snorted. So did his sister—she was the one to speak next, voice high and nasally, but hushed like her brother's. "Protects us? That doll's never saved *anyone*."

"Yeah!" one of the other children said, a little boy with a birthmark splotched across his nose. He and the other two little boys scurried to join their friends, clustering around the tall siblings and collectively glaring at Shean. The anxious girl joined them but at a distance, shuffling behind the group and giving Shean a look more apologetic than aggressive.

Shean frowned. "What do you mean?" She shot a dubious look at the doll, clinging to its chosen house like a cliff bat to its sleeping hole, dangling by its claws. Its head cocked at her, freezing for a moment before springing back into its original position, producing a hollow clacking noise. Shean's nose wrinkled. "That doll can't be the work of an artisan."

"It's not a toy!" the tall boy said, exasperated.

"Then what do you mean, it's never saved anyone? If it's a guard doll, then its very design dictates that it protects you from the Shod, and is therefore deserving of your resp—"

"Shod!" the tall boy echoed, disdain dripping from the single syllable. His sister rolled her eyes, the trio of littler boys mirroring her when she folded her arms across her chest. The tall boy sneered, voice scathing. "How could it fight the Shod, when the Shod aren't real?"

Shean's mouth opened. No words came out. She stared at the tall boy, sure he was making a joke. A bad one.

But his face was serious. As was his sister's. Shean looked between them for a bewildered moment, voice betraying confusion. "You . . . you don't think the Shod exist?"

"*I've* never seen a Shod," the gangly girl said.

"You haven't?" Shean asked. The gangly girl shook her head. Shean looked at the rest of the children. "Have any of you?"

Five more negating shakes of little heads. Shean shook her own head, baffled, though the next moment she realized that she shouldn't be—the children in front of her were all easily under the age of fifteen. That meant they'd been born after the Red Tide and the resulting recession of the Shod. There hadn't been a Shod attack in Pearl since the Tide, and the same went for most cities along the far shore. Even so, Shean had thought that in the village called Web, it being so far away from the coast and so close to the untamed lands of One that were historically notorious for Shod clusters, attacks would still be common.

Apparently not.

"Your parents have told you about them, though," Shean said.

The birthmarked boy batted his hand through the air in dismissal. "Grown-ups lie about everything."

Shean frowned at him. "No they don't."

"They lie about the Night Foxes!" The birthmarked boy's brow set, and he shook his finger at Shean, as if scolding her. "I tried it—I went to a river and stood in its center all night and sang the thousand-rains song and clapped three times between each verse, and no midnight-furred foxes came to give me sugar flowers to eat or to take me to their palace of shadow and starlight to meet the Wise Princess Who Always Weeps!"

Shean rested a hand on her hip, exasperated. "Night Foxes are myths!"

The birthmarked boy flushed. "So are the Shod!"

"No. They're not."

"How do *you* know?"

"Because my entire family was killed by them," Shean said. That silenced the birthmarked boy, along with the other children. They shuffled, eyes dropping to stare at the ground as she went on, speaking in firm tones. "I assure you; the Shod are very real. And it's the most despicable form of stupidity to bully the dolls made to keep them from tearing you apart. Let alone an affront to all the dollmakers of the country called One."

The children's abashedness faded as quickly as it'd come, replaced by sullenness, hunched shoulders, and glowers. Shean suspected they'd heard what she was saying before and had long ago stopped believing the words. Their parents probably told them these things often, receiving the same pouting, rebellious looks she was now getting from the little imps.

Shean straightened, an idea occurring to her of how to, if not get through to the children, then at least see them properly punished. An idea that'd get her started on the business she'd come to Web for in the first place.

"Where are your parents?" she asked, looking from the children to the houses ringing the square. She couldn't see where the doors of the structures were amidst the weave of twigs encircling them, but that didn't stop her from gesturing to a house, taking a step in its direction. "Is this where you live?"

The children let out a collective, protesting gasp, leaping forward to block her path with many outstretched arms, fanned and waving hands. With the exception of the anxious girl, who made no attempts to block Shean, they began talking over one another, voices a torrent of pleas:

"No!"

"Don't wake them up!"

"My father will be furious if he knows I got up early again!"

"My manma will make me skip first meal!"

"Ilo will scold us!"

"We were just playing Kill the Shod!"

Shean gave a sharp look to the speaker of this last excuse—the gangly girl—temper flaring. "'Kill the Shod'? That was a *doll*, not a Shod, you insufferable little urchin—and you're lucky that's the case!"

"What do you know about anything?" the gangly girl asked, face flushed red with anger and distress, words turning petulant in the face of parental threat. "Who *are* you?"

Shean drew herself to her full height, pleased when, right at that moment, the sun reached a point in the sky that sent light rays bouncing off the jewels of her dress in a veritable shower of gleams and sparkles. “A dollmaker.” As she spoke she stepped aside, gesturing to Silver, who stepped out from behind her and dipped a bow, straightening with a smile. The anxious girl gasped aloud, hands lifting to her lips in what first appeared a shocked gesture, but revealed itself to be a sign of delight when the girl’s eyes widened, a pink blush flashing across her features. Shean gave her a smile, flipping the hair back from her face and declaring herself fully: “I am Dollmaker Shean of Pearl.”

That took a bit of wind out of the children’s sails. They stared at Silver, none of them sharing the open delight of the anxious girl, but the gangly girl unable to hide her curiosity, her brother’s expression impressed. But only for a moment—the next they shared worried looks, the little boys edging to hide behind the tall siblings.

“You’re a dollmaker?” the tall boy asked.

“Yes.”

“Oh.”

The reaction wasn’t as grand as Shean had hoped. Or expected. Sensing she’d now gained at least a smidgen of respect from her audience, though, she repeated herself. “I’ve dollmaking business to attend to in the village called Web, so I ask again: Where are your parents?”

“Asleep.” It was the anxious girl who spoke, in a voice that brought to mind the silky ripping noise of a moth’s wing being torn. Her words elicited glares from her friends, whom she shuffled a step back from.

Shean frowned. “It’s the middle of the day.”

“They’ll be up at sunset,” the tall boy said.

“Why?”

“To work.”

“They don’t work during the day?”

The gangly girl let out a belabored sigh, resting a hand on a bony hip that jutted through the fabric of her trousers. She answered in a tone that made clear just how stupid a question Shean had just asked. "Of *course* not. The spiders are awake at *night*."

Ah, of course. The spiders. Shean shot a look at the town square's statue, then turned back to the children. "They're nocturnal?"

The tall boy imitated his sister's sigh and pose, rolling his eyes. "That's what it *means* to be awake at night."

Ignoring his disdain, Shean looked up at the Shod-like doll, still clinging to its chosen house. Another realization struck her, obvious now that she thought about it. "Is that one of Ikiisa's dolls?"

The children shared another look, faces strange. The tall boy was the one to answer, voice suspicious. "Yes."

So *that's* what Nock had meant by saying Ikiisa's dolls were hard to explain. But what was so hard about saying they looked like Shod?

But, no. Staring at the doll, Shean realized she wouldn't describe it that way, either. It was lopsided and sort of patched together like the Shod, almost as if it, like a Shod, was built out of things stolen from humans—this doll certainly looked like it could've been cobbled together from many pieces of better-made items. And there was that whistling noise it made, close to the Shod's Cry.

The doll's demeanor, though, was nothing like a Shod. Nothing like the screaming, staggering terror that was the essence of the monsters. And its eyes didn't glow white. So, no. Shean wouldn't say Ikiisa's dolls were Shod-like. But she wouldn't say they looked like *dolls*, either. Lips pressed together, she felt Nock's conundrum.

She also felt a thrill, a spark of delight, as she realized the significance of what she'd just witnessed the children doing. If Ikiisa's dolls were this hated by the youths of Web, all of them too young to even *recall* the Shod, Shean could only imagine what the dolls did to the adults of Web, people who'd lived through the Red Tide and survived many Shod attacks. One look at the doll had made Shean relive the worst day of her life—no doubt the people of Web had similar experiences.

Shean suppressed a smile. *This'll be easier than I thought.*

"Right," she said aloud, the children giving her wary looks as she waved Silver out of the way, gesturing for him to stand beside her as she took a step forward. "Do you know who hires people here?"

If it was possible, the children's faces became even more guarded.

"The person in charge of village employment. Who is it?" Still, nothing. Shean frowned. "If you don't tell me, I'll have no choice but to just start knocking on . . ." She glanced at the nearest house, head cocking. "Twigs."

The tall boy looked at his sister. She nodded and he looked back at Shean, lips pressed into an unyielding line.

"Ilo," the anxious girl said. Shean looked to find her staring at the ground, flinching when her friends whipped around with protesting gasps. The anxious girl lifted her eyes to look at Shean, voice diminished to a whisper. "Ilo's in charge of work."

"Shut it, Dola!" the tall boy said. He spat, and she stepped back to avoid having his phlegm splatter across her boots. "Doll lover!"

The anxious girl, Dola, looked at him with a withdrawn expression. Shean had never heard the phrase "doll lover" before, but in this context it clearly wasn't a compliment.

Clearing her throat, she drew the children's attention back to her. "Master Ilo, is it?" she asked. "That's who I speak to?"

The tall boy's expression was sullen, voice flat and hostile when he answered. "Yes. But he's asleep, too, and only people who want to lose fingers wake him up this much before sunset."

Shean waved a dismissive hand. "Yes, yes. Where does he live?"

The tall boy scowled. "Not telling!"

Then he was running and, moved by some unspoken signal, so were the other children, scattering in a flurry of feet and snap of embroidered sleeves. Before Shean had time to react they were gone, disappearing down paths besides the houses, launching into the tree line of the forest called Deep and vanishing in a disharmony of rustles.

The only child who remained was the one called Dola. She turned away from Shean with the other children, but instead of finding a hiding place she ran toward the house that Ikiisa's doll clung to, lifting her arms and making cooing-clicking noises. The doll scurried back down the house, dropping into the girl's arms and making her stagger. The moment her balance was caught she turned around and ran too, slower than her friends, but fast enough that she'd be gone in moments.

"Wait!" Shean cried. Dola glanced over a shoulder but didn't stop—if anything she ran faster, barreling down a path between two houses, Ikiisa's doll jostling in her arms.

"Oh, for the love of the First Dollmaker!" Shean huffed. She turned, shoving Lintok's reins into Silver's hands. "Watch him," she ordered.

Then Shean picked her skirts up high enough not to trip her, located Dola vanishing behind the edge of a twig-woven house, and gave chase.

THE PATH DOLA TOOK WIDENED PAST WEB, BECOMING SOMETHING OF A PROPER road leading away from the village and ending in a house. A normal house that lacked the woven twigs of the other houses of Web. It stood a good distance from the main village and reminded Shean of an awkward uncle at a family gathering: tucked into an isolated corner where one could watch what was going on without being a part of those goings-on, dim and shuttered windows, tall, lanky, and hunched, three levels of slightly crooked floors and a peaked roof missing more clay shingles than it had.

Fast despite the doll she carried, Dola reached the house before Shean, stumbling to a stop at the front door and bending to set the doll down. As Shean slowed her own pace, panting and seeing spots, the girl knocked on the door. Wiping sweat from her eyes, Shean waited for the door to open. It didn't. Dola knocked again. Harder. When that effort yielded no results, she lifted her tremulous voice.

"Master Ikiisa? I-it's Dola."

The door slid open a fraction, just enough for an eye to come into view, gazing at Dola before dropping to the doll at her feet.

"Bobble!"

The door flew open and Dollmaker Ikiisa threw herself to her knees in front of Dola, gathering up her broken doll, cradling its odd shape. "Oh, look at you. So many cracks!" The doll, Bobble, let out a soft, mournful whistle.

Ikiisa continued to fuss over her doll, but Shean was distracted from her words by her appearance. She was young. So young that if what Nock said was true and she'd fought in the Red Tide, she must've been a teenager at the time. Her hair was short, bobbed around her jaw in a line of dark golden brown, and she had an olive complexion typical of the western cities. Her eyes were too big for her face, sitting wide and hazel blue on either side of a very thin nose. Sparse lips, a sharp chin, a scar roping down the left side of her face, stopping just above her jawline. Dressed in a sleeveless brown tunic worn soft by too many washings, she had a long, sloping neck around which hung a black cord. On the cord was a pendant, a light green, teardrop-shaped rock with a hole drilled through its top and an unfamiliar symbol carved into it.

When Shean had been traveling, when she'd lain stretched out on horrendously uncomfortable mattresses in dingy, stilted seaside inns and distracted herself from dismal surroundings by picturing her first encounter with Ikiisa, she'd imagined the fiercest, most intimidating woman. Tall and broad, ugly, wiry hair pulled back in a bun so tight her widow's peak was frayed and thin. Hulking and aggressive, with bloodshot eyes and a voice husky like a man's. Shean had imagined herself facing down a sweaty, foul-mouthed ogre of a dollmaker, the two of them a perfect, aesthetically pleasing contrast. In this story, she, Shean, was the ravishing heroine, her triumph spoken of for centuries, passed on by the faithful, adoring voices of her children and their children's children's children.

If they were standing on equal footing, Shean felt certain she'd tower over Ikiisa. And she was bigger than Ikiisa, who had no figure to speak of beneath the shapeless cut of her clothing. *If I was to take a firm step*, Shean thought, *I'd flatten her.*

This *waif of a woman is the greatest dollmaker in all of* One?

"Master Ikiisa? Is there anything I can do?" Dola said, her voice drawing Shean from her thoughts. Ikiisa was fiddling with Bobble's broken leg, muttering as she did.

"You have to run faster, and don't let them lure you into their traps—I know you like the way acorns look, but they aren't worth it," she said. Bobble let out a sad whistle, drooping. Ikiisa patted it in a consoling way. "You need to learn to curl up and shield yourself, if they're attacking you. Don't worry. I'll fix you."

She picked Bobble up, carrying it back into the house. Crooning, she made to shut the door behind her.

Shean straightened, taking a step forward. She wasn't sure what she wanted to say to Ikiisa (a greeting, an introduction, a declaration of war?), but the thought of their first meeting transpiring without a word between them was unacceptable. "Excuse me!" she said. At the sound of her voice Dola jumped, spinning around and staring at her with surprise, as if she'd completely forgotten Shean existed.

Ikiisa ignored her. The door slammed shut, a firm click followed by the distinct *shunk* of a lock sliding into place.

Shean let out a hissing breath. She hadn't much time to linger on Ikiisa's rudeness, though—shoulders slumped and head ducked, Dola was hurrying down the steps from the house, back toward the village. There was no way for her to get to Web without passing Shean, though, and before she could escape again Shean caught her arm, not hard enough to hurt, but firmly enough to pull her to a stop.

"Dola, right?" Shean asked.

Dola nodded, staring at the ground. "Yes, ma'am."

"Is Ikiisa always like that?"

Dola shuffled. "Like w-what?"

"She ignored you," Shean said. *And me*, she added silently, with no small amount of irritation.

"She doesn't like talking to people."

"Even people who bring her dolls back to her when they've been damaged?" Shean asked. Dola winced as if Shean had hit her. She offered no response to the question, so Shean asked another one. "Does this happen often?"

Dola's brow furrowed. "What?"

Shean flicked a hand toward Ikiisa's house. "You and your friends torturing her dolls."

Dola let out a protesting gasp, head jerking. She looked up at Shean, eyes made wide by the dark circles under them and gaze pleading. "I never! I never throw anything o-or use Slink and Una's sticks, o-or set any traps with the triplets. Never!"

Shean frowned, letting go of Dola and folding her arms across her chest. "But you don't stop them from doing those things, either. You let it happen."

Dola opened her mouth, hesitated, then closed it. Her head bowed, her hands curling in the fabric at the bottom of her tunic, wadding up the cloth. After an awkward, silent moment she lifted her eyes. "T-thank you for stopping them." As she spoke, her ear tips pinkened.

Shean studied her. "You're very fond of Ikiisa's dolls, aren't you?"

Dola's face brightened. She nodded.

"Even though they look scary?"

"They aren't scary!" Dola protested, so loudly she made herself jump. She shrank back from Shean, stammering, "I mean, t-they're nice. Gran says dolls don't hurt people, only help them, and Master Ikiisa's dolls are like that."

"Still, you have to admit her dolls are . . . strange. Wouldn't you prefer beautiful dolls to work for Web? Like the doll I showed you earlier?" Shean asked the question sweetly, with all the persuasion she'd learned in years of winning fights with Nock. Dola frowned, yanking harder at the bottom of her tunic.

"M-maybe?" she said. Her face puckered with confusion. "As long as dolls are kind, does it matter what they look like?"

Not the response Shean would've preferred. She pursed her lips, pushing back the annoyance nipping at her—Dola was a child. Her opinion meant little in the grand scheme of things. Forcing a smile, Shean changed the subject.

"Of course. Dola, please show me where Master Ilo lives."

Dola took a step back. "It . . . it's still early—"

Shean pointed at the sky. "It's sunset."

And it was—colors streaked the sky, long trails of red and orange and yellow leaching the blue from the heavens, bronzing the clouds and turning the wings of a passing flock of birds from dull black to burnished. Even the air spoke of approaching night, the muggy heat of day turning into a more breathable cool. Dola followed Shean's gesture to the sky, then looked back down. Fidgeted, then relented.

"All right. I-I'll take you to Ilo."

"Thank you," Shean said. She shot a glance at Ikiisa's house, wondering if she imagined movement at one of the windows overhead—a shiver of curtains, a shadow darting back from glass that caught the glare of sunset on its surface in a blinding flash. Then she turned and followed Dola back to the village called Web.

SHEAN AND DOLA FOUND LINTOK AND SILVER ON THE EDGE OF WEB. LINTOK WAS off to the side of the road, grazing on tall grasses that produced loud ripping noises as he made his way through them. Silver was sprawled on his back next to the elk, staring at the sky with unblinking eyes. He sat up at the sound of approaching feet and, at the sight of Dola and Shean, stood up, waving his arms in greeting. He ran to Dola, bowing low to her and holding the pose until, looking a bit startled, she returned the greeting. Then he straightened, bouncing on the balls of his feet and smiling at her in a very charming way.

"His name is Silver," Shean said, bending to grab Lintok's reins and, with some effort, pulling the elk's head up from the grass he was murdering. She patted his muzzle, scratching the spot under his chin she knew he liked as Dola looked up at him, expression awed. "This is Lintok."

As if on cue Lintok lowered his head, nudging Dola with curiosity, making her giggle. She petted the sides of his face, rubbing her forehead against his cheek.

When Lintok finished greeting Dola, the group followed her back into Web. They returned to the town square to find life creeping into the village. Or, more accurately, creeping out of it—people stepping from the tangle of branches encircling their houses, emerging from unseen gaps in the weaves. They were all dressed the same, drab gray or brown tunics ornamented with white thread fashioned to resemble spiderweb, handspun trousers, and boots. Some had satchels slung across their bodies, swinging on their hips in time with their steps. They trickled into sight in slumped lines, moving forward in small, slow clusters that, after brief pauses, dispersed and moved to the tree line of Deep.

The villagers moved in silence but for the sound of feet on cobbles and the loam under the trees, kicking the occasional fallen leaf. Some of them were old, white-haired and hunched, walking with the aid of canes or younger arms. Most were middle-aged, brown or black hair showing hints of gray but still thick and full, faces creased but not yet wrinkled. The youngest, and fewest, of the procession were children, some close to adulthood and others barely past infancy. A few of the children from earlier were among them, shooting Dola dirty looks as they passed with parents or grandparents who looked at Shean with some curiosity, but mostly suspicion.

No one approached her. Nor did they speak—even the smallest figure was quiet, the youngest child she spotted (a little boy holding on to his mother's hand as they emerged from one of the woven houses) stumbling along without a word, head bobbing with exhaustion.

Shean had never seen a group of people so pale. It was like none of them had seen the sun in years. Seeing as they were nocturnal, she supposed they hadn't.

"Where're they going?" Shean said as more and more villagers disappeared into Deep. She spoke softly, almost in a whisper. Any louder, and a silly part of her suspected she'd spook the villagers and they'd run away. Or, like ghosts, vanish.

"To work," Dola said. Without further explanation she pointed. "That's Ilo."

Shean followed the gesture to a man. He stood in the center of the town square next to the spider statue, the only villager not heading toward the trees. Instead he spoke to those who passed by him, scanning the villagers and picking out one or two to go to, touch on the shoulder, softly query and warrant a nod or shake of the head. He also appeared to be counting the people, lips moving as he looked over the sparse crowd. In one hand he held a small book, in the other a stick of lead that he used to write notes and, Shean guessed, a head-count tally. Though he was lacking the proper burgundy uniform, the long plaited hair, and the distinctive neck scarf that adorned head employment officers in the country called One, this Ilo had the correct gaze—calculating and careful, sharp and quick and sure to miss nothing. Of importance, anyway.

Shean braced herself. This was it. She turned and untied the strings of the travel bag on Lintok's saddle, pulling out the five dolls she'd selected for this journey: Jewel, Glass, Marble, Crystal, and Coin. All of them were still asleep and stood dead as mannequins while Shean arranged them around her, their Breath Marks shiny curls of black ink on cheeks or arms or hands. Even without animation they were stunning—all roughly as tall as the length from Shean's wrist to her elbow, these dolls were her most recent, and most exquisite, work. Each wore a hand-stitched outfit with personalized embroidery to match the decorations she'd painted on their faces and shoulders and chests (patterns ranging from intricate floral arrangements to a minimalistic design of a single golden carp against a lovely silken blue), and each had heads of lush horse hair that ranged from shades of brown and black and blond, styled in the bobs and braids and loops popular in Pearl.

Shean leaned forward, touching each of the dolls' Breath Marks gently, a brush of her pinky along the familiar lines. When she finished she straightened, smoothing her hair and stroking wrinkles from the front of her skirts. Once satisfied that the ruffles to her outfit caused from her chasing Dola were tamed, she snapped her fingers. At the sound her dolls sprang to life, joints limbering and heads swinging from side to side, taking in the town square and the gray people of Web. Coin and Glass, the showiest of the group, performed a few cartwheels and flips before Shean told them to be still, acrobatics that made Dola gasp in delight.

The girl's admiration, small as it was, filled Shean with confidence. Arranging a winning smile on her face, she stepped forward, checking that her dolls kept pace with her as she strode to Ilo.

Villagers looked up as she did so, startling before shying back to give her room to pass. They looked at her dolls' steady, proper steps and then back at her. She was sure to smile at everyone whose eyes she met, putting on an especially charming face for the sleepy little boy she'd spotted earlier who, at the sight of Silver, straightened, eyes stretched wide in fascination as he pulled on his mother's sleeve.

"Manma, look!"

His manma did look, but not at the dolls. She looked at Shean, eyes wide like her son's. Shean was aware that sunset was catching on the jewels of her dress, producing spinning refractions of light that danced on the faces of mother and child, making her a spectacular sight indeed when she inclined her head in greeting. The mother nodded a hasty reply to the courtesy before pulling her son away, disregarding his protesting, "No!"

The next to look at Shean was Ilo, turning at the stir she was causing. Up close, the village employer looked older than he had from a distance. Older and short, broad-shouldered but thin. Like all the other villagers he was pale as fresh snowfall, eyes a watery brown that lifted, bloodshot, as Shean stopped before him.

He stepped back and looked Shean up and down, face setting with a familiar enmity. His furrowed brow made him look very much like the tall boy and gangly girl from earlier. Their father, perhaps? Or an uncle?

Shean greeted Ilo, bowing the way Nock had taught her to when meeting a potential employer—her right hand placed over her heart, her left curled into a fist and pressed to the small of her back. Her dolls mirrored her, just as she'd told them to do a few days ago in the city called Drift, when she'd rehearsed this meeting with them.

"Master Ilo of the village called Web," Shean said, straightening. Ilo was looking at Silver, expression subdued but calculating eyes failing to hide that he was impressed. As Shean moved, his attention snapped back to her. She inclined her head. "It's a pleasure."

Ilo looked past her. "Dola," he said, voice gruff. "What's this?"

"Shean of Pearl. S-she's a dollmaker," Dola said, stepping forward. She addressed the cobbles of the ground. "S-she wants to speak to you."

"About what?"

"A matter of business," Shean said, primly, in the tone of voice she used when demanding the attention of whom she addressed. Ilo eyed her.

"Business, is it? What business?"

"Business concerning the dollmaker employment currently functioning in Web."

"Dollmaking business," Ilo said, brusque. He sighed, casting a mournful look at the reddened sky. "And right at sunset."

"It'll only take a moment," Shean said. After what she'd seen of Ikiisa's dolls, and how the village children felt about them, she was certain her words were true.

Ilo frowned. "Fine," he said. He looked at Dola. "Don't you have work to do?"

"Y-yes, sir," Dola said, bobbing a bow and scurrying off, joining other villagers heading into Deep. Ilo watched her go before turning back to Shean, expression wary.

"What do you want?" he asked.

"I've come to Web seeking employment." As she spoke, Shean flicked a hand and her dolls stepped forward, lining up before her to ensure Ilo couldn't miss a single detail of their splendor. "As you can see, I offer dolls of a very fine quality."

"They're pretty," Ilo said, glancing at the dolls. "Some of the parents might be interested in buying one or two as presents for the children. I doubt anyone in Web can afford your fees, though."

Shean's smile threatened to twist into a snarl. To combat the transformation, she smiled wider, the edges of her mouth straining. "I'm afraid you've misunderstood. I'm not an artisan."

Ilo's eyebrows lifted. "A guard?"

Not trusting herself to speak without seething, Shean nodded. Her hand shifted to her hip, searching for and finding the hard shape of Nock's license amidst the folds of her skirt, tucked in a secret pocket she'd been thrilled to discover and utilize, currently tied shut and secure with maroon ribbons. Her fingers pulled the ribbons loose and closed over the card, presenting it to Ilo. He made no attempt to take it, eyebrows lifting even higher at the sight of the First Dollmaker's boar. Just in case he upended her expectations and recognized the outdated licensor brand, Shean covered the symbol with her thumb.

"Oh," Ilo said. "I see."

"Then we understand one another," Shean said, tucking the license back into her pocket and knotting the ribbons twice.

Ilo's eyes narrowed. "Maybe. We don't get many dollmakers coming here looking for work. What's your interest in Web?"

Shean spread her hands wide in a disarming gesture. "Web is a village in my beloved country and, thus, in need and deserving of as much protection as any other."

Ilo didn't look impressed. He shook his head. "We already have a dollmaker, and she's done fine for us. We haven't had a Shod incident in years. Why would we want a new dollmaker?"

"With all respect, Master Ilo," Shean said, smile sweet, "you asking that question is quite a sad thing—in any other town such words would never be spoken."

"Why do you say that?"

"Because it's common as moss for towns to have multiple choices when it comes to dollmakers, sir. Here in Web you've had so few options—you say your dollmaker has done well for you, and I'm sure that's true, but have you ever had the chance to compare her to other dollmakers?"

"We've had plenty of dollmakers in Web."

"May I ask what you thought of those dollmakers?"

Ilo's face darkened. "Cowards. All of them."

Shean nodded, all sympathy. Of course she already knew Web's dollmaker history—Nock had explained the basics, and on her journey to Web she'd gone to the trouble of minor research, stopping by a couple dollmaker archives in the cities she'd stayed in and wading through records that, to varying degrees, contained accounts of dollmaking history in each area of One. She knew full well that the longest a dollmaker had worked in Web before Ikiisa was half a year, with over fifty dollmakers coming and going from the forest called Deep in the past forty years alone—each one giving different, but similar, excuses for leaving: "The townspeople are unfriendly and callous," "The forest is overrun with monsters and it's impossible to purge them, for the wood is too thick to successfully penetrate," "To be so far from civilization is a burden I cannot, and shall not, bear any longer."

And Shean's personal favorite:

"I hate Web."

Ikiisa really was the first dollmaker, ever, to linger. Shean wasn't surprised to find Ilo resistant to a change.

But it'd be easy enough to make that resistance falter.

"Master Ilo, forgive my frankness, but I fear your basis of comparison, the bar you've set for a successful dollmaker, is not how *effective* she is at her work, but whether or not she's abandoned Web at times of need. Is that any way to judge the skill of a craftswoman?" Shean shook her head, sighing. "It saddens me, *ashames* me, that my predecessors have handled Web so poorly. But, as you said before, it's not often that dollmakers wish to work so far from cities—it's rare to find someone who doesn't mind independence from the collective whole of our work." She leaned forward. "I don't, Master Ilo. I only wish for my dolls to do the best work they can, and I believe that work is to be done here, in Web. I implore you, don't settle for a dollmaker simply because she's treated you marginally better than those in the past have treated you and your predecessors. Don't settle for something you are in any way dissatisfied with because you feel you have no other option."

The words were perfect—Shean was sure of that. But Ilo was shaking his head before she finished speaking, waving a dismissive hand to accompany dismissive words. "I understand what you're saying, but, as I've said, we already have a dollmaker. And no reason to be discontented with her work."

"Yes," Shean said, unable to keep the stiff edge from her voice. "I'm aware. But," she said, indicating her dolls with a flourish, "the craftsmanship of my dolls is far superior to Dollmaker Ikiisa's work, is it not?" As she spoke she nudged the doll on the far end of the line, Marble, forward. At the small kick he jumped, performing a spin that was picked up by the doll next to him, Jewel, and then the doll next to her, Coin, and so on and so forth until all six dolls had spun about, showcasing both the ease of their movements and the fine shape of their figures.

Ilo watched the display with pinched lips. When it was over he shrugged, resting a hand on his hip. "You're very skilled. But Ikiisa's dolls work for us. I see no reason to replace her."

Shean's patience began to fray. "No reason? Not an hour ago I witnessed a group of your children treating one of the current guard dolls of Web as if it was a Shod!"

Ilo's face darkened, eyes darting a glare to Shean's left. When she turned to follow his look, she found the tall boy and gangly girl from earlier standing next to a woman with their same narrow eyes.

They huddled close to her when Ilo looked at them, the gangly girl giving Shean a look of pure loathing before scurrying off into Deep with her family. Shean turned back to Ilo, more certain than ever that she saw the children's faces in his when he turned his attention back to her, scowling.

"Despite what you may've seen, Web has no need of a replacement dollmaker. For all their . . . faults, Ikiisa's dolls are effective. I've seen them fight Shod with my own eyes."

"With all due respect, when?" Shean asked. "From what I've heard, there hasn't been a Shod attack in Web in the past ten years."

"Heard from who?" Ilo asked, voice gruff.

Shean waved a vague hand. "People."

Ilo's eyes narrowed, but after a moment he said, "Nine." He folded his arms across his chest. "The first year Ikiisa was here we had five attacks. But no deaths, because her dolls are, as I've said, effective." He grimaced. "Ugly as sin, straight out of nightmares. But effective."

"You admit yourself that Ikiisa's dolls are terrifying creatures, and still say you have no interest in my dolls?"

"They can be as terrifying as they want, so long as they keep the Shod away."

This man was irritating. He clearly held those hideous dolls in as much contempt as the children of Web, and that should be enough for him to see that Shean's dolls were superior to Ikiisa's, to get down on his knees and beg her to be the dollmaker of Web, to give him dolls that, in contrast to Ikiisa's nightmares, were lovely dreams. And yet it wasn't. Shean ground her back teeth together for a frustrated moment, deciding to switch tactics.

"If effectiveness is your main concern," she said, "I assure you, what my dolls lack in bulk they make up for in intelligence. You won't find cleverer dolls, not in all the country called One; I'd be happy to prove to you that my dolls are *just* as capable of fighting the Shod as Ikiisa's."

"Oh? And how do you propose to prove that?"

"I'll have my dolls go into Deep, find a Shod, and bring it here to Web, where they will then decimate the monster under your watchful eye." Shean turned to her dolls, all of which were looking up at her, their sea glass gazes inscrutable, and their expressions, usually so animated, blank. Silver's especially—he looked as wooden as a lifeless mannequin.

Shean was taken aback by the strange expressions, but decided she hadn't the time to worry about her dolls' glazed faces. "Understood?" she asked them. All six dolls nodded. "Good, then—"

"Wait!" Ilo's distress was palpable, not only in his voice but on his face, in the hand he raised and stretched toward Shean, coming close to grabbing her shoulder, as if holding her back would prevent her dolls from obeying her half-spoken order. His expression was haunted by familiar fear, the fear Shean had seen in many faces in the city called Pearl; the fear of someone who's met the Shod.

"Is something wrong?" Shean asked, voice sweet innocence. "It's no trouble, really—as you've said, my dolls are very beautiful and well-crafted. The Shod, as I'm sure you're aware, are drawn to two things: well-made, beautiful creations, and humankind. They will be attracted to my dolls' workmanship and, then, the people of Web—it will be quite simple to draw them out."

"There's no need to bring a Shod to Web!"

"That'd be the fastest way to prove my dolls superior to Ikiisa's, wouldn't it?" She looked at her dolls. "As I was saying—"

"Stop!"

Shean suppressed a smirk at the note of panic in Ilo's voice. Of course he'd react just like Nock had to this threat. Though she still didn't understand *why*—it wasn't as if anyone would be in danger if she found one little Shod and had her dolls tear it apart. That *would* be the simplest way of proving her dolls were the guards she'd made them to be, if anyone had the guts to let her provide such proof.

She doubted she'd ever find such a willing soul, at least not among those from whom she sought employment. It never ceased to amaze Shean, how frightened the older generations were of the Shod when she herself, a victim of the Shod's most vicious attack, felt nothing but an intense, raging desire to destroy the monsters. *Especially* when she recalled the Red Tide.

What was the use of succumbing to fear, when she could channel her emotions into destroying the Shod instead?

"Master Ilo," she said, "I'm afraid I don't understand—you wouldn't have me prove my dolls to you, but at the same time you'll not even *consider* my petition to be dollmaker of Web? I'm afraid I have no *choice* but to prove myself to you, and, as I've said, the Shod—"

"Decisions such as what dollmaker is employed in Web are made by the entire council of Web," Ilo interrupted, face pale and brow sweaty in the diminishing daylight. "I'm in charge of employment in the village, but I don't have the authority to change dollmaking appointments."

"I wish to speak to the council of Web, then."

"I'll discuss your proposal with them," Ilo said, voice desperate.

Shean smiled, dipping her head slightly. "Thank you, Master Ilo. I appreciate your cooperation."

Ilo grunted, mopping his sodden forehead with a sleeve. He made to turn from her, to follow his fellow villagers into the forest. "Very well. Tomorrow morning—"

Shean grabbed his arm, stopping him. He tried to pull away and she didn't allow it, taking a step forward and leaning close to him. She smiled her most winning smile. A smile to inform those who viewed it that she wasn't to be taken lightly.

"Now," she said.

THE COUNCIL OF WEB WAS COMPOSED OF FIVE INDIVIDUALS, AND ALL OF THEM had earned their spots due to seniority—that, as a plethora of predecessors had proven, was the only way to force a villager of Web to find the time and energy to function in a leadership position. The five of them sat in the front room of Ilo's house, resting upon kneeling cushions flattened from use and threadbare, but still preferable to folding their aching legs on the hard wood of the floor. The space was lit by a glow lantern hanging from a hook mounted in the ceiling, the imported stones from the far shore cities of One casting a muted light over the proceedings.

Ilo sat in front of the other four council members, kneeling on his wilted cushion with his hands fisted and resting on his thighs. Already in a bad mood from his interaction with that fussy dollmaker, he fought to keep his temper in check as four people gave him glares that ranged from furious to tired to curious.

"What's this about, Ilo?" Mont asked, scowling. Never a handsome man, age had filled his jowls into large rolls of skin that creased around his round face. A face flushed with irritation to match the bite of his croaking voice. "Sending us out to work only to call us back—you're delaying the harvest!"

"I am aware. But we have a situation," Ilo said. "As some of you may've noticed, there's a stranger in Web. She calls herself Shean of Pearl, and she's a guard dollmaker. She requests employment."

"Here?" Tana asked, voice skeptical. She fiddled with the neck of her tunic, plucking at fraying embroidery and cocking her head. The gesture made her white-streaked hair fall over her eyes and that, combined with her hooked nose and pebbly lips, caused her to resemble a large, quizzical bird. "Are you sure?"

"Yes."

"But we already *have* a dollmaker," Mont grumbled.

"So?" Plonk mumbled in his low, baffled voice. The eldest of the council, he sagged on his cushion, shoulders frozen in a hunch with age, eyes all but lost in the folds of wrinkles drooping down the loose skin of his face while long, wispy eyebrows draped his temples. He shivered in a nonexistent draft, a few key wrinkles shifting so he could lock Ilo in a watery gaze. "When I was a child, we had a new dollmaker every week."

Tana let out a frustrated noisc, crossing her arms and pursing her lips at Plonk. "This is *today*. And we've had the same dollmaker for *ten years*. Her dolls are disturbing, true, but they don't do any real harm. They're effective against the Shod, as limited as the attacks have been. And she hasn't abandoned us like the dollmakers before her. What rational reason do we have to replace her?"

"I told this Shean that," Ilo said.

"Her response?"

"A threat."

Mont scoffed. "What sort of threat?"

"She said she'd bring the Shod to Web if I didn't consider her."

An appalled babble of words rose at this information, talking over one another in a tired groan:

"By the First Dollmaker, *why*?"

"Is she disturbed?"

"When I was a child, all dollmakers were disturbed."

"But *why*?"

Ilo shifted uncomfortably, feeling a prickle of guilt—though he knew he hadn't forced Shean to say such a terrible thing, a part of him felt responsible that she had. If he hadn't so quickly dismissed her, if he'd had some tact . . .

Clearing his throat, he lifted a hand for silence, which fell with a final sigh of "Insanity!" from Plonk. In the quiet Ilo lowered his hand, pressing it flat to his knee.

"Just as you've said, I told her that I saw no reason for hiring a new dollmaker," he started.

"What did she say to that?" Tana asked.

"She showed me her dolls, and said they were smarter and more finely crafted than Ikiisa's, and thus more deserving of employment."

A pause. "Well," Mont said, gruffly. "Are they?"

"They're very . . . pretty. And small. Delicate-looking; I thought she was an artisan before she showed me her license." Ilo waved a hand, shaking his head. "But that's beside the point—I told her it would be foolish of us to hire a dollmaker based on how her dolls look, and that Ikiisa's dolls have been tested against the Shod and are, therefore, trustworthy."

"And she offered to show you the effectiveness of her dolls?" Tana said. She sounded amused, appalled. And a bit impressed.

"Essentially."

"She sounds mad," Mont said.

"Ambitious," Tana corrected with a snap, glaring.

"Ambitious to the point of insanity, maybe," Mont shot back, returning the scowl. He looked back at Ilo and tossed his head with a snort, jowls swinging. "But I fail to see why this is a matter of such importance that you thought to call us together—if she wants to find a Shod, let her try! There hasn't been a sighting in years. For all we know, the Shod left Deep years ago."

"But if she really brings one—" Ilo started.

"Why are you frightened of this girl?" Tana interrupted, impatience in every line of her face.

Ilo set his jaw, frustration flaring. "I'm not frightened. I simply recognize recklessness when I see it."

Tana shrugged. "Then send her away. Banish her from the village."

"If I do that, she might set her dolls on us. Or just take my refusal as an invitation to send her dolls out Shod-hunting, thinking that if she can 'prove' herself to me, I'll reconsider sending her away."

"And how do you know that's how she'd react?"

Ilo hesitated. Why *was* he so certain that Shean of Pearl wouldn't let herself be driven from Web? Something in the way she'd spoken to him, or the way she'd carried herself, or maybe how she'd forced her dolls to spin for him, as if once he had a better look at them he'd change his mind. His brow furrowed, fingers tightening their grip on his knees.

Across his mind flashed an image of Una and Slink, his youngest, most exhausting, children. And suddenly he understood.

He looked up at the council, voice confident. "She has the look of a child who's never been told no. That's why."

A soft noise, a mild clearing of the throat. All eyes turned to the woman sitting in the far left corner of the room, silent until this moment. She sat tall and slender on her cushion, clothing faded with age but pressed neat and free of creases, her face lined more than wrinkled in a peculiar effect that made her appear ageless. Her hair, though, betrayed her years, a shock of white pulled back and tied in a loose chignon at the base of her neck. With calm amber eyes she looked at Ilo, face expectant.

"You've something to say, Lenna?" he asked.

Lenna smiled. "Yes. Why not hold a pageant?"

Tana let out a sharp, startled noise. Mont frowned so deeply the rolls of fat around his face swelled. Plonk let out a small, delighted wheeze, head lifting with his voice, which was more excited than it'd been in years. "A pageant!"

"Yes," Lenna said, eyes bright with confidence. "It seems a logical way to settle things, I think, in a way this new dollmaker might accept. A pleasant change of pace for the village and a way to show her that we're taking her seriously. Then, once it's over, we can simply pick Ikiisa as our preferred dollmaker."

"That . . ." Ilo said, trailing off. He hesitated, then nodded. "That might work."

"But the harvest—" Mont started.

"Have you forgotten?" Lenna asked, turning to look at Mont. Her voice was gentle, not meant to offend, but inform. "Tomorrow night is the new moons. This is the perfect time to take a respite."

"Oh," Mont said, a bit red in the face. "Of course. You're right."

Lenna inclined her head in acknowledgment, turning back to Ilo. "We can hold it tomorrow—I'd suggest during the day. It's been a long while since our children have experienced sunlight."

"Our adults, too," Tana said, voice wistful.

"But to hold the pageant tomorrow, we'd have to stop the harvest tonight," Mont said. "We'd need to sleep from now until morning, or we'd never last the day."

"I see no issue with that," Lenna said. "The spiders are growing restless enough to bite. And besides—there's no harm in missing one night of silking; we're currently a day and a half ahead of the production schedule for the year."

No one could argue with that—Lenna kept the time charts of Web, making sure they harvested and wove enough silk to be able to sell cloths to the merchants who came every year just before and after winter. If she said they were ahead of schedule, they were.

"Let's turn this unfortunate conflict into a pleasure, shall we?" Lenna asked. She looked around the council, smile bright. "Are we agreed?"

Ilo looked at the other council members, all of whom nodded. "Yes," he said.

"Splendid. Shall we call her in?"

Ilo stood. "Yes."

He walked across the room, pulling open the door and walking down the hallway to the front of his house. He opened the door to find Shean sitting on the step leading up to the entrance, her elk and dolls standing in a cluster next to where she sat. She stood at the sound of his arrival, turning with a clink of jeweled skirts, her strange and beautiful dress catching the light of the slivered moons in an array of iridescent flickers. She smiled, her lovely features enough to make some of the irritation he felt toward her ebb. A little.

"The council's made a decision," he said with as much sternness as possible, hoping the night was dark enough to conceal the effectiveness of her smile. He stepped back, motioning for her to enter the house. She did with a gracious dip of her head, striding in and following him to the council room, head erect and eyes meeting each of the council members' in turn. Ilo moved his kneeling cushion next to Tana and sat down, leaving Shean alone to stand before them.

"Lenna, if you'd explain," Ilo said.

"Gladly," Lenna said, drawing Shean's attention, a gaze so focused it could penetrate stone. Lenna was unfazed by the dollmaker's intensity, smile remaining pleasant as she spoke.

"Shean of Pearl, Ilo has told us of your request to become the dollmaker of Web. To simply hire you over a dollmaker who's served us well for many years, though, is impossible. As a compromise, we," Lenna said, gesturing to the council, "have decided to hold a pageant."

"A pageant?" Shean repeated, both her voice and the look on her face suggesting Lenna's words were senseless to her. And a bit silly.

"Yes," Lenna said, with more patience than Ilo could have mustered. "It's tradition—a way of deciding between two candidates who desire the same thing, be it a job or some favor, who are seemingly matched in worthiness for the desired prize. You'll be given three tasks to complete to demonstrate your merit as a potential dollmaker of Web. Of course, Ikiisa will complete these tasks as well; the pageant is, first and foremost, a competition. In the name of fairness, as a council we'll set the first task, but you and Ikiisa will set the other two. At the end of the pageant, the entire village will vote, and things will be decided. Can you agree to this?"

"Yes," Shean said. There was no reluctance in her voice, no hesitation. Or fear. Ilo wondered what that would be like, having such unwavering confidence.

"Good," Lenna said. She stood and Ilo followed suit, the other council members rising with various pops of protesting backs and joints. "The first trial will start at daybreak. Do you have a place to stay?"

Shean shook her head.

"Dola and I will be happy to house you."

Shean's face betrayed surprise, and Ilo wondered if hospitality was that uncommon in far shore cities like Pearl. She composed herself quickly, though, schooling her face and bowing. "Thank you, Master Lenna."

"It's my pleasure." Lenna looked at the other council members over her shoulder as she crossed the room, ushering Shean away. "Until daybreak, friends."

And then she and Shean were gone. Silence hung in the room for a moment, the sound of four people unsure what to do next.

Plonk broke the quiet with a cough. "Someone needs to get everyone back from the Veil," he said.

Tana sighed. "I'll do that."

"I'll come as well," Mont said.

As the two walked away, Plonk turned his ancient head in Ilo's direction, eyes a faint gleam among the creases of his face. "Someone needs to tell Ikiisa of the pageant," he mumbled.

Echoing Tana, Ilo sighed.

"I'll do it," he said.

IKIISA STOOD IN THE DOORWAY OF HER HOUSE, GRIPPING THE FRAME AND STARING AT Ilo. He stared back, face pale in the light cast by the glow lantern he held in one hand, his dark eyes reflecting the radiance in helix swirls.

He'd just said something, and the words bounced around Ikiisa's head in a jumble, a confusion that made no sense. Just noise. Noise.

"What?" she said, voice scraping from disuse, making her croak.

"A dollmaker," Ilo said, repeating himself. "She says she's from the city called Pearl. She wants to work in Web, and we've decided to settle the matter with a pageant."

Ikiisa knew what a pageant was. Master Coen had told her once, a long time ago. Explained the pageants he'd experienced as a child in Web with wistful tones, lying on his back next to Ikiisa on the grassy side of the hill their school sat on, gazing at the stars like old friends.

"It's a beautiful way to settle arguments," Master Coen had said. *"A civilized way to fight."*

"But I . . ." Ikiisa said, shoving Master Coen from her head as best she could, which wasn't very well—he was always wedged there, saying something or gesturing or laughing. Missed. She swallowed, fingers squeezing the doorframe until she felt pain, which she latched on to to keep herself anchored in the present, dealing with the current problem standing in front of her and looking at her and waiting for her to say something. "I, um . . . Why didn't . . . why didn't anyone tell me?"

Ilo frowned. "I'm telling you now."

He misunderstood. That's not what Ikiisa meant—she meant before. When they were deciding things. She was the dollmaker of Web, but even when discussing dollmaking in Web they hadn't come to ask her opinion.

Then again, why would they? She kept herself locked up in this house all day and night, didn't she? Bolting doors and windows, not even speaking to Dola when the girl defied her peers and brought Ikiisa's dolls home in mendable pieces. Telling herself she was just doing her job, not bothering anyone, making dolls and fixing dolls and keeping the Shod away so well, no one would ever get angry with her. No one would ever tell her she'd ruined their life ever again.

Ikiisa's mouth soured. Why *would* the villagers talk to her, when they probably all thought she kept away from them because she hated them? Why would they talk to her when they probably hated her just as much as they thought she hated them?

She didn't hate them. She kept away so *they* wouldn't hate *her.* But they still did. They had to, to do this to her. To decide these things without her. To try to get rid of her.

She did this to herself. Every time. It was always her fault that things turned out this way again and again and again. Behind her back, whispers. Heated, hating looks. And then there would be stones, aimed at her dolls but hitting her as she ran away, as she tried to shield the littlest of her creations from rocks that'd smash them to splinters. Big bruises, round and red and then black, raised inches from her arms and legs and jaw. And there was the cut that'd led to the twist of scar tissue down the side of her face, the hot breath on her cheeks, the snarling face above her, so much anger in the hand pinning her by the chest to a brick wall that dug into her spine. She tried not to think about that. And so, of course, thought about it.

Ikiisa felt dizzy.

"Ikiisa?" Ilo said, and she jumped. He startled at her surprise, taking a step back so his lantern swung, the glow stones within clicking like beetles. Or like something wooden and twisted and scurrying. She shuddered, wanting to slide back into her house, away from the light and Ilo's eyes. She held tight to the doorframe to stop herself from doing that.

"We start two hours after sunrise," Ilo said, eyeing her with a wary look on his face. "Meet in the field called Pond, and bring a few of your dolls—not all of them." He waited for her to acknowledge his words. When she didn't, he sighed. "Do you understand?"

Ikiisa swallowed the imaginary stones plugging up her throat (so hard to breathe with them there) and nodded.

"Good."

Ilo turned and left, walking away without a backward glance. Ikiisa watched him go, shivering, eyes on his lantern's light until that was snuffed by the shape of houses down the road, down the road in Web. Only when her eyes readjusted to the dark did she peel her fingers from the doorframe.

She waited to panic until the door was closed and bolted. Once the lock slid into place she sank to her knees, hyperventilating.

It was happening. Again.

"We want you to leave."

She flinched at the voice, old but still clear, ringing through her insides.

"It'll be best for you, you'll see. Better if you aren't around. I'm doing this for you."

Ikiisa crushed her ears with the heels of her palms, but that didn't stop the voices.

"Our children are getting nightmares. Even some of the adults can't sleep at night, thinking your dolls are walking through our city."

"We've received complaints about you refusing to talk to the employment office, avoiding them when they try to approach you, locking your door so they can't get in. We can't live with a dollmaker like that."

"There are plenty of other dollmakers. Plenty of people who can replace you!"

"You! This is all your fault!"

It went on. Of course—years of it, years of voices. An endless supply. Ikiisa was on her side, curled in the fetal position, wheezing. All she could think was *Not again. Please, please. No. Stop. Stop it.*

Useless, useless words for old, old voices.

Something bumped against her. She ignored it, eyes squeezed shut. It bumped again, harder this time. A sound, a hollow whoosh like what you hear when you hold a seashell to the side of your head. Hissing breaths between clenched teeth, Ikiisa forced herself to open her eyes.

There was Bobble. He stood next to her, lopsided because the new leg she'd given him was from a mannequin with different proportions than his. She'd lacquered his recent chips and cracks and filled them with clay so they wouldn't spread, and the wounds glistened in the light of the candle stands flickering on either side of the front door. When she looked at him he twisted his head and sat next to her with a thump. He whistled, and Ikiisa recognized the call as one for aid, the signal she'd taught her dolls to use if one of them needed help. Hearing him use that signal made Ikiisa's chest squeeze—no one would hear him. Though all her dolls had suffered injury over the years, Bobble was the only one she kept back from Shod patrolling. The damage the children of Web had inflicted on him over the years was simply too great, his body too weak, now, to serve the purpose she'd made it for.

Once Bobble had been Ikiisa's strongest doll. Since coming to Web, he'd turned into a house pet.

Bobble bent down, shoving his long snout against Ikiisa's chest. His prod produced a click. Ikiisa looked down to see him pushing at her pendant.

For one moment hope and relief surged through her. Then she shook her head, hand closing around the stone, squeezing it tight as she told herself she was being ridiculous—how many times over the years had she looked at the pendant and hoped? How many times had she decided that such hope was fanciful nonsense? The man who'd given the stone to her, who'd told her what words to say to the pendant if she was ever in dire need . . . She'd been a child when they'd met. Seven, eight years old at most. She remembered him being so strange, so otherworldly, with hair of copper and white marks all over his face.

She'd had these same thoughts, this same debate with herself, dozens of times before in dozens of "dire" situations. And she always came to the same conclusion, didn't she? She'd imagined the man. This pendant was something Master Coen or maybe her father had given to her, and she'd made up a story to make it seem magical, a lucky charm that'd save her in her hour of greatest need. Silly. And useless. That's why she'd never tried to speak the words she thought the man had told her, not when any of the other towns she'd worked for drove her away.

But this was Web. If Ikiisa was forced to leave the village called Web, where would she go? Was there a single city or town or village left in the entire country of One that hadn't already thrown her out? Ikiisa couldn't think of any, and her hand tightened on the pendant, squeezing until tears of pain pricked her eyes. If she lost Web, she'd lose her last chance to have a home.

"As thanks for helping me, use this pendant if you're ever in an emergency," the man had said, or Ikiisa imagined he'd said, his voice soft and burring. She swallowed, a hard lump in her throat. If she'd ever been in an emergency, this was it.

Shaking, Ikiisa let go of the pendant and used Bobble to sit up, arms wrapping around his rounded back as she shoved herself upright. Her movement made dust from the floor rise and she sneezed, hanging on to Bobble and coughing.

When she could breathe better, she stared down the hallway, down into her house, dark with night and oh so quiet. It was musty. She always forgot how musty until she opened a door or a window and fresh air came in, stirring the stale of the house up and giving it a second, fragrant life. Ikiisa rested her cheek against Bobble's head, wondering when she'd last gone outside, not to use the waste area behind her house but to *be* outside, to *see* outside.

Merchants had been in Web. Someone had thrown something

at her, sharp. Cut her cheek. It hadn't hurt much, but she'd been so surprised she'd stopped breathing. Long enough that her knees buckled under her.

Ikiisa shook her head, dispelling the memory. Scooting back from Bobble, she propped herself against the wall, clasping her pendant. She rubbed her thumb over the symbol carved into the stone. She hesitated.

"It won't hurt," she said, looking at Bobble. The doll whistled a questioning note, and she swallowed, eyes turning back to the pendant. "It won't hurt to try, will it? Even . . . even if nothing happens. No harm done."

Ikiisa hesitated. Then she ignored the flush of embarrassment in her face and held the stone to her lips. Her hand trembled so hard she had to wrap her other hand around her wrist to hold herself steady long enough to whisper the strange words a strange man had taught her long ago.

"Roque, I need you."

SHEAN WOKE WITH A CRICK IN HER NECK. AND NO WONDER—SHE WAS CURLED on a mattress hard as a pile of tubers. When she sat up her whole left side throbbed, various aches and pains running from her ankle to her shoulder. Rubbing a knot at the base of her neck, she glanced toward the window set in the wall across from her. Hues of red and orange shone through its warped glass, refracting in whirls and lopsided circles—the paint-splatter colors of sunrise, tiny and diminished without an ocean to reflect off of.

Staring at the colors, Shean remembered where she was. After the council meeting, the woman called Lenna had led her to this house, showing her a small clearing in which to pasture Lintok. She'd left her dolls to look after him and her travel bags, then Lenna had taken her inside, through hallways fragrant with the scent of tree branches and up a set of steep stairs that ended in a loft room small, hot, stuffy, and containing nothing but a deflated sleeping pallet with a storage chest arranged at its foot.

Lenna had offered some sort of ghastly sleeping shift, so worn it was faded to limp nothing. Shean recalled confliction, torn between exhaustion and forcing her aching limbs back down to Lintok and her saddle packs to find something more suitable to sleep in, scolding herself for the oversight of not thinking to bring a change of clothing with her in the first place. Looking down at herself now, Shean found exhaustion had won. She grimaced, plucking at the discolored front of the borrowed night dress and wondering if she imagined a slight itching wherever its fabric touched her.

She hadn't time to be appalled, though—dawn had come, and with it the pageant that'd prove her dolls to Web. Deciding the first thing to do was to stretch away her aching, Shean slid out of the bed, the wooden floor creaking under her feet. The moment she stood hunger struck her—her stomach was an empty gourd, hurting as if someone was scraping her insides with a spoon. She pressed her hand to her abdomen with a grimace. How long had it been since she ate? A day and a night, she realized.

Shean took a step toward the stairs. Then she stopped, remembering she was wearing the awful sleeping shift. She couldn't leave the room dressed in something so abysmal, so she turned back, lifting her Gleam dress from where she'd folded it atop the chest at the end of the bed. Fingers shaking with hunger, she removed the shift, pulling on and lacing the ties of the dress quick as she could.

Once finished, Shean descended from the loft, at first swiftly, but forced to slow down on stairs that were even steeper going down than they were going up. Skirts lifted so as not to trip herself and one hand on the wall for balance, she eased down to the main floor of the house. The hallway was dimly lit, and, pausing in its gloom, she realized she had no idea which way to go.

She heard a noise, a clink and shuffle of feet. Following the sound down the hall and around a corner, she caught sight of an open window from which flooded the bright light of sunrise, broken up by the shadow of someone moving. She hurried forward, stepping into the room.

The moment she crossed the threshold a scent struck Shean, so heavenly it stopped her short. Meaty and spiced, sugar-cooked and tender. She closed her eyes and inhaled, the fragrance a full-force delight moving from her watering mouth to her aching stomach, consuming her senses.

"Good sunrise, Dollmaker Shean."

Shean opened her eyes to find Lenna standing across the room from her, smiling. The woman's hair was untied, long, and an even snowier white in daylight than it'd appeared at night, stark in the light coming from the window opened to her left. She wore the same work clothing she had the night before, and she stood in front of a steaming pan atop a fire stove—a counter built out from the wall with a flat metal top flanked by slabs of heat-absorbing marble, a chimney set into the top of the stove and sticking up through the roof to funnel smoke.

"And to you," Shean said, eyes tracking the swirl of Lenna's prongs in the pan, a gesture from which came divine fragrance.

"Hungry?" Lenna guessed.

"Very."

"I've just finished."

Lenna lifted the pan from the stove and set it on the marble countertop. With a leisure that made Shean's stomach cramp with protest, the woman crouched, opening the little door beneath the cooktop and using a poker to spread a layer of ash over the stove's fire. When the flames were smothered to embers she straightened, refastening the door and picking up the pan. She sidled to three serving plates set across the counter and split the contents of the pan between the dishes. As she did Shean was awarded a view of strips of tempting beef in a dark broth thick as seaweed sauce, steamed-brown vegetables, and the distinct, glossy tops of mushrooms.

When she finished pouring Lenna set the pan aside, picking up one of the dishes and carrying it, steaming, to a dining table standing on the right side of the room, unnoticed by Shean until the moment food was set upon its scuffed top. Lenna gestured for Shean to come to the table, which she did with eagerness, sitting with her legs to the side atop a deflated kneeling cushion and taking the eating utensils offered her.

Wasting no time, Shean lifted spoon and eating hook, bending over her meal and skewering a mouthful of meat and mushroom. The food tasted as good as it smelled. Better, even, for the way Lenna had cooked the meat was inspired—the sauce a sugary glaze that mingled with the juices of the meat to create a mixture so delectable, Shean resisted the urge to swallow until she'd chewed the beef to tangy mince.

Focused as she was on filling the hollowness of her stomach, Shean didn't notice Lenna wasn't eating until her plate was half-empty. She looked up to find the woman sitting across from her, watching her. Not with judgment, but curiosity, the steam rising from Lenna's own meal diminishing by the second.

"Are you not hungry?" Shean asked, face warm with self-consciousness. What was she doing, shoveling food into her mouth with a potential employer watching her? Lenna would think her an ill-mannered slob. She straightened, forcing herself to forgo taking the next bite, tempting as another mouthful was.

"I am," Lenna said. "I just mean to wait a few minutes more."

She gestured to the left, pointing. Frowning, Shean followed the wave, surprised to find that she'd failed to notice that the room she sat in was not, in fact, a cooking room. Well, half of it was—the room appeared to be a combination of eating area and rest area, half taken up by the stove and dining table, and half covered in long body cushions and pillows made for lounging social events. Or, in this case, for sleeping children; Dola was curled on one of the cushions, breaths soft and quiet, steady with a sleep undisturbed by the ruckus of cooking or voices.

To Shean's shock, Silver was wrapped in Dola's arms, his own eyes closed in an imitation of sleep. One of his arms returned Dola's hug, the other draped over the girl. His hand clutched some sort of writing pad or journal, leather-bound with straps tied around it.

What was Silver doing inside after Shean had told him to stay with her other dolls, watching Lintok? Thinking back on it, she supposed she hadn't instructed Silver, specifically, to watch Lintok, but still. Him being here smacked of defying orders.

Borderline disobedience aside, Shean disliked seeing Silver held like that, as if he belonged to Dola. And what was he thinking, pretending to sleep? She'd half a mind to get up and yank him from the girl's arms, scolding the both of them for acting like a child and her toy. With Lenna watching, though, it was best not to do something quite that drastic. In fact, it was probably best not to address the matter at all. Shean forced herself to look away, smiling in a way she hoped wasn't strained.

"Your daughter?" Shean asked. Lenna smiled a faint smile.

"Granddaughter," she corrected, in a tone of voice that let Shean know she'd caught, and was amused by, the attempt at flattery. Shean felt heat in her face again and cleared her throat.

"I see." Shean picked up her utensils to take another bite of beef before saying, "I was surprised last night when you mentioned Dola—I met her yesterday."

Lenna's eyebrows lifted. "Oh?"

"Yes. She and her friends had cornered one of Dollmaker Ikiisa's dolls." She lifted her gaze to meet Lenna's. "They were tormenting it."

"Not Dola, though," Lenna said, words not a question but a statement of fact. Shean shook her head in confirmation, and Lenna's smile grew a little, eyes proud. "She's too sensible for that."

Thinking of how Dola had stood back from the doll-teasing, Shean wondered if the girl was sensible or just cowardly. Which wasn't a thought to voice in front of her adoring grandmother—Shean took another bite and indicated the little book clasped in Silver's hand while she chewed. "What's that?" she asked.

"Something I gave Dola to practice her writing in. She was up most of the night, showing your doll her work. I kept telling her to sleep, only to hear whispering a few moments later." The words were exasperated but fond, with no real annoyance in them.

"She likes writing?" Shean asked, surprised. Most children she knew who weren't training to be dollmakers disliked practicing penmanship. When she'd been young enough to attend a general school, she'd been driven to insanity by the endless complaints of her classmates over the writing drills their teachers gave them as homework. One boy had irritated her so much, going on and on about how useless good, or even legible, handwriting was, Shean had smashed his workbook into his mouth one day, an attack that knocked out one of his front teeth. Given his age the damage hadn't been permanent, but it'd left him with a satisfying breathing whistle for months.

"Writing and drawing, yes," Lenna said. "Her manma's an artist—a good one, too." She flicked a hand to indicate a picture hanging on the wall above where Dola slept.

Shean looked at the picture, which was a portrait of a man. She studied the curves of the face, the delicate, precise shape of the nose and eyes and chin, the features realistic enough to breathe. Impressive.

"Her manma teaches her?" she guessed.

Lenna shook her head. "She left four years after Dola was born."

"She died?"

"No. Left." Lenna sighed. "Tiry's art made the entire village happy, brought joy and beauty into our lives. But that wasn't enough for her." She waved a hand through the air, looking tired. "She was convinced her art had a greater destiny than to decorate the walls of the houses in the village called Web, a higher calling than the purpose it was serving. She refused to 'settle' for how her art was being used in Web, whatever that meant. So she left. And with her gone . . ." Lenna looked at the portrait hanging on the wall. "Dola's father did his best, but he never had good health. He pushed himself to keep working every night and spent every morning playing with Dola. He wanted her to be happy, more than anything. He died within a year of Tiry leaving." Lenna paused, gaze dropping to Dola. "He wouldn't have lasted much longer than that, anyway."

"Oh," Shean said. She looked at Dola and felt a pang of kinship; she'd been abandoned by her family, too. Though, admittedly, not by any choice of theirs. "Do you ever hear from your daughter?"

"No. We didn't part on good terms. She never told me where she was going."

"I see."

"Yes, well, we may hear from her someday yet. Time will tell—it always does." Lenna grunted, glancing at the window across the room, which now cast a golden light over the table, the sun finished rising and throwing rays of early morning light. "And speaking of time," she said, pushing herself to her feet and walking to Dola. She shook the girl awake.

"Gran?" Dola said in a croaking voice, sitting up and blinking groggy eyes.

"Time to eat, love."

"I was dreaming about Papa," Dola said, yawning. "He was singing the Spider Queen song. Do you remember that song?"

"I remember."

Dola knuckled one of her eyes and looked over at the dining table. Her gaze cleared at the sight of Shean, arms dropping from Silver so quickly he slid to the floor, landing on his face before he could catch himself. He stood, dusting himself off and, with a flourish, handing the notebook he held to Dola. She took it, casting a nervous look in Shean's direction as she scrambled to her feet.

"G-good sunset—rise," she said, words squeaking as she corrected herself.

"And to you," Shean said, looking past Dola to Silver. Smiling so as not to alarm her hosts, she did her best to spell danger with her eyes, letting him know just how displeased she was with him.

He beamed back at her, and Shean noticed he was still holding something, something flat and thin. She stood up, recognizing Nock's license.

"What are you doing with that?" Shean asked. She did her best to keep her voice pleasant, tone exasperated but charmed, like she was scolding a pet. This was difficult, as a zing of panic zapped through her, paranoid scenarios of someone with sense seeing the card and realizing it was outdated plaguing her. She walked over to Silver with controlled steps. Bending forward so her hair swung down around her face, she stuck out her hand. "Give it back," she said with a forced smile, words strained through her teeth. Silver passed the license to her without protest, pressing the card into her palm. "Thank you," she said, tucking it into her skirt and knotting the pocket's ribbons five, tight times. Knowing that Dola and Lenna couldn't see her face, Shean gave Silver a scowl. At the glare he held a finger to his lips, smiled, and winked.

"All right," Lenna said, and Shean turned to find her ushering Dola to the table. "No more delay. You and I need to eat, love, then show Dollmaker Shean where she needs to be. It won't do for one of the guests of honor to be late to her own pageant."

THE PAGEANT FIELD STRETCHED BETWEEN THE EDGE OF THE VILLAGE CALLED WEB and the forest called Deep. The villagers had already arrived by the time Dola and Lenna led Shean and her dolls to the field; they sat in cross-legged clusters at the fringes of the clearing, some on kneeling cushions but most sprawled in the grass. Their skin was so pale their faces reflected the light of the sun, and they spoke to one another in soft murmurs broken by the occasional squeal from children chasing one another around, bursting with energy as they played catch-pursuit games and raced one another across the lea.

Ikiisa stood apart from the villagers, near the center of the clearing and pacing through a patch of trampled-flat grass. Seven dolls of varying sizes and shapes sat in a group next to her, heads tracking her as she walked one direction for a few steps, stopped, swung on a heel, and paced back the way she'd come. The dolls let out the occasional twarp and twitter, speaking to one another in a language of warbles and whistles.

Ilo stood between the villagers and Ikiisa, striding over to meet Shean as she stepped onto the field. "Good sunrise, Dollmaker Shean," he said, nodding to her, her companions. "Lenna. Dola."

"Good sunrise," Lenna said. "We apologize for being late."

Ilo waved a hand. "I took the time to explain the situation to the others. We're ready to begin if you are, Dollmaker Shean."

Shean glanced at her dolls, confirming the five she'd selected were ready. She'd left one doll, Crystal, behind to watch Lintok, and she felt his absence—she would've liked to have all her dolls present for the pageant. Nevertheless, confidence warmed her as she looked from Marble to Glass to Jewel to Coin. And, of course, Silver.

Her masterpieces—how could they fail?

Shean faced Ilo, inclining her head with a smile. "I'm ready."

"Good." Ilo turned, voice raising. "Ikiisa!"

Ikiisa stopped pacing with a jerk, eyes snapping to Ilo, then dropping to the ground. She turned, saying something to her dolls before trudging across the field. Lenna and Dola excused themselves, settled amidst the other villagers by the time Ikiisa reached Ilo and Shean.

"Dollmaker Ikiisa," Shean said, bowing a bow intended for someone who's of a status just slightly below one's own—both hands behind her back, fingers clenched together as she bent and lifted herself in one quick movement.

Ikiisa didn't return the greeting. She stared at Shean, face pale, brow creased, and expression one of pained confusion. After an awkward moment Ilo cleared his throat.

"Right," he said. He turned to face the villagers, lifting a hand for quiet. When it fell, he spoke.

"As you know, this pageant has been called as a means to determine who will hold the position of dollmaker in the village called Web. The candidates are Dollmaker Ikiisa of the city called Glass, and Dollmaker Shean of the city called Pearl. Per tradition, the pageant will consist of three tasks, the first of which is set by the council." He turned to face Ikiisa and Shean, continuing to speak loud enough for all to hear.

"The Shod are notorious for their ability to move faster than any beast or man—to fight them, a doll must be able to match their pace. As such, the council has decided that the first test of this pageant will be one of speed. You'll each select three dolls to complete a lap of the village before returning to their respective master. Whichever dolls return first will win the task."

Shean suppressed a smile. A test of speed. What good fortune, the first task being so nicely tailored to one of her dolls' greatest strengths.

"Neither of you may move from where you stand at the start of the race, or you'll forfeit this test," Ilo continued. He looked from Ikiisa to Shean as he spoke, as if glaring would make them obey. He folded his arms across his chest. "Is that understood?"

"Yes," Shean said.

Ikiisa nodded.

"Good. Pick your dolls."

Shean chose Glass, Marble, and Jewel. She ignored Silver's look of disappointment and Coin's dejected slumping as she did so—really, it didn't matter which dolls she picked for this task. They were all equals, or close to equals, in speed. But Glass, Marble, and Jewel were smaller than Silver and Coin, and it'd be more impressive when they outpaced Ikiisa's dolls, which were mammoth in comparison.

Shean instructed her dolls to step up to Ilo and Ikiisa did the same. Side by side, the contrast between Shean's work and Ikiisa's was stark. The villagers noticed—they murmured at the sight of Shean's lovely dolls next to Ikiisa's monstrosities. Shean stood a little straighter.

Ilo stepped aside, out of the dolls' way. He lifted an arm, and as he swung it down he said, "Begin!"

The dolls sprang forward, dashing toward the village. All six kept pace with one another, neck and neck up to the moment they rounded the corner of a house and disappeared from sight. An excited chatter rose from the villagers, a few standing and craning their necks. One of the children cupped his hands around his mouth, calling to Ilo.

"Can we watch?"

Ilo grunted, waving a relenting hand. With squeals of delight children split from the other villagers and ran off. Shean saw Dola look at Lenna, waiting until her gran gave her an encouraging nod before scrambling away too.

"This won't take long," Shean said, folding her arms across her chest. Silver and Coin mimicked her.

Ikiisa said nothing in response, eyes glued on Web, unblinking. Shean eyed her, then ignored her, returning her own gaze to the village.

She was right—the race began and ended swiftly. No sooner had the children run off to track the dolls than they were returning to the field, arms waving and shouting that the dolls were coming back. Shean held her breath for the second between the children's return and the first doll appearing around the far corner of Web. She let the air out in a triumphant whoosh as Marble zipped into view, followed closely by Glass and Jewel.

All three of her dolls were in the lead, but Ikiisa's dolls weren't far behind, galloping around the curve of Web seconds after Jewel. Shean's shoulders tensed as the race became a final sprint, all six dolls picking up speed. Shean's dolls became three specks of shimmering color and whipping hair, Ikiisa's dolls brown arrows shot from an invisible bow. Shean resisted the urge to step forward, to close the gap between herself and her dolls as Ikiisa's dolls bit at their heels.

In the end there was no need to worry. Shean's dolls reached her first, stopping in a neat line and bowing as Ikiisa's dolls came to a belated halt in front of their creator. A cheer went up from the villagers, mostly from the children, but with a few adult shouts added to the mix. Ilo's voice rose above a smatter of clapping.

"Dollmaker Shean wins the first task."

Shean shot a triumphant look at Ikiisa, but, to her annoyance, the woman wasn't looking at her. She was crouched in front of one of her dolls, fiddling with its leg joint. The fussing made it look like Ikiisa's dolls had lost because of some injury, and Shean bristled.

"Well done," she said to her dolls, loudly. Ikiisa looked at her, but said nothing.

"Dollmaker Ikiisa," Ilo said, voice edged in impatience. Ikiisa looked at him, letting go of her doll to stand. "You set the next task."

Ikiisa's lips pressed into a line. She glanced at Shean, then looked away, gaze lowering to her dolls. Her hands were shaking, fingers trembling until she folded them into fists at her sides. For a painfully long time she said nothing, standing so still she could've been a mannequin. Only when rustles of boredom began rising from the villagers did she look up, clearing her throat.

"The Shod are strong as oxen and can withstand more damage than any living creature before falling," she said, eyes lowering as she spoke until she was staring at her shoes. "An important aspect of a guard doll is its ability to match that strength."

Shean stifled a snort. The words were practically quoted from the First Dollmaker's fourth edict—it'd taken her that long to decide to repeat a section of law?

"As a test of strength," Ikiisa went on, "we'll each select a doll and have them hold a stone. We'll give them more and more stones, and whichever doll can no longer support the weight of their stack first loses."

Shean wasn't surprised by the challenge—if she had dolls as big and bulky as Ikiisa's, her mind would go to a task involving strength, too. Ikiisa was mistaken, though, in thinking that Shean's dolls were at a disadvantage. Small as they were, Shean had given them reinforced limbs and torsos, going to lengths and pains to ensure they were sturdy enough to lift entire buildings, if such was required of them while saving victims of the Shod.

"Very well. Where are we to get these stones?" Ilo asked, frowning.

Ikiisa turned to her dolls, saying a low word to them. Two dolls whistled in acknowledgment, turning and running into the forest. A few moments passed, then the dolls returned, dragging stones behind them. They pulled one rock in front of Ikiisa, the other in front of Shean. Then they turned and ran back into the forest, returning with two more stones. They repeated the process twice more, then Ikiisa whistled a note that made them stop.

"They can get more if we need them," Ikiisa said.

Shean eyed the four stones piled in front of her. Though they ranged in size and shape, her pile and Ikiisa's appeared evenly balanced. If anything, one of the stones in front of Shean was slightly smaller than the ones in front of Ikiisa.

Shean looked up to find Ikiisa and Ilo watching her, waiting. She gave a crisp, consenting nod.

"Choose your dolls," Ilo said.

Ikiisa, of course, chose the largest of her dolls, a great behemoth that, when standing on its five, many-jointed legs, was nearly as tall as Ilo. Shean eyed her dolls, and, a bit annoyed with herself, chose the largest as well.

"Silver," she said. He saluted her and stepped forward, taking his place behind Shean's pile of stones. The rock nearest him was so large, only his head was visible over its top.

"Begin," Ilo said.

The dolls picked up their first stones. Ikiisa's doll lifted its rock with ease, holding the stone aloft with a merry whistle. Silver took longer, and for one terrible moment Shean thought he'd fail. But he didn't, holding his stone over his head with a calm look on his face. He winked at Shean when their eyes met, and she relaxed.

Ikiisa bent, picking up one of her rocks with a grunt. She offered it to her doll, who looped an arm around the second stone and placed it atop the first. Shean followed suit, picking a flat rock and setting it atop Silver's first stone. Ikiisa gave her doll a third rock. Shean did the same. The fourth stones were placed, and, when neither doll showed signs of faltering under their burdens, Ikiisa's dolls brought four more stones from the forest.

The stacking continued. And continued. On stone nine, Shean found herself standing on tiptoe, straining to reach the top of the stones already balanced atop Silver. When she failed she flattened her feet and let out a frustrated breath. Her arms ached from lifting so many rocks, pulsing as she spun to face Ilo.

"How much longer is this going to go on?" she asked. Her voice broke the quiet of the field, the villagers sitting in a shroud of eager hush while they waited for one doll or the other to falter. Tucking the rock she held under an arm, Shean waved a hand to indicate the sun, which had passed the midpoint of the sky. "Are we to continue stacking to sunset?"

Ilo glanced at the sky, then over his shoulder, looking toward where the other council members of Web sat. After a moment, he turned back to Shean.

"One more stone," he said. "If neither doll flags under one more stone, we'll call this task tied."

Shean glanced at Ikiisa, who'd stopped stacking to listen. She was staring at Ilo, a protest struggling across her face. When Ilo looked at her, that struggle died. Expression resigned, she nodded.

"Fine," Shean said, turning back to Silver. "One more stone." She stared up at the stack of rocks Silver held, brow furrowed. She had no idea how she was going to reach the top.

Something bumped against her leg, startling her. She looked down to find one of Ikiisa's dolls crouching next to her. It had a flat back that was just large enough to stand on.

Shean looked at Ikiisa. She was already standing on one of her dolls, boosted high enough to hold her last stone over her doll's pile. She didn't look at Shean. Just waited.

Well, there wasn't really an alternative, was there? Shean stepped onto Ikiisa's doll. It lifted itself, slowly enough that Shean kept her balance without trouble. When she was high enough to see the top of the highest stone Silver held, the doll stopped lifting her.

"Place the stones at the same time," Ilo said, counting down. "Three, two . . . one."

Shean let go of her stone. In the corner of her eye she saw Ikiisa do the same. The moment the rocks landed, a great *crack* split the quiet of the clearing, followed by a gasp from the villagers.

Triumph rising in her, Shean looked at Ikiisa's doll, searching for what part of it had just fractured. But there was nothing wrong with the doll.

Its head was turned, though. Ikiisa's was too. Toward Silver.

Shean's breath caught. She leapt from the back of the doll holding her aloft, landing with a stumbling step before spinning to look at Silver.

His arms. His beautiful arms that'd taken her over a week apiece to carve and shape and assemble.

They had cracks in them.

Instinct buzzed through Shean, sending her lurching forward. She shoved her hands against the stack of rocks Silver held, scraping her palms raw as she knocked the tower over. With a mighty noise the stones fell behind Silver, thumping into the ground and tearing up grass, striking one another in loud percussions that made Shean's ears hurt. When the noise ended all Silver held was his first stone.

"Put it down," Shean said, heart pounding. Silver cocked his head to the side, as if he didn't understand. "Now!"

Silver dropped the stone, stepping back and out of the way before the rock could land on him. Ignoring the hubbub coming from her audience, Shean knelt next to Silver, taking his arms in her hands. She scowled at the lattice of hairline cracks lining the wood—nothing that put his arms in danger of shattering, but blemishes to the smooth grain of his limbs. To her relief, that was the extent of the damage; she found no cracks when she pulled up his shirt to check his chest and shoulders, rolled up his trousers to inspect his legs and knees.

"Is he all right?" Ikiisa asked. Shean looked up to find the woman standing next to her, bent at the waist to better see Silver's arms. A few steps away Ikiisa's doll was setting its own stones down in an orderly, quiet manner. Because, Shean realized, the task was over.

"Dollmaker Ikiisa wins the second task," Ilo said, and Shean felt cold.

She'd lost.

Her jaw clenched. "No!" she spat, jumping to her feet. Ikiisa rose, too, taking a step back from Shean when she swung a hand, gesturing at Silver's poor, broken arms. "Look what you did to my doll!"

"I didn't—"

"Liar!" Shean interrupted. "On the very last stone, the stone that would've tied us, my doll cracks? Impossible!"

She fought to keep her voice steady as she spoke, her distress over Silver's injuries warring with her frustration over the thought of conceding a victory to one of Ikiisa's hideous, subpar dolls. It wouldn't do to lose her temper now, though. Not with such a large audience watching her—an audience with the ability to decide whether or not her journey to the village called Web had been pointless.

And it hadn't been. It *couldn't* be; she hadn't come all this way, worked so hard to prove her dolls could fight the Shod, to fail now. She had to be upset without being enraged. Rational and convincing. Logical enough to make them see that her dolls were in no way inferior to Ikiisa's.

With that in mind, she whirled on a heel and faced Ilo, planting her hands on her hips. Addressing him directly, she spoke with the same no-nonsense tone she used whenever she was having an argument.

"You can't declare Dollmaker Ikiisa the winner of this task. Not after such circumstantial success."

"Circumstantial?" Ilo echoed, voice wary. But not immediately dismissive.

Good. She could still salvage this situation.

She flung a hand toward Ikiisa, the woman flinching as she did so. "Not only did she select this task in a clear attempt to give her lumbering dolls an advantage, but she had her dolls select the very stones we used—including the last stones we placed," Shean said. "The stones that oh-so-conveniently broke *my* doll, but spared hers." She settled her hand back on her hip, leveling her gaze at Ilo and putting all the conviction she could into her voice. "She did something—told her dolls to give Silver heavier stones. How else can you explain him failing at the very last moment?"

As she spoke, Shean realized she believed what she was saying. What had started out as bluster and protest, determination to not let her dolls fail in any regard, became truth—Ikiisa really *had* to have rigged that final stone. There was no other explanation for why Silver would fail at the last, not after withstanding every stone placed on him before that moment.

Folding her arms, Shean raised her chin and spoke loudly enough for all the villagers of Web to hear. "I demand this task be declared a draw."

"But—!" Ikiisa started, protest cutting off with a strangled noise when Shean looked at her. Her eyes were wide, face drained of color. She was trembling. "I didn't—"

"Don't deny it!" Shean said, voice rising close to a shout as her frustration peaked. Arms dropping and hands fisting, she took a step toward Ikiisa that made the woman blanch, scowling. "Silver's rocks were heavier!"

"And if they were?" Ilo said. When Shean looked at him, there was color in his cheeks. His eyes were hard, and the hesitation that'd been in his voice before had changed. Settled into determination. Bordering on anger. "The task was one of strength. If your doll's stones *were* heavier, he should've been strong enough to hold them."

Shean stiffened.

No one was *listening* to her.

Again.

She saw the same flash of hot red she'd seen when Maton refused to give her a proper license, and, just like then, her hands clenched tighter, the urge to lift a fist, to resort to violence where rationality had failed, surging.

Before she could, a cough interrupted her.

It was a soft cough. But it was so close and so unexpected, it made Ilo, Ikiisa, and Shean herself jump. All together they turned.

A man stood on the edge of the forest called Deep, presumably just emerged from the tree line, though there wasn't a stray leaf or bit of dirt on any part of him to suggest a trek through the tangled undergrowth of the woodland. Composed to a fault, he was only a step or two away from Shean, and with calm, lancing gray eyes he looked from her to Ikiisa to Ilo before turning his attention to the villagers of Web. Expression thoughtful, he pushed a stray copper lock out of his eyes, away from the white markings curled at his temples. Shean gasped.

The man from the city called Ports. He was here. In Web. Clearing his throat, adjusting the blue-ended travel pack on his shoulder, and smiling a subdued smile.

"Forgive me. Am I interrupting something?" he asked.

SHEAN HAD ONLY BEEN TRULY SHOCKED THREE TIMES IN HER LIFE. FIRST ON THE morning following the Red Tide, when she'd seen the bodies of her family amidst the casualties, her manma's face ripped asunder, her father's arms missing, and Giko's eyes turned to pale, vacant marbles over a slit throat. Second when she'd been ten and a tidal wave came racing from the ocean to the city called Pearl, a miles-long ridge of water that slapped against the world, washing away the cove docks and fishermen houses built along the rocky shore beneath the city. The sheer *power* of the sea that day had stolen Shean's breath away, making her tremble with a mixture of admiration, envy, and fear.

The third and final time Shean had been shocked was when she was eighteen and Borden the elk herder's apprentice, two years her junior and caretaker of the herd she pastured Lintok with during winter, had arrived without warning on Nock's doorstep. She'd met him at the gate, and when she'd asked him what he needed he'd grabbed the straps of her woodworking apron and yanked her mouth to his. A very sloppy, wet moment later, Borden the elk herder's apprentice had turned and run, never to be seen again.

In all three instances Shean had experienced a disorienting disbelief, a confusion that dulled her senses and slowed her thoughts to silence. She felt that same numbness now, staring at the man from Ports. She stared and stared and, like corpses and tidal waves and stolen kisses, she could make no sense of him.

Then Ilo spoke, hostile voice yanking Shean from her stupor. "Who're you?"

"Roque, a traveling linguist and translator," the man from Ports said, bobbing his head in greeting. Ilo didn't return the favor, folding his arms across his chest and giving the man, Roque, the same look he'd given Shean when they'd met—a glare of suspicion.

"Why are you here?" Ilo asked. "What do you want?"

"I want nothing," Roque said, "and I'm here because I was requested."

"Requested? By who?"

Roque cocked his head, gaze sliding from Ilo. "A good question," he said. He looked around the clearing, eyes meeting Shean's with a glint of recognition that made her think, for one confused moment, that he was referring to her. Then he looked away, attention settling on Ikiisa.

"Her," he said.

The word sent a jolt through Shean. She stared at Ikiisa in horror—*she* knew the man from Ports?

By the First Dollmaker, *why*?

"Ikiisa?" Ilo said. "Who is this man?"

Ikiisa was staring at Roque, mouth hanging open. At Ilo's words she flinched, looking at him with wide, alarmed eyes. "I . . . I-I'm not . . ."

She trailed off, expression baffled. Roque cleared his throat, drawing Ilo's attention back to him. "As I've said," he said, voice patient, "I am Roque, a language specialist. Ikiisa asked me here, and I've come. It's that simple."

Shean could tell Ilo didn't believe him. *Shean* didn't believe him—who came to Web without a personal reason, be it to buy a bolt of spider silk or to make an attempt to displace their current dollmaker? This was the *village called Web*—the least important village in all of One. What sort of work could a linguist hope to find here?

"We've no need for a language studier in Web," Ilo said, echoing Shean's thoughts.

"Ikiisa is my client," Roque said. "Her need of a language studier is all that concerns me."

Ilo scowled at that, but didn't argue. How could he? It was against the laws of One, and all the country stood for, to block anyone from fulfilling an employment request. Even a foreigner. "How long do you intend to stay?" he asked.

"However long Ikiisa has need of me."

Ilo let out a frustrated huff, face reddening.

"Ilo," Lenna said. Shean jerked in surprise—she hadn't notice the woman's arrival. Based on how Ilo jumped, he hadn't, either. Lenna placed a hand on his shoulder, eyes moving from Roque to Ikiisa to Shean in turn. Her expression was calm, but her gaze was firm.

"Master Roque," Lenna said, "it's none of our places to send you from Web if you've work to be had here." She looked at Ikiisa. "You *did* send for him?"

"I . . ." Ikiisa hesitated, looking at Roque. She nodded. "I did."

The confirmation made something within Shean wail, distraught.

"Very well," Lenna said. She lowered her head to Roque. "Forgive our rudeness, Master Roque. We aren't used to visitors in Web, and we didn't intend to offend you."

Roque inclined his head in return. "No offense taken."

"Good. Now, I think," Lenna said, turning back to Ilo, "that it'd be best if we ended the pageant here."

The words sent a bolt of alarm through Shean. She took a breath to protest.

"We can finish with the final task tomorrow," Lenna said. She looked at Shean. "Once everyone's heads have had time to cool."

Shean bristled. "I—" she started.

"A wise suggestion," Ilo said. He shot a glare at Shean, Roque. Then, without another word, he turned and stalked away, passing the silent villagers and marching to the village called Web. After a pause, everyone but Dola and Lenna followed him.

"Shall we go as well?" Roque said, turning to Ikiisa. She looked at him like he was speaking gibberish, but she nodded, turning to lead the way to her house. Roque didn't spare a look for Shean as he passed, and on impulse she took a step to follow him, reaching to grab his wrist and hold him back, to demand he explain his presence in Web and how (*why*) he knew Ikiisa. She was stopped by Lenna grabbing *her* arm, pulling her back toward the village.

Before Shean could protest, Roque was gone and the first, disastrous day of the pageant ended.

IKIISA'S HOUSE WAS CLUTTERED. SHE DIDN'T MIND THAT—CLUTTERED DIDN'T mean dirty, and she found a certain comfort in having a house that, large as it was, felt tight and close on the inside. The dozen or so rooms of the three-story structure were like the chambers of a burrow, crammed with things important to her, kept safe by sturdy walls.

With Roque standing in the doorway of her workroom, though, looking at the dozens of incomplete dolls shoved and stacked against the walls, Ikiisa regretted never bothering to tidy up.

"S-sorry," she said, pushing past him and into the room. "I'll just, ah—" She cut off, hurrying to clear off one of her work tables, leaving the glow lantern shining fitfully on its top and scooping up the three medium-sized, in-progress dolls sprawled across the table. She threw them onto a pile of smaller projects to her left, wincing at the resulting rattle and scrape, then shoved a clutter of retired Shod-fighting armor she'd been mining for parts off to the side, stacking leather bracers and a chest piece cracked from age against the wall. After a frantic search she located a kneeling cushion under a particularly large, half-complete doll that she could only move by wrapping both arms around its barrel-like chest and lifting. A fair amount of scrambling, shifting, grunting, and fluffing later, she managed to set the kneeling cushion down behind the table, gesturing to it.

"Here," she huffed, struggling to catch her breath while an embarrassing amount of sweat dripped down the sides of her face. Never before had she so wished she hadn't blocked all the windows of the room with her piles of incomplete work—a cool breeze from outside would do wonders for the stuffiness in the air.

"Thank you," Roque said. He stepped across the room, and Ikiisa backed away to give him space to pass her. She still couldn't believe it, but it *was* him—the man from her childhood. The man from the ditch. Not a figment of her imagination after all, and not as disheveled as when they'd met, of course. Not covered in blood, either. But that was the metallic hair, the dark skin and pale eyes, the strange white marks spread across his face and hands. The man who'd given her the pendant, who'd told her what to say to have him come to her.

And here he was. Here. Come. To her.

Roque sat down, untying the travel pack from his back and setting it beside him. He looked up at Ikiisa and, after an awkward pause, she sat down across from him, deciding against searching for another cushion and sitting cross-legged on the bare floor, hands clasped over her ankles.

Roque smiled once she settled. A small, polite smile. "It's good to see you again, Ikiisa. You look well."

He looked exactly how she remembered him, which was impossible. Over twenty years had passed since they'd met. If she remembered him being a young man back then, he should be close to middle-aged now. But he looked younger than her, not older.

Impossible. Strange. Confusing.

Almost as baffling as the fact that he was here in the first place.

"You . . . you're really him?" Ikiisa asked, tentative. "The man in the ditch?"

Roque grimaced at the word "ditch." Then his smile returned, voice pleasant. "I am."

"How?" Ikiisa asked, the single word insufficient to convey the confusion and pleasure and slight tingle of fear that swirled in her at the confirmation.

He gestured to her pendant. "When someone in possession of a Summon Mark evokes my name and speaks, I hear their words. You evoked my name and requested help. You called me, and I came." His smile softened. "It's that simple."

That didn't sound simple to Ikiisa. Half of the words he'd just said made no sense to her. But she nodded anyway.

"Only those to whom I owe a great debt have the right to call me," Roque continued. "As such, allow me to thank you again." He pressed his hands flat to the table between them, lowering his head until his forehead touched the wood. Ikiisa wasn't expecting the gesture, and it made her uncomfortable and embarrassed, like she was being given an award for something she hadn't done.

"Thank you," Roque said.

"Um, you're, ah, welcome," Ikiisa said, and to her relief he straightened. She pulled at the collar of her shirt, not sure what to say or do next. What would a polite host do?

"Are you, ah, hungry?" she asked. "Thirsty?" She paused, then blurted, "Tired?"

"I'm fine, thank you," Roque said. "Would you mind telling me why you need my help?"

"O-oh," Ikiisa said, blushing. "Right."

She explained. Roque was an attentive listener, asking the occasional, clarifying question, but, for the most part, remaining silent as Ikiisa told him of Shean and the pageant.

"And you called me because you're afraid Shean will take your place as the dollmaker of Web?" Roque said when she finished detailing the outcomes of the first two trials, lapsing into silence.

"Yes," Ikiisa said, eyes lowering as she spoke. "I, um. I don't know what I'll do if they make me leave Web, so I, ah . . . I remembered what you said. About using this," she said, clutching the pendant, "to reach you."

Saying it aloud, her reasons for using the pendant sounded trivial. Stupid. Ikiisa didn't dare look at Roque, frightened of seeing amusement, or even anger, in his expression.

"I see," he said, and he didn't sound upset. Just regretful. "I'm grateful that you thought of me, but I'm afraid I'll be of little help in this situation."

Ikiisa toyed with the hem of her tunic, twisting the fabric in an attempt to mask her disappointment. What had she expected him to say? He was a linguist—and even if he wasn't, even if he was a warrior or a trickster or a minstrel, what could he, or anyone, do to save Ikiisa from her employers finding someone they preferred over her?

"R-right," she said. "I . . . I suppose words can't save me."

"It's unwise to underestimate the power of language," Roque said, voice suddenly sharp. Ikiisa looked up, surprised at his tone and cringing back when she found his gaze searing with intensity, his entire body tilted forward with an urgency that could be heard in his voice. "Some words have the ability to achieve wonders—your Breath Mark, for example."

"The Breath Mark?" Ikiisa echoed, surprised. She shook her head. "It's not a word."

The passion in Roque's eyes flagged. He settled back, removing his hands from the table and straightening, adjusting the collar of his shirt and speaking in a more composed tone. "Not in a language anyone knows, no. It's not." He waved a dismissive hand. "But that's beside the point—what concerns me about your situation is that I doubt anyone in Web would listen to me if I tried to protest their treatment of you. Which sounds quite terrible."

Ikiisa appreciated him saying that, saying that the people of Web weren't nice to her. It'd been . . . Well, *no one* had ever said something that kind to her when referencing her work. Especially not a veritable stranger. She fought back the sudden, irrational urge to hug him.

"They're not that bad," she said, rubbing the pad of her thumb against the edge of the work table. "Not as bad here as other cities, anyway."

"You've had similar troubles in the past?" Roque asked. Ikiisa looked up to find him watching her with concerned eyes. She swallowed, but forced herself to hold his gaze, nodding.

"The longest I've worked anywhere is Web. Everywhere else I was only employed for a few weeks, a month or two at the most."

"And then you were . . . ?"

"Asked to leave." Ikiisa let out a short, sharp bark of laughter that fizzled into a painful gulp. "Or made to leave."

Roque frowned. His gaze shifted to her scar.

"Made?" he echoed.

Ikiisa turned her head so her scar was less visible to him. Its long, tight shape suddenly felt more uncomfortable than usual, a stiff line down the side of her face. "Y-yes. But that's not . . . I wasn't thinking when I . . ." She took a deep, steadying breath and paused long enough to sort her thoughts. "I, um, understand if you decide to leave. I wasn't thinking clearly when I . . . called you." She looked down at the table, fingers curled and nails digging into the wood. "I was panicking."

"I'll stay," Roque said. Ikiisa straightened in surprise. And unexpected delight.

"Really?" she said.

Roque nodded. "Yes. And I'll do what I can—I owe you that much for rescuing me from that unpleasant situation."

Ikiisa doubted anyone else in the entire world would refer to a pack of Shod tearing them to pieces as just "unpleasant." She was too happy to find his nonchalance unnerving, though—she had no clearer idea than Roque did as to how he could help her, but the fact that she had an ally was such a rare, sweet realization she didn't care if he did nothing at all but *be* there during the last task of the pageant tomorrow, watching. Buzzing with relief, she leapt to her feet.

"Thank you!" she said, hands clasped in front of her.

"My pleasure," Roque said, standing. He bent to pick up his travel bag, and Ikiisa wondered how fast, and far, he'd had to travel to reach Web just a day after she called him.

"You're tired—you should rest," Ikiisa said. She spun on a heel and ran across the room, waving for Roque to follow her. He did, and she led him through the narrow hallways of her house, all the way to the guest room, which was the one room she hadn't completely filled with mannequins.

Not completely, though, didn't mean not at all—there were half a dozen mannequins propped against the walls and sprawled across the floor. She removed five almost-dolls from the bed that served as the only piece of furniture in the room, stacking them with their fellows as Roque entered the room.

"You're very prolific," he said as she dragged the largest mannequins out into the hallway, voice impressed and amused.

Ikiisa let out a strained chuckle. "More unfocused than prolific—I start more dolls than I ever finish," she said, abandoning the hallway mannequins and standing in the doorway. Roque was sitting on the edge of the bed, his pack next to him. She held on to the doorframe, feeling like there was something more to be said but at a loss as to what those words were. She gave up and said, "Well, um. Good night."

"There's one more thing I wanted to ask you," Roque said.

"Yes?"

"You're the dollmaker of Web. That means you're aware of the whereabouts of the Shod in this area, yes?"

Ikiisa hesitated, a sliver of guilt that'd been embedded in her for years making itself known with a wiggle. "Yes," she said, slowly.

Roque nodded, tucking a strand of copper hair behind his ear. "I admit," he said, "it's been decades since I was in the country called One, but in the past month I haven't seen a Shod. If memory serves me, that wasn't the case twenty years ago."

Ikiisa held the doorframe a little tighter. "No."

"So there *are* less Shod about than normal. Is there a reason?"

"You've heard of the Red Tide?" Ikiisa asked, wondering if just that question was saying too much. Foreigners weren't supposed to be told about the workings of One, especially when those workings concerned dolls or Shod. But Roque already seemed to know so much—was there really any harm in telling him a little more?

"I have," Roque said.

Ikiisa swallowed her nervousness and said, "Ever since the Tide's recession, there's been less Shod."

Roque's eyes flashed with curiosity. "And why is that?"

"I don't know."

"And here in Web?"

"What?"

"Are there less Shod in Web than usual?"

The guilt digging into Ikiisa grew sharper. She looked at the ground. "My dolls drive any Shod that come close to Web away."

"How often?"

"A . . . a few every month," Ikiisa said. An exaggeration, but she just couldn't bring herself to admit that it'd been half a year or more, now, since she'd last seen or had her dolls report a Shod.

"Are the villagers of Web aware of that?" Roque asked.

Ikiisa wet her lips, voice a whisper. "No."

"Why not?"

Ikiisa shuffled her feet, eyes moving to the side, to study where the door met the floor. She wasn't doing anything wrong. She told herself that as she stared at the ground. She was a dollmaker, hired to keep Shod away from Web. And she did. When there were Shod to be kept away.

She wasn't doing anything wrong.

"Ikiisa?" Roque said, voice soft.

"I don't know," she said, forcing herself to look up. "We don't . . . we don't discuss it."

Roque stared at her for a long moment, expression neutral. Then he nodded. "I see," he said. "Thank you, Ikiisa. And good night."

Relieved at being released from the conversation, Ikiisa nodded, backing away from the door. "I'll see you in the morning," she said.

"In the morning," Roque agreed as she shut the door between them.

SHEAN STOMPED FROM ONE END OF LENNA'S LOFT ROOM TO THE OTHER. HER hands fisted in the folds of her skirt, grip clenched so hard the jewel beading bit into her. It hurt, but she didn't care. The pain made her pace faster.

"Ridiculous!" she spat. "Refusing to let me defend myself when I'm being taken advantage of! Telling me my dolls aren't strong enough. Clearly playing favorites—" She cut off with a jerk and a revelatory gasp, whipping around to face the bed. Silver sat there, arms wrapped in linen bandages to give the sealing lacquer Shean had dug from her travel packs and applied to his cracks time to set. Her other dolls had been sent down to Lintok.

Silver smiled at Shean when she faced him, a serene expression she returned with a scowl. "I wouldn't be surprised if they never *meant* to pick me as the pageant's winner!" she said. "The tasks are just a front, something to make me think I have a chance—their intentions have always been to choose Ikiisa in the end anyway!" She stomped a foot, seething. "They're just like Nock and that damn Maton—they won't even give me a *chance*!"

She let go of her skirts, letting them fall in a clicking swish around her legs. Her hands itched for something to tear or smash, something, anything, to let her frustration out on. But the only things in the room were the bed and Silver and her. The bed wasn't hers and, furious as she was, tearing up a stranger's bedsheets was a damning option. She wasn't going to lay a hand on Silver, of course, and the thought of ripping up her beautiful Gleam dress was unbearable. She ended up doing absolutely nothing, standing stiff and furious and bursting in the middle of the room.

"What's the point of a test of strength, anyway?" she asked Silver. "Holding up a bunch of lousy rocks only makes sense if all you want from dolls is aimless, brute strength—which doesn't even work against the Shod! Not in the long run!" She pressed her hands to the sides of her head, the heels of her palms digging against her temples as she clenched her teeth, eyes squeezed shut as she strove to grimace through the anger. "I keep *telling* them that, but no one *listens* to me! This whole country has just *one* way of thinking, *one* idea of how dolls should work, and I *hate* it."

Her eyes opened, narrowing as her hands dropped, digging back into her skirts and twisting as her mind pivoted toward another frustration. "And that man—that Roque!" she said. "Why does he know Ikiisa? How did she contact him? If I'd known they were friends, I would have, have—"

What? What *would* she have done?

"Something!" Shean said, flinging her arms through the air in an exasperated grab at nothing. "I don't know! I don't know anything! None of this is fair! Not that strength task, not Roque knowing Ikiisa. *Especially* not Roque knowing Ikiisa. He's, he's—"

Shean cut off, realizing she was about to say "mine."

Hers? A stranger she'd met once, had one conversation with, and shared a meal with? Hers?

Yes. She'd met him her first day out of Pearl. *She* was the one who'd talked to him about his homeland and the Shod. Not Ikiisa. Her. Shean.

She saw him first.

"D-Dollmaker Shean?"

Shean spun around, snapping. *"What?"*

Dola jumped, almost dropping the tray she carried. She cowered away from Shean, shuffling back as far as she could without tumbling down the stairs she'd just climbed to reach the loft. "I-I'm s-sorry." She extended her arms. They shook, making the bowl and utensils on the tray clatter. "I've b-brought dinner."

The sight made Shean's stomach growl. Teeth a-grit, she stalked across the room and took the offering from Dola with a jerk and a curt thank-you, sitting down on the bed and shoveling food into her mouth.

She expected Dola to leave. But she didn't, continuing to stand near the entrance of the room, watching Shean with a pale face that displayed an increasingly irritating amount of hesitation.

When she was halfway through the food, Shean couldn't stand it anymore. She slammed her utensils down, glaring at Dola. "Do you *need* something?"

"I, um . . . Is Silver all right?"

"As you can see, he's fine," Shean said, gesturing to Silver. He waved at Dola, the gesture making the girl's shoulders relax a little.

"That's good," Dola said.

Shean snorted. "Right." She looked down at the half-eaten bowl in front of her, decided she was full, and stood, marching to Dola. She shoved the tray back into her hands, then straightened, flipping the hair back from her face and folding her arms. "I don't know *what* Ikiisa was trying to prove with that task—as if any doll would have to hold that many stones for any reason outside of a silly test!"

Shean eyed Dola, waiting for her to either agree that Ikiisa was out of line or defend her. When she did neither, Shean planted her hands on her hips, rolling her eyes.

"Was there something else you needed from me?"

"N-no, I, ah, um." Dola shot a look at Silver, who returned the look with a smile and wink, a finger held to his lips. Dola gained a little color in her face and looked back at Shean, speaking in a voice that, if not clear and confident, at least didn't stammer. "Yes."

Shean tapped her foot in an impatient rap, eyebrows raised. "Well?"

"There's something I want to show you, Dollmaker Shean. You *and* Silver."

NIGHT HAD FALLEN AND NEITHER MOON HUNG IN THE SKY. IN PITCH DARKNESS disrupted by the small glow lantern in her hand, Dola led Shean and Silver into the forest called Deep.

They walked in silence, Dola having begged Shean not to speak until she said it was safe to do so. Silver brought up the rear of the procession, bandaged arms swinging at his sides with a faint rustle barely distinguishable from the rustles of the trees standing close to them on all sides.

The trail they followed wasn't much more than a strip of trampled grass and dirt, more a deer trail than a path suitable for people. It snaked, weaving around knobby trees and prehistoric ferns with soft, itchy fronds that brushed their faces as they passed. Shean had expected whatever Dola wanted to show her to be close to Web, but she was wrong—minutes trickled by into what felt to be at least an hour, and still Dola walked. Shean's feet began to hurt from treading on unpaved ground, soles throbbing on the occasional errant tree root worming across the path and heels rubbing raw inside her shoes. The branches of bushes caught on the beads of her skirts, plucking at her hem and forcing her to untangle herself more than once. With each such effort she managed to prick a new finger on a thorn or splinter, her hands joining her feet in their misery.

Shean had just gotten a piece of her hair caught on a low tree branch, forcing her to pause to yank herself free, and was about to demand Dola explain where they were going when the girl stopped. She turned and waved for Shean to join her, crouching behind a line of shrubs. Shean glanced to check that Silver was still with her, then did as instructed, crouching next to Dola. Silver squeezed in between them, resting a hand on each of their shoulders.

Shean peered over the shrubbery, seeing they were on the edge of a large clearing. The space was full of bushes with purple-black leaves and thorns poking out of them in haphazard directions. There were dozens, if not hundreds, of these bushes, growing in sporadic clumps and clusters with the occasional crooked line of shrubbery visible here and there.

A white haze stretched across the clearing, and at first Shean thought it was frost. A bead of sweat trickled down the side of her face, and she realized it was far too hot for frost. Or snow. When she looked closer, she noticed a faint light was lifting from the haze, a soft glow that made the cottony whorls seem like threaded stars, stretched in a mesh across the bushes. Rustles came from the shrubs, a gentle shush suggesting small, unseen creatures scurrying.

There was only one explanation for the white fuzzing the dark leaves before her. Only one Shean could think of, anyway.

"Is that . . . spiderweb?" she said.

"Yes," Dola said, whispering. She turned to Shean, face anxious in the light of her lantern and the snowy glow of the webbing. "You can't tell anyone I showed you—outsiders aren't allowed to go to the Veil."

"The Veil?"

Dola gestured to the clearing. "Here—where the spiders live."

Shean glanced at the bushes, then back at Dola, confused. "If you're not supposed to show me this, why are you?"

Dola leaned forward. "Because he said to—" she said, cutting short and biting her lower lip.

Shean straightened. "He? Who's 'he'?"

Dola looked at Silver. Shean did as well, eyebrows raised. He looked between them, and shrugged.

"S-Silver did," Dola said, looking at the ground.

"Silver," Shean repeated.

"Yes."

"My doll. Silver."

"Yes."

"Told you to bring me here."

"Yes."

Shean suppressed a sigh. This was why she didn't like children—they were pathological liars, making up excuses and pinning their actions on anything, anyone, to avoid criticism.

So Dola didn't want to tell Shean why she was showing her the Veil—fine. She could at least be honest about that, rather than claiming a *doll* had told her what to do.

"Right," Shean said, swallowing her annoyance. "Silver told you to bring me here. Why?"

"You believe me?" Dola asked, looking up.

"Sure," Shean said. Dola beamed, looking at Silver.

"See?" she said. He winked at her, smiling. Shean cleared her throat, patience fraying.

"Dola, *why are we here*?"

"To see the floating cities," Dola said.

"The what?"

Dola looked at the sky, covering her glow lantern with her hands to make the stars easier to see overhead. "It's almost midnight," she said. "It should start soon."

"What should?"

Dola pointed into the clearing. "That!"

Shean turned to see shapes rising from the bushes. Square shapes and rectangles, pyramids and circles, and all of them made from luminescent spiderweb. Like tree saplings surfacing from the ground, the figures rose and unfurled, at first compact shapes and then spinning out, expanding by some unfathomable mechanic. Shean gasped as the woven sculptures began to fly between bushes, launched into the air and landing with bounces and the rustles of leaves. They were followed by dark silhouettes that could fit in the palm of Shean's hand, clear against the backdrop of glowing web and waving sets of eight spindly legs.

"Spiders," Shean said. She craned for a better look. "What're they doing?"

"What they do," Dola said. "On the night of the new moons, the spiders raise their cities."

"Cities?" Shean echoed. As she spoke Silver tapped her shoulder. She looked at him and he lifted his arms like a child. She picked him up, holding him high enough to see the spiders.

"They look like houses, don't they?" Dola said, gesturing to a pyramid that'd just landed in a bush near where they crouched. This close, Shean could see the spiders crawling all over the woven structure: red bodies swollen and shiny like boils about to burst, legs covered in black hair to match the smatter of dark eyes that gleamed above massive dun pincers. As she watched them squirm, situating themselves in positions of unknown importance, she realized why the shapes of their webs felt familiar.

"They look like *your* houses," Shean said, watching as the spiders got under the pyramid of web and, together, heaved it toward another bush, following its arc with far-reaching jumps.

"Gran says the people who made our houses wanted them to look like the spiders' cities," Dola said.

"I see." Shean followed the arc of a circular bundle of web as it flew across the clearing, adjusting Silver in her arms when he started feeling heavy. "What makes it glow like that?"

"No one knows. The spiders' silk only shines when there's no moons, and after it's woven into cloth it doesn't even glow then."

A huge spider, as big as one of Shean's hands, sprang from a nearby bush, creating such a noise she jumped. Unlike the other spiders, this one looked like sunlight filtering through leaves; even in the dark, its round, taut body sparkled gold. As it flew, a long, equally golden thread followed in its wake, unspooling in a swirl that cut through the silvery light of the rest of the clearing. A blaze of gilt in the dark.

Dola gasped. Shean looked to find the girl watching the golden spider, no longer crouching and on her feet, hands buried in the bush in front of them. Her lips parted, eyes stretched wide.

"Dola?" Shean said. Silver wiggled in her arms until she set him down. He grabbed the bottom of Dola's shirt, face concerned.

"I'm fine. I-it's a Queen," Dola said, voice trembling. She didn't take her eyes off the golden spider as she spoke. "I've never seen one before."

"Queen?" Shean echoed, looking back at the field.

"Female spiders. The only ones who make gold silk."

"Are they rare?"

Dola nodded. "Gran says there are only three Queens in Deep. We hardly ever see them, and when we do, Gran's the only one allowed to touch them." Dola paused, hesitating. Then, softly, she sang:

"Come, missy Queen Spider, spin me a golden thread
I'll weave a fine silk scarf
To tie 'round my lover's neck.
When chilly winter comes, I'll beg another thread
I'll knit a quilt of sunlight
To drape 'round our child's bed."

The tune was simple and bouncing, Dola's young voice ringing through the clearing. Shean wondered if it was her imagination that, just while she sang, the spiders' throwing and jumping matched the rhythm of Dola's voice.

"My papa taught me that song," Dola said, crouching back down next to Shean. She folded her hands over her knees, staring across the Veil. "He wrote it after he saw a Queen. Gran says he sang it to my manma a lot, just before I was born." She was quiet for a long moment. Then she said, "I like nights with no moons. I like it when the spiders raise their cities and are restless and bite too much to be handled. When there *are* moons, and when we're not having a pageant, the whole village comes to the Veil every night at sunset. We harvest until moonset, then we go home and weave. We have to, or we won't finish cloths in time to sell to the merchants who come before and after winter." She lowered her head, eyes downcast and voice growing not bitter, but upset. "Sometimes we have to weave through the morning, past sunrise, and we only get a little sleep before sunset. Gran says it's not good for people to work that long and to never be outside in the sun. Some people get sick. I get sick sometimes, and Papa was sick all the time."

Dola paused again. This time for so long Shean couldn't stand the silence.

"If life is so difficult, why don't you find an easier place to live, work that isn't so taxing?" she asked.

"Some people leave. My manma did."

"Why don't you?"

The look Dola gave Shean was one part horror, two parts guilt. "Leave Web?"

"Yes."

Dola shook her head. "I can't do that."

"Why not?"

"Because . . . because if we leave, there won't be anyone to look after the spiders. There won't be anyone who knows how to harvest and weave their silk, or make the cloths we sell."

"And? Would anyone notice?" Shean asked, impatient with the weakness of the excuse—she hated when people endured unnecessary burdens. And the troubles of Web qualified as such; maybe Dola didn't know, but the adults of Web *had* to be aware that they lived in obscurity. By the First Dollmaker, Shean hadn't even known they *existed* until Nock had told her! Spider-silk cloths were famous enough, but even then no one sensible ever bought such luxury items—only recently rich merchants wanting to show off their newfound prosperity. What nobility was there in an entire village slaving to make a scarf or handkerchief to go around the necks and wipe the noses of magnates who didn't care about, and most likely didn't even know of, their existence?

Who would notice, really, if Web ceased to be?

"We would," Dola said. Her brow was furrowed, a hurt expression on her face. "*We* would notice."

Shean felt a prick of guilt. She pushed it aside with a wave of a hand, shaking her head. "Fine," she said. "But what you people are doing to yourselves is insane." She stood and turned away from Dola, looking out across the Veil. She had to admit, as silly as she thought the villagers of Web were for worshipping at the altar of spider silk, the spiders' work was beautiful. They were throwing their "houses" in earnest now, a flurry of shapes arcing through the night. Unlike anything Shean had ever seen, and something she'd never forget.

Too bad pretty silk sculptures couldn't help her redeem herself in the last task of the pageant.

The thought made Shean frown, mood souring. She was wasting time, standing out here in the middle of the forest called Deep watching spiders jump around. She should be back at Lenna's house, thinking up a task for tomorrow.

She would set a test of intelligence. From the moment Lenna had told her she'd be allowed to pick one of the pageant's trials, she'd known that—with her dolls being as they were, finding a way to demonstrate their cleverness was the logical choice.

But what would impress the villagers of Web? How could she get through to these denizens of the forest called Deep, these misguided souls who slaved away every night in a field of spiders for the sake of a thankless art? Especially after coming so dangerously close to losing her temper in front of them?

Shean knew she shouldn't give in to anger so easily. But she just got so *mad*. Some of the children she'd known when she was young had teased her for her bouts of rage, the boys calling her "blown top" in reference to the reef volcanoes whose eruptions were visible off the shore of One, and the girls saying no boy would ever want to vow with her if she didn't become sweet and soft, like them. She'd proved the girls, at least, wrong plenty of times (with plenty of men), but now she wondered if there was some sense in what they'd said when it came to Web.

It was too late, though, to change what'd happened. She could only move forward—a step that required her to not linger here, staring at dancing spiders. Shean turned to leave.

She felt a tug on her hand and stopped, looking down to find Silver gazing up at her. He lifted his arms, wanting to be picked up again. His hair and bandages glowed, reflecting the light of the Veil—he looked like he had spiderwebs for hair, like his injuries were bundled in spider silk. Staring at him, an idea struck Shean.

"Dola," she said, turning to the girl. "You say the entire village harvests and weaves every night?"

"Yes."

"And because of that people often fall ill?"

Dola frowned, standing and picking up her glow lantern. "Yes."

The solution to the disaster that'd been the second task of the pageant filled Shean, clear as the next note in a song.

"What if you had someone, someone more trustworthy than anyone in the entire world, harvest the silk *for* you, so you could sleep at night and weave during the day?" she said. "Wouldn't that make life in Web better?"

"I . . ." Dola started, trailing off. She glanced at Silver, looked back at Shean. "Yes?"

“Yes,” Shean echoed, smiling. She took a step closer to Dola, leaning forward.

“Dola, I’ve decided what pageant task I’m going to set tomorrow. And I need your help.”

IKIISA FELT GOOD AS SHE AND ROQUE MADE THEIR WAY TO THE PAGEANT FIELD the next morning. With the sun warm on her skin, her dolls around her, and Roque’s reassuring presence at her side, she could almost, *almost* believe that the villagers would pick her to continue as the dollmaker of Web.

“You’ve high spirits today,” Roque said. His hair was tied back, and, as always, he looked fresh-faced and alert. She smiled at him, fingering her pendant.

“After what happened yesterday,” she said, “I think I might have a chance in the pageant.”

“From what you’ve told me, I don’t doubt that,” Roque said, looking ahead of them, toward the pageant field. The side of his mouth lifted, slightly. “Dollmaker Shean is . . . an interesting person.”

Ikiisa agreed with him, with one caveat: not only was she interesting, she was terrifying. Ikiisa had never met anyone so driven, so talented, so intimidating.

And familiar. Shean was also familiar. Ikiisa remembered that as she and Roque reached the edge of the pageant field—yesterday, when she’d first looked at Shean, she could’ve sworn she’d seen the woman somewhere before. Something about her eyes. Or her face? Ikiisa was terrible with remembering people, a weakness that wasn’t helped by a lifestyle that had, for five long years, consisted of moving from one city to the next, an endless cycle of faces and names that blurred into one. Had she met Shean in one of the cities or towns that'd made her leave after just a week or two? Had they shared words, a whole conversation, even, that Ikiisa couldn't remember?

"Ikiisa?" Roque said, and she realized she'd stopped walking. They were on the edge of the pageant field. She could hear the murmur of voices, people waiting to either choose or banish her. Yesterday, those voices had frightened her so badly, she'd struggled to breathe. Now she ignored them. She also put Shean out of her mind, focusing all her attention on Roque. In a moment of brazen bravery, she took his hand.

He cocked his head. "Is something wrong?"

She shook her head. "No. I just . . . Thank you." She held his hand tighter. "Thank you for coming. I'm glad I'm not alone."

Roque's expression softened. "I'm glad I could come."

Ikiisa swallowed, throat feeling tight. She nodded, not trusting herself to speak, and let go of him. Together they entered the pageant field, walking to where Shean stood, waiting. She was talking to Ilo in front of the villagers, her dolls clustered around her, and she looked up as they arrived, eyes zipping to Roque, then away, full lips pressed into a tight line.

The grimace surprised Ikiisa. If she didn't know better, she'd say Shean knew Roque. And was mad at him.

"We'll speak after the task," Roque said to Ikiisa. Then he walked to the edge of the field, sitting down next to a boy named Slink. Roque smiled when Slink looked at him, and the boy scowled, standing up and walking away, pulling his twin sister with him to settle deeper in the ranks of the villagers. Roque seemed unbothered by the shunning, swinging the travel pack off his shoulder and setting it to the side before leaning back on his hands, eyes closed and face turned to the sun.

Ikiisa watched him, envious of his nonchalance, for as long as she could, until the feel of Shean and Ilo watching her grew unbearable. Then she swallowed and turned, forcing herself to walk up to them, her dolls clustered close around her.

"Good sunrise," Ilo said in greeting. Ikiisa nodded to him, to Shean.

"You're late," Shean said.

Shean had been late yesterday. But Ikiisa suspected that would be an unwise thing to point out. Instead she looked at her shoes and said, "I apologize."

"You're here now," Ilo said with a shrug. "Let's get this over with." He looked at Shean. "Ready?"

"Yes."

"Good." Ilo turned to the villagers, silencing them with a wave of his hand. He spared no breath on formalities, gesturing to Shean. "Dollmaker Shean," he said, "please announce your task."

"With pleasure," Shean said, voice agreeable and charming. Ikiisa wondered how she did that—how did someone have a voice like daggers one moment, a voice like a blooming rose the next?

Shean was wearing the same jeweled dress she had the day before and she flared as she faced the villagers, too blinding to look at. "First," she said, "I would like to apologize for my actions yesterday. I was upset at the damage done to my doll, and allowed my pain to influence me." She lowered herself in a polite bow, first to the villagers, then to Ilo. "I should not have contended the results of the second task. Forgive me."

Ilo's face softened, his acceptance of the apology obvious. Ikiisa felt a stab of resentment; if it'd been *her* apologizing, he wouldn't have been so forgiving so quickly. If he forgave at all.

Shean straightened, giving the villagers a dazzling smile. "For the pageant task today, I set a challenge of intelligence." She turned, hands on hips, and addressed the tree line of Deep. "Now, Dola."

Ikiisa frowned, confused. She looked toward the trees and there was Dola, stepping out with her hands cupped, holding something. The girl was hunched, eyes down, and, even from a distance, she was clearly trembling. She rushed to Shean, looking at no one. Ikiisa glanced to where Lenna sat, the woman's face tight with surprise and concern as she watched her grandchild.

"Show them," Shean said. Dola glanced at one of Shean's dolls, the one called Silver. Then she did as Shean said, turning and opening her hands. Ikiisa leaned forward with everyone else, wondering what the girl could be holding. Her stomach dropped when she saw what it was.

A spider.

Gasps of protest rose from the villagers of Web, many leaping to their feet. Even Lenna stood, face drawn.

"Dola!" Ilo snapped, anger so obvious and sharp the girl cowered. "What do you think you're—"

"There's no need for concern," Shean interrupted. She placed a hand on Dola's shoulder, smiling at Ilo. "I'm allowed to set any task for the pageant, am I not?"

"Not one involving our spiders! Outsiders are forbidden from touching them! How did you even—"

"I don't plan on touching your spider," Shean said. She patted Dola's shoulder. "Dola is. And she's allowed to."

Ilo scowled. "But—"

"The Shod aren't only strong and swift; they're intelligent," Shean said, interrupting him again. Ikiisa was surprised at the bravery—Ilo looked like *he* was going to be the one yelling today. Ignoring his red face, Shean addressed the villagers. "As such, dolls who combat the Shod must be clever. They must be able to outsmart their opponents, and that can include being capable of performing delicate, complicated tasks that are beyond the Shod."

That was an interesting view—one Ikiisa hadn't heard before, at least not in Shean's particular terms. She agreed that dolls had to have a degree of cleverness to them, the ability to act on their own when they fought the Shod and their maker wasn't close enough to give direct orders . . . but the Shod, intelligent? Ikiisa frowned. In all her time as a dollmaker, in all the battles she'd fought, the Shod had never struck her as smart. Desperate and frenzied and lethally strong, yes. Capable of crushing entire cities simply by swarming and surging, like a writhing, screaming, crazed tidal wave.

But that was it. There was no coherent thought behind them. At least, not any that Ikiisa had ever sensed.

The Shod were like a force of nature. Mindless. Devastating. And, outside of trying to match their strength with dolls, impossible to combat.

Turning from the villagers of Web, Shean looked at Ikiisa, halting her misgiving thoughts on the woman's theories with a challenging, confident smile. "To test the intelligence of my and Dollmaker Ikiisa's dolls," Shean said, "I set the task of silking a spider from the forest called Deep."

Ikiisa stiffened, dismay and shock tightening her chest. The murmurs of the villagers shifted to shouts, protests, cries for Ilo to end the pageant. Ilo made to do so, trying to reach Dola but prevented when Shean made a gesture and four of her dolls sprang forward, grabbing his legs and holding him back.

"Stop this!" Ilo shouted, struggling against his tiny captors. But before Ikiisa or anyone else could do as he said, Shean turned to Silver.

"Silver," she said, "silk the spider."

The doll stepped forward, taking the spider from Dola, who was looking between Shean and the villagers with a dismayed, torn look on her face. Ikiisa knew she should do something, leap forward and snatch the spider from Silver, or at least tell her dolls to stop him. But her mind was faster than her tongue—and so was Silver.

He'd already found the spider's thread, pulling a length of it out with a delicate movement. With the spider cupped in one hand, Silver used the other like a spool, wrapping silk around his fingers by rolling his wrist, rotating his hand in a way no human could and extracting silk so quickly that within minutes he'd collected so much it stood inches out from his wooden digits.

The villagers fell quiet. Even Ilo stopped struggling against the dolls holding him back, mouth gaping as he leaned forward, expression moving from furious to thrilled in a heartbeat.

"That . . ." he said, trailing off. He cleared his throat, straightening and looking at Shean. "That's well done."

Shean smiled a smug smile. "That's enough, Silver."

The doll stopped silking, snapping the thread connecting his hand to the spider and handing it back to Dola. She took the spider with a grateful gasp, staring at the silk wound around his hand as if she couldn't believe her eyes. Ikiisa knew she couldn't.

She understood how her legs were trembling, though. She recognized the terrible drop of her stomach, the dizzy of her head. The feel of the world closing in on her, this time not because every person nearby was glaring at her, but because they were looking at Shean with adoration. Smitten.

"Dollmaker Ikiisa?" Shean said, voice sweet. She turned to Ikiisa, all smiles. She made a deferential gesture.

This was bad. Ikiisa tried to swallow but her mouth was dry. She looked at her dolls. Some of them had hands. Or, at least, something that resembled hands.

"Ikiisa," Ilo said. "Pick your doll."

Alarm shot through Ikiisa, and without thinking she blurted. "No."

Shean snorted aloud, folding her arms. In contrast Ilo stood very still and very silent. Staring at Ikiisa, expression impossible to read.

"No?" he echoed.

Ikiisa flushed. Everyone *was* looking at her now, and she hated it. Too many eyes, too much judgment, too much hostility. All the happiness Silver's actions had brought to the gathering was gone, replaced by silence laced with irritation.

Irritation bordering on anger.

Ikiisa forced herself to swallow, wetting her lips. It was all she could do to stop herself from bolting, gaze slipping past Ilo and finding Roque. The man stood on the fringes of the watching villagers, standing like they all were, a hand wrapped on the strap of his traveling pack. When their eyes met, he nodded. Gave her a reassuring—and urging—smile.

At the encouragement, Ikiisa found the strength to speak. "I . . . I don't believe this is a proper task," she said, forcing herself to look from Roque and back at Ilo. "The Shod . . . they aren't . . ." She paused, taking a steadying breath. Her eyes started to drop to the ground, but she caught herself, mustering the strength to keep looking at Ilo, willing him to listen to her, to understand, as she said, "Intelligence in dolls can be important. But something like this—being able to silk a spider—would never do anything against the Shod."

It was the most assertive words she'd spoken to Ilo since moving into his village. The first time she'd ever said what she really wanted to say while in his presence. Gazing at him, she felt a faint spark of hope. A gentle belief that she might've been heard.

"If you'd wanted to contest this task, you should have done so earlier," Ilo said.

His voice was flat, and, heart sinking, Ikiisa knew he was right. She should have protested Shean's claims about the Shod being smart the moment they were made. But she'd been too distracted by wondering about that statement to actually say anything.

And now the whole village had seen Shean's doll silk one of their spiders. Now they were all watching the possibility of dolls helping them in their work unfurl before them, thoughts of what dolls were *actually* meant to do—guard them from the Shod—fading in the face of rescue from the long, exhausting nights they spent in the Veil.

Now it was too late.

"But—" Ikiisa started. Weakly.

"Pick your doll," Ilo said again. Voice hard.

Ah, right. For a moment, Ikiisa had forgotten. That Ilo didn't like her. No one liked her.

Why would anyone listen to someone they didn't like?

Feeling lightheaded, Ikiisa pointed. "Cadence," she said, voice a shaky, faint croak. The doll stepped forward on three-toed feet, the closest to fingers any of her dolls had. Aware of Ilo watching her, Shean staring at her, all the villagers of Web glaring at her, she said, "S-silk the spider."

Cadence's responding whistle was confused. But the doll turned to Dola, lifting two front feet. Ikiisa held her breath as Dola tipped the spider into the doll's grasp. She didn't want to watch as Cadence began fiddling with the spider, but she couldn't bring herself to look away, despair rising higher and higher as Cadence poked and prodded and tried to pull the delicate end of the spider's silk out. The sun overhead was making the spider sluggish, so it didn't struggle, but that did Cadence little good—her toes were just too large for something like this. Too suited for climbing trees and throwing rocks, to clinging onto Shod and ripping them asunder.

A discontented murmur rose from the villagers, whispers and hisses. In the corner of her eye she could see Roque, standing and watching.

She didn't look at him again. He couldn't help her.

"It's going to ruin the spider!" someone shouted. Ikiisa recognized the voice—council member Mont.

"Stop this, Ilo!"

"Take that spider away before it gets hurt!"

"Or killed!"

"Her doll can't do it!"

"*She* can't do it!"

Ilo stepped forward. Ikiisa's attention snapped to him, her vision stinging from the sweat dripping into her eyes. Their gazes met, and she hoped against hope to see some compassion. Some hint of the past ten years, all those years her dolls had taken care of and watched over Web, driving the Shod to the very borders of the forest called Deep and keeping them away, keeping the villagers safe.

Ilo's eyes were cold. And thankless.

"Stop. Tell it to give the spider back to Dola."

Ikiisa wet her lips. "But—"

"Now. Before you crush it!"

No. No, this couldn't be happening. Not again.

"No," Ikiisa said. Ilo's eyes narrowed. She lifted a trembling, pleading hand. "Just, please—give her more time."

"There's no point. Your doll can't perform this task. Which means that Dollmaker Shean—"

"Wait!" Ikiisa said. She didn't mean to shout, but the world was slipping from her fingers. Things were unraveling. Everything was falling to pieces, to pieces. Everything, ruined.

"Give the spider back to Dola!" one of the villagers shouted.

"Yes! Stop this, Ikiisa!"

"You're going to kill it!"

"Stop!"

"You can't do this!"

It was hard to breathe. It was hard to think. Ikiisa stumbled back from Ilo, moved toward Cadence. The doll, *her* doll, was still trying, still doing her best to obey Ikiisa's orders. She could do it. She had to. They couldn't be driven from another town. Not again. Not another.

Please. Not again.

Ikiisa reached for the spider. *I'll do it*, she thought, mind spiraling out of logic as desperation seized her. *I'll silk the spider. I'll show them I can do this, that I don't have to be sent away.*

Just as her hand closed around the spider, Ilo grabbed her, yanking her back so hard her shoulders struck his chest. Ikiisa felt her fist clench, an involuntary reaction to her balance vanishing. There was a crunch. Ilo cursed and let go of her, and she uncurled her fingers, finding them covered in a sticky, pale blue liquid. The spider was folded up in her palm, legs drawn in toward a flattened torso.

Ikiisa stared at the dead spider. Ilo was shouting. Other people were, too. She didn't hear them. The only noise was the roaring in her ears. The only thing to see in the whole world was this dead spider, its blood all over her hand.

Tears filled Ikiisa's eyes. *Over*, she thought.

Then she fell to her knees and wept.

THE TRAVEL PACK ON IKIISA'S SHOULDER WAS HEAVY, CRAMMED TO BURSTING with her belongings; which was to say, full of dollmaking tools, most of which were an inheritance from Master Coen. Hand clenched on the bag's strap, she stood looking up at what'd been her house for the past decade. Overhead the sun was at the midpoint of the sky, its edge covered by the house's roof to create a shadow that fell on Ikiisa's face. Even with the shade her eyes ached from the light, the edges of her vision searing, as if the house was being burned into her memory.

"This is extreme," Roque said. He sat on the step leading up to the front door, chin resting in the palm of his hand. "Insisting you leave before nightfall," he clarified when she looked at him.

Ikiisa felt too dull, too drained and numb, to answer.

"Is that all you're taking with you?" Roque asked, indicating her bag.

Ikiisa mustered up the energy to shrug, then gestured to the dolls sitting around her, all forty-seven silent and still, their normally merry whistles and hoots fallen to uneasy quiet. Those dolls who'd been thrown from towns before crouched low to the ground, ready to run. Other, newer dolls sat up, heads cocked with puzzlement, but keeping the peace set by their elder siblings. Bobble sat next to Ikiisa, and he alone let out the occasional, faint wheeze.

"What about your works in progress?" Roque asked.

"Ah," Ikiisa said, straightening as she thought of all those almost-dolls filling up the burrows of her house. Consumed by the desire to run from the yells, the spitting, the anger in the eyes of the villagers, she'd forgotten about them.

Reality's teeth sank into her. Her shoulders slumped. She shook her head.

"I have to leave them. I can't carry them. And none of them are ready for Breath Marks."

"I see. Where will you go?"

"To the city called Glass."

"That's where we met."

"Yes. It's where my master's school is. It's been . . . I want to hold a vigil for him."

Ikiisa didn't say that she feared she wouldn't be allowed to do so. She'd been Master Coen's last apprentice, but not because Coen was old—he'd been young, not yet forty. He'd died in an accident, and the only other student he'd fully trained, Darin, blamed Ikiisa. Coen had gone to town that day to buy a replacement whittling knife for Ikiisa, after all. If not for her he never would've been knocked into the street by a pickpocket fleeing capture, landing under the wheels of a passing lumber cart.

It didn't help that Darin resented Ikiisa for receiving a license only a few days after he had, despite being ten years his junior. The moment the funeral arrangements were carried out for Coen, Darin had exercised his right as senior apprentice to claim the school, taking Coen's place in looking after the younger, fledgling apprentices and kicking Ikiisa out with a sweet-voiced, "It's for your own good."

She'd wanted to argue. But, steeped in pain and sadness over Coen's loss, the words and will had escaped her. So she'd done as Darin said. And left. With Coen gone, it wasn't like she'd had a reason to linger in the city called Glass, anyway.

Until now. As dictated by the First Dollmaker's second edict, though the Dollmaker's Graveyard was not far from Web, a vigil for a dead dollmaker had to be held in their last place of residence. That meant Coen's school in Glass. Whether or not Darin would let Ikiisa through the gates, though, was a mystery.

Not that it mattered, really. Ikiisa was going to Glass with the slim sliver of hope that Darin's temper had cooled enough in the past fifteen years to allow her to stay at the school for a while, but she harbored no hope that her former peer would be so generous as to offer, or allow, Ikiisa to become a teacher at Coen's school. Even if she got down on her knees and begged, lied and said that to be a teacher was what she desired more than anything else, Darin's thin eyebrows would only bunch with contempt, his voice lashing like a whip.

"Who would ever want to learn how to make dolls from you?"

Or something like that. Darin had never made it a secret how little regard he had for Ikiisa's dolls.

Most people hadn't.

"Ikiisa? Are you all right?" Roque asked. She blinked to clear her vision of Darin's sneer and saw he was watching her with concern. How long had she been standing here, thinking? Coen used to tease her about that, saying her thoughts caught on the wings of passing birds, getting lost in the sky.

"Where will you go?" Ikiisa asked, forcing herself to focus on the moment. She'd worry about Darin when she got to Glass.

"I'm staying in Web."

The words stung more than they had any right to; Ikiisa barely stopped herself from flinching, stomach in knots of dismay. It wasn't like Roque was her friend, not really—he was someone she'd helped a long time ago, and who'd been willing to help her. It wasn't his fault he hadn't been able to save her from Shean. And it was foolish to think he'd continue to stay with her, now that her crisis had come to an end.

She'd still hoped, though.

Ikiisa resisted the urge to grab at her pendant, fingers aching to squeeze the stone the way she always did when she was upset. Instead she clenched the bottom of her tunic. "O-oh," she said, voice small. She looked at Roque's feet, afraid he'd notice her eyes were welling with tears. "Why?"

"I met Dollmaker Shean before I came to Web."

Ikiisa looked up. "What?"

"We met in the city called Ports two weeks ago. And then you called me to Web, and she was here." Roque's eyes gleamed. "Such feels like fate. Like my Dead led me to her."

"Dead?"

"Yes. Our Dead, be they family or friends or lovers, have the power to guide our lives, for good or ill. In that way they move our fate, but only if we listen to them. And I confess I seldom listen—not that my Dead choose to speak to me very often." His eyes lifted to the sky, expression gaining distance as he continued. "To have met Shean in Ports, and then again here in Web, though, is too contrived to be coincidence."

Ikiisa wasn't a religious person. She'd held vigil for Coen when he'd died, and occasionally recalled the Goddess of Stone her mother had spoken of before the mine collapse that'd taken her, along with Ikiisa's four elder sisters, to the grave. While traveling after the Red Tide, Ikiisa had been introduced to the worship of the Sea Children; shrines dedicated to the dozen deities included in that title were erected in every sector of every city along the far shore. She'd occasionally glanced into such shrines to glimpse prostrate figures stretched over prayer altars, men and women draped in robes the color of sea foam and decorated with embroideries of the Children, worshippers who sang their desires in lovely, mournful voices.

She'd never heard of a pantheon composed of ghosts, though.

The thought made her skin crawl, this time unable to stop herself from wrapping a hand around her pendant.

"I feel there's something I'm meant to learn from Shean," Roque continued. "She interests me. As do her dolls. So I'll stay in Web a bit longer."

Ikiisa nodded, unnerved enough that her hurt at Roque's abandonment now felt foolish. She took a step back, looking down at her dolls. "I-I should go."

"Why?" Roque asked.

Ikiisa paused, looking up at him. "Ilo asked me to leave."

"Would it really matter if you stayed a few days longer?"

"Where? They . . . they gave my house to Shean."

"You know the forest called Deep—I'm sure you can find somewhere to camp."

Ikiisa imagined lingering after being dismissed, after Ilo had looked at her with such anger and told her to leave Web, that her services were no longer required and Dollmaker Shean would replace her. She imagined the villagers seeing her about and glaring, spitting at her feet, encouraging their children to capture her dolls and torture them. The idea made her chest squeeze with an alarm that told her she needed to run, to get away *now*, or she'd be hurt. Badly.

She took another step back from Roque. "*Why* would I do that?"

"I have a feeling that it'd be better if you stayed," Roque said, folding his hands in his lap, fingers lacing as his head tipped to the side. "That's all."

"A feeling," Ikiisa echoed. She had one, too. A bad one.

"I ask only that you consider it. If you don't wish to stay, you don't have to." Roque smiled. "If you'd like, once I'm finished in Web I can meet you in Glass."

Ikiisa's chest loosened a little. "Really?"

"I still have a debt to repay."

"Oh," Ikiisa said, looking down at her pendant. It deflated her a bit, that Roque was willing to extend their interactions out of obligation. But not so much that she'd refuse his offer. "Right. We can meet in Glass, then. Thank you. I'll . . . I'll be going now."

"Good travels," Roque said.

Ikiisa turned from him, waving for her dolls to join her as she headed for the edge of Web. She looked back once, to catch a final glimpse of her house, and Roque was gone.

His absence was echoed all the way through Web, the village empty and all the houses closed tight. She thought she felt eyes watching as she and her dolls crossed the town square, passed the statue of Bashin, the Spider Mother, and began down the road through Deep. But no one called out at her, not even in insult. The only noise that followed her into the forest was the whistles and chirrs of her dolls, their steps thumping on the stone of their path.

As she walked through Deep, trees growing thicker together the further she went from Web, branches encroaching on the sky overhead and making her feel suffocated, Ikiisa had no intentions of staying, not even for another night. Roque's "feeling" made no sense—the villagers wanted her gone. So she'd go.

When she reached the edge of the forest, though, she stopped. She stared at where the road moved out from under the trees, growing wider and sun bleached.

Ten years. Ten years since she'd left this forest. Ten years since she'd faced the daunting reality of an entire country of cities and towns and villages, all of them unfriendly to her and her dolls.

Ikiisa tried to swallow. Her mouth was dry, her throat an aching strip of sandstone. She was trembling, and not because she was tired, though she was.

Scared. She was scared to leave Deep. Scared to go back to Web, too. Scared to move.

Shaking, Ikiisa turned. She left the road and walked into the trees. Her dolls followed with questioning whistles and she kept walking, at first aimlessly, not sure where she meant to go or do. Then she recognized a tree with a great white burl growing from it. Realizing where she was, she turned right at the tree, searching for and finding a faint animal trail, almost rain-washed away to nothing and overgrown from lack of use. She followed the trail to a cluster of boulders, moss covered and ancient. Dolls watching her, she knelt on the far side of the rocks, fingers poking at the layer of spongy moss growing on the stone until she found a lever. She pulled it, expecting resistance; it'd been years since she'd used this place for anything. But at the tug the lever lowered with ease and the side of one stone lifted, revealing the boulder's hollow insides.

Ikiisa didn't know who'd made the hideaway. She'd found it by accident during her early days in Web, tripping the lever when she'd tried to climb the boulders to get a better look at the surrounding area. She assumed the hideout was the property of a previous dollmaker, as the mechanism that lifted the side of the rock was similar to the springs and joints that gave dolls mobility. She used to stake out here, wanting to get a good sense of the areas of the forest the Shod frequented. After weeks of never encountering a single Shod around the boulders she'd abandoned the spot and, in the years since, had all but forgotten the lair.

Stepping into the boulders, Ikiisa was forced to duck to avoid hitting the stone ceiling, inhaling the musty scent of long-trapped air. Her eyes caught on a glow lantern, glass panes grimy from lack of use, shoved into the far left corner. She couldn't remember if that was something she'd brought, or something that'd always been here. Not that the distinction mattered.

Pack sliding from her shoulder and thumping to the ground, Ikiisa sat down, pressing her back to a cold stone wall and appreciating the gloom of the space, a relief from the mugginess outside. Closing her eyes against the daylight filtering through the open doorway, she decided to stay in the forest called Deep, close to the village called Web, a little longer. Just for the rest of today and through the night. Tomorrow she'd go, as she'd been asked to go. Her journey would start anew. And, come sunrise, she'd be able to handle that.

With a few uncertain hoots, Ikiisa's dolls crept into the boulders, the smaller ones climbing the sleeves of her jacket and nestling against the sides of her neck while larger dolls formed a ring around her. Bobble crawled into her lap, settling like a cat.

"We'll be fine," Ikiisa said, stroking the top of Bobble's head. The doll whistled and sighed, wrapping his arms around her wrist, and the touch was comforting. Right now was a moment when Ikiisa needed to be touched.

"Don't worry," she said, voice cracking. "We . . . we'll be all right." She rubbed the back of a hand across her burning eyes, wrapped her arms around Bobble, and whispered.

"Someday, everything will be fine."

SHEAN STOOD JUST PAST THE VILLAGE CALLED WEB, ON THE EDGE OF THE FOREST called Deep. Her dolls were lined up in front of her, faces expectant. Lintok, fetched from Lenna's pasture, grazed beside her, his reins clutched in her right hand while her left rested on her hip, the gems beading her sleeve casting shimmers as the sun beat upon her from above.

"We've succeeded, and I'm pleased with you," she said, meeting each doll's gaze in turn. The dolls straightened at the praise, heads lifting higher, shoulders becoming a bit straighter. "For now," Shean continued, "we are the dollmaker and dolls of Web. As such, I want you to search the forest for Shod. If you find any, dispose of them. Once you've checked every part of the forest, come back and report to me. Understood?"

The dolls nodded.

"Good. Now go." The dolls turned and a thought struck Shean, causing her to amend her orders. "Except you, Silver—you stay with me." He frowned at her over his shoulder. "I'm worried about your arms," she said, gesturing to the bandages still wrapped around the limbs. Silver looked down at himself, slumped, then, with clear reluctance, turned back to face her. The other dolls, at a nod from Shean, dove into the forest called Deep, disappearing in five different directions with rustles and snaps that quickly faded to silence.

"Come on," she said to Silver, tugging on Lintok's reins until the elk lifted his head, following her as she turned her back to the forest. "Let's go."

She headed for Ikiisa's house, which was, now, her house. She thought—she was *almost* certain that was what Ilo had told her. The events in the wake of the pageant were something of a blur; any upset Shean had caused by commandeering a spider had been dwarfed by the killing of said spider, and the sheer amount of venom directed at Ikiisa as a result had amazed—shouts of derision, curses, most of the children throwing sticks and stones until their parents forced them to stop (which they did only after allowing them to carry on for long, noisy minutes). All order had broken down, all sense of pageantry swept away in a tide of fury, and everything surrounding Shean being hired in place of Ikiisa had been rushed. A vote happened—amidst the outrage, Lenna had insisted a tally be taken as to who would be the dollmaker of Web. Only one person had voted for Ikiisa: Lenna.

It was good, then, that Shean no longer needed to stay with that woman and her granddaughter. Even if the alternative *was* Ikiisa's leftover house.

Walking up the road to her temporary abode, Shean wasn't thinking about any of that, though. Nor was she thinking of the contract an irate Ilo had dragged her to his house to sign, or the promise he'd forced out of her to assign at least two of her dolls to spider-silking duty once she was done patrolling Deep, or even the glimpse she'd caught of Ikiisa slinking out of Web with her dolls in tow.

Walking to Ikiisa's house, Shean was thinking about the strained expression on Roque's face when the pageant had fallen to pieces. She was experiencing persistent disappointment over the fact that she hadn't had a chance to demand he answer her many questions about him before he'd disappeared again. This time, she felt, for good.

Despite everything, despite him showing up and declaring himself in the service of an enemy, despite his frown when she'd won the pageant, Shean yearned to speak with Roque again. To explain why it'd been necessary to displace Ikiisa, how this was the only choice she'd had. The only *dignified* choice, anyway—the only option her master had given her that didn't include groveling at someone's feet, begging to be allowed a proper license and relying on others to shape her destiny.

Shean *wouldn't* allow someone else to decide her future for her. She alone deserved that privilege.

But she was being silly, fretting like this. She didn't need to excuse herself to Roque. Or anyone, for that matter. She'd done nothing wrong, and wouldn't be made to feel any differently.

Telling herself such with brisk firmness, Shean straightened her shoulders and lifted her chin, determined to enter the house she'd won with pride and high spirits. Which she did minutes later, eliciting Silver's help with carrying her saddlebags and glow lantern inside once Lintok was unsaddled and released to graze in a nearby grassy area.

Ikiisa's house was narrow—tight hallways with slender doors that opened into small, cluttered rooms. There were unfinished dolls everywhere, some small as Shean's hand, others the size of a human adult, and therefore outside the designated craft-size parameters set by the First Dollmaker. Those charts only mattered if the Breath Mark was applied, though, so, technically, nothing Shean saw was illegal. Even so, the mannequins were irritating—the sheer number of them meant Ikiisa was prolific. Even more so than Shean; a feat no dollmaker had managed before now, and a reality that made Shean's rather good mood sour.

Now that her dolls were out looking for Shod, the first matter of business Shean needed to attend to was writing a letter to inform Nock of her success. He and Licensor Maton needed to know that they'd been wrong about her dolls, and that she could now prove as much. This task in mind, Shean searched for a room with enough space for her to sit down and write.

Her efforts were in vain; every door she opened revealed stacks of wood scraps and shavings, mannequins upon mannequins upon mannequins. One room even had a pile of moldy Shod-fighting armor shoved up against the wall, leather bracers and a chest piece that might've been of a high quality once, but was now cracked and peeling with age, the First Dollmaker's boar nothing but a smudge on limp fabric when Shean picked the bracers up for inspection.

"What a disgrace," she muttered, dropping the neglected armor and wrinkling her nose at the flakes of leather that remained on her hands, refusing to detach from her skin until she rubbed her palms on her skirts.

How anyone could live in such a cluttered, disorganized mess, Shean couldn't imagine. Eventually she gave up on finding a good place to write, picking a random room and, with Silver's help, dragging enough mannequins into the hallway to clear a space to sit down at a lopsided design desk. Doing her best to ignore the precarious towers of half-finished dolls around her, she shook her glow lantern into shining, put it on the writing desk, and pulled out a sheaf of design paper and a pencil from one of her travel packs.

She couldn't find a kneeling cushion, so she settled for sitting on the bare floor behind the desk, Silver wandering off when she failed to give him an order to stay with her. She didn't bother to call him back; he wouldn't go far, and she preferred to be alone while writing. Before she could begin, though, she had to do a fair bit of shifting and rearranging, moving her skirts until their beadwork didn't dig into her.

She was growing tired of wearing the Gleam dress—not only was sitting in it difficult, but she wasn't accustomed to wearing the same clothing for days on end. Of course, she'd had no option but to do so; this dress was the only presentable thing she had to wear. After three days, though, it was starting to be less so: dust on the hem, smudges on the jewels, the stale scent of perspiration wafting from its fibers. Her other travel clothes weren't much better, but some of them, by a slim margin, were cleaner. She decided she'd change after she finished writing.

Shean spread the design sheets out on the desk, turned the pencil in her fingers twice, gave herself a moment to think, then began.

To my dear master,

I have news.

MARBLE, THIRTY-FIFTH DOLL OF DOLLMAKER SHEAN, WALKED THROUGH THE forest called Deep, listening, watching, and learning.

There was much to be heard, seen, and learned. The call of birds holding discussions across the canopy, the bustle of little creatures and the hissing, soft-pawed prowl of larger predators. The huge-leafed ferns that sprang from the spaces between rocks furred in moss, tree roots squiggling across the forest floor and making each step a hike. The overall breathing and shift of the forest, each part of it moving in a distinct way that Marble took note of, details he filed away for future reference.

He longed to sit and observe one rock for an hour, a day, to see all the lives that scuttled over it and lived under it and grew from it before moving on to the next rock, or perhaps a tree. Or a berry bush. What would it be like to find the burrow of a honey badger and live there with the creature? What would Marble learn from such an experience? And what about bird nests, and streams, and little lakes and ponds, and whatever that creature over there watching him with five eyes and a long, forked tongue was—

But, no. He wasn't to be distracted by the plethora of information surrounding him. The Mistress had sent him out to look for Shod, and he would do so with pride; there was no greater honor than serving the Mistress. Not even in the nobility of pure study.

Shod. He was looking for the Shod.

But the Shod were nowhere. Hours passed, the sun closer to the far horizon through the gaps in the canopy overhead when he looked, and still Marble found no sign of something unnatural in the forest.

Marble had only a vague notion of what the Shod looked like, which didn't help matters—having never seen one himself, he had only the sketches the Mistress and Master Nock had made of the creatures to go by. His head swung back and forth as he climbed over tree roots, pushed through extended lines of bushes with thorns that scraped his face, and there was no sign of glowing white gazes or red-streaked, asymmetrical bodies, flat heads with cobbles of eyes and big, gaping mouths. He didn't hear anything louder than the twirl of birdsong, which sounded nothing like the alleged wail of the Shods' Cry.

Marble began to wonder if his siblings were having greater luck than he (and if so, wouldn't it be all right if he took a small break to study that interesting lizard hanging upside down from a branch of that tree?) when a scraping noise sounded to his left, a sharp chipping noise followed by the rustle of something large in the undergrowth. The noise was nothing like any noise he'd heard an animal make.

Perhaps it wasn't an animal, then?

Being stealthy, Marble whisked toward the noise, which continued at a steady beat while he tiptoed around mushrooms, ducked under ferns and leapt over a spatter of dead, crackly leaves littering the forest floor. Careful not to make a sound, Marble hid behind a flower bush, pushing aside great white-and-yellow trumpet-shaped blossoms to glimpse the creature crouched in front of him, hunched at the base of a giant tree.

The noise-making thing was not a Shod. It was a person. A man, who stopped whatever it was he was doing to look at Marble.

The man's eyes widened with surprise that mirrored Marble's own. How had the man known Marble was there? He'd been stealthy!

Then the man's expression settled. He smiled, turning to face Marble. He held a knife in one hand, and next to him lay a travel bag with blue ends. Like a doll he had glassy-pale eyes and shiny copper hair, his face and arms and hands covered in white lines. Marble vaguely recalled seeing him in the field where the Mistress had ordered him and his siblings to compete against the big, friendly dolls that whistled a lot.

If Marble remembered correctly, the Mistress wasn't happy with this man. He'd been distracted by a cloud shaped like a spoon the last time the man had been close to the Mistress, though, so he couldn't recall why.

"Hello," the man said, and his voice was friendly. "You're one of Shean's dolls, aren't you?"

Marble stepped out from behind the flower bush and nodded, proud to be recognized as belonging to the Mistress.

"Are you looking for the Shod?" the man said.

Marble nodded again.

"I as well. But I can't find any." The man looked off into the trees around them. When he frowned the white symbols on his face, particularly the lines and triangles near his mouth, warped. "I can't find *any* signs of them. That worries me."

Marble was familiar with the concept of worry, though he himself had never experienced it. Worry was something dollmakers and other, less talented people felt—sibling Silver had a theory that, unlike dolls, human people didn't know what to do with themselves. This caused a range of emotions outside of confidence and certainty (the two standard emotions of dolls) to plague them. Emotions that sibling Silver enjoyed imitating.

Sibling Silver was strange that way—Marble couldn't fathom why anyone would want to experience things that made them frown the way this man did. Marble felt disappointment on occasion, and just that emotion was strong enough to make him squirm—and sibling Silver suspected that "worry" was a hundred times worse than disappointment. To Marble, that meant it was to be avoided at all costs.

Dismissing thoughts of "worry," Marble stepped forward and around the man, curious to see what he'd been doing before being interrupted. He found a symbol carved into the wood at the base of the giant tree, which would account for the strange scraping noises Marble had heard (knife on wood). He crouched, trying to read the symbol and failing. It wasn't in the language of the country called One—it didn't resemble any of the characters Marble had painstakingly learned to read. He tapped the symbol, tracing its four swooping lines, all of which peaked up at the center, a bit like a picture of a mountain.

"Curious?" the man said. Marble nodded.

"It's a Mark. Like this." The man bent to touch Marble's Breath Mark. He was the first person other than the Mistress to ever do that, and Marble shivered at the pressure of a stranger's finger on the source of his life. Thankfully, the man didn't touch the Breath Mark long, hand retreating as he continued. "But not for the same thing—this Mark," he said, tapping the symbol carved into the wood, "is for protection. It makes this tree a sanctuary." The man placed a hand on the tree, skin distinguished from bark by the white banding his fingers. He sighed. "I hope I'm being paranoid."

Marble straightened and tapped the man's hand, touching the white symbols curving up the side of his wrist, then pointed to his own Breath Mark.

"Yes—these are Marks as well," the man said. He rubbed his palm over his knuckles, fingers massaging his Marks as he gave Marble a wry smile. "Sloppy, hasty ones."

Marble cocked his head, wondering what the man wasn't saying. If he was sibling Silver, maybe he could've asked.

But he wasn't, so the man turned from Marble after a moment, using his knife to score a few more lines into the tree. Marble folded his hands behind his back and watched. When the man finished with a horizontal line slashing straight through the center of the Mark, the tree shuddered, leaves from high branches falling in a shower of green. One leaf fell over Marble's eyes, and by the time he pulled it off the man was standing, tucking his knife away and pulling his pack over his shoulder. They stared at one another for long moments. Then the man bent forward, placing a hand on Marble's head.

"I've always admired dolls. You're loyal to a fault. Kind. Fearless, even of death."

Marble straightened at the praise, all of which was true. He *was* loyal to the Mistress, willing to do whatever she asked without hesitation; he *was* kind to humans, no matter what they did or said. And what *was* there to fear when it came to oblivion? Marble came from a place of quiet, and he'd return there when his Breath Mark was broken. That was how things were.

"I wish I could learn the language of dolls," the man said. "Maybe you could tell me the answers I seek." He sighed, as if the idea was both appealing and exhausting. He lifted his hand, hesitated, then said, "I don't suppose you know where the Shod come from, or how they're made? From personal experience I know they can only be killed by dolls, but I still don't understand how they come to be."

Marble didn't know the answers to those questions. He knew that sibling Silver had ideas about the Shod based on the stories the Mistress told about her family and the Red Tide—he'd been writing them down, but he wouldn't show anyone except Dola. For some reason, sibling Silver had taken a liking to her.

So in response to the man, Marble could only shake his head. The man let out a long breath, shoulders slouching.

"Of course not," he said. Then he straightened, smiling a smile that Marble recognized, from years spent with the Mistress, as forced. "Would you like to look for the Shod together?"

The Mistress had said nothing about working with someone, but Marble found the man intriguing. He wanted to study him a little longer, so he nodded.

"Excellent," the man said.

Together they headed through the forest. As they walked, the man spoke.

"I suppose it would do for me to introduce myself. My name is Roque. I'm from the country called Steep. Have you heard of it?" Marble nodded. The man, Roque, ducked under a low tree branch, slipping out into a small meadow. "That was a foolish question," he said, pausing to gaze at a stream running through the meadow, ringed by a thick growth of wildflowers colored a deep violet blue. Marble inspected one of the blooms, noting its star-shaped pattern as Roque continued. "The whole world has heard of us, in one manner or another." He hesitated, as if considering saying more on that topic. He didn't, moving to step over the stream, Marble hopping to follow as they reentered the tree line.

"This isn't my first time in One," Roque said. "I come fairly often, but I usually remain on the coast. The city called Ports is a good place to hear all sorts of stories from all over the world—I'm searching for something, you see. Something that could be anywhere, disguised as practically anything. So, when I've hit a dead end, I sometimes go to Ports to find leads and find where I should be looking *for* leads." They ran into a pile of rocks, mossy stones on which their feet slipped as they scrabbled up them. Roque's voice grew ragged with exertion. "The reason I came to One in the first place was because I heard of the Shod. I wanted to study them, to understand where they came from. I guessed they had a Mark that made them how they are, like you and I do. I still believe that. But I can't tell what Mark—a Mark of rage? Fear? There are several of those, but I've never seen any of them create monsters." He grimaced. "Not out of the people who have those Marks placed on them, at least."

Much of what Roque was saying made no sense. Marble knew what the Breath Mark was, of course—it was what the Mistress used to give him life and purpose. He'd just seen Roque use another Mark, and the man's white symbols were Marks, so clearly there was more than just the Breath Mark in the world. But the Shod having a Mark? That seemed strange to him. Wrong. Perverse, even.

"Ah," Roque said, stopping. "We've reached the edge."

They had—the forest called Deep was over, trees behind them and a flat expanse of stone stretched out ahead, a smooth and pale line extending into the distance before dipping away into rises of stone that formed top-heavy shapes that looked purple against the sky. The parts of the plateau nearest to Marble and Roque were raised, rectangles and circles of stone sitting up a few inches above the ground in a purposeful way. Almost directly in front of them stood a sign, one of many stretching in either direction of the forest's border, dozens of posts forming a fence of words.

Marble stepped forward, feet inspiring puffs of dust to rise into the air, and looked up at the sign. It said, THE GRAVEYARD, RESTING PLACE OF THE FIRST DOLLMAKER AND HIS HONORED COMPANIONS.

"I don't read much of the written language of the country called One, but I believe it says 'Graveyard, Resting Place of First Dollmaker and Honored Companions,'" Roque said. Marble nodded, waving a hand. Roque cocked his head. "You already knew that?" Marble nodded. "You can read?"

Yes, yes, Marble could read. A little. Not as much as siblings Glass or Jewel, and he couldn't write the way sibling Silver did. He nodded anyway.

"I've never met a doll who reads," Roque said, tucking a strand of copper hair behind an ear, head tipping to the side. "Then again, I've never met a doll as human as you."

The way the words were spoken, Marble wasn't sure if they were a compliment or an insult. Before he could figure it out, Roque stepped past the sign and walked out into the Graveyard. Marble hurried to follow.

"So this is where they bury dollmakers," Roque said. "I'm surprised the location is so remote." He paused next to a grave and crouched. Marble did too, studying the words written on the stone placed over the tomb. He recognized the characters for "Died in Honor" and "wife."

Roque stretched out a hand, tracing the grooves of the words with long fingers. His touch swept away the bits of dirt and sand blanketing the tomb, creating glimmering clouds of gold that lingered for a moment before the wind came and blew the gilt away.

“Hundreds of them,” Roque said. He was looking across the Graveyard, gaze moving down the lines of tombs. “I wonder how many of them were killed by Shod.”

Marble had no answer to that, but something told him Roque wasn’t asking a question he wanted answered. He stood as Roque did and followed the man through the Graveyard, pausing at the occasional tomb before moving on. Eventually they reached the end of occupied tombs, finding three rows of holes with stones beside them, waiting to be put in place once the graves were filled with bones.

Roque stopped at the grave nearest the empty tombs. It was new, the dates on the stone from only a week ago. Roque sighed, bending to touch the top of the grave.

Before he could, the gravestone rattled. Roque straightened. The gravestone shook again, this time lifting up a fraction before falling down with a thump. Marble heard something scratching beneath the ground, something clawing at stone in a rhythmic screech.

Instinct told Marble to grab Roque’s leg, pulling him back until the man stumbled, then complied, running with Marble back to the forest called Deep. They reached the trees just as a grinding noise swept across the Graveyard, the both of them turning to see the stone lift and then shift from the top of the now-distant grave, sliding to the side. There was a pause. A gust of wind whistled by.

Then something crawled from the grave.

It was small. Hunched. And in some way wounded; it collapsed the moment it appeared, trying to stand only to fall and crawl, dragging itself forward with painful effort. A moment later a second something clawed out of the grave, going through the same process of standing and falling, worming forward with twisted, jolting movements. A third creature emerged, a fourth and a fifth and so on—Marble stopped counting after twenty.

"They aren't the Dead," Roque said, voice soft. Marble agreed. The things crawling from the grave weren't human—not even dead ones. From what Marble could see, they were made of wood and each had two arms and two legs and a head. There was only one type of creature similar to the things that Marble knew of; one creature buried with dollmakers.

Dolls.

Marble wasn't sure if Roque realized that or not. It felt important that he did, so Marble tugged on the man's arm, making him look down. Marble tapped his chest, then pointed at the dolls rising from the grave. Roque frowned at him, and he repeated the action two more times before that frown cleared into understanding.

"Dolls?" Roque said.

Marble nodded.

"You're sure?"

Another nod.

Roque looked back at the Graveyard. Marble did likewise, seeing that the number of dolls had doubled. A final doll heaved itself up onto the plateau and some unspoken signal passed through the convulsing ranks of its fellows; while most crawled away from the grave, a few turned and dragged the stone back over the tomb, replacing the grave marker and hiding their escape in the process.

The dolls lurched across the plateau until they reached its edge. Then they disappeared, sliding or leaping over the lip of stone and dropping out of sight. Roque, who'd fallen into a crouch as they watched the odd procession, stood. When the last doll disappeared from sight he stepped back into the Graveyard, swift steps propelling him after the dolls. Marble followed.

As did siblings Glass, Jewel, Coin, and Crystal, all four emerging from Deep when Marble did, looking at one another not in surprise (dolls were rarely surprised) but greeting, lifting hands and waving, dipping heads, and, in the case of Coin, blowing kisses the way she'd seen a man do at one of the Mistress's parties. Together they trotted after Roque, and sibling Jewel, ever cautious, held a finger to her lips in a shushing gesture as they bunched together, forming a cluster of feet and swinging arms. There was no need for her worry—Marble was being stealthy, as were his siblings. Even Roque was being quiet, his steps inaudible as a doll's as he crept to the edge of the Graveyard and knelt, leaning over to peer at what lay below. Marble and siblings joined him, hands curling on the lip of the stone and heads tipping forward.

At the edge of the Graveyard was a break in the world; a deep crack through stone that dipped down into shadow. A handful of the grave-dolls skittered down the walls of the crevice, descending at a rapid pace that hinted at falling. And they weren't falling into darkness—on the contrary, they fell into light. Many circles of white light, flashes that slashed the walls of the fissure to highlight ruptured stone and erosion grooves. The illumination came from a seething mass of something that clicked and groaned, had many arms and heads and feet, and was not one something at all but many, many somethings. A clutch of things locked together in either battle or passion or both—it was impossible to tell. All Marble was certain about was that the creatures were in the hundreds, maybe even the thousands, lining the bottom of their canyon like ants bubbling up from a broken anthill. Where one creature ended the next began, and Marble began wondering if he was looking at a river, a living current of many red-streaked, white-eyed things.

Roque inhaled sharply. In a hissing voice he gave a name to the creatures below.

"Shod."

Marble felt a zing of excitement. The Shod! He'd found them, just as the Mistress wanted! There they were, hundreds of Shod, a tangle of monsters! He leaned forward, enthralled by his first glimpse of the Mistress's great enemies, that which she wished destroyed. Which he'd be glad to do, of course. He just needed to know more about them. In fact, he needed to know *everything* about them. If he could get a better look—

Marble's hand slipped on a patch of loose dirt. He pitched forward, and he was going to fall, head over heels, into the bosom of the Shod below. *Good*, he thought. *I'll get a real look at them.*

Roque's hand caught on the back of Marble's shirt, yanking him out of danger. But not before his mishap knocked a shower of dirt and rock down into the crevice. The airborne stones fell with clunks atop the Shod, and the monsters froze. They looked up, hundreds of shining eyes casting a light that Roquc flinched back from. Marble, being a doll, was unaffected by the flare. He witnessed the moment the Shod unhinged their jaws and let loose a deafening Cry.

Like the stories said, the wail sounded like children screaming. And then the Shod were leaping up, breaking into separate units and climbing the walls of their crevice in frantic lunges. Over the resulting din Marble could barely hear Roque jumping to his feet.

"Run!" Roque said, shouting over the Shod before turning and following his own advice.

Siblings Glass and Crystal followed him. Siblings Coin and Jewel stood, but didn't run, eyes locked on the rising Shod. They probably felt the same way Marble did, standing still for the same reason he couldn't force himself to rise; the Mistress had told them to find the Shod. And they had. Which meant this was their chance—they were seeing the Shod up close, close enough to study. Marble counted their forms, the variations in their build and how those variations mimicked his own composition.

Dolls. They were dolls! Like him. But different. Why different? They came from a tomb, and he didn't. But when the Mistress died he'd be buried with her the way her family's dolls were buried with them, per the second edict of the First Dollmaker. Would he become a Shod then? Did being buried turn a doll into a Shod? No, no. That felt simplistic.

What, then, was the secret? Why did dolls become Shod? Why was Marble's own future climbing toward him, so close now he saw the way their shining eyes rolled and spun, their hunched and lopsided shapes speaking of many disassembled dolls and human bones wedged into one hideous form?

Roque was shouting. "Not that way!" he yelled, presumably at siblings Glass and Crystal. "You'll lead them to the village!" Then, "Why are you standing there!" That was probably meant for Marble and siblings Coin and Jewel.

Even to respond to Roque, though, Marble couldn't turn from the Shod. They were almost upon him, and maybe if they got just a little closer he'd learn their secrets, why they were him and he was them. And then he'd work hard and get good enough at writing to put his findings into words, reports to help the Mistress fight the Shod.

The Mistress had said to destroy the Shod. But how could Marble destroy something that so clearly needed to be studied, inspected, *learned* from? To destroy something before learning its secrets—knowing all the information in every line and dip of its shape—would be a shame. A great disappointment.

The first Shod reached the top of the crevice. It rose high, as tall as a human, towering over Marble with a body that brought to mind giant centipedes. Only instead of narrow, spiky arms, this centipede had the arms of dolls with hands of grasping fingers, spindly legs that rammed into the stone on either side of Marble, making the ground crack. He looked up as the Shod stretched over his head, blocking the sky and casting him in a long, inescapable shadow.

He saw something on the Shod's belly. Nine lines twisted into an odd shape that, even warped, was familiar. Still recognizable as the Mark that'd given Marble his first breath.

And which gave him his last as the Shod fell, tore into him, ripped him limb from limb in a splintering burst that was the last thing Marble, thirty-fifth doll of Dollmaker Shean, ever knew.

SHEAN LET OUT A FRUSTRATED GROWL, SCRATCHING OUT HER MOST RECENT AT-tempt at a letter to Nock. She scrunched the wasted paper into a ball, throwing it across the room to strike one of Ikiisa's ugly mannequins, making the figure's limp arms flop before the paper fell with a rustle, joining the other nineteen failed letters on the ground. She was down to one sheet of paper—the last piece she'd brought with her from Pearl.

Several hours' worth of aches tortured her back, her hand cramping from writing for so long. To top off her discomfort, when she forced herself to pick her pencil back up, a headache made her forehead pulse. Groaning, she shoved her head into her hands, squeezing her temples with sweaty fingers and shutting her eyes.

She didn't understand why this was so difficult. All she had to do was tell Nock that she'd faced the "strongest dollmaker" he'd ever met, defeated her, and was now the dollmaker of Web, taking on all the responsibilities such a position entailed. Which meant she'd proved that he was wrong, that her dolls were on par with a fully licensed guard dollmaker's. And *that*, in turn, meant Licensor Maton was wrong, and had to be told as much immediately.

Every time Shean tried to put that information into words, though, the task complicated itself. Just beginning the letter was proving impossible—every address to Nock she tried sounded trite or cute or overly formal: *My dear master, Honored Master Nock, My dear Nock, Nock*. And no matter what she wrote after those faulty addresses, the words somehow always ended up describing Ikiisa collapsing on her knees in the pageant field. Weeping.

That didn't convey the way Shean felt, her triumph or her pride to have done what her master had thought she could not. But, try as she might, she couldn't get that image of Ikiisa out of her head. That pathetic, wretched moment kept replaying in her mind, over and over again.

Ikiisa crumpling, the already small woman growing smaller, dropping to her knees and pressing her hands to her face while sobs wracked her. Her face streaked with spider blood and tears when Ilo hauled her to her feet with unsympathetic roughness, shouting reprimands in her face that made Shean's own ears ring. Throughout the scolding Ikiisa had continued to cry, though at some point her face closed off, expression blanking and eyes growing distant. An invisible wall raised against Ilo's rebukes, against the shouts of the villagers who'd joined in his admonishments.

Shean had never seen someone openly weep before, not even Nock. The sight was shocking. Repulsive. And pitiful.

Pity was dangerous. Pity led to shame, and shame led to guilt. And there was nothing Shean felt guilty for—she'd won the pageant fairly, her dolls perhaps not the superior to Ikiisa's in strength, but making up for that with speed, dexterity, and cleverness. There was absolutely no reason for her to feel uneasy or to keep picturing Ikiisa's downfall.

Then why did the image of Ikiisa crying like that feel so—

This is why I came to Web, Shean thought, cutting her own question short and banishing the image of Ikiisa from her mind. She set her jaw. *I've done what I set out to do, and now my life will go the way it's intended to go.*

But, a soft voice whispered, a voice that sounded terribly similar to Nock's, *you ruined someone else's life to get here.*

Shean slammed her hands on the work desk in front of her, shoving herself to her feet. She needed to clear her head before she could go on, so she swept across and then out of the room, striding down the hall and to the front door, which she yanked open, stepping outside.

The sun wasn't quite set yet, close to the horizon but still bright and warm. The oppressive heat of the day hammered into Shean, accompanied by the sawing of cicadas in the forest, the droning buzz of bugs flitting about their dull lives. She turned to place a hand on the house, steadying herself. Her head spun.

She hadn't ruined Ikiisa's life. She *hadn't*—Ikiisa had a license. She could get a job anywhere. She could even reclaim her job here in Web; it wasn't like Shean planned on staying! A week at the most, just long enough for her dolls to find, and dispose of, some Shod. That would solidify her victory, make it impossible for anyone to accuse her of failing to live up to the standards of a guard dollmaker. Once Shean achieved that last goal, she'd go home to Pearl and forget all about Web and Ikiisa and Dola and Queen spiders and Lenna and Ilo and, and . . .

Shean's hand curled on the side of the house, the wood panels of the structure digging into her with a threat of slivers. Ridiculous. She was being ridiculous, feeling like this, thinking like this. Her only crime was working harder than Ikiisa, being more passionate and clever than Ikiisa. What was *wrong* with being passionate? What was *wrong* with trying harder than everyone else to be better, to be more, to be the best?

She'd had to do what she did. There wasn't any other way to prove herself. Nock said he'd petition the licensors to give her a guard license if Ikiisa approved of her dolls, but what did Ikiisa, a stranger, know? She'd be just like Licensor Maton, taking one look at Shean's beautiful dolls and dismissing her. The way Ilo had tried to. The way everyone, Shean realized, for all their praise of her work, did.

Except . . . she hadn't tried, had she? She hadn't even *considered* talking to Ikiisa, reasoning with her until she met Nock's requirements and approved Shean's dolls. Even if Ikiisa had refused to do so, Shean could've tried, couldn't she? She could've at least asked. And then, maybe, the villagers wouldn't have turned on Ikiisa.

Shean's throat felt tight. Her eyes were prickling. To her horror, she realized she was about to cry.

Someone whispered, too soft to understand, but audible. Shean lifted her head and saw a foot sticking out around the corner of the house. A familiar foot.

Straightening, Shean rounded the house. She found Dola and Silver sitting against the wall, Lintok dozing on the grassy plot in front of them. They were bent over something, heads close together. Shean shifted a step to the side and saw they were looking at Dola's work journal, which was opened across Silver's legs, pages crammed with a long list of words Shean was too far away to read.

"What're you doing?" Shean asked, grabbing on desperately (and gratefully) to the distraction child and doll provided.

Dola jumped, looking up. "Dollmaker Shean!"

"Are you showing Silver your writing practice?" Shean asked, remembering what Lenna had said earlier. Curious, she reached for the journal.

"No!" Dola yanked the journal from Silver's hands, slapping it shut and tying its straps into knots.

Shean pulled her hand back. "Dola? What's wrong?"

Dola clutched the journal to her chest, pulling her legs up as if protecting the book. "I, um, I-I don't want you to see."

"Why not?"

Dola looked at Silver, as if he could help her. He shrugged, waving what looked like a stick of writing lead in one hand. Shean frowned at that—had Dola been playing pretend with Silver again? Only this time, instead of speaking, she was pretending he could write?

"Because, um, I . . ." Dola said, trailing off.

"Yes? You what?" Shean prompted.

"I want to be a dollmaker!" Dola said in a rush, words spilling out in a single breath.

Shean pushed the hair back from her face, tucking it behind her ear to hide her surprise. "Really?"

Dola hugged the journal, nodding. She looked at the ground, voice quavering. "Yes. I-I really like dolls. I want Dollmaker Ikiisa to take me as an apprentice, but I don't think she's noticed." She looked up, eyes bright with hope. "Will *you* take an apprentice, Dollmaker Shean?"

Shean had never considered having an apprentice before. The thought had never even crossed her mind—she was on the cusp of her career, at the very beginning of her legacy. She was too young by far to be thinking of taking on a student.

Well, not *too* young; technically, any full-fledged dollmaker could start taking apprentices at any time. Nock had taken one at the age of twenty-five, during his first year of service. But that was Nock. He'd raised an entire school of dollmakers by himself, and enjoyed doing so.

Shean wasn't like that. She was no good at teaching others how to make dolls—in all fairness, she'd never actually *tried* to teach anyone how to make dolls. But she'd also never desired to.

All of that, though, was beside the point; an unlicensed dollmaker couldn't take an apprentice. Even if they wanted to.

I'll be licensed soon, Shean thought. But even that reality failed to fill her with the desire to have an apprentice.

"Maybe," Shean said, reluctant to disappoint the excitement brightening Dola's face. She sat down next to the girl, legs sprawled out in front of her and the skirts of her dress caught up in bunches and twists around her knees. She sighed, leaning her head against the wall and staring at the sky. "But becoming a dollmaker isn't easy. You have to pass the Breath Mark exams, and then you have to spend years training under a master—I trained for ten years, and I was ready to be assessed for licensing earlier than most."

The words made her feel old. They made her remember being Dola's age, excited by life and unable to wait until she was an adult, a licensed dollmaker working as a guard in Pearl. Those days felt so long ago, so spectacular with anticipation and hope. So unlike today, with the sun refusing to set so Shean could sleep and escape thoughts of Ikiisa's tears and the terrible pricks of self-doubt plaguing her, if only for a handful of hours.

"Dollmaker Ikiisa passed her licensing when she was my age," Dola said, interrupting Shean's melancholy.

Shean sat up straight, looking at her. "That's impossible."

"It's true—she was twelve."

Shean's eyebrows raised. The outrageous idea of a dollmaker being licensed at such a young age (and the annoying fact that, given they were talking about Ikiisa, Shean believed it) aside, Dola was *twelve*? The girl was so tiny, Shean had thought her eight, nine at the oldest. She wondered if Dola was small because her parents had been, or because of the long hours she was made to spend in the Veil every night.

Maybe that trick with the spider silking had been even more astute than Shean had thought.

"I know I'm not like her," Dola continued, taking Shean's surprise for skepticism, "but I-I've been practicing the Breath Mark every day, and Gran says she'll take me to the city called Swamp for the exam when I turn thirteen next year. Then I can find a master, but I want to stay in Web if I can." She ducked her head, voice growing shy. "Maybe my dolls can work in the Veil, too."

Shean dismissed her shock with a smile. "What sort of dolls do you want to learn to make?" she asked.

Dola's head rose with excitement, her eyes shining. "I want to make dolls that help people!"

Shean bit back a snort of laughter—trust a child to say such an obvious thing with the enthusiasm of one presenting a groundbreaking concept. "No, I mean what *kind* of dolls—guard or artisan?"

"Either!"

"Either?" Shean echoed, head tipping to the side. "Don't you know what sort of dollmaker you *want* to be?"

Dola frowned. "Won't that be decided when I learn to make dolls?"

"What do you mean?"

DOLA
Touches her face when she's concentrating - motivated, studious, smart
Gentle
Quietly brave - too quiet?
Fidgets when nervous
struggles to speak her mind; doesn't seem to believe anyone will listen if she does.
Shy? Frightened? Why?

"I . . . I thought that was how it worked. Doesn't an apprentice learn how to make dolls, and then what license they're given depends on what their dolls are like?" As she spoke she looked at Silver. To Shean's annoyance, he nodded.

"But that . . ." Shean started, protest trailing off as she realized what Dola said was, technically, true. She pursed her lips. "Most apprentices know what they want their dolls to be. It gives them a goal to work toward, an artistic vision to emulate."

Dola's brow furrowed. "But what if I think my dolls are one thing, but they're not? Isn't it better to just want my dolls to help people?"

Shean opened her mouth. No words came out. She shut it again, tried to think of a good argument because there *was* an argument to be had—what Dola was saying was simplistic. After a minute of struggle, though, Shean couldn't think of any point to make that didn't sound like petulant whining. So she said, lamely, "Yes. I suppose it is."

Dola smiled. "Then that's what I want."

The girl's certainty was unsettling. And foolish. Without a more specific goal, Dola's journey as a dollmaker (assuming she passed the Breath Mark exams) would be drifting and confused. If she didn't aim toward guardhood or artistic craft, there would be no guide for her to follow when she began to design her own dolls. Shean had studied Nock's dolls, as well as designs drawn by her brother and parents, when making her first dolls; it was a combination of their styles, and her own personal flair (earned through relentless practice and work), that'd resulted in her current arsenal of dolls. Including Silver—Silver more than any doll, in fact, showcased years of imitation leading to personal discovery and design.

But what would a dollmaker apprentice with no ambition, no desire to make one type of doll or the other, do when learning to make her own dolls? What models would she use to propel her to success? And what success was there to be had, if she had no idea what it was she even wanted, what goal she was even working toward? That way of thinking wasn't logical. Or normal.

That way of thinking made Shean uncomfortable.

Before Shean could say as much, a crashing came from the forest called Deep. A cacophony of cracks and thrashes, like a bear blundering, blind and enraged, through the undergrowth. Shean leapt to her feet, Dola and Silver joining her as a figure broke from the trees, bursting into view in a shower of leaves and branches. Lintok reared at the unexpected arrival, letting out a warning bark, the whites of his eyes showing with surprise.

The figure staggered a step and paused, panting, and Shean recognized Roque. He looked more flustered than she'd thought him capable of—lips a strained line, cheeks flushed, hair in disarray, and the neat tuck of his tunic coming undone. Lintok was still kicking, spooked to a degree Shean had never seen before and tossing his head with dismay. She swept forward to calm him, grabbing the side of his neck to steady him and wishing he had his bridle on, or something equally easy to grab onto and hold. To her relief he ducked his head low enough for her to snag one of his antlers, holding his head down with a jerk until his barks settled to alarmed huffs.

As Shean calmed her elk, Roque straightened. He ran to her and Dola, grabbing their wrists and yanking them forward, toward Web, before either of them could protest.

At the handling, Shean's hold on Lintok broke. The elk reared again, blaring, and, to her horror, he turned and bolted, dashing into the forest called Deep, bounding into the foliage. Within a heartbeat he was gone.

"Lintok!" she cried. She yanked against Roque, digging her heels into the ground and yelling. "Let go of me! My elk—"

"Leave him," Roque said, and Shean had never been spoken to with such firm command, in a tone of voice that so stoutly refused disagreement. Roque yanked her forward again, casting her a sharp look over his shoulder. "He's better off on his own."

"What's happening?" Shean gasped as Roque dragged her down the road, her heavy skirts making it difficult to keep up with his pace. She still wanted to chase Lintok, but Roque's intensity was scaring her. She looked at Dola, who had ahold of Silver, pulling him along with her. There was fear in the girl's face, the way she clung to Silver, desperate as Roque barreled down the road, dragging them with him. He said nothing, and Shean swallowed the tremor in her voice, trying again. "What's wrong?"

Roque didn't answer until they reached the town square. There he released Shean and Dola, cupped his hands around his mouth, and bellowed.

"Shod!"

Shean flinched at the cry, mouth going dry at its implications and all her worried thoughts about Lintok fleeing in a rush of cold that filled the spaces of her body. Roque shouted again, louder, and there was a slam of doors opening. People stumbled from houses, dressed in sleepwear and looking disoriented. And afraid.

"What's going on?" The voice was Ilo's, preceding him as he stomped across the town square, red-faced and scowling.

"Shod are coming," Roque said, head turning as he scanned the square. "Is this everyone?"

Ilo spluttered. "Shod? What, *when* did you—"

Roque cut Ilo's stammering short by turning, shouting.

"Shod are coming to Web! We have to leave! Now!"

Dola let out a noise, half whimper and half sob. Shean looked to see the girl trying to cower behind Silver, despite him being a head shorter than her. Her trembling snapped Shean out of her stupor and she marched to Roque, grabbing his arm.

"Roque!" she barked, forcing his attention to her. She scowled. "What are you *doing*?"

She expected him to yank away from her, to yell. He looked angry enough to. Instead he stepped closer to her, eyes steady on hers as he said, "There are Shod coming to Web."

Fear, old and primal, spiked through Shean. She ignored it and said, "Then my dolls will handle them!"

"I saw the Shod destroy your dolls," Roque said. Shean recoiled at the lie, letting go of him and taking a step back. He grimaced. "And it's a good thing they did—without that distraction, they'd be here already."

"Liar!" Shean said, anger leaching away her fear. "That isn't—"

"We need to leave," Roque said. He turned to Ilo, who was watching their exchange with a face drained of color. "There's a place, a shelter I created in the forest that can stand against the Shod. We have to go there and hide. Now."

"He's lying!" Shean said, shoving past Roque and stepping toward Ilo. She stopped when the man backed away from her, his expression betrayed. With horror, Shean realized he believed Roque.

"If you were being chased by Shod, where are they?" Shean demanded, turning on Roque. "You expect me to believe you can outrun the—"

A rustle stopped her short. A soft, crying noise. Like a wounded animal. Or a weeping child.

Shean's hair stood on end. She knew that noise. She'd heard it before. Fifteen years ago. In Pearl.

She spun around, taking a step back as a fern on the forest's edge swayed, the sounds of cracking branches peppering the forest called Deep.

And then Shean, Roque, and all the villagers of Web were confronted by a wall of white eyes. Glowing white eyes and voices raised in a collective, shrieking scream, a Cry like a hundred children wailing. Before Shean could process what was happening a Shod burst from the forest called Deep, huge and red and moving in that jerky, lopsided way. It had a head the size of a boulder, split wide by a mouth full of giant shards of glass, human bones thrust through a thick chest in a nonsensical pattern of fractured spikes, a long, sectioned body thrashing the ground with each step.

The Shod lifted its head and Cried. As it did, Shean saw the inside of its maw. Her entire body seized.

In the jaws of the Shod were the broken, fractured, unmistakable remains of her dolls.

IKIISA WOKE TO A SOUND FROM NIGHTMARES.

She stiffened, curled on her side on the cold stone ground of the hideaway. Eyes snapped open, she listened to the shriek of suffering, weeping, pleading the likes of which she hadn't heard in years. She held her breath as she waited to wake up from whatever dream she was having about hearing the Shod lift their Cry in the forest called Deep.

Then Bobble stood, hooting a concerned hoot that stirred her other dolls to their feet. She sat up, the press of the heel of her palm into the gritty ground, along with the throb of her body from sleeping on rock, painful enough to convince her that she was awake.

What she'd just heard was real.

"Shod," she gasped, shoving herself to her feet and trying to run to the front of the hideout. She tripped over her dolls instead, landing hard and scraping her knees and palms on the floor. Ignoring the resulting burn of pain and the alarmed whistles of her dolls, she crawled toward daylight, pulling herself outside and standing, head whipping from side to side as she tried to pinpoint where the Cry was coming from.

It didn't take her long to realize it was coming from Web.

She launched herself forward, knowing her dolls would follow. Sure enough, their loping gaits pounded after her through the undergrowth. A few dolls even overtook her, swinging from the branches of trees overhead as they flung themselves through the forest.

The boulder hideout was close to Web—a five-minute walk at most. Running, Ikiisa would reach the village in a minute or less. She felt each second of that minute acutely as she ran, tearing through Deep and doing her best not to catch her feet on anything, praying she wouldn't stumble and prolong the precious time she was wasting in running.

By luck or providence, she managed not to fall, reaching Web with sprint-winded lungs and burning limbs, breaking from Deep just in time to witness a wave of Shod break over the houses of the village.

Ikiisa's breath caught as blurs of red streaked through Web, slashing the woven branches around each structure, shredding the careful plaits. Debris spewed in all directions. Roofs caved in with clatters of broken tiles and the mighty snap of support beams. The Shod swarmed over every structure they tore down, so numerous they looked like a thick, garnet liquid rolling and slapping against Web.

Ikiisa hadn't seen this many Shod working in tandem since the

Red Tide. She hadn't been so deafened by the Cry since it rang over the city called Pearl. She hadn't so much as *seen* a Shod for months now, not even a footprint in the mud or an awkwardly broken branch on a bush suggesting a lingering presence of monsters in the forest called Deep. From the gossip she'd heard from the merchants who came to Web twice a year, the rest of the country was experiencing a similar lull. Some people even believed the Red Tide had been the end of the Shod, the monsters' final push that, once thwarted, had resulted in, if not extinction, then something close.

Ikiisa had never believed that. Given that no one knew how the monsters reproduced, thinking that the Shod had died off completely, or had even dwindled to unthreatening numbers, was naïve. She was glad peace had fallen over the country called One—after decades of living in fear and losing hundreds every year to the Shod, a respite was nothing to turn one's nose up at. But not once had Ikiisa thought she'd seen the end of her, and her dolls', enemies.

That being said, she hadn't expected to find not just dozens, but *hundreds* of Shod attacking the village called Web. For a moment the sight was too much to comprehend, as terrible as the Shod pouring over Pearl had been. Ikiisa stood frozen in place, each breath searing, thoughts fractured and scattered and spiraling in a frenzy, then condensing into one clear question:

Where had they all *come* from?

Another house fell, this one so close bits of wooden shrapnel struck Ikiisa, slicing into her cheeks and splitting the bottom of her lip. The house caved under the weight of the Shod piling atop it, and she flinched, woken from her shock. Her ears strained for the cry of human voices amidst the Cry of the Shod. She heard none, which meant one of two things: the villagers had escaped Web before the Shod had arrived, or they were all dead.

Choosing to believe the former, but knowing that either possibility was out of her control, Ikiisa pressed her pointer finger and thumb together, shoving them into her mouth and making the shrill, high-pitched whistle that worked as a signal between herself and her dolls to attack. At the sound her dolls flew past her, diving at the Shod with high-pitched shrills to match the baying of their targets. One doll stayed behind—Bobble. A personal guard to make sure Ikiisa herself was defended from any Shod that broke through her dolls.

It was the fate of dollmakers to both fight and not fight the Shod. Ikiisa spent days and dozens of hours slaving over each doll she made, but when the time came for those dolls to face the Shod she could do nothing for them but stand nearby, watching, letting out the occasional whistle to warn about the movements of their opponents. Guided by these signals, her dolls began to rend the Shod, her heart lifting when the monsters were driven back from the remnants of the houses they'd crushed, kept from taking up the wreckage and, as was the way of the Shod, using the remains to build upon themselves, reinforcing their cobbled forms and growing more durable in the process. That was something Ikiisa *did* know about the Shod, a point of clarity among the many mysteries surrounding the monsters; as noted in the eighth edict of the First Dollmaker, the Shod were attracted to man-made things, as with such they could build themselves into new, stronger forms.

Of the hundreds of Shod in Web, dozens already boasted armor made from house fragments, shields of woven branches cocooning their heads and torsos—reinforcements that made it harder to destroy them. But there'd been twice this many Shod in the district of Pearl Ikiisa had fought in, reinforced not with twig and stick but stone and brick. And—terribly—fresh human corpses.

The monsters attacking Web had no such advantages. As they had in the Red Tide, Ikiisa's dolls began to drive the Shod back.

That fact could only ease so much of Ikiisa's worry, though. Keeping her eyes on the wrestle of her dolls among the Shod, she did the only thing she could think to do; she yanked her pendant up, holding it close to her mouth and shouting what she hoped weren't futile words.

"Roque! There are Shod, in Web! I don't know where the villagers are, but if you can find them, please—help them!"

SHEAN COULDN'T THINK. NOTHING MADE SENSE—NOT HOW SHE WAS RUNNING through the forest called Deep, not the people surrounding her who were weeping as they, too, ran. Her foot caught on something hard, toes stubbing. She almost fell, knocking into the people around her, some of whom shoved her away with curses, only one fellow refugee grabbing her and steadying her, dragging her forward for a few steps with a hand clenched on her shoulder before letting go.

How had she gotten here? She remembered her dolls, her poor, broken dolls dangling in fractions and severed limbs from the teeth of a Shod. Glass's torso, limbs ripped away, impaled on a long, sharp spike. Coin's hands wedged in the space between two fangs. Marble's head rolling from the Shod's mouth and tumbling to the ground, eyes open and lacking the light that'd filled them when she'd given him his Breath Mark, turned him from mannequin to doll. From piece of work to companion.

Then a blur, shouting voices, someone shoving her forward and finding herself fleeing from Web. She was holding her skirts up to her thighs to keep herself from tripping, and her arms ached nearly as much as her legs. Her heels felt like two bruises pounding against rock, her knees itching with many small cuts gained from the whipping branches of the thorn bushes she dashed through. All around her were trees, a thick canopy overhead that let only slivers of sunlight fall to light her path. The further she ran, the more packed together the trees became; she and her fellow runners had to swerve around thick trunks and tangled roots, darting like hares through the undergrowth but lacking the swiftness of rabbits, the agility to maintain a breakneck pace while veering. They were slow. And growing slower.

Which was bad, because Shod were following them. Shod were *catching up* to them. Shean listened to the monsters' baying at her heels, ever louder and accompanied by cracks and groans and thudding impacts that made the ground shudder. Unlike people, Shod had no need to dodge around trees—they could simply knock them over, clearing a path for themselves through the forest with unprecedented speed.

The Shod should've had all of their heads already. Their only luck, really, was that the Shod had been distracted by Web for a few minutes—just long enough for the villagers to start running and get enough of a head start to still be alive. In the corner of her eye, as she rounded a tree with sparsely leaved branches that twisted overhead like serpents, Shean could see younger villagers carrying older ones on their backs, children dragged through the undergrowth by parents who, with furtive glances over their shoulders, relented and scooped their sons and daughters into their arms, speeding up for a handful of moments before their new burdens slowed them. And slowed them.

Behind Shean, the Cry of the Shod grew louder.

Breathing was difficult—the air was thick and hot, matching the burn of Shean's chest, the heat of the tears cascading down her face and making it difficult to see, all the harder to keep herself from falling or crashing into a tree, a person, a tall fern. She kept seeing her dolls in the blur of her vision, picturing their remains in the smear the world became each time she blinked.

But she couldn't think about them. She couldn't think about what it meant, the fact that her dolls lay in fragments within a Shod. The implications of that were unfathomable when she was running for her life.

"Here!" a voice shouted over the Shod, the gasping of the people around her. Shean looked up and saw Roque.

He was at the front of the pack, and he wasn't running. He was standing next to a tree, a giant tree, larger than any Shean had ever seen. If five people stood with their arms stretched wide and their fingertips touching, they'd barely reach across one side of this tree.

A part of the tree was open, a swath of bark pulled back like a door to expose a jagged silhouette of darkness. Roque was waving, gesturing to the depths of the tree—this must be the "shelter" he'd spoken of earlier, the safe place he'd told Ilo he'd made. As Shean slowed because those in front of her were no longer running, she watched Roque grab the villager nearest him, shoving the man into the tree. The villager fell with a cry, swallowed by darkness. Another villager followed, then another. The fourth was not thrown in by Roque but stepped forward of her own accord, dragging a pair of familiar, tall children with her. And then all the villagers were surging toward the shelter tree, dashing inside it, pushing the elderly and children forward while Roque waved an encouraging hand.

When it was Shean's turn, she hesitated. People shoved past her, bumping her and making her stumble as they ran into the shelter. All too aware of how loud and close the Cries of the Shod were, she looked over the villagers' heads at Roque, meeting his eyes.

She wanted to ask him if it was true. If what she'd seen was right, and not some nightmare. Were her dolls really gone? Had the Shod really taken them from her?

Roque grimaced and she saw her answer. Her eyes misted, a sob wedging itself in her throat. The familiar grief of loss strangled her.

Loss, and defeat.

No! No, no, no, no—

Shean's internal scream was cut short by a real scream. A shriek slicing through the gasps and sobs of those around her, making her turn.

The Shod were visible through the trees. They were upon the villagers of Web, reaching for those still running toward the shelter tree. Reaching for Dola, who was on her hands and knees, tripped by something—a rock, a hole, a fallen tree branch. Lenna was with her, dragging her upright and holding her hand and running.

But something was wrong. Dola ran for only a moment—then she ripped her hand from her grandmother's and turned around, shouting something, running back the way she'd come. Running toward the Shod who, at the sight of her approach, tossed and jerked themselves in a frenzy of anticipation. Dola ignored them, staggering forward and reaching for something that she snatched from the undergrowth. Something small and compact, tied shut with strings. Her notebook.

Protest rose in Shean's mouth like vomit. Lenna was screaming at Dola, kept back by villagers who dragged her toward the tree. Roque had left his post next to the tree and was barreling through the remaining villagers, making his way to Dola, hand outstretched and fingers straining, as if doing so would make him reach the girl in time.

Dola was standing with her journal clutched to her chest, and she must've realized her mistake because she was staring up at the Shod, trembling so violently her head swung back and forth. She didn't run, and Shean knew why; she was stuck in place with an overwhelming fear, a fear Shean had experienced for the first time when she was half Dola's age.

The Shod would reach her in the next heartbeat. They'd tear her the way they tore down trees, coating themselves in the red of her blood. Taking her apart and using her pieces to build upon themselves.

Shean didn't want to watch.

She couldn't look away.

A flash of white. The blur of a small figure leaping out from the trees, diving from the foliage and thrusting itself between Dola and the Shod. Shean's eyes widened as Silver planted himself in front of the girl, arms spread wide, the glimpse of his face she caught displaying a twisted scowl of fury. He opened his mouth, and screamed a single word.

"No!"

IKIISA'S DOLLS WERE DYING. THEY WERE DYING, AND SHE DIDN'T KNOW WHY.

The first doll, Shard, fell in minutes, overcome by a flock of small, sharp Shod that pecked him to pieces. Kindling and Twig were knocked down together, crushed under the overly large feet of a Shod with a tiny body, oversized limbs, and a head that hung so low it dragged in the dirt. Tripper and Caterpillar were reduced to splinters next, followed by Flower. Another doll, Beat, threw herself at three Shod at once. The monsters turned, catching Beat across her chest with five long, whipping arms and sending her flying backward with a crack that made Ikiisa wince. Beat tried to stand and split in half. She didn't die, though, the half of her with the Breath Mark struggling to rise in the moment before a dozen Shod fell upon her, ripping her limb from limb.

Ikiisa stepped back, away from the village and into the edge of the forest called Deep. She was trembling. Her mouth tasted like chalk.

This wasn't right. There weren't more Shod here than there'd been in Pearl, and during the Red Tide her dolls had held off hundreds of monsters with ease. Why wasn't that the case now?

The doll called Merry perished with a mighty crack and Ikiisa whimpered. She felt something push against her leg, looked down to find Bobble looking up at her, an arm lifted in a gesture she didn't understand. Did he want to fight? Did he want her to pick him up? Was he worried because of how she was shaking?

The arm he had lifted was his newest one. The arm she'd replaced after the children of Web ruined his old one. Staring at the limb, something clicked in Ikiisa's head. She knew the answer to all her questions, why her dolls were dying; they weren't succeeding in Web the way they had in Pearl because they weren't as strong as they'd been in Pearl. None of her dolls were free of cracks or replaced parts, weaknesses made from stones thrown at them, boots kicking them here in Web or one of the many other cities she'd dragged them through over the years. As she watched in horror, the Shod shattered her creations with single, pointed blows to weak points she'd never designed, never intended them to have.

This was pointless. Hopeless. As things were, Ikiisa's dolls were all going to die, and then they'd become a part of the Shod, reinforcements to make the monsters stronger.

They had to stop.

Ikiisa tried to whistle the signal of retreat, a small tune she'd only ever used when urging her dolls to run from people. The notes were lost amidst the cacophony, three more of her dolls shredded before her eyes, falling to pieces and making her chest ache with loss.

Tears pricking her eyes, Ikiisa cupped her hands around her mouth. She shouted.

"Hide!"

Then she turned and, Bobble at her heels, Ikiisa ran.

SILVER DIED IN A SINGLE BLOW. ONE SWIPE OF ONE SHOD'S LONG, POINTED ARM, a spike that cleaved him into two Silvers, severing his Breath Mark and splitting him into halves that fell to the ground in a limp tumble. Immediately these two Silvers were scooped up, further ripped apart and distributed among the line of Shod, which paused as the monsters bickered over parts.

Shean watched two Shod fight over Silver's legs. She felt dizzy. She felt sick.

Had . . . had Silver just spoken?

A hand on her wrist, turning Shean and pulling her toward the shelter tree. Ilo, face set and pale, gaze meeting hers as he dragged her back. Head spinning, she stumbled into sap-smelling gloom and Ilo let go of her. Her eyes adjusted to the dark, taking in the hollow inside of the tree, a space large enough to hold every villager of Web, all of whom, at a glance, seemed present.

But could it hold what remained of Silver? Could it hold that single word he'd shouted, his voice a chill down Shean's spine?

Could it hold her fragmented dolls, her ruined masterpieces?

Could it hold the sick rising in her, ready to spill out in a mighty heave?

Suppressing bile, Shean turned, looking through the door of the tree. Roque had Dola. He'd scooped her up and was running, meeting Lenna and pressing her granddaughter into her arms, shoving the both of them toward the tree.

They wouldn't make it. Dola and Lenna would, yes. But not Roque.

He wasn't even trying, staying behind Lenna and shepherding her to the tree at a trot that was too slow. Shean staggered toward the door, stumbling as Lenna arrived, bumping shoulders with her as she carried a sobbing Dola past.

"Roque," Shean said, though she couldn't hear herself over the Shod. The monsters were done distributing Silver's corpse and were running toward the tree now, faster than any animal. Roque grabbed the door of the tree, tugged. It began to close.

Still, Roque didn't enter the tree. The door was closing, and he was on the wrong side of it. The Shod were almost here. He was pushing the door shut. The Shod were going to reach him.

They were going to destroy him, sunder him, rip him to pieces and use those pieces on themselves, paint themselves in his blood the way they'd painted themselves with Giko's blood, with Manma and Father's blood. They were going to dismember him the way they'd dismembered Silver.

And it was Shean's fault.

No. Please.

No.

Shean dove for the closing gap of the door. She thrust herself into the space, digging her hands into the front of Roque's shirt, fingers wrapping around the strap of his travel bag. She had a glimpse of his wide, startled eyes as she heaved him into the tree, forcing the door open wide enough for him to pass. She spun, swinging him away from the door and thrusting him toward the villagers huddled against the far wall of the hollow tree.

Something impaled Shean's ankle. The pain was sharp and sudden and breathtaking, but she still found the air to scream as her leg jerked back. She fell on her face, unprepared for the collapse and thus failing to catch herself. The air was knocked from her lungs and she struggled for breath as she was dragged across the ground, chin and neck rubbed raw as she was pulled from the shelter of the tree and into grass that pricked her face, the earth she clung to too soft to impair her momentum. Clumps of dirt came up in her hands as she tried to dig her fingers down, to find a hold to stop herself from being taken away. Her fingernails tore in raw flashes. The skirt of her dress bunched painfully, digging into her abdomen and ribs and then falling around her head as she was picked up by the leg, lifted with an agonizing jerk.

Gooseflesh rose on Shean's naked skin, a chill offset by the extreme hot of the blood oozing down her leg. Her uninjured foot kicked in an attempt to free herself, swinging at nothing while heat filled her head and set her ears to roaring like the waves of the ocean. She was blinded by her dress, hands clawing at the heavy skirts that covered her face as her captor swung her like a ball on a string. There was a click, a *shunt-shunt-shunt* noise muffled through fabric and head-rush. Then lines of fire erupted around Shean's leg, ripping down in a spiral from her bleeding ankle to her hip.

This time the pain was too much for Shean to scream. Instead her entire body seized, black lights bursting like squashed berries across her vision. Her mouth opened in a contortion that made her lips feel like they were being ripped from her face. Wet warmth slicked her left side, the scent of blood accosting her senses. Her eyes rolled and she felt unconsciousness rising in the back of her skull, ready to crash down, to sweep her away to a place where she'd feel no pain.

Then there was a snap, like a tree branch breaking. Shean fell, landing on the ground in a heap, just barely covering her head in time to prevent herself from breaking her neck.

Staving off the urge to black out, Shean struggled upright, shoving her skirts down and turning to look behind her. Two of Ikiisa's dolls struggled with the Shod, pushing the monsters back into the trees. A third doll appeared, intercepting a Shod making a flying leap toward Shean. Doll and monster exploded overhead, and Shean flinched, cowering when bits of wood showered down, a few cutting her arms and hands. Through the rain of splinters, she saw that the door to the tree was shut. Closed, and, now, invisible. The tree looked like nothing but a tree. And there was no sign of Roque.

Then Ikiisa was there, grabbing Shean, pulling her to her feet and yelling in her ear.

"Run!"

IKIISA'S DOLLS BOUGHT HER TIME TO HALF LEAD, HALF CARRY SHEAN FROM THE great redwood tree that stood like a cornerstone in the far west side of the forest called Deep. Through the sacrifice of more dolls they reached the boulder hideout without being attacked, but the Shod were howling after them, gaining on them, the sound of Web being ripped to pieces adding to the din.

Ignoring the mounting noise, Ikiisa dragged Shean into the shelter, flinching every time the woman cried out in pain. Once Shean was inside, Ikiisa scrambled back to the hideout's entrance, pausing for a moment as she thought of leaving what remained of her dolls alone in the forest called Deep. Then the undergrowth across from the hideout shivered, a Shod careening into view in a shower of torn leaves and snapping jaws, three huge, protruding eyes rolling in three separate directions. Ikiisa hit the switch that made the door slide shut. A moment after it did the Shod rammed against it, making the whole hideout shake.

Ikiisa held her breath, imagining how it would feel if the boulders above her fell. But they didn't, not even when the Shod continued banging on the door of the hideout, joined by companions that shrieked and clawed at the stone. After a few fraught moments, Ikiisa turned from the hideout's entrance.

She was shaken, and therefore had lacked the foresight to ignite the hideout's glow lantern before shutting the door. In darkness she fumbled and found the lamp, juddering it to life and swinging it toward where Shean huddled.

The aquamarine light of the lantern showed puddles of brackish brown on the floor around Shean's left leg, pooling under her ankle and oozing from under the drape of her skirt. The sight sent sparks of alarm through Ikiisa and she half crawled, half stumbled in a crouch to her travel bag, left behind when she'd run for Web. She set the lantern aside and opened the bag, rifling through her dollmaking tools until she found the other items she'd brought with her.

"I don't have bandages, but I have shirts," she said, babbling because talking calmed her in terrible situations. The night Master Coen had died, she hadn't stopped talking until Darin screamed at her to shut up.

"And water," Ikiisa continued, pulling out a half-full canteen, setting it aside. "And a jar of methylated spirits." She yanked out a few of her shirts and a knife, cutting the garments into strips as she went on. "We need to stop the bleeding, wash out the wounds with water, then clean them with the spirits. Then wrap your leg up to keep out infection."

Shean's only response was a moan, followed by a hiccupping sob that turned into full weeping. Ikiisa finished creating makeshift bandages, snatching up her water jug and the flask of alcohol. Ignoring the continual thump and scratch of Shod trying to break into the hideout, she crawled over to Shean, not waiting for permission to shove the woman's skirt back to expose her injuries.

They looked awful. Five black claw marks wrapping from her ankle up to her hip, a spiral that oozed, turning her pale far-shore skin cerise. And sticky. But, thankfully, the bleeding looked like it was stopping already. Ignoring how her hands shook, Ikiisa decided to forgo wasting her few bandages on stemming the trickling blood and uncapped the water jug, pouring it over Shean's leg and doing her best to get an equal amount of water across the injury before she ran out. When she was done, she wadded a couple makeshift bandages into a ball, saturating the result with alcohol. The sharp, dizzying smell filled the hideout and Ikiisa sneezed twice before pressing the wad of fabric to the first cut.

Shean screamed, lashing out. Ikiisa wasn't fast enough to duck, the back of Shean's hand catching her across the face. She winced at the resulting sting but didn't stop, gripping Shean's leg when the woman tried to squirm away and scrubbing until her bundle of rags turned dark. Shean tried to kick her, but this time Ikiisa was ready and knelt on her foot to stop her from doing so.

Ikiisa swapped the first set of bandages for a second bundle, lifting Shean's leg despite the woman's loud, cursing protests and making sure to dab every part of each cut with alcohol. Then she poured another general layer of spirits over the wounds, Shean hissing as she did.

"Keep your leg up from the ground," Ikiisa said, letting go. Shean obeyed, planting her foot on the ground and pulling her leg toward her chest. Ikiisa leaned close as the alcohol did its work, rewarding her a cleaner view of the cuts. She let out a sigh of relief.

"They're shallow," she said. "They'll stop bleeding, soon." She began wrapping the remaining bandages around the wounds, thankful that she'd cleaned her clothing recently.

Shean's ankle worried her the most—its injury was deeper than the other cuts, a puncture wound that'd probably done more damage than the naked eye could see. Ikiisa had no idea how to treat anything that wasn't skin-deep; she settled for wrapping extra bandages around the ankle, tying a tight knot when she finished. As if that made a difference.

She was double-checking her work when Shean spoke, voice rough with pain.

"How do you know how to do this?"

Ikiisa looked up. Shean's face was pale and splotchy, and, though she was no longer crying, her eyes were damp in the light of the glow lantern. With one hand she clutched a wad of her skirt, knuckles whitening from the grip.

"First aid?" Ikiisa said. She looked down at her hands, realizing they had a coating of blood on them. It was drying, making her skin stiff. She flexed her fingers and sat back. "I . . . I've had to do it on myself before."

"Your face," Shean said, like she was answering a question. "What happened to it?"

Ikiisa flinched. She didn't want to talk about that.

But Shean's own face was shiny with sweat, tight with pain and injury fever. She cringed every time a Shod rammed against the hideout, and by her expression Ikiisa could tell she was desperate for distraction. She wanted *Ikiisa* to be a distraction. A combatant to the fear of being trapped and hurt.

It was a desperation they shared.

"It happened in the town called Marsh," Ikiisa said, forced to raise her voice to be heard over the scream of a nearby Shod. She tried to scrub her hands clean of blood on the hem of her shirt, rubbing so hard it hurt. "A Shod killed a little girl, and someone who saw it happen mistook the Shod for one of my dolls. I was arrested and charged with murder."

"Oh. How far into the penalties did they get?"

Ikiisa rubbed her knuckles down the side of her face and couldn't bring herself to answer. The question made her feel sick—sick, and resentful. For a moment, she regretted answering Shean's first question, when she could've just ignored the query and steered the both of them away from her face. Her past. Things she didn't talk about.

But getting upset about Shean's prying felt silly right now, with the Shod Crying all around them, the walls of their sanctuary vibrating with attacks that might end this conversation at any abrupt moment. So Ikiisa let go of feeling annoyed and lifted the hem of her shirt, answering Shean by exposing one of the scars rippling across her abdomen. A cut to match the slice down her face.

Shean sucked in a loud breath. She met Ikiisa's gaze.

"Hot knives," Ikiisa said, letting her shirt drop back into place. She touched the blemish on her face, fingertips tracing the bump of scar tissue. "They were just about to cut out my eyes when evidence came in that cleared me."

Shean stared at Ikiisa with an unreadable expression. Quiet

stretched between them, broken by the scrambling of Shod around the hideout, claws raking on stone as the monsters tried to reach them. The Shod weren't Crying anymore. And as Ikiisa stared back at Shean, the scratches on the walls diminished, falling silent. Not that silence meant the monsters were gone.

Still Shean said nothing. Ikiisa found she couldn't bear the pity gleaming in the woman's eyes any longer, so she cleared her throat, looking away.

"What happened?" Ikiisa asked.

"What?" Shean asked.

"To Web," Ikiisa said.

"The Shod attacked."

Ikiisa felt a prick of frustration. *Obviously*, she thought. Aloud she said, "What happened to your dolls?"

Shean didn't answer. She stayed quiet for so long Ikiisa looked at her. To her surprise, tears were rolling down Shean's face.

"My dolls," she gasped, hands lifting to press over her eyes. She hunched forward, sobs making her entire frame jerk, her voice breaking into stutters. "T-they destroyed m-m-my dolls!"

Feeling guilty, Ikiisa crawled forward, sitting next to Shean and patting her back. The gesture felt awkward, but not as awkward as just sitting and watching the woman weep. "You're all right," she said, the way Master Coen would when she cried over how the other apprentices chased her dolls around, making up cruel rhymes to mock her and her work.

"I couldn't do anything!" Shean sobbed. "I just stood there and watched! And Silver, he—" She broke off into fresh, louder sobs, speech losing to grief.

Ikiisa made sympathetic noises, remembering losing her own dolls for the first time. It'd happened during the Red Tide, and she'd cried, too. Though not until she'd left Pearl—crying over dolls when all those around her were mourning the loss of loved ones had felt insensitive. She'd waited until she was alone on the road to the next town. Then she'd sat down on the wayside, buried her face in her hands, and wept for hours.

"Do you think dolls hurt when they die?" Shean asked, lifting her face from her hands with a loud, wet sniff. She looked at Ikiisa with despairing eyes.

"I wondered about that, too, when I lost my first dolls," she said, patting Shean's shoulder. "But a dollmaker can't afford to think like that."

Shean rubbed the back of her hand under her nose, wiping away dribble as her gaze dropped. "The first edict," she said.

Ikiisa nodded, quoting. "'Dolls are to serve their masters and perform their purpose of protecting human lives without hesitation. From doll *or* dollmaker.'"

Ikiisa didn't say that she had, for a long time now, felt the first edict of the First Dollmaker a cold, unfeeling rule. She understood that dolls were made to fight Shod. She understood that a doll dying wasn't the same as a human dying. But her dolls, if not people, were at the very least alive—the Breath Mark *gave* them life, just as thoroughly as a human heart or brain. And they had personalities, things they liked and disliked; like Ikiisa's doll Flower, who'd gotten his name because he always picked flowers from the forest and brought them back to her. He'd done so with a pure simplicity that might've put him at a level of cognition lower than Ikiisa, but she'd never *ordered* him to pick flowers. He'd picked flowers because he enjoyed picking flowers.

Now, though, he'd never pick another flower, never hold a bloom up for Ikiisa to inspect or pluck velvety petals from their sepal and arrange them in color-gradient patterns around the front steps of her house. He was another sacrifice to the Shod, dead so Ikiisa could live. An existence she'd brought into the world taken out of it to protect her.

A lump formed in her throat. She swallowed it with the ease of practice, relegating her grief over the dolls she'd lost today to the back of her mind, to be acknowledged and dealt with at a time when she didn't have a young dollmaker falling to pieces in front of her.

"I didn't want my dolls to die," Shean said, voice cracking.

"They died doing what they were made to do. There's comfort in that," Ikiisa said, half addressing herself.

Shean pressed her face to her knees and said nothing.

"Does your leg hurt?" Ikiisa said, trying to change the subject. Shean made no reply, and Ikiisa pulled her hand back from the woman's shoulder, realizing that was a silly question. She rested her hands in her lap and tried again. "You shouldn't feel guilty about Web—you only had six dolls, and there're so many Shod. My dolls couldn't drive them away, either."

Shean lifted her head a fraction. "They couldn't?"

"No." Ikiisa looked down at her hands, thinking about the cracks in her dolls that'd turned into mortal wounds. Thinking about how, if her dolls had never been kicked or whipped or gouged by human hands, they could've driven the Shod back.

She didn't say any of that. She just said, "I wonder where all those Shod came from."

"I don't know." Shean straightened, staring at the ground. "Roque ran into the village yelling that the Shod were coming and . . ." She hesitated, breath catching in a hitch of pain. "And that we needed to run away," she finished.

"And then you left the village?" Ikiisa said.

"Yes. Roque took us to a giant tree that was hollow."

Ikiisa cocked her head. "The tree where I found you?"

Shean nodded.

Ikiisa hadn't known the redwood was hollow. "Is that where the villagers are hiding?"

"Yes."

Ikiisa relaxed, a little; at least all of Web wasn't dead. Then she frowned. "If there was a place for you to hide," she said, "how did the Shod catch you?"

Shean placed a hand on her leg, touching the bandages. "Roque was closing the door behind us. He was going to be left outside. I pulled him inside the tree, and when I did the Shod caught my ankle." Her face set with a flash of grim victory. "I *saved* him."

"That was . . . brave of you," Ikiisa said. As she spoke, she thought about what she knew about Roque. His agelessness. The position he'd been in when they'd met, being torn to pieces by the Shod but, somehow, not dying.

She wondered if he'd actually needed saving. She wondered if he'd *meant* to be left outside of the redwood tree.

"This is all my fault," Shean said, voice wretched.

Ikiisa tucked thoughts of Roque away for a later time, refocusing on the hunched, hurt woman sitting next to her. She shook her head, speaking gently. "No, it isn't. Like I said, there're just too many Shod and—"

"You're wrong!" Shean interrupted, voice rising to a shout that made Ikiisa jump. She shuffled back, out of range of any hands or heels. Shean's head was down, lowered with the force of her yell, and Ikiisa watched warily as she straightened. Slowly. "You're wrong. Do you remember a dollmaker called Nock?"

She didn't look at Ikiisa as she spoke, but her voice wasn't despondent anymore—it was hard with determination.

Ikiisa furrowed her brow. "Master Nock of the city called Pearl?" she said, the kind face of an aging man flashing through her mind. "The guard dollmaker?"

"Yes. My master." Shean stretched her legs out in front of her, grimacing and clutching at the top of her injured leg. Her fingers curled tight against her upper thigh, nails digging into her bandages. "He sent me to Web. To meet you."

"Me?" Ikiisa said, brow pinching with confusion.

"He wanted me to speak with you."

"Why?"

"He said that I'd learn something if I did."

"Like what?"

Shean's head jerked up, voice rising in anger. "I don't *know*! He said you found a way to be content, to survive and be the person you are without worry, but I don't see how that's true—you were charged with murder because of your dolls and almost *killed* for it!" Shean shook her head and looked at Ikiisa, pity and rage at war with one another on her face. "Everyone in Web is scared of you and your dolls, and you treat the villagers like a plague, never talking to them or telling them anything about yourself. You don't even talk to Dola—she wants to be a dollmaker, she practically *worships* you, and you haven't even noticed!"

"I noticed," Ikiisa blurted, one retort to the painful truths Shean was flinging about.

Shean hesitated. "What?"

"I know Dola wants to be a dollmaker. Sometimes she tries to repair my dolls by herself. But I-I *can't* take an apprentice."

Ikiisa was trembling so hard she almost couldn't get the words out, her tongue a great, choking thing behind clenching teeth.

It was happening again. Another person was telling her why she was terrible, why she was unsuited to be a dollmaker. And with Shean staring at her like that, the way so many people had stared at her before, it all hit Ikiisa again, all over again, again.

Web wanted her gone. Like all the other villages and cities and towns, they'd sent her away. Yet again, despite trying so hard to make sure this time would be different, she'd burned bridges and made people hate her and yell at her and accuse her of making their lives difficult and she *didn't know why*. How could she have ruined anyone's life when she didn't *talk* to anyone? She hadn't hurt anyone. She hadn't frightened anyone, not intentionally, not on purpose, and they had to know that, didn't they? They had to know that she didn't mean for her dolls to be scary—they didn't know her, they couldn't assume she wanted to scare them. She hadn't even fought back when the villagers hurt her dolls, turned a blind eye to their children hurting her dolls! She'd kept to herself, spared everyone from having to deal with her and her work as best she could. And, somehow, things had *still* fallen apart.

Ikiisa wanted to run away. Every inch of her burned with not just the desire, but the *need* to flee. But she couldn't, not this time; she was holed up in a hideout, Shod running amuck outside—softly scratching at the stone walls around her even now, searching taps and scrabbles seeking weakness—and few, if any, dolls were available to keep her safe from the monsters.

Well, she *could* run. It'd just mean dying. And, as terrible as she felt, Ikiisa didn't want to die.

In pathetic compromise she scooted away from Shean, getting as far away as she could, shifting until she was tucked in a corner of the hideout with her legs drawn to her chest and her arms wrapped around her knees, a posture to make herself as small a target as possible. Shean stared at her but, blessedly, made no move to pursue her.

"Why not?" she asked instead, continuing like she didn't notice Ikiisa's shaking, didn't notice how desperately Ikiisa wanted her to stop. "Why *can't* you have an apprentice?"

Ikiisa shook her head, fighting off the fast, panicky breaths rising in her chest. "I can't make anyone live the way I do," she gasped.

Shean let out a huff, hand slamming against the stone floor. "*That's* what confuses me! Nock said you were strong and confident. He must be remembering you wrong!"

"Probably," Ikiisa said, agreeing too fast. Shean stared at her like she was trying to do a handstand on the peak of a mountain—like she was senseless. Still, Ikiisa couldn't make herself shut up. "I might've seemed that way to him when he met me." Laughter, insane and loud, burst from her, making her throat raw before choking into a gasp. "That was fifteen years ago," she said, digging her fingers into her legs, focusing on the resulting pain to steady her voice. "I'd only been turned away from seven cities when I tried to find a job in Pearl."

"How many have turned you down now?"

"Forty-nine," Ikiisa said. Her head was spinning and she closed her eyes as she continued. "Five of those hired me, but my contracts were always cut short."

"*Why?*"

"Why?" Ikiisa echoed. She swallowed another laugh, hands moving to slide into her hair, clutching her head. "*Why*? You just said why! My dolls give children nightmares. People mistake my dolls for the Shod and destroy them. People mistake Shod for my dolls and try to destroy *me.*" Ikiisa fought the urge to rock back and forth, continuing in a rush, in a tumble of words that could be dammed no longer. "They ask me to leave. *Tell* me to leave. Say it's for my own good, or don't even try to be nice about it and say they can't stand having me as their dollmaker. By the time I got to Web I'd decided the best thing for everyone was if I kept to myself. I made sure my dolls stayed in Deep and only patrolled the outer edges of the town. The children took to capturing my dolls anyway, calling them Shod and beating them. I didn't do anything. Sometimes one of my dolls would wander into town. They always came home broken in some way when that happened, and maybe the damages were from an accident, someone mistaking them for a Shod. Maybe not. Either way, I *didn't do anything.*"

She was talking too much. Saying too much. And it was all pointless—why tell Shean this? Nothing would change. Nothing ever changed.

"Why didn't you tell the villagers your history?" Shean asked, relentless. "Why didn't you talk to them?"

Ikiisa wanted to cry. She didn't. "I tried that once," she said, eyes cracking open. The light of the glow lantern hurt her eyes. "Not in Web. In a small village close to the grazelands—I told the employment officer there about my past experiences because she seemed . . . nice. Trustworthy. The next day I was asked to leave the village. When I asked why, I was told they didn't need someone like me disturbing the peace."

Shean made a frustrated noise. "That's ridiculous."

Ikiisa agreed. She should've known better than to try and make friends like that.

"Why didn't you retaliate?" Shean said.

Ikiisa blinked, uncomprehending. "What?"

Shean leaned on a hand, glaring, her pretty face sharpened by the lantern's light to pointed, painful intensity. "If they wouldn't listen to your words, if you couldn't *talk* to them, why didn't you *fight back*?"

Ikiisa laughed weakly, lifting a halting hand and shaking her head. "I couldn't fight."

"Why *not*?"

"Because . . ." Ikiisa trailed off, swallowing. Hard. "Because it was my fault."

"What was?"

"All of it. Everything."

Shean stared. Her eye twitched. "I don't understand. Do you make your dolls like that on purpose? To look similar to the Shod? To scare people?"

Ikiisa shook her head. "No. That's just how they come out. I've tried to *not* make them like that, but I can never finish the dolls I try to make look . . ." She hesitated.

"Look?" Shean prompted.

Ikiisa ducked her head, eyes lowering. "More like *your* dolls." She whispered her next word: *"Beautiful."*

Shean had no immediate response to that. Silence stretched between them—painful and awkward—for a few minutes before she spoke, voice quiet. "It's the same with my dolls. I can't make them any way but the way I do; that's my style, just like your dolls are made in *your* style. You can't change how you make dolls any more than I can, and you shouldn't, either." Her voice hardened, slightly. Developed an edge. "So how is it *your* fault that people react to your dolls, and you for that matter, the way they do? That's *their* choice."

Ikiisa shook her head, wondering how someone as intelligent

as Shean could fail to understand. “If I could just act the way they want me to, do what they want, be the way they want me to be—”

Shean interrupted with a derisive noise, her tone snapping with impatience. “Then you’d be even more pathetic than you already are!”

Ikiisa flinched. But didn’t argue. How could she? “You’re right,” she murmured, feeling deflated. Feeling seen. “But I . . . I’m afraid.”

As she spoke, Ikiisa realized that was true, the reason she was the way she was. She’d always known, really, though she’d never admitted it aloud—at the root of her, the very core of her being, was fear. She was frightened. So *frightened*, terrified to the point that, if she wasn’t careful, she’d stop breathing. She hugged herself instead, squeezing her eyes shut.

“The people around me terrify me more than the Shod,” she said, “because I *can’t* change. I’ve tried; I *can’t* act how they want me to act, or make dolls the way they want me to make dolls. So I’ll never belong anywhere.”

“Only if you decide you won’t,” Shean said. Her voice flattened. Bittered. “Or the Shod break through these walls and kill us both right now.”

Ikiisa managed a weak laugh at that, cutting off when Shean made a noise, a growl that broke into a sob. The slap of her hand hitting the ground for a second, then a third, time. Silence. The sound of something dripping, something wet hitting the floor.

“What am I doing?” Shean said, voice a whisper. “This doesn’t matter. None of this matters.”

Ikiisa lifted her head. Shean’s chin was lowered to her chest, and she was leaning forward, bent double. Tears dripped from her face while her fingers curled against her bandages. She looked like she was bracing for pain.

“It doesn’t matter who you are or if you’re different than what

Nock said," Shean said. "What's happened in your past *doesn't matter.*" She lifted her head, fixing puffy eyes on Ikiisa. Her lips trembled, and she looked very young and disheveled; a far cry from the smoothly confident Dollmaker Shean who'd swept into, and quickly come to own, Web.

"Doesn't matter," Shean said. The side of her mouth twitched, not becoming a smile or a grimace. Just a spasm. "I can't deny it anymore, can I? I'd be insane if I did."

"Deny what?" Ikiisa said.

"That this is *my* fault." Shean pressed a hand over her eyes. "My fault that Web was destroyed. My fault that my dolls died."

Ikiisa's panic was receding. So quickly, for one bizarre moment she thought it was leaving her and entering Shean, moving like an ocean retreating from its tide pools, recoiling toward the horizon and leaving a gulf of damp, pockmarked sand in its wake.

That was her, wasn't it? That hunched figure sitting across from her in a rumpled dress with hair in tangles, her leg in bandages, tears dripping between the gaps in her fingers? Wasn't that another Ikiisa softly weeping right there? A reflection. A mirror.

Ikiisa crawled out of her tide pool, across the damp sand. She reached for Shean, wondering if touching her would make one of them shatter.

"I'm not a guard dollmaker," Shean said, voice a whisper.

Ikiisa paused. Her hand lowered, flattening on the cool stone floor.

"I saw your license," she said after a confused moment.

Shean shook her head. She shifted, struggling for a moment before, with a faint whoosh of ribbons coming undone, she pulled the license in question out from a fold in her skirt. She slid the card across the floor and Ikiisa caught it, picking it up. Her eyes went to the licensor seal in the corner of the card, recognizing it, and its age, immediately.

"I stole Nock's license," Shean said. "At *my* licensing, Licensor Maton assessed Silver and gave me an artisan license. I was . . . upset, and ended up getting my license revoked." Shean took a deep breath. "I threatened to go and find a Shod with my dolls, to prove to everyone that they could be guards. To stop me from doing that, Nock begged me to come and meet you instead. He told me that if you approved of my dolls he'd ask the licensors to reconsider their decision. I agreed, but not because I wanted to talk to you. I thought that if I could replace you as the dollmaker of Web, I'd prove to Nock on my own terms that I was a guard dollmaker." Complexion ashen, Shean turned her face away from Ikiisa, the motion making her long hair fall down her shoulder, swinging forward to hide her expression. "I used that same threat of finding Shod to get Ilo to agree to consider me as Web's dollmaker."

"Oh," Ikiisa said, hand tightening on the edge of Nock's license. She wondered if it was surprise or shock or pain she was feeling. A combination of all three, probably. A thought struck her and she straightened. "*Oh*. Then your dolls . . ."

Shean shook her head. "They didn't fight the Shod. Roque told me the Shod killed them, and then I saw Silver die without fighting at all and I . . ." Her face puckered, scrunching up as fresh tears spilled from her eyes. She shook her head again, too overcome to speak.

Ikiisa wasn't sure what to say. A question as nebulous as "Why?" would profit an unclear, confused response. And asking Shean why she didn't want to be an artisan was foolish—she obviously wanted to be a guard dollmaker instead.

Ah. But that was the question, wasn't it?

"Why do you want to be a guard dollmaker?" Ikiisa asked, doing her best to speak gently. Harshness would do no good, not when Shean already had the look of a kicked hound.

Shean sniffed, pushing the hair back from her face. Pieces stuck to her damp cheeks, dark lines against flushed skin as she answered, voice raspy. "My family died in the Red Tide."

"You want to be a guard dollmaker to honor their memory?"

Shean heaved a sigh, sitting back against the wall and tilting her head up. Her eyes were closed, tears still sliding down her cheeks. "No. I was six when they died; I barely remember them. Sometimes I have flashes. My brother's eyes, or my father's laugh. My manma is all but gone, except for her hands. I remember how her hands felt when she braided my hair for me." She looked down at her own hands, fingers curling. After a moment she shook her head, looking at Ikiisa. "I honor my family's sacrifice. But I don't wish to be a dollmaker for their sakes."

"Why, then?"

Shean took a deep breath, closing her eyes again. When she opened them, she spoke in a rush.

"When the Red Tide swept Pearl I was almost killed. I was cornered between burning buildings, dozens of Shod climbing over one another to reach me. I was about to give into despair when a doll saved me." Her gaze grew distant with memory. "I can still remember the Shod struggling to reach me, gouging one another in their desperation to be the first to have a piece of me. I was dizzy and confused; I thought I could hear the Shod speaking to me. Terrible voices begging me for something:

"*'Please, please, please. Save me.'*"

Shean paused for breath, looking away from Ikiisa before continuing, as if she couldn't bear having an audience to her memory.

"I know those words were just my own thoughts, my own pleas that I confused with the Cry of the Shod. And then, as if answering me, help came from above." Shean looked up, as if seeing someone dropping down to carry her to safety. "I remember something grabbing my arms, the sensation of being lifted, the air roaring in my ears and the Shod Crying out after me. Their Cries faded and I was on a roof. Pearl stretched in all directions around me, all in flames for one moment before I was turned and held against a wooden chest. The doll that saved me protected me until the Red Tide receded. It stayed with me until its maker found us, until the flames died to embers. My rescuers. My heroes."

Shean's face was red with blush. She looked at Ikiisa, their eyes meeting as she finished.

"I wish to be a dollmaker to repay the debt I owe to the dollmaker who saved me—once I become renowned throughout the country called One, I'll seek out my saviors. And thank them."

"I understand," Ikiisa said, and she did. What Shean described, that great desire to repay someone who'd helped her, was similar to what Ikiisa felt toward Master Coen. Such emotions had driven her to keep trying to be a dollmaker all these years; the pain of letting Master Coen's teaching go to waste was worse than any abuse she received from clients.

Shean's gaze became pleading. She pressed her hands to the ground between her and Ikiisa, leaning forward. "I was sure. I was certain that my dolls were meant to be guards. That's what I've spent my whole life doing, making dolls to be guards. I didn't believe that I'd failed. I didn't want to . . . but now, how *can't* I?" Her head lowered, forehead almost touching the ground. "I'm sorry. I'm sorry this happened to Web because of me. I'm sorry my dolls are . . . that my dolls are what they are."

There were a few things Ikiisa could've said in response to the apology. A reprimand. A curse. Laughter, ironic as it would sound and be.

But those were unfair responses. Ikiisa's dolls *were* guard dolls, and little good that'd done them when the Shod attacked Web. If Shean's dolls weren't guard dolls, if they'd fallen to the Shod without a fight, that was only marginally worse than Ikiisa's dolls falling after a few minutes of struggle.

Ikiisa reached out. She touched the top of Shean's head and said what she wished people had said to her after so many mistakes, so many misunderstandings and incorrect conclusions.

"It's all right."

Shean's head jerked up, knocking Ikiisa's fingers away. Her eyes were wide, disbelieving. "You're not angry?"

Ikiisa forced a smile. "I don't think it's fair to blame you for what happened in Web."

"My dolls couldn't protect the village," Shean said, voice a protest.

"Neither could mine," Ikiisa said.

"They might've, though. If you'd been there at the beginning of the attack," Shean said. She pressed a hand to her chest. "If *I* hadn't made you leave Web."

Ikiisa waved a hand, feeling a little bubble of amusement. She'd never met anyone who'd *insist* on being reprimanded.

"There's no way of knowing if my being there would've done any good," she said. "From the sound of things, Roque was the only one who did anything *really* useful when the Shod attacked."

Shean opened her mouth to further protest, hesitated, and closed her mouth. She nodded.

"And," Ikiisa said on impulse, smile less strained, "for what it's worth, if *I* was the dollmaker who saved you, I'd be happy to see that you grew up to make such beautiful dolls." She thought of Master Coen as she spoke. He'd said something similar to her, once, when she'd been upset about her dolls being so different from those of other dollmakers. And not in a good way.

"Whose approval do you seek?" Coen had asked, tousling her hair as she leaned against him, weeping. "If it's mine, you have no need to fret. I'm proud to have an apprentice who makes such wonderfully unique dolls." He'd laughed when Ikiisa looked up at him in amazement. "Be proud of your work, little bird! Don't apologize for being different."

Shean snorted, disrupting Ikiisa's memory and turning the image of Master Coen's smile to mist. She sat up, rubbing her knuckles over her eyes. "Useless dolls, you mean," she said, voice full of disdain.

"Just because they can't fight the Shod doesn't make them useless," Ikiisa said.

"Right. They're plenty suited to being toys," Shean said, tone despairing.

Ikiisa frowned. "They don't have to be that, either."

Shean gave her a withering look. "If not art or guard, what *can* a doll be?"

"Anything they want!" Ikiisa said, tilting forward slightly. "Anything they *are*."

She was quoting Master Coen, and she spoke with too much conviction, too much passion—Shean gave her a funny look and Ikiisa's face flashed hot. Eyes dropping, she fiddled with the hem of her shirt, embarrassed by her own outburst. She didn't take the words back, though. They were true.

"Did you always know?" Shean asked.

"What?"

"That you were a guard dollmaker."

Ikiisa nodded.

"How?"

Now it was Ikiisa's turn to give Shean an odd look. "I asked my dolls."

Shean peered at her, like a child looking at a puzzle. "You . . . what?"

"Before my licensing, I asked them what they wanted to be. They told me they were guard dolls. Is that . . . is that odd?"

"They *spoke* to you?" Shean asked, questions of sanity buried behind the words.

Ikiisa blushed. "No. I asked if they wanted to be artisan dolls and they shook their heads 'no.'"

Shean blinked, looking owlish. After a moment she said, "I never thought to do that."

"So it *is* odd," Ikiisa said, laughing a weak laugh. She wasn't surprised—why had she assumed that something she'd done was something all other young dollmakers did? That'd never been the case before—why would it be true in this? Sighing, she ran a hand back through her hair, gaze dropping to her crossed legs.

"What made you think to ask?" Shean asked.

Ikiisa shrugged. "A part of me was hoping they'd be artisan dolls."

"Why?"

Ikiisa dropped her hand, clasping her ankles. "Artisan dolls are only bought by clients who really want and appreciate them."

"Oh." Shean was quiet for a moment. Then she heaved a sigh. "None of that really matters, now. What are we going to do?" She gestured as she spoke, indicating the walls of the hideout. Ikiisa couldn't hear any Shod trying to break in right now, but she doubted that meant they were gone; the Shod could be quiet if they wanted to be.

"We could wait until they leave Deep," Ikiisa said. "Shod tend to travel—once they finish with Web they'll move on. I doubt they'll stay for longer than a week. We could stay here until then."

Shean shook her head. "That won't work."

"Why not?"

"I doubt the villagers have food. Or water." Shean looked at the empty water flask next to her. "We don't, either."

Ikiisa's shoulders hunched. Shean was right—in her panic over Shean's wounds, Ikiisa hadn't thought to preserve a swallow of water. And she didn't have any food with her, either—she was used to foraging while traveling. Ducking her head, she let out a mumbled, "Sorry."

Shean shook her head, a strange pucker twisting her features. "No. *I'm* sorry. You were helping me by using up the water. I . . . appreciate that." The words were strained. And awkward. As if this was the first time Shean had ever thanked someone.

But that was ridiculous. Ikiisa gave an acknowledging nod, and the both of them lapsed into silence. Minutes ticked by, Ikiisa's back growing sore from leaning against the stone wall of the hideout. She tried to think up a plan to escape the Shod, but she couldn't imagine a course of action that didn't require a few dozen dolls being at her disposal.

"I wish we could make more dolls," she said, lamely. An impossible wish that, once voiced, didn't make her feel any better.

Shean straightened at the words, eyes widening. "More dolls?"

"That's the only thing I can think of that could hold the Shod off," Ikiisa said.

"You're right," Shean said, voice excited. "We need more dolls."

Ikiisa frowned, confused. "Yes, but . . . we can't *get* any."

"Maybe . . . you said your dolls were all killed by the Shod?"

"Almost all of them, yes."

"Then there are a few that survived?"

"Possibly. I called a retreat before all of them were destroyed."

"How many escaped?"

Ikiisa thought for a moment, settling on an estimation. "A dozen or so?"

"If you called all of your remaining dolls to you, how long do you think they could keep the Shod away?"

"Away from what?"

"You. Me."

"I . . . A few minutes? Ten at the most."

Shean nodded, a slow, thoughtful nod. A smile turned up the edges of her mouth, growing larger as she said, "Ten minutes. That's long enough."

"For what?" Ikiisa said, perplexed.

Shean's smile widened. "I think I know where we can get new dolls."

"What? Where?"

"Your house."

Ikiisa squinted. "There aren't any dolls in my house."

"I know. But there are mannequins." Shean leaned forward. "Many, many mannequins."

Ikiisa hadn't thought about that. Now she did—all of those abandoned projects, dozens of dolls in varying degrees of completion. She worried the hem of her shirt, torn between excitement at the idea and unease.

"But . . . the third edict of the First Dollmaker," she said, quoting: "'Dolls are to be of the finest caliber, crafted to a state as near to perfection as possible before the Breath Mark is placed upon them.'"

Shean waved away the edict. "Ideally, yes. Of course. But there's no edict that says incomplete mannequins *can't* be made into dolls, is there?"

There wasn't—piecemeal as they were, turning Ikiisa's mannequins into dolls was as simple as putting a Breath Mark on them. They wouldn't be very *good* dolls; dolls that'd be missing limbs and heads and other necessary things. But, as far as Ikiisa knew, they'd be able to fight the Shod, one way or the other. Maybe even long enough to give the villagers time to escape the forest called Deep.

However.

"The Shod have probably destroyed all of them already," Ikiisa said, hating to defuse the enthusiasm sizzling in Shean's expression but seeing no way around doing so.

Shean shook her head. "'The Shod are drawn to fine craftsmanship—they use our greatest creations to build themselves into stronger, deadlier forms,'" she said. Her eyes were shining, excited. "Edict eight of the First Dollmaker. The Shod are attracted to *well-made* things. Are unfinished mannequins well-made?"

"Well, no," Ikiisa said, slowly. What Shean was saying was making sense. Or, a sort of sense; her words were starting to sound less and less crazy.

"I suppose not," Ikiisa continued. "But that's for the Shod to decide, isn't it?"

"It's a risk," Shean said, nodding agreement. "We could find your house gutted and empty. And then we'll die. But if we find mannequins, new dolls to use against the Shod, we can drive them out of Deep!"

"But even if we do find mannequins, what if they aren't enough? What if the Shod win?"

"Then at the very least we can buy enough time for thc villagers to get out of Deep and head toward a city for help," Shean said. She patted the stone ground. "If that happens, we can hide here until more dollmakers come." She paused, cxpression sobering. "We'd have to find a way to let everyone know it's safe to escape, though."

Now it was Ikiisa's turn to smile, experiencing a faint spark of hope.

"You said Roque's with the villagers?" she asked.

Shean frowned. "Yes?"

"Then I have a way."

Ikiisa picked up her pendant. She held it to her lips as Shean stared at her in confusion.

"Roque," Ikiisa said, smiling at Shean. "We need you."

ROQUE, TRAVELING LINGUIST AND TRANSLATOR, THUMBED THROUGH HIS LEXIcon, looking for a useful Mark and having no luck.

The Marks filed under *Destruction* were wild, untamable as forest fires—a wise man wouldn't use them when there were people around he'd like to keep alive. And Roque really would like to keep the villagers huddled across from him, all shivery and weepy in the dark of the sanctuary tree, alive. Given that, the Water and Wind Marks were also bad. The few Weather Marks he had were useless in context (if only the Shod had some silly weakness, like being vulnerable to sunlight and clear skies, or a tendency to melt in the rain), and the handful of Health Marks he had were only advantageous if the Shod needed head colds and mild abrasions cured. Even the

Marks he'd just gathered from the country called Structured—what he was calling the Build Marks—powerful as they were, would do nothing against the Shod. Craft-based as those Marks were, and given the Shod's notorious love of well-crafted things, they might even make things worse.

The Unnotice Mark would be an option, if Roque was certain it'd be effective on the Shod. The Unnotice Mark didn't fool most animals, and, even if they'd once been dolls, he felt the Shod were closer to animal than person; there was also a strong possibility that if he put the Unnotice Mark on the villagers of Web, one of them would go missing. Forever. A possibility that'd lead to a furthering of an already healthy guilty conscience on Roque's part, which he didn't like.

And, besides all that, it didn't sit well with him, the idea of giving a Mark to the villagers of Web. He wasn't in the habit of spreading Marks; on the contrary, a key component of his travels was taking Marks *away*. To do otherwise would be counterintuitive.

Not that counterintuitivity was lacking in his existence. As complicated (and, by and large, negative) his feelings toward Marks were, Roque couldn't deny their usefulness. Time and time again he'd seen people rely on Marks to the point of detriment, but, just as often, Marks had stood as a singular defense for societies against dangers of various forms. Without Breath-Marked dolls, for example, the country called One would've languished into Shod-orchestrated ruin long ago. Similarly, without Roque finding it within himself to overcome his distaste and think of a Mark or two to help the villagers of Web, their dire situation could become deadly.

Even if the cost of him helping was the risk of introducing new Marks into an environment that might (as so many had before it) suffer greatly from the addition.

Hurt and help. Benefit and punish. That was how Marks worked. Sometimes it took a while for the good to leak away to reveal the bad, but, no matter *how* long that revelation took to come, it always did. Marks *always* warped the people and places around them.

No one understood that better than Roque himself. Sighing, he made a conscious effort to push aside his misgivings, hoping good would last longer than bad in this case as he moved past the sections of known Marks at the front of his lexicon and flipped through the dozen or so pages he had of untested Marks, symbols gathered during his travels that might or might not be powerful and useful. Might or might not be Marks at all, for that matter—so many aesthetics had sprung from the original Marks, it was sometimes difficult to tell an allusion from a genuine. Even for Roque, who'd seen many of the Marks created.

Still, he scanned his notes on a few of the unknown Marks, impatience tempting him to throw caution to the wind and try one or two of them. Especially the one he thought was a Time Mark—it was either that or a Destruction Mark, though, capable of disintegrating any living thing in a three-mile radius. And right now just wasn't an appropriate time for experimentation. Especially experimentation that could end in explosions.

Roque spread his lexicon out in front of him, smoothing its pages down and tapping its corners with thoughtful fingers. From his experience with the Shod he knew that no Mark was effective in killing the monsters—not the Incendiary Mark or the Rend Mark or the Wound Mark. Even the Death Mark, a Mark so wicked Roque had to be forced to the brink of desperation (which was no small feat) before resorting to using it, had only made the Shod he wrote it on shudder, pause, then continue to try and strip away his flesh with renewed fervor.

Perhaps if he drew the Rend Mark on the ground at the Shod's feet . . . but, no. The size of the resulting rend was out of his control—the ground would open up under the Shod's feet, yes, but there was a fair chance it'd open up under his and the villagers' feet as well. He'd experienced being stuck in a crack of the earth before, and it was *not* a situation he was eager to repeat.

He could use a Cut Mark to fell a few dozen trees on top of the Shod. While the monsters were trapped, the villagers could run for the edge of the woods, and, hopefully, escape. After a moment of thought, he decided that was a reasonable option, filing it away for later consideration.

Just then the Shod, who'd fallen relatively quiet in recent minutes, chose to renew their attack. Roque jumped as the wall he leaned against bucked, replying to the impact of something large striking its other side. He lifted his head and listened to the Shod, who really were doing their best to break in: scuffling around the tree's roots, raking through dirt and pawing handfuls of soil to the side with steady, rhythmic thumping while other monsters barraged the tree with rapid pummels, ramming themselves against the bark as they tried to create an opening for themselves. And all the while they sobbed, wailed, wept.

Cried.

They wouldn't succeed. What they scored their claws on was not wood but something stronger than metal, more unrelenting than stone. With the Shelter Mark in place, this tree was made a fortress. One under siege.

Roque abhorred sieges. They were simultaneously stressful and exceedingly boring.

A cry sounded, much closer and more immediate than the muffled sobs of the Shod. The noise was quickly hushed, and Roque looked at the villagers huddled across from him, a tight knot of shaking arms and hunched heads. At first they'd tried to shuffle as far back from the front of the tree as they could. When the Shod had started attacking from every direction they'd scurried to the center of the sanctuary, now a cluster gathered as far away from all walls as possible. They reminded Roque of the crag birds back in the country called Steep: typified by traveling in flocks, easily frightened, and prone to congregating when a threat larger than a grass mouse was nearby.

No one had spoken a word to Roque since Shean had dragged him inside the tree, forcing him to seal himself in with the villagers or risk the Shod breaking in and slaughtering everyone. Not being spoken to was fine, though; Roque wasn't in the mood to deal with the spiraling, irrational logic of frightened people. What was needed right now was calm thought.

Not that calm thinking was getting him anywhere. The way he saw things, they had two options in regards to surviving the Shod. First, they could wait and hope the Shod would go away. This was the least appealing idea for several reasons, the least of which being that the villagers had no supplies to sustain them if the Shod decided to linger in Deep like the smell of rotting milderberries in high summer—rancid and thick and persisting for months. If Roque had a Sustenance Mark things would be different, but he didn't. For years he'd searched, and never before had he so wished he'd found one—the idea of the villagers of Web dying from starvation or dehydration, each new death adding a stench of rot to the tree until Roque gagged with each breath, was extremely unappealing.

The second option was for him to open the door of the sanctuary and leave, using a Mark or two to do his best to handle the Shod. The thought of giving himself over to the monsters made his heartbeat quicken with dreadful memories of the last time he'd done so, but it'd been a long time since he'd felt enough fear to stop him from facing anything, be they fiends or ghosts or people.

If he opened the door, though, there was a good chance the Shod would get in. He'd keep most of them from slithering into the tree, but just one Shod was enough to kill the couple hundred people shivering and sweating before him. They all had just one life. One fragile, easily stolen, life.

Like Shean. She'd sacrificed her delicate life to try and save his. For all he knew, Ikiisa was dead, too.

Two more regrets to add to an already long list.

Roque rubbed a hand down his face, exhausted in a way that had nothing to do with his physical state. He couldn't open the door. And he wouldn't sit here and watch dozens of people starve to death, either. Neither option was viable. Which meant he was back to square one.

A thought struck him, and he glanced at his travel pack, unbuttoned and laid out at his side. Through its opened top he could just see the bone handle of the paintbrush he'd picked up in a place simply known as the King's Lands, the carved grip white and stark in the dim light of the tree. The brush could make portals into worlds you painted with it; a reality Roque had experienced in a very intimate, maddening way.

Roque considered the brush, for a moment tempted—a painted portal to another world seemed a sure way of escaping the Shod.

But getting out of those damned paintings had been one of the most unpleasant things he'd ever done—he'd had to use the Transport Mark, arguably the most unstable of all Marks, to return to reality. The first time he'd used such a Mark, when he was younger and foolhardy, he'd found himself thrown into a vortex in the middle of a cerulean sea. The second time he'd used the Mark, when he'd been desperate enough to leave those paintings to risk another vortex, he'd fallen out of the sky and into a city, by luck avoiding impaling himself on any spires but breaking every bone in his body when he crashed down onto a cobbled street, barely avoiding taking a passing woman into the dust with him. An event that'd led to a whole slew of troubles.

Roque folded his arms, resisting the urge to spiral into the unfathomable debts of his own memory. Instead, he focused intently on the feel of the hard ground under him, the whimpering of the villagers of Web, the relentless wailing of the Shod. Anchoring himself to these realities, he turned himself away from his own regrettable tendency to dwell on the past and focused on the now; the point was, there was no telling where the Transport Mark would take a person. And with about two hundred people in tow, using such an uncertain method to escape, either from this tree or from the dimensions the paintbrush could create, would be even riskier. Maybe even impossible.

So no to using the brush. Or the Transport Mark.

Unless there was no other option.

Wistfully, Roque imagined having the Marks of getaway and evasion: the Escape Marks. True, he had no concrete proof such Marks existed, but he knew Feah. He was sure she'd thought up Marks that provided avenues of escape in the case of emergencies, as little good they'd done her in the end. But he'd never seen such Marks used, had no idea where to look to find them—for all he knew, they were among the Lost Marks, burned away from the memory of humankind in the many decades since the Mountain Queen's fall.

He also wished that knowing what he did about the Shod now, that they were the dolls of the dead, sparked ideas for new ways to fight them. But the information had yet to elicit any revelations—nice as it was to know the origins of the monsters, at the moment he couldn't think of how that knowledge was of any practical use.

The only idea he had, in fact, was that the Shod could, perhaps, be turned back into dolls if their dollmakers were brought back to life. But Roque, fool as he was in many ways, was not quite foolish enough to attempt raising the dead.

He was, after all, living proof of why such should never be done.

So he sat against the wall and listened to the Shod, lexicon spread pointlessly open before him, hoping the monsters would eventually lose interest and leave. Knowing they wouldn't.

One of the villagers was crying. A little girl. The one Shean's doll had sacrificed itself for. She'd been crying since Roque had sealed the door, but only now did he watch her. She huddled against her grandmother's side, clutching the notebook she'd risked her life for, sobbing so hard, yet softly—her face was contorted in a quiet twist of agony. And guilt.

Roque sympathized. He'd enough deaths on his head to last fifty lifetimes—he knew what it was like, seeing someone die because of you. It wasn't something that ever ceased to haunt you, even when enough days passed for you to not see her face every time you closed your eyes, hear his last words every night while you lay awake, frightened to sleep.

The little girl wasn't the only one crying. Many of the villagers sat hunched, hands cupping mouths to muffle sobs. The adults, more practiced at bottling grief, wept silently, wiping at their eyes with the sleeves of their shirts. The young adults were similarly discreet, as were the eldest children. The young ones, though, wailed, increasingly ignoring the urges to hush from parents as their fear made their small frames tremble, their pale faces splotch with distress.

The tears were unpleasant to watch. They made Roque start remembering things again. Think about things better not thought about.

He wanted to turn away from the villagers. But he didn't. The day he looked away from someone's tears was the day he gave up for good. Sometimes he thought that day had already come. But no. Not yet.

Not just yet.

"Roque. We need you."

Ikiisa's voice arrived in a crash, vibrating Roque's bones and swelling between his ears, intimate as his own private thoughts. He lost a breath in surprise, never prepared for the moment someone called out to him. Surprise gave way to relief, though, his body relaxing with the knowledge that Ikiisa was safe. He knew at once where she was—sheltering in a pile of boulders, a hideout made some decades ago by a dollmaker of Web who'd liked privacy. Roque felt an intense, deep compulsion to go to Ikiisa. To answer her summons, the way he'd answered another's long ago.

There'd been a time when Roque couldn't resist such an impulse. At the mere whisper of his name he'd be on his feet, lunging toward wherever the person speaking to him was, desperate to reach them and help them in whatever way they needed helping. Over the years, though, he'd grown practiced in resisting that desire until it became a mere thought, a fancy that, if he chose, he could ignore for varying lengths of time (his record was five, highly uncomfortable, years). Ultimately he had no choice but to answer the call of the person speaking to the Summon Mark. But he could take his time getting to them.

As he did now. His legs twitched and, with firmness, he stilled them, the moment of intense desire to run to Ikiisa passing and settling into a dull pressure at the back of his head. He relaxed, listening as Ikiisa went on.

"Shean and I have a plan. We're going to fight the Shod to give you a chance to get the villagers out of Deep."

So Shean was alive. With a soft, grateful sigh, Roque mentally struck her from the list of lives he'd taken.

"This is our plan," Ikiisa said. Roque listened to her explain an idea involving mannequins and buying time that was more reasonable than any of the ideas he'd come up with. Dangerous, but far less likely to end in Roque getting people killed or accidentally creating a new gorge through Deep.

Ikiisa finished by saying, *"I'll tell you when it's safe to run."*

Roque nodded, a silly thing to do given Ikiisa couldn't see him. A smile lifted the side of his mouth. *This is the Ikiisa I remember,* he thought, mind turning to when they'd met, some twenty years ago. It'd been during his first trip to the country called One; having heard of their dollmakers and dolls, he'd come to study both the Breath Mark and the Shod, suspecting the Shod themselves had a Mark.

Dolls had been easy enough to come by—everyone in One seemed to own one or more, and, though it was illegal for foreigners such as himself to study the Breath Mark, Roque had managed to pin a doll down long enough to find, and record, the Mark. Finding Shod, though, had been trickier. He'd been forced to leave the coastline and travel deeper into the country, where guard dolls were infrequent and less efficient. He'd nearly reached the city called Glass when he'd finally found Shod.

Many Shod, in fact. Dozens that swarmed and latched upon him, dragging him from the road and into a ditch with pleading wails, desperate cries that, wordless as they were, implored for relief from endless torment.

He could offer no such relief. He could, though, serve as a distraction. And he did. For hours the Shod had carved into him, trying and failing to make him a part of themselves. But no matter how hard they tried, he couldn't be dismembered or killed.

The pain had been tremendous. And endless. Being eaten alive in a body that couldn't die . . . More than once Roque had tried to run, pushing himself to his feet and attempting to throw the Shod off him. When he proved incapable of such a feat, he'd crawled with the Shod dragging behind him, almost making it back to the road several times but, ultimately, always pulled back into the ditch.

I'm trapped, he'd thought, hands gripping the gore-slick ground and finding no purchase, holding on to nothing. *Maybe these monsters will actually succeed. Maybe I'll die.*

At that thought he'd stopped trying to escape. The Shod had torn at him, pulled strips of skin from his body, sometimes digging deep enough to strike bone before his muscles reknit, his skin resealed. He'd endured the agony and waited to see if it'd ever stop.

And then he'd heard her voice.

No words, but a shout—a cry of alarm, and then the hiss and whistle of new creatures, creatures pouncing on the Shod and driving them away. A face above Roque's, two bright, wide eyes, a mouth that moved fast and spoke words muffled through the blood pooled in his ears. A child. A little girl. First she'd dragged him from the ditch. Then she'd gathered him in her twiggy arms, holding him as if he was fragile.

"Don't die," she'd said, the first of her words Roque understood. She'd begun crying, tears warm through the blood on his face.

"Don't die! Don't die! Please!"

"I won't," Roque had said. She'd lifted her face, staring at him with such amazement, he knew she'd thought he was already dead. "I won't die."

And then Roque had cried, weeping in a way he hadn't in years because it'd been years, *decades*, since someone had wept over him, and he'd forgotten what that felt like. Years, decades, since he'd come so close to the brink of despair. He'd forgotten what *that* felt like, too.

So he'd lifted his hands and pressed the heels of his palms against his eyes, curled on his side in Ikiisa's lap, and let her hold him as he cried.

More than her intervening to drive off the Shod attacking him, her letting him cry like that was why Roque gave Ikiisa a Summon Mark. A reward for her compassion, as well as for her willingness to help someone in need, even when doing so put herself at risk. Just like she was doing now.

Heart feeling lighter with the knowledge that he could—*finally*—do something, Roque gathered his lexicon, slid it into his travel bag, and stood. Some of the villagers flinched as he did so, watching him with wary eyes as he approached their protective huddle. He stopped close to them, pulling the strap of his bag onto his shoulder and speaking in a voice loud enough to be heard by all.

"Dollmakers Shean and Ikiisa are going to give us a chance to escape."

"How could you know that?" the man named Ilo asked, voice gruff with accusation.

"I've methods of contact with Ikiisa," Roque said.

"*What* methods?" Ilo asked. He stood, the other villagers doing the same, until Roque faced hundreds of frightened, untrusting eyes.

"Methods," Roque said. He rested a hand on his hip and met the gazes of the villagers of Web, gesturing to the sanctuary tree. "I've already saved your lives once. I've given you no reason to believe I'll harm you. So you *must* trust me. It's that, or death." He looked at Ilo. "I'm not lying."

Ilo hesitated, sharing looks with those around him. After a long moment, he looked back at Roque, not happy, but no longer outright hostile, either. "Fine," he said.

"Good," Roque said. "Allow me to explain."

SHEAN WAS FORCED TO STOOP WHEN SHE STOOD, THE CEILING OF THE HIDEOUT so low the top of her head brushed rock before she was even halfway risen. Her resulting, cramped discomfort wasn't helped when putting weight on her left leg made her ankle sear, the cuts on her leg blazing. She grimaced, but forced herself to stand as normally as possible, taking the skirts of her dress up around her legs, wrapping and tying them in a way that eliminated their power to trip her. The weight of the jeweled beads in the fabric, once so appealing, made her wish she was wearing something lighter.

"You're sure you're going to be all right?" Ikiisa asked. She was crouched at the front of the hideout, ready to pull the lever that'd open the door. Once she did that she'd call her dolls to her, and she and Shean would have to run. Fast.

The thought of running made Shean's knees wobble. But she nodded as she limped forward, stopping next to Ikiisa. "I'll be fine. It doesn't hurt that much," she lied, batting Ikiisa's hand away when it reached out to touch her bandages. "I'm *fine*. I'm not even bleeding anymore."

That would change when she started moving around—they both knew that. But Ikiisa was wise enough not to offer any further protests; they'd already wasted breath arguing about Ikiisa going and executing the plan alone, weighing the pros and cons of Shean staying behind in the hideout. Shean had won the argument in the end by pointing out that, firstly, Ikiisa's chances of getting enough mannequins turned into dolls quickly enough all on her own were slim; secondly, Ikiisa couldn't *stop* Shean from following her into Web; and thirdly, that leaving Shean behind would just mean leaving her vulnerable to the Shod.

"All right," Shean said, setting her feet and gritting her teeth. "I'm ready."

Ikiisa looked at her, the light of their glow lantern, currently clutched in her hand, casting a faint blue nimbus around her. "Remember, if the mannequins are gone or they don't hold against the Shod, we come back here."

Shean suppressed the urge to roll her eyes. "Yes."

"And if the mannequins *are* working, we tell Roque so he can get the villagers out of Deep."

Shean still had a hard time believing the claims Ikiisa made about her pendant. She nodded anyway.

Still Ikiisa hesitated. "The fastest way to my house is straight through Web," she said, "but the town square will be full of Shod. I think it'll be safer to run around the edge of Web, and avoid being seen for as long as possible."

Shean waved an impatient hand. "Fine. Whatever you think is best."

"All right," Ikiisa said. "Ready?"

Shean squared her shoulders and put from her mind her injuries, the memory of her dolls in pieces, the image of Silver exploding after letting out one, haunting word. She would think about all that later. For now, her attention had to be fixed on getting to Web and finding Ikiisa's mannequins. She focused on that.

"Ready," she said.

Ikiisa nodded. She grabbed the lever and took a loud breath, bracing herself. Then she pulled down, and with a grind of stone on stone the hideout opened. Starlight spilled over them, a silver radiance that outlined Ikiisa as she darted outside. She emitted a warbling whistle that, if Shean wasn't looking at the source of the sound, could be taken for birdsong. Dark shapes dropped down from the trees, surrounding Ikiisa with responding whistles as Shean staggered outside. She counted ten dolls, including the one she recognized as Bobble.

Close by, a Shod let out a Cry. The shriek was answered and joined, the crack of trampled undergrowth filling the night and racing toward where Ikiisa and Shean stood.

So fast, Shean thought.

Ikiisa whirled, grabbing Shcan's hand. She was surprised by the gesture, her initial instinct to yank her hand away. Then she looked at Ikiisa's face. Their gazes locked for a heartbeat, and Shean saw her rapid, nervous pulse reflected by the bright alarm in Ikiisa's eyes.

Ikiisa was shaking. So was Shean.

Shean curled her fingers around Ikiisa's, holding her hand back.

Together they ran.

IKIISA MUST'VE CHANGED HER MIND ABOUT WHAT ROUTE THEY'D TAKE TO HER house because the moment they reached the edge of Web she led

Shean toward the town center. With Shod snapping at their heels, Shean didn't protest.

If it was possible for Shod to be glutted, the ones in Web were. They bumbled around in irregular staggers, bundled so thickly by the woven branches of destroyed houses they resembled coarse, prickly sheep. Running into the village with Ikiisa, already breathless and left leg wet and frighteningly numb, Shean hoped that meant the Shod would be sluggish. Or, at the very least, too preoccupied with the new additions to their bodies to pay her and Ikiisa any mind.

No such luck. The moment they broke into the village, sprinting for the path to Ikiisa's house while her dolls ran in a tight circle around them, the Shod charged.

The night was dark, the moons barely twin slivers in the sky and the stars' light not enough to go by. Ikiisa still held the glow lantern, the lamp swinging in a frantic blur that gave Shean flashes of clear sight as the dolls running next to her intercepted the Shod diving to tackle her. She heard more than saw Ikiisa's dolls fight, the clash of wood on twig, cracks and shrills as Shod howled and dolls let out piercing, whistled notes.

Shean flinched as something brushed her good ankle, not hard enough to hurt but with a snap that spoke of a near-miss. Something snagged on the edge of her dress, yanking her an unplanned step to the right before, with a rip of fabric and a faint click of jewel beads falling to the ground, she tore free. Sweat ran down the sides of her neck, making her dress stick to her back as, in the corners of her eyes, indistinct shapes writhed and twisted, some protecting her, some reaching for her, the difference impossible to tell.

Ikiisa's pace picked up, the tight grip she had on Shean's hand relentless, compelling her to run faster. They crossed the town square and reached the path to her house, forced to jump and scramble over rubble from the homes that had, just hours ago, flanked the road. Now the structures lay in fragmented piles that spanned twice the amount of area they had as houses, all spiky edges of ruin. As they navigated the debris Shean was glad to have Ikiisa's hand; she almost fell twice, rescued when Ikiisa used their laced fingers to pull her steady.

Only two dolls were still with them by the time they cleared the rubble and ran the final stretch to Ikiisa's house, guards flanking their sides. The sound of conflict was a racket behind them, the Shod held back by Ikiisa's dolls long enough to allow them room to breathe.

Which was good, because breath was *not* coming easily—Shean could feel herself slowing down. The pain of her injuries was no longer stark, but her leg was starting to refuse to respond to her, dragging behind her when she tried to run faster. Ikiisa noticed her lagging, glancing over her shoulder. By the light of the lantern her concern was evident. Her mouth opened, as if she was about to ask a question. Before she could a scream broke through the night, loud enough to make Shean's ears ring. She looked back toward Web, and wished she hadn't.

The Shod had broken through Ikiisa's dolls and were shooting out of the village. They appeared to have latched on to one another, many individual Shod becoming one huge Shod that, framed against the starry sky, looked like a giant, twiggy insect, haphazard bulges and spikes rising from a cylindrical shape. Its shadow fell over Shean, her view of the heavens blocked. In this new darkness she found a final burst of energy, her leg half-cooperating again for the last, breathless moment it took for her and Ikiisa to reach their destination.

They had to pause before entering the house, long enough for Ikiisa to yank the door open. In that brief moment Shean saw, with blurry relief, that the house was, for the most part, intact; missing parts of its roof and decidedly more lopsided than it'd been before, but still upright. Which was more than could be said of any other house in Web.

Ikiisa had the door open. Shean was forced inside, her hand released while the two dolls escorting them rushed into the hallway, Ikiisa bolting the door behind them. Shean slumped against the wall, left leg shaking so hard she almost fell. One of Ikiisa's dolls, Bobble, pushed up against her before her leg gave out, giving her something to lean on, which she did. She also bent over, resting a hand on her good knee and taking deep, gasping breaths. In the gloom she could just make out the dark stains soaking the bandages over her wounds. The sight made her dizzy.

Her respite was short-lived—the next moment Ikiisa grabbed her hand again, forcing her forward.

"The door won't hold, and they might try to crush the house!" Ikiisa said, forced to shout over the howls of the Shod.

Shean couldn't argue with that—before they were even halfway down the hall the door behind them cracked, splinters striking the back of her neck. She dared a look over her shoulder as Ikiisa pulled her around a corner, skin crawling as her gaze was met by dozens of white, glowing eyes.

While the Shod's Crying (which never before had so reminded Shean of weeping children) grew in volume and pitch, Ikiisa led the way around another turn, into a room fragrant with the scent of ink and paint. Shean gasped in relief to see piles of mannequins stacked around the room, rifled through, knocked over and left lying crooked on the floor, but otherwise untouched. She shared a hopeful look with Ikiisa.

"I'll get something to write with," Ikiisa said, letting go of Shean's hand and rushing forward. She nearly tripped when the house lurched around them, rocking to the side as if a large hammer had smacked into its side. Shean grabbed onto the wall to steady herself, watching the ceiling shift and creak ominously while Ikiisa shoved mannequins aside, looking for and then finding an art chest, which she ripped open with the shrill of old hinges. A thumping noise came from near the front of the house, the Shod growing louder, and Shean flinched, glancing back the way they'd come. When she turned Ikiisa was on her feet, thrusting a paintbrush into one of Shean's hands, an inkwell into the other. She ran back to the art box, grabbed supplies of her own, and scooped up the glow lantern, setting the lamp at Shean's feet.

"You give Breath Marks to the mannequins here," Ikiisa said, words thrown over her shoulder as she dashed out of the room. "I'll go upstairs and get those ones!" Then, like an afterthought, "Bobble, stay with Shean!"

Bobble whistled a confirming note while the other remaining doll followed Ikiisa. Wasting no time, Shean limped to the nearest mannequin, crouching next to it, uncorking her inkwell and dipping her brush into the smooth black liquid. She started painting a Breath Mark across what might've been intended to be the mannequin's face. The wood was unfinished—lacking polish and rough, in need of sanding. Shean's teeth gritted together as she struggled to draw smooth lines, her efforts resulting in the ugliest Breath Mark she'd ever drawn. Ugly, but effective; the moment the ink dried the mannequin shuddered, pushing itself upright on its two arms, Breath-Marked head swinging toward Shean.

"Good!" Shean gasped, standing to hobble past the new doll, brush outstretched to the next mannequin. And after that one, the next. And the one after that. And after that. And after that.

There were so many mannequins, some the size of her palm, others as large as people. When they came to life she ordered them away from remaining mannequins, but before long she was having trouble shifting past dolls to reach their unfinished siblings. It didn't help that Bobble stuck to her side like a needy hound pup, holding the glow lantern up and coming close to tripping her more than once before she told it to stay back.

The house continued to sway as she worked, a constant reminder of the urgency of the situation and the need for speed. Luckily, Shean was well-practiced at drawing the Breath Mark—her childhood schoolmates hadn't called her "Scribbles" for nothing. She painted the Mark on mannequins so fast her wrist ached, finishing every figure in the room just minutes after Ikiisa left.

The result of her efforts was a room crammed full of truly pathetic dolls. Shean took in their incomplete shapes, their asymmetrical stances and torsos that lacked sufficient support, many a doll slumping on the ground like exhausted old men. Staring at them, Shean felt doubt about their usefulness against the Shod.

But it wouldn't do for her to second-guess herself now. She ignored her worry and the trembling of her hands. She even ignored the blood sliding down her foot, oozing from under her bandages and filling her shoe with thick, sticky wet.

"Shod are attacking us!" Shean said to the mannequin-dolls. She pointed. "Barricade the doors of this house for as long as you can!"

The mannequin-dolls hooted and wheezed consent, trundling

off in painfully slow lopes. What speed could be hoped for, though, from incomplete dolls? Ignoring the panic ramming through her like a spike, Shean followed the mannequin-dolls out of the painting room, moving on to the next room and its mannequins. Once she finished that room she went on to the next. And the next, until she'd gone into every room on the bottom floor of Ikiisa's house and emptied it of mannequins.

As she worked things grew increasingly quiet. And still. By the time Shean was drawing the final line of the Breath Mark on the last mannequin in the last room, minutes had passed since she'd heard a Shod wail, or felt the walls around her shake. This fact didn't register until she'd finished the last mannequin and the thing wobbled upright, consenting to her order to fight the Shod with a wheeze and staggering off. Shean stood, wiping sweat from her brow with the back of her hand, blinking through the gloom of the room she was in, a part of her overwhelmed by its emptiness, her hands twitching and telling her she had to keep going, to keep drawing the Breath Mark even though her fingers hurt and her leg was still bleeding and she felt lightheaded.

But there were no more mannequins to work on. Things were so quiet. Shean looked at Bobble the doll, standing a few paces from her with the glow lantern lifted to help her see.

"Are there any rooms we missed?" she asked. Bobble swung its head in what Shean took as a negative gesture. The doll emitted a whistle that sounded pleased.

Shoving the inkwell and brush Ikiisa had given her into the pocket of her dress, Shean limped out of the room, into the hallway. Her head turned as she heard the pounding of feet to her left, a steady *thunk-thunk-thunk*, like someone coming down a set of stairs. Shean headed toward the sound, voice lifting through the quiet.

"Ikiisa?"

"Shean!" came the reply, louder than expected.

They rounded a corner at the same time, colliding. Ikiisa came in at a run; Shean was thrown back against the wall with a jar that made her leg scream and her vision, for one fraught moment, go black. When her eyes cleared she saw Ikiisa had fallen, kneeling in the hallway with both her dolls hovering around her in an anxious way. Murmuring soft words of pain, Ikiisa picked herself up, wincing when she looked down at her knees, her trousers torn to reveal scuffs and blood.

"Sorry," Ikiisa said, and for the first time in what felt like hours her voice wasn't a shout.

"I finished all the mannequins," Shean said, voice winded as she pushed herself away from the wall. Ikiisa's eyes widened.

"Really? All of them?"

"All the ones I could find on this floor."

Ikiisa pointed at the ceiling. "I finished all the ones upstairs."

"I sent mine out to the Shod."

"I did too."

A crashing noise from outside echoed through the house, muffled and distant. Shean shared a look with Ikiisa. They both turned, hurrying to the front door.

The night air was blessedly cool, making the sweat on Shean's face prickle as she stepped outside. She only enjoyed the relief from the stuffiness of the house for a moment; the next her attention was stolen by the giant shapes wrestling on the path between her and the remnants of Web.

At first glance, it looked like Shod fighting each other. Two of the massive insect-shaped Shod from earlier snapping and curling, taking turns throwing each other to the ground, creating massive clouds of dust and making the trees ringing Web sway. It was impossible to tell which was winning, and equally difficult to tell the two monsters apart. Except, of course, in the moments when they broke apart, heartbeats when their separate shapes were distinct.

Ikiisa let out a gasp. Shean looked to find the woman pointing at one of the giant Shod.

"Mannequins," she said, and Shean realized she was right. The distinction was subtle; one of the giants was covered in the woven walls of Web, looking like balls of spiderweb knitted together. The other giant was edged in unblurred spikes, lacking a sense of conformity in the absence of twigs.

It wasn't two monsters made from hundreds of Shod fighting in front of them. It was *one* monster made from hundreds of Shod and one *protector* made from many faulty mannequin-dolls. The mannequin-dolls were mimicking the Shod, combined together into one giant doll.

A giant doll driving a giant Shod back.

"We . . . we're winning," Shean said.

"Yes!" Ikiisa shouted, so loud Shean winced. The woman threw a fist into the air, jumping up and down. Shean would've jumped for joy too, if doing so wouldn't have made what remained of the scabs on her left leg crack open and bleed. She settled for smiling a wide smile, heart lifting as she watched the Shod recoil from the pummels and snaps of the mannequin-dolls, overwhelmed by the sheer number of dolls and falling back, getting closer and closer to the edge of Web, moments from being driven into the forest called Deep, chased through the trees and forced away, away from the hollow tree where Roque and the villagers sheltered.

The plan, *Shean's* plan, was working.

She'd made a mistake with Web. With her dolls. She'd been wrong about everything she'd thought was true. That fact still made her head spin.

But, if nothing else, she was finding a way to correct her mistakes. The sight of the mannequin-dolls smacking into the Shod so hard the monsters' construction fell apart, individual Shod showering to the ground in spins and bounces, brought tears to Shean's eyes. A smile of relief trembled across her lips.

With a cry of triumph to match what Shean felt inside her chest, Ikiisa lifted her pendant, shouting.

"Roque! Now!"

"NOW!"

This time, when Ikiisa's voice swept through him Roque was ready. Without hesitation he pushed on the door of the tree sanctuary, opening the shelter while Ikiisa's voice echoed in his head.

The sounds of Shod trying to get into the tree had ceased some time ago, and Roque was relieved when he stepped outside to find only traces of the monsters: claw marks in the ground and upon the tree, footprints in the loam too wide and long and three-toed to be human. Fresh leftovers, but leftovers nonetheless—even when he stooped to pick up a rock, whipping it into the canopy over his head and then performing the same check on the undergrowth nearest him, nothing stirred. His thrown rocks didn't bounce off wood or strike hollow heads with telltale thumps. The Shod, it seemed, really were gone.

For now.

"Quickly," Roque said, turning and waving for the villagers of Web to come out of the sanctuary. They did, and he waited until every person passed him before following, taking the rear of the pack as the villagers, far more acquainted with the forest called Deep than he, raced through the trees, headed to the edge of the woods with a surefootedness comparable to the fleet, springing sprints of deer.

As he ushered people forward, watching for stragglers, Roque listened to the forest behind him. He could hear Shod Crying, still. Distantly. He felt vibrations under his feet, subtle lurches that reminded him of his days in the country called Steep, especially during the great upheavals before the Mountain Queen's ascension. Explosions couldn't be causing the shaking of the ground—he'd hear them. Something very large falling, then? Something very large being knocked over?

Roque was distracted enough by these questions that he didn't notice the girl until he ran into her. She let out a squeak and he caught her before she fell, hand seizing her shoulder to keep her upright. He felt a shock at how bony her frame was; she felt delicate enough to snap in response to an accidentally rough touch.

She pushed back against his hold, staring up at him with wide brown eyes, and Roque recognized her as the child from before, the one with the notebook. Which she currently had wrapped in her arms, held against her chest the way he'd seen some children hold comfort rags and what Roque personally thought of as dolls (soft-fabricked and cotton-stuffed constructions, like the wolf doll he'd had as a child).

"What're you doing?" he asked her, noting that she was turned around, not facing the way out of the woods like the rest of the villagers. Her grandmother was nowhere to be seen, perhaps under the impression that the girl was at her side, or at least close behind her. Roque frowned. "Your gran will worry."

Distress and fear and guilt mingled across the girl's features, tugging at her eyebrows and pinching her mouth, the emotions congealing into a general sense of desperation that came out in her quivering, quavering voice.

"Y-you said that Dollmaker Shean and Dollmaker Ikiisa are back in W-Web."

"Yes."

"W-will t-they b-b-be okay?"

She sounded like she wanted to cry. She looked it, too.

Roque let go of her. She took a step back, hunched like she was scared of him. Given how she looked at him, she probably was. He was used to that—he unnerved himself, even. In more ways than anyone knew.

Given his effect on people, he was also used to putting them at ease. Which he did now, smiling and speaking gentle words. "You're very kind to worry for them. But Dollmakers Shean and Ikiisa are just that—dollmakers. They've studied and dealt with the Shod their entire lives. We can trust them."

"But what if they need help?" the girl protested.

"Then they have each other," Roque said, firmly. He stepped forward. "Go. Don't look back." He took the girl's hand, turning her around. Once she was again facing the edge of Deep he shifted his grip to press into her back, urging her forward. "Those who live are those who keep their eyes on the cliff edge before them."

He spoke the adage without thinking, the ancient words—something his own people had taught him—registering and souring on his tongue only after they escaped him. The girl nodded, running after where the other villagers had vanished into the undergrowth. In seconds she, too, was out of sight.

Roque didn't follow. He turned, looking back toward Web.

What Roque knew of dolls and the Shod was limited. He knew where the Breath Mark came from, and why it'd been made. He'd witnessed the birth of one of the first dolls ever created, and when he closed his eyes that scene was there, *Feah* was there, just like she always was: crouched on the beach, cradling a figurine of driftwood with one hand, the other using her damp hair like a writing brush, sweeping the pitch strands across the doll's chest. A gesture that'd left behind lines, even though there was nothing on her hair, no charcoal or ink to write with. She'd sat back with a satisfied noise, the doll stirring and standing up in her hands, bowing to her and, with a pounce, tapping her nose before lunging away from her, starting a game of chase that'd included many shrieks of laughter and giggles, Roque watching with puzzled (and slightly alarmed) amusement until Feah had come up to him, breathless, and clasped his hand in both of hers.

"Come," she'd said, eyes gleaming, taciturn and shy, but thrilled enough with her doll to brave approaching him. To find the courage to invite him to join her in play.

That was what dolls were for, what they'd originally been meant to do—play. Provide companionship. When Roque had heard they'd been repurposed into serving as guards against monsters, he'd felt grief, a sense of loss as his memories of Feah's impish little dolls were tainted by images of combat dolls built like storm walls and made to die like intelligent shields, thrust between vulnerable human flesh and the Shod.

Dolls weren't alive, he knew. Not the way people were. But, still; to see creations that'd once brought joy and relief to a child's life serve as the weapons of adults in an endless war had been, and still was, disheartening.

Roque would do anything, give anything, to have such activities end. Anything to rid the world of the Shod—of the Marks in general. But, as he currently was, he hadn't the knowledge to do so. And that was why he stood still as the sounds of the villagers retreating diminished and then vanished. Why he gazed toward Web, fingers curling on the strap of his travel bag, making the pack move in such a way that his lexicon pressed through the burlap, against the small of his back.

Did Shean and Ikiisa know? Did they know that the Shod were dolls? Twisted, demented dolls, dolls that, if Roque were to guess, became Shod after their creators died—that would explain why the tradition of One was for dolls to be buried with their dollmakers in remote, isolated locations, why he and Shean's dolls had seen the monsters crawling from a dollmaker's grave. Dolls perverted by the death of their own creators . . .

Perhaps that was something all dollmakers knew. Information kept hidden from Roque until now, shielded from sight by oaths of secrecy.

But maybe they didn't know. Maybe the dollmakers of the country called One fought their battle against themselves in ignorance. Roque had seen such large truths concealed before. He'd seen the detriment such secrets caused.

If Shean and Ikiisa knew what the Shod really were, would that help them in some way? Would what they knew from lifetimes of studying dolls be enhanced by this added piece of information? Was this truth the tip of the scale that'd allow one, or both, of them to realize a way to free their world from monsters?

The chance that such was the case felt slim. But if there was one thing Roque had learned over years of searching for and studying the Marks, it was that even a chance the width of a spider's thread was worth pursing, if one had the time to pursue said thread to its end. And time was something Roque had in abundance.

Roque thought of Feah. He held the memory of her fresh in his mind, reminding him, as she had so many times before, why he was here. Why he remained when the Mountain Queen was gone, and all her peaks fallen. Why it was not only his obligation, but his sworn duty, to pursue any leads he had pertaining to a way to end the Marks.

Even leads as thin as spider's thread—a fitting guidance, here in the forest called Deep.

With such thoughts came the death of uncertainty, and Roque made up his mind. Trusting the villagers to flee their forest on their own, he ran toward Web.

THOUGH SUCH WAS THE NATURAL STATE OF THINGS, IN THE ABSENCE OF SHOD the village called Web struck Shean as eerie. Night was halfway over, the delicate splinters of the moons in the sky beginning to set and taking with them what wane light they'd provided while stars gave faint illumination to the wreckage. Ikiisa supporting her, Shean limped through the debris of the village, taking in piles of rubble that looked like awkwardly sprawled creatures in the dark, laid low by hard blows that none would rise from anytime soon. They stopped at the tipped-over statue of the massive spider in its stone web, still in the center of the town square. Shean slipped her arm from Ikiisa's shoulders, reaching out and touching the edge of the sculpture. The stone was cold against her skin.

"We did it," Ikiisa said, and her voice was loud. Shean winced. "We should go look for the villagers and Roque."

Shean dropped her hand from the statue. "Right," she said.

"Do you need help walking?"

"No. I'm fine."

Ikiisa nodded and turned, heading toward the edge of Web. Her two remaining dolls followed her, flanking her. Shean hesitated, looking back at the toppled stone spider. There was a crack down its face, right over its huge, glassy eyes. The fracture was deep, a crevice through pale stone that gathered shadow like a leaf gathers rainfall.

Staring at the fissure, Shean realized her skin was crawling. For a moment she didn't understand why. Then her head jerked up.

Something was wrong. She turned to face the forest called Deep and recognized its stillness. Not only were the Shod no longer Crying, but, outside of what the wind made rustle, there was no hint of sound in the trees at the edge of the woods.

Where were the mannequin-dolls? If they were still chasing the Shod away, Shean should've been able to hear that pursuit. If they'd killed all of the Shod, they should be coming back to Web. And making a racket as they did.

Second wave, Shean thought, cold sweeping through her as the phrase brought to mind her brother's death.

Though she'd lived through the Red Tide, her recollection of the actual events of the attack were limited. She'd seen the part of the city she lived in decimated, the burning of the district called Reef known to her in an intimate way. The destruction of the other nineteen districts of the city, though, she knew only from hearsay and reading official accounts. And the story she'd sought out most often was that of the collapse of the district called Coral.

One of the smaller districts, Coral had sat on the far eastern tip of Pearl, on a jutting bluff overlooking the sea. Of all of Pearl, Coral had been hit the hardest at the beginning of the Red Tide—the Shod had used it as an access point to the city, coming from the sea and climbing the undersides of the cliffs, ripping through Coral like hail through wood and leaving a chipped, decimated wreck behind.

Dollmakers had been sent en masse to clear Coral and stem off the steady stream of Shod rising over the edge of the district to reach the rest of Pearl. Including Shean's brother, Giko. Together, over two dozen dollmakers had succeeded in driving the Shod from Coral, bottlenecking the monsters on each end of the district, sending many into the sea and some further into Pearl, toward other dollmakers waiting in other districts.

This success had come swiftly, within minutes. Made confident by easy victory, the senior dollmaker in Coral had ordered all but one dollmaker to return to the other districts of Pearl, instructing her troops to turn their energies toward purging the Shod from the rest of the city. The dollmaker chosen to stay behind experienced roughly fifteen minutes of peace before the Shod returned, leaping up from beneath the cliffs and crashing over Coral even more fiercely than before, overwhelming the hundred or so dolls left to keep them at bay. Killing the dollmaker who'd been left behind.

Killing Shean's brother.

Shean had often wondered if Giko protested his orders. Had he suggested it was best to wait a little longer before sending the other dollmakers away, that the Shod might've been driven back for a time, but would surely return? Or had he readily agreed to his commander's orders, confident that his dolls could hold the line on their own? All she knew for sure was that by the time his body was recovered and brought to Nock for burial preparation, his throat had a slash so deep you could see bone, his eyes had been empty green marbles, and his limbs had displayed the violence of trampling. For years afterward she'd woken up screaming from nightmares of having a Shod cut her throat, a Shod kick her down so more and more Shod could run over her, drive her into the ground until she was nothing but another stone to be stepped on, each foot that fell on her driving air from her body and making the world darker, darker, until all was dark and there was nothing but the jerk of waking up, the damp of tears on her face, shed while she slept the sleep of the haunted.

Shean hadn't thought about Coral in many years—when she was a teenager, she'd realized obsessing over her family's demise wasn't healthy. Or productive. So she'd stopped reading the reports concerning their deaths. Now, though, she recalled what she'd learned from reading about Coral—that the Shod *could* be driven away. They *could* be sent running.

But there was a reason their attack had been called the Red Tide in Pearl.

They always, always returned.

Always.

Shean spun around, shouting.

"Ikiisa!"

Ikiisa was to the edge of Web. She jerked at Shean's cry, turning to look back at her. Even in the dark, even though they were standing half a town apart from one another, Shean made out the startle of Ikiisa's features, the question forming on her lips.

A question she never had the chance to ask.

The edge of Deep erupted. Shod surged from the trees, slicing a divide down the center of the village called Web. Packed so closely together they resembled a dark, glistening liquid, the monsters were no longer simply covered in the woven orbs of Web's houses—now they had a new layer slapped onto their sides, fresh armor made from dolls that'd already been missing limbs or heads before the Shod touched them. Mannequin-dolls, the ink barely dry on the Breath Marks used to bring them to life.

There was no edict of the First Dollmaker that said that dolls *couldn't* be made from incomplete mannequins.

In one terrible moment, Shean realized there should be.

"Ikiisa!" Shean shouted again, but her voice was lost in the rising wail of the Shod. They were filling up Web again, each Shod bigger and bigger than the last, growing so rapidly in size that Shean had to stumble back or risk being crushed underfoot.

So big. She'd never seen Shod of such sizes—even the monsters of her nightmares, the demons who'd shredded Pearl to ruins, had been a third of these Shods' statures.

And not only were the Shod huge, they were white. *White?* With a spike of horror, Shean realized the Shod were covered in spiderwebs, great bundles of the sticky stuff clinging to their irregular sides, stretched over their grotesque faces and swiping hands.

The Veil. The spiders. Not only had the village called Web's houses fallen, but its livelihood, too, displayed like trophies on the Shod destroying both.

Shean caught a glimpse of Ikiisa over the swelling rise of spiderwebbed Shod, their eyes meeting before the wall of monsters blocked their path to one another. The Shod were leaping toward Shean, screaming. Seeing no other choice, she turned and ran.

She headed back to Ikiisa's house, not because she hoped to find more mannequins (there were no more mannequins) but because it was the only available shelter. She could take her chances and try to flee through Deep, but with her leg like it was, she doubted her ability to keep up a decent pace through the undergrowth. Her instincts told her not to run but to hide, to find a place to curl up and pretend to be small.

She'd nearly reached the house when a Shod caught her. The collective Cry of the monsters was so loud she didn't hear her attacker, unprepared for when a weight smacked into the back of her legs, making them cave. She fell on her hands and knees, the heels of her palms skidding on the grass under them. The Shod climbed up her back and what felt like lightning shot through her, giving her the strength to regain her feet and shake herself until, to her immense relief, the Shod fell off.

The victory was short-lived. Before she could take another step there was a flash of movement in the corner of her eye, followed by the weight of the Shod returning, this time on her right leg. Staggering, Shean looked down at her attacker.

Unlike the monsters currently thrashing through Web, this Shod was the size of a toy. But it Cried fiercely as it crawled up the bunches of her skirts, reaching her waist before she could react and stretching out a two-fingered hand to swipe at her face. Shean screamed, smacking at the monster. She knocked a fist against it, but the imp continued to cling, and its shrieks started to sound like weeping, like great, heaving sobs.

More Shod were coming. They'd jump on her while she was distracted and drag her into their collective embrace. They'd kill her. Just like they'd killed her family. Her dolls.

"No!" Shean yelled, so loud her throat burned. Gritting her teeth, she did the only thing she could think to do—she dropped to the ground and rolled. The movement hurt something awful, both in her injured leg and in the press of the Shod against her chest. There was a brief but terrifying moment of knowing the creature would

either be knocked off of her or take this as an opportunity to thrust its small, sharp hands through her.

Thankfully, when Shean finished rolling and pushed herself to her feet the Shod was left behind in the grass, lying flat on the ground, stunned.

Shean meant to run away at once. Staring down at the small Shod, though, she paused.

There was a blue streak down the monster's front. It was faint, the color muddied by grime and the webbing of branches laced around the Shod's torso. But she saw it. And recognized it—the doll, her brother Giko's last doll, the one she'd placed with her own hands upon his burial-wrapped chest. It'd had that same blue streak. And, now that she looked more closely, could it be possible that the two-fingered hands of this Shod weren't natural? They weren't symmetrical, those hands—the fingers were at different spots on each hand. Like the Shod had had other fingers before. Ones that'd been ripped off.

And its face. Two glowing white eyes, a gaping hole of a mouth above which could be something that had, once, been a nose. Or something similar to a nose.

Something very much like a doll's face.

The Shod was getting back to its feet. Shean didn't have time to stand here staring at it. In desperation she shoved her confusion over its appearance into the crowded corners of her mind, to be thought about when her survival wasn't in question. She turned and ran the remaining steps to Ikiisa's house, shutting what remained of the door behind her before hobbling down the hallway, turning until she found a suitable room near the center of the house, a bedroom with a set of drawers standing at the end of a bed.

She entered the room and shut the door behind her, grabbing and dragging the drawers and then the sleeping pallet across the room, arranging them into a hasty barricade. Finishing, she half-expected a Shod to burst in after her. When none did she stumbled back from the door until her back pressed to the wall. Her knees gave out and she sank to the floor, huddled. She curled a hand over her heart, which was beating so fast her chest hurt.

The mannequins hadn't lasted. What's worse, they'd become fuel for the Shod. The monsters would overwhelm Ikiisa's few remaining dolls in no time, and if that stone of Ikiisa's really worked, Roque had told the villagers to make a run for the edge of the forest called Deep. From the hollow tree they were hiding in, it would take an hour of sprinting to leave Deep. They had children with them who couldn't keep up that pace. Elderly who'd fall behind. Shean imagined the noise hundreds of people running through a forest would cause.

The Shod would find them: the villagers, Ikiisa, Roque.

They'd find them. And kill them.

What did Shean do now? What *was* there to do?

Die. That's what.

Something crashed nearby, the wail of the Shod growing closer to her hiding spot. She felt no spike of fear at the sound—what more fear could she feel than what she'd been feeling for hours? A stupor locked into place around her, so heavy she sagged, gaze dropping to her knees, to the scuffed floor she sat on. The bandages on her leg were brown with bloodstain, stuck to her like a second skin. Her other leg trembled with exhaustion. She had cuts and bruises all over; what wasn't cut or bruised ached from strain. Her eyes burned from watching the same village fall to the Shod twice in the past day because her dolls couldn't protect it, her plan to save it hadn't worked.

For the first time in her life, Shean felt truly, horribly numb.

The Shod were in Ikiisa's house. She heard them, banging through doors and tearing at walls, Crying and Crying and Crying. They'd find her soon. Minutes. Seconds. And no one was coming to help her.

I wonder how much it will hurt.

Shean's head tipped back against the wall. She closed her eyes, hand reaching for the pocket of her dress. She searched for and found Nock's license, pulling the card out because she was going to die and she wanted to die holding something familiar, something from home. Hoping that doing so would make the trembling of her fingers stop, or at least lessen. Knowing it wouldn't.

She lifted the card. The room was dark, but she could still make out the design on the license's front. She saw the mighty boar of the First Dollmaker. The symbol she'd been so sure it was her destiny to carry. The symbol she'd been so sure would prove that her dolls were as strong and wonderful as she felt they were. Tears blurred her vision, turning the lines of the boar into indistinct squiggles. Her hand shook and she dropped the card.

It clattered to the floor, flipping over. To Shean's surprise, there was something drawn on its back, faint lines in the gloom of the room. A Shod screamed so close her ears rang, but she ignored the Cry, bending forward and picking up the card. She held it close, eyes straining.

Words. There were words written on the back of the card, etched in unfamiliar handwriting:

GIVE THE SHOD BREATH MARKS?

Shean stared at the words, reading them over and over and finding it impossible to wrap her mind around them.

Shod. Breath Marks.

Shod? Breath Marks?

"Why?" she said, voice cracking. She flipped Nock's license over, searching its familiar front for some clue as to what the words on its back meant. When she found none she turned the card back over, tracing the strange suggestion with a fingertip.

Shean knew this card. She'd played with it as a child, games of pretend about being a grand master, a famous guard dollmaker like Nock. There'd never been any writing on its back. No carving. Who'd written this?

But, more importantly, what did they mean by this message? People had tried putting Breath Marks on all sorts of things in the past: pots and kettles, beds and houses and jewelry. It'd been irrefutably proven by the First Dollmaker himself that the Breath Mark only worked when put on dolls, but that didn't stop idiots from trying anyway.

But, put a Breath Mark on a *Shod*? The Breath Mark was meant to bring dolls to life, to make them loyal to their dollmakers and bind them to the bidding of their masters. If the Mark affected the Shod in a similar way then, yes, it would be wonderful to put a Breath Mark on a Shod, assuming you could get close enough to do so. But Shod weren't dolls—a Breath Mark wouldn't do anything to them . . .

Would it?

Shean's mind swiveled to the Shod that'd grabbed ahold of her outside. That blue streak down its chest, just like Giko's doll. Its hauntingly familiar face and missing fingers. She listened to the Cry of the Shod searching for her, and for the first time really wondered why they sounded like lost, wailing children. Children calling out for parents.

Something clinked against the floor, making Shean jump. She glanced down to see the inkwell Ikiisa had given her, fallen out of the pocket she'd shoved it into upon finishing with the mannequins. A moment later, the brush Ikiisa had given her fell out of her pocket, too, landing on the floor with a thump. Holding Nock's license in one hand, she picked up the inkwell and brush. She stared at them.

Her fingers curled over the writing tools. Her grip on the edge of Nock's license tightened, so hard the wood of the card creaked.

"Do I have anything to lose?" she whispered, already knowing the answer.

No.

No she did not.

SHEAN ENJOYED THINKING. LOGIC WAS A COMFORT—AS LONG AS SHE HAD A plan, she had direction, a guide to follow and mull over and think and rethink until she'd thought of every possible outcome to every possible event.

This time, though, Shean didn't think. The moment she made up her mind she scrambled to her feet, dropping everything and yanking the Gleam dress off. Underneath she wore only undergarments, a thin, black shift and shorts, but that was as good an armor as the dress had been, and far easier to move in. After a slight hesitation she decided to keep her shoes on—impractical as the wooden clogs were, she worried that running barefoot would make her slower than she already was.

Dropping the Gleam dress on the floor with a heavy clink, Shean dragged away her barricade. Then she scooped up the dress, the inkwell and brush, and Nock's license. Shoving the latter into the waistband of her shorts, she flung the door of her hide-out open. Gleam dress flapping over her arms, she ran through Ikiisa's house, past the Shod overrunning the structure, kicking at the ones that got too close, dodging the ones too big to kick, and stumbling all the way to the front of the house. The door was now fully ripped off its hinges, a Shod the size of an elk blocking her way. Gritting her teeth, Shean threw herself at the monster, knocking it back with her own weight.

She and the Shod fell to the ground outside. There was a moment of confusion, a mess of flailing, spiky legs and the shimmer of her dress. Then Shean rolled to the side, off the Shod and onto grass. She forced herself to stand, to ignore the frightening tremor of her legs and half run, half limp toward the village called Web.

Shean had never run this slowly in her entire life. Every part of her was screaming for her to go faster, faster, and she couldn't. She squeezed the ink brush in her hand so hard she nearly snapped it, feeling the yield of the stick just in time to relax the pressure.

She heard the Shod closing in. Whistles and clacks, rustles, that hollow voice, that collective Cry announcing the Shod had locked in upon new prey. Just like fifteen years ago.

But, also, nothing like then; Shean wasn't a child. She was no longer helpless.

She had a plan.

By some miracle she managed to move for several seconds without being grabbed or tackled, dragging herself a few steps before a Shod latched on to her leg.

Her injured leg, of course. Shean screamed, whirling and using her undamaged foot to kick the Shod off. The monster was solid, her clog breaking and her toes jamming as she kicked. She felt her big toe crunch and crack, a shock of heat lancing up the length of her foot. But her painful efforts were worth it—the Shod detached, falling away with a flail of limbs that, for all the woven twigs and mannequin parts fortifying and obscuring the creature's shape, were very doll-like.

Not that Shean had long to marvel at that new, possibly insane, way of viewing the Shod—as soon as her assailant was down she turned to continue running. She only managed a step, though, before dozens of Shod were blocking her path forward. Tears of pain and exhaustion and fear streaming down her face, Shean spun on her good heel, glaring. She backed away from the Shod in front of her, whipped around at the sound of the Shod coming up behind her, then twisted left, right, spun in a circle that made her dizzy—everywhere she turned there were Shod. She was surrounded.

That was fine. That was *good*, even. Shean had never meant to make it all the way to Web. She just needed Shod to come to her. And here they were.

"Do you want this?" she yelled, holding the Gleam dress aloft. The Shods' heads tracked the dress, lifting as she lifted it, swinging as a wind gusted by and picked up the jeweled skirts, making them swirl and shine in a billowing dance. Overhead, night was ending, sunrise seeping into the sky in lines and splotches of reds and blood orange, stars expiring as the sun experienced its diurnal rebirth. Sweat trickled down the sides of Shean's neck, her eyes squinting against the increasing light, the dawn a halo against trees in the distance, around the collapsed remains of Web. Her hand clenched on the fabric of the best-made thing she owned, the last finely crafted item she had left that the Shod might want. Besides her own skin and bones, of course.

Jaw set, Shean yelled hard and loud, so loud she screamed.

"You can have it!"

Shean spun, using the momentum of the twist to fling the Gleam dress into the air. The garment swirled, a helix of shimmer framed against the red sky, all its many facets displaying deep tones of purple and blue and flaming green, a gradient of iridescent hues, its sleeves whipping in refractions of light. After a breathtaking moment the dress landed, cresting the heads of the Shod and falling into the grass with a flutter and collapse, becoming a heap of diamonds and emeralds, sapphires and opals and onyx.

Watching the dress fly, for one terrible moment Shean thought she was wrong. She thought the Shod would choose her over the Gleam dress. That she'd overestimated their desire for beautiful, well-crafted things.

But she wasn't wrong. The moment the dress landed the Shod were after it, wailing, racing to be the first to reach the clothing. The Shod that chose to launch themselves at Shean instead were few enough for her to dodge, though one almost got her, the monster leaping at her head and clearly set on decapitating her with two long, spiked arms. It would've succeeded if at that moment her injured leg hadn't given out, sending her to her knees. She felt the Shod pass overhead, the breeze of its flight stirring her hair and cooling the sweat on her forehead.

Teeth gritted, Shean dragged herself upright. And ran to the Shod gathered around the Gleam dress.

Now came the hard part.

She picked a small Shod, one without too many twigs bundling it and almost no spiderwebs, only one arm from one mannequin-doll reinforcing its body. She clamped her hands down on its back and dragged it from the squirming mass of Shod ripping the Gleam dress to pieces. The Shod turned as she touched it—it had a jewel clasped in its hands, a sapphire drop attached to a piece of burgundy fabric that, torn at the edges, looked like a ripped piece of skin. Even when Shean pinned the Shod down, it wouldn't let go of its bead. Which was good—Shean doubted she'd be able to hold it flat if it chose to use all five of its limbs to smack at her. As it was she managed to kneel on its kicking feet, using one hand to hold it down while she uncorked her inkwell with her thumb, set it to the side, and shoved her brush into its murky depths.

When she made to write the Breath Mark the Shod bucked its head, throwing her hand off with a shriek so piercing Shean feared her ears would burst. The brush was knocked from her hand, sent spinning. She snatched at it, and she was forced to stretch as she did, making her knee slip. The Shod surged upward, almost knocking her off and causing her grab to go wild, her fingers missing the brush as it tumbled away from her. Before her captive could squirm free, she replanted her knee, driving the monster back into the ground with an effort that made her see spots.

The brush had fallen well out of reach—to reclaim it Shean would have to let the Shod under her go. And catch another one. Which she didn't have the energy left to do.

Shean set her jaw and shook her head, hand clenching into a fist.

"I will do this," she said. "I *will*."

She lifted and planted her injured foot, blood-slicked as it was, on the Shod's chest. Putting all the weight she could bear on that foot, she dipped her finger into the inkwell, the ink cool and thick on her skin, and bent forward.

She made a mistake the first time she drew the Breath Mark, her hand was shaking so hard. The distraction of her dress would only last so long, and she felt that reality in the quaver of her finger—the first line she drew was crooked, jerking in a jagged line to the side when the Shod writhed. She took a deep breath and tried again, making it halfway through the Mark this time before the Shod wiggled and ruined her attempt.

She was running out of time. The Shod were starting to scream less, the sounds of ripping fabric and jewel beads clattering against hard-shelled backs diminishing by the second.

One more time. Just one more time.

Shean bent double, digging her foot into the Shod with all her remaining strength. She painted the next Breath Mark behind her heel, drawing the Mark in nine swift strokes that, finally, were the smooth and clean lines she'd memorized from years and hundreds of hours of practice. Then, with no small effort, she pushed herself to her feet, snatching up her inkwell and stepping back, clutching her ink-stained hand to her chest and watching the Shod with bated breath.

The Shod lay in the grass, limp and silent. After a moment it stood, rising with a sway to its three legs, its hands releasing the sapphire bead. Shean traced the wink of the jewel as it fell into the grass, then looked back to the Shod. It stood frozen in place.

No. Not frozen—moving, still. Slowly, very slowly. As if wading through a bog, each limb sluggish, oblong head tipping so far to the side it appeared on the cusp of breaking free of the monster's thin neck. Behind it Shean could see the other Shod were finished with the Gleam dress, dispersing from their excited cluster and turning toward her, their faces studded in gems, bits of fabric tied and tucked around necks, wadded into cracks and crevices. She didn't look from the Breath-Marked Shod.

A crack, loud and dull like the *thwump* of a bow's string after shooting an arrow. Then there was a rending noise, a grind and crunch. With a shudder the Breath-Marked Shod ripped in two.

One side, the side with Shean's Breath Mark, collapsed on the ground, stiff and curled inward like a dead bug. The other side staggered and fell, spinning and churning up the ground with a thrash, the flash of wide, staring white eyes. This living half of the Shod flopped like a fish, trying to regain a semblance of balance and motion, but only managing to spin in a futile circle.

Shean barely noticed the Breath-Marked Shod's struggles; she was no longer looking at it. Instead her attention was on the other Shod, all of which had gone still. They stared at her from amidst the weave of twigs and spiderwebs wrapped around them, the new parts they'd gained from the mannequin-dolls hanging limp and awkward off their sides. Their Gleam-dress ornaments shone like extra eyes, a bizarrely beautiful addition to their horror.

The first Shod to move was one of the largest ones. It took a step forward as creeping as a bashful child's, stepping over the Breath-Marked Shod and looming over Shean. She had to look up to see its wedge-shaped head, feeling a dull and distant pain as she recognized Coin's face set into the side of the monster's neck, staring at nothing with empty eyes. The Shod sat down, a motion that made the ground lurch and Shean stumble a step back. With a click the monster extended an arm, the flat disc that served as its hand stopping in front of her.

Shean stared at the offering for a moment. Then she reached out, gripping the Shod's wrist. She half expected the monster to attack the moment she touched it, but it didn't. It didn't move at all as she set her inkwell down, wetting her finger in it. The Shod didn't stir when she began drawing the Breath Mark, and it didn't follow when she finished and backed away.

A pause. Then the same crack, the same rending noise. The Shod fell into two parts, one unmoving and the other flailing the moment it collapsed into the grass. Like the first Breath-Marked Shod, the living half of this second Shod couldn't even stand. It struggled and softly Cried, but didn't rise.

Shean's knees weakened. She sank to the ground and pressed a hand into the grass, feeling dizzy. With a vision that swam, she watched another Shod sit down before her, bowing to expose the back of its head.

Shean leaned forward. Feeling as if all of this was a strange, incomprehensible dream, she lifted her hand. And wrote.

IKIISA RAN THROUGH THE FOREST CALLED DEEP, PANICKED AND TORN. BEHIND her came the Shod, breaking trees into shards, trampling ferns into pulp, and spurring her to speeds she hadn't thought her body capable of. Beside her Bobble and Cadence sprinted, keeping pace with her and serving as a guard against the monsters that'd catch up with her soon.

Each breath Ikiisa took as she ran seared and reminded her that she'd told the villagers of Web to run, that the villagers of Web were now running just like she was, with no one and nothing to protect them from the Shod she'd failed to defeat. And each step she took, each stride that cracked through bushes and slammed atop hard tree roots, reminded her that Shean was alone, Shean had nothing and no one to protect her from the Shod.

Ikiisa had to do something. But if she sent her two remaining dolls away, not only would they probably do no good for whomever she sent them to (the villagers or Shean), but she'd be left alone and exposed.

Then *she'd* be dead.

Ikiisa didn't know what to do, which was why, outside of running, she hadn't done anything yet. Running was easy, thoughtless, legs pumping and arms swinging, ducking under low tree branches, skirting rocks too large to jump over, blundering through the forest called Deep with very little care for direction or finesse.

Her panic mounted every second. *I have to do something, anything*, she thought, desperate to shake off the paralyzing fear spurring her onward, making all other concerns but her own seem small and trivial. *Send one doll to help Shean and one to the villagers, or try to lead the Shod away from where the villagers might be, or call Roque and tell him what's happening or, or* something!

"Something!" she screamed aloud. Knowing it to be the only way to make herself think, she forced herself to stop running, gripping the trunk of a nearby tree to steady herself as she panted. Trying, and failing, to ignore the sound of Shod getting close to where she stood, Ikiisa looked down at her dolls, mouth opening to order them away, Cadence to the villagers, Bobble to Shean. Then Ikiisa would start running again, turning deeper into the forest and baiting as many Shod as she could away from where the villagers were headed.

Before she could speak, a shout stopped her.

"Ikiisa!"

Her head whipped up, turning to see Roque. He charged through the forest toward her, copper hair reflecting the color of the brightening sky, flashing in the dapples of light falling through the canopy of Deep. In seconds he'd reached her, looking from where she leaned against the tree to her two dolls to the direction of the oncoming Shod.

"What's happening?" he asked.

Ikiisa's mouth opened and closed, the relief of his arrival potent enough to render her speechless.

"Ikiisa!" Roque said, the urgency of his voice snapping her from the trance.

"You got my message?" she asked. He nodded. "The mannequins didn't work—we thought they would, we thought they *were*, but the Shod overwhelmed them and used them to build themselves up." She gestured the way she'd come, toward the ever-increasing roar of charging Shod. "They're coming!"

"Where's Shean?" Roque asked.

Ikiisa shook her head, eyes welling and voice cracking with distress. "I don't know. We were separated, we—"

The Shod arrived, cutting Ikiisa off. They crashed through the trees behind her and she leapt back at the sight of their giant, cobbled forms, squeaking in alarm. She felt Roque grab her wrist, tugging her behind him in one smooth, powerful movement.

"Go!" he shouted, and Ikiisa meant to, willing to trust Roque to make the decisions she, in her panic, was incapable of making.

Before she could resume her flight, something happened. At first she wasn't sure what, so disoriented by all that was already happening that she ran a few steps before noticing things were quiet. *Very* quiet. She stumbled to a stop, turning.

The Shod stood behind her, unmoving. Cocooned in twigs and spiderwebs, they blended into the forest, great, blocky sculptures of wood tall as trees with white eyes casting a milk-skim glow over Roque and the undergrowth around him. He stood with his back to Ikiisa, head tipped to look up at the Shod.

The Shods' heads were tipped as well. Tipped to the side and back, as if listening to something. Ikiisa found herself straining to hear, to catch whatever sound had brought the monsters' rampage to a halt. She heard nothing.

But the Shod must have; as one they turned. Still silent, they began walking back to Web.

Walking. Not running.

Ikiisa had never seen a Shod *walk* before.

She and Roque shared a look. Without a word, they followed.

THE SHOD KEPT COMING. AND COMING. DOZENS TO HUNDREDS, CLEAVING IN HALF and thus multiplying, piles of dead and squirming halves rising up around Shean like towers, stacking so high she couldn't see what lay on either side of her—there was just the Shod, living and dead, in pieces and soon to be joined by more pieces. Many of them boasting bits of her own dolls, ghosts that made tears spill down her face.

At first she counted, but she gave up after hitting one hundred and ninety-seven. Instead, she focused on peeling back tangles of branches from faces and torsos and hands, wiping away spiderwebs to find spots to draw the Breath Mark on each new Shod that appeared before her. She collected splinters in her palms, her fingertips. Tiny pains that registered in faint tingles.

And she wrote. She wrote until her hand was numb, her ink-soaked fingers stiff and her vision blurred. Some of the Shod came to her like the first two, crawling or slithering up and fixing their hollow, sightless eyes upon her, gazes that stayed steady up to the moment she drew a Breath Mark that stole the light from them. When Shod stopped coming to her she rose and came to them, walking to the monsters standing around Web. Most of those waited for her, making no protest as she drew Breath Marks on their splintered sides. Some ran from her, emitting high-pitched Cries of terror, wails of fear that were so human, Shean almost broke under the sound. She watched as other Shod caught the runners, holding them still long enough for her to limp up and write on them, step back to avoid the living and dead halves that fell to the ground.

Hours might've passed. Or minutes. When all the Shod in Web and the surrounding areas were reduced to heaps at her feet, more Shod emerged from the forest called Deep. Big ones, trundling up to her and sitting down in a ring that encircled her. She dragged herself to them, shoving aside twigs and one of Glass's arms to draw a Mark on this one, then the next, the next, the next.

By the time she finished, her hands were shaking and her knees were weak. Each breath was an effort and her chest burned with them. When the last Shod collapsed to pieces she waited for the next to arrive, unable to believe the ordeal was over. She stood with a hand fisted around her almost-empty inkwell, the other limp and pulsing at her side, arms shaking. She waited for a Shod to leap from the trees to her left, the wrecked village to her right. Instead a hand touched her shoulder, sending a shock through her. She was too tired to jump—it took all her remaining energy to turn.

Ikiisa stood behind her. *We're the same height*, Shean realized. She'd never noticed that before.

Ikiisa was looking at the Shod on the ground, eyes wide and face pale. "They're dead?" she asked.

Shean shook her head. "Not quite," she said, voice a croak. She watched one of Ikiisa's remaining dolls step forward. It bent to inspect a living half of Shod that was trembling and thrashing in the grass. There was a pause. Then the doll leapt into the air, bouncing high and pouncing like a fox diving through snow. There was a crack, and the Shod fragment ceased moving. The doll gave a delighted hop and moved to the next Shod fragment, destroying it with one blow. Which was all it took to destroy the next fragment, and the next. Ikiisa's other doll joined in, the two leaping across the wreckage that'd once been the village called Web, slaying Shod that were already half dead.

Shean watched the dolls work, only looking away when Roque's voice tugged at her, drawing her attention to where he stood, a step back from Ikiisa.

"What happened?" he asked.

Shean was too tired to explain. Instead she reached into the waistband of her shorts, pulling out Nock's license. She handed it to Ikiisa, who frowned with confusion.

"The back," Shean said. Ikiisa flipped the card, Roque stepping forward to look over her shoulder. Together they peered at Nock's license. Watching them, Shean had a hazy moment of doubt. Maybe she'd imagined the writing on the card; it was so strange, so impossible, that it was there. Maybe she'd dreamt up the idea to write the Breath Mark on the Shod. Maybe it'd been a stroke of inspiration, manifested as imagined words scratched into wood. She leaned forward to see the back of the card herself.

Something yanked on her leg. She looked down to find a half-Shod squirming at her feet, clinging to her with a desperation she identified with. A thin wail escaped it and the creature stabbed her leg, making her flinch as one of its spindles pushed through her bandages, bit into flesh. Her leg was too stiff to move away from the small attack. One more step and she'd collapse.

Which was fine, because she didn't want to move away. Staring down at the half-Shod, the weak remains of a monster that, minutes ago, had threatened her life, Shean thought of how the Shods' Crying sounded like wailing children. Like calls for help. Of how, during the Red Tide, trapped and about to die, she'd stared into the faces of a thousand Shod and thought she heard them speak:

"Please, please, please. Save me."

Back then she'd taken those words to be a projection, her own mind shouting out as her lungs seized with fear, unable to utter the plea for help she'd longed to make. Now she knew she'd been mistaken—the Shod *had* spoken to her. Told her the truth, even though, at the time, she'd been unable to understand them.

Why were the Shod attracted to well-made things? Why were they drawn to humans? Why did they build upon themselves, patching together their bodies as if trying to mend themselves? Why did they fall upon people and grab ahold of them and squeeze and slash and pound as they Cried and Cried and Cried, until there was nothing left but broken bone and torn flesh?

What if they stayed within the borders of the country called One *not* because of the effort of dollmakers who could be outnumbered and overrun, but because they were beholden to the land and its people—because One was their home?

They were dolls. The Shod were dolls—she *had* seen Giko's doll, that blue-streaked doll from her cherished childhood memories, attacking her as a Shod. Somehow, for some unfathomable reason, Shod were twisted, tortured, frenzied dolls. Striving in their wrong, violent way to be repaired, healed. Instead destroying, and being destroyed in turn.

Tears filled Shean's eyes as she understood. All this time the Shod had been broken dolls. Trying to get help. Trying to make all of One understand their pain. Failing miserably, but still—*dollmakers* had made these monsters, the very monsters they swore to destroy. Their own fallen dolls.

Dollmakers had failed the Shod, the country called One, their own dolls.

Dollmakers like Shean.

Shean wondered if Ikiisa could've discovered the truth. Ikiisa, who treated her dolls like people—if Ikiisa herself had been treated like a person all these years, could she have figured out the Shod's secret before now? Before so much death and pain and ruin?

The half-Shod let out another pitiful Cry, its hold on Shean tightening. Her leg shook under her, and she realized she didn't need to take another step to collapse. She heard a rushing in her ears and fell.

Before she could land on her injured leg, arms caught Shean, lifting and steadying her. Familiar arms, and a grip that took her back to a night of fire and terror, of Shod screams and human screams and yelling for her brother and manma and father. Back to being cornered by that mass of Shod, unable to escape, half-fainting and feeling herself snatched up before the monsters could take her.

Breath catching, Shean looked up. She looked into a doll's face, a face she'd seen fifteen years ago when the arms holding her had rescued her from the Shod. As they did now, a lopsided, strange doll dragging her out of reach of a half-Shod and its cruel stabbing. Tears ran down Shean's face as she stared at Bobble, at the doll that'd saved her when she was a child.

How had it taken her this long to recognize him?

Ikiisa was making noises of alarm, crouching next to Shean and putting a hand on her back. With a whistle Bobble let go of her, deferring to his mistress.

"Shean!" Ikiisa said. "Are you all right?"

Shean shook her head. She closed her eyes, head dropping and hands curling on the ground. She bent forward, shaking.

"Shean?" Ikiisa said, gripping her shoulder. "What's wrong?"

Shean looked up, and for a moment the nature of the Shod meant nothing to her at all because, for the very first time, Shean saw Ikiisa. She saw the woman who'd saved her fifteen years ago. Her hero.

How hadn't she realized?

"Ikiisa, you . . . you were in the Red Tide," Shean said, voice cracking. "You were in Pearl."

Ikiisa frowned. "That doesn't matter right now, Shean, you're hurt—"

"Do you remember a little girl?"

"I . . ." Ikiisa trailed off, hesitating. "Yes. There were many little girls in Pearl. I saw a lot of them that day."

"This one was on the roof of a house. One of your dolls had her. He'd taken her up high to get away from the Shod, and then he stayed with her." Shean looked at Bobble. "*That* doll."

Ikiisa looked from Bobble to Shean and back again, brow furrowed. After a moment her expression cleared, eyes widening. She pointed at Shean, mouth an O of surprise.

"*You?*" she said.

Shean could barely see through the tears she was shedding. She sat up, even though doing so made her hurt all over and her head spin in circles, and reached out, blind, finding Ikiisa's hands and holding them. Her fingers squeezed Ikiisa's wrists, her head bowing until her forehead touched her knuckles.

"I wanted to be a dollmaker because a dollmaker saved me. I wanted to be like my hero. I wanted to save people, just like I was saved." Shean held on tight to the thin, calloused hands she grasped, lifting her head and meeting her savior's startled gaze. "Ikiisa, I wanted to be like *you*."

And then everything was too much, too close, too loud and soft and bright and dark. Shean shook her head to clear it of a noise that wouldn't clear, gave up, and flung her arms around Ikiisa's neck, holding on with all her might.

"Thank you," she sobbed, closing her eyes against the sunrise and the half-Shod and Roque.

She buried her face in Ikiisa's shoulder, and wailed.

SEVERAL WEEKS LATER, A KNOCK SOUNDED ON SHEAN'S DOOR, SOFT AS A HUMmingbird's heartbeat. She looked up from the desk she sat at, setting down the doll she was working on.

"Come in."

The door slid open. Dola appeared, carrying a tray holding a steaming bowl and a tall, lacquered cup.

"Lunch," Dola said. Shean smiled.

"Thank you," she said, gathering up her unfinished doll, whittling knife, and the array of paints spread over the top of her desk, setting them to the side so Dola could place the tray in front of her. She inhaled deeply, enjoying the sweet smell rising from the bowl, which was full of rice with honey drizzle and a half-cooked egg cracked over its top.

"Sorry it's the same as yesterday," Dola said, kneeling next to the desk. Shean shook her head, picking up the wooden spoon next to the bowl.

"It looks delicious," she said, meaning every word—she'd been working since before sunrise. Her stomach felt like a growing, empty pit, the hunger pains enough to distract her from dollmaking.

Dola smiled, and Shean felt a wave of affection for the girl as she took a spoonful of the meal. In the month that'd passed since the destruction of Web, Dola had been Shean's constant companion—bringing her meals, helping with checking her wounds and lending a shoulder to lean on during the daily walks Lenna insisted she take. Shean wasn't alone in this care; she, along with those villagers who'd been wounded in the Shod attack, had been placed in Ikiisa's house to rest and recover while the rest of Web was rebuilt, and Dola, being too small to be of much help in the reconstruction, had been designated the caretaker of the wounded. Once houses began being raised in the village again, the injured had filtered away, moving back in with family or friends until Shean was the only one still at Ikiisa's house. Which was probably for the best—the villagers had been less than pleased upon finding out their homes and a large (but thankfully not complete) portion of the Veil had fallen to the Shod. Even less pleased when Shean had confessed to lying about her license.

To stop them from stoning her, she'd gotten down on her knees and begged for forgiveness. That, and offered to make first, enough dolls to work in the Veil, and second, additional dolls to be sold for sufficient coin to replace lost supplies and looms and construction materials as compensation for the damage she'd caused. Those proposals had managed to calm some of the rage directed at her. It hadn't hurt, either, that she'd been the one to put a stop to the Shod's rampage—a rampage they were *almost* convinced hadn't been her fault in the first place.

Even so, the repercussions of her blunders were a tall order, and one that only now, weeks later, was close to being resolved. Food supplies had been purchased in the nearby town called Bog, new looms brought in from the city called Shoal, and the reconstruction of Web was well on its way to completion. Many of the dolls Shean had rushed to complete in the first week after the attack were busy silking and nursing to health what spiders remained in the Veil, while additional dolls helped the villagers weave; the spider-silk cloths that'd been lost in the attack were set to be replaced in time to be sold to the merchants scheduled for arrival in Web in a few weeks' time. Shean had made over forty dolls in the past four weeks, more dolls than she'd thought herself capable of making in such a short amount of time, and with the doll she'd finish tonight, the debt she owed to Web would, at least in a superficial way, be settled.

There'd been a moment, though, when Shean had almost gotten away with lesser penalties. It'd happened just after the attack, when Ikiisa told her part of the story, admitting in the process that all her dolls combined had been unable to drive the Shod from Web.

"You had almost fifty dolls and *still* couldn't fight the Shod?" a pinched-face villager with hair like tangled cotton had spat. "Then of *course* Dollmaker Shean's dolls didn't stand a chance! There was only six of them!"

"You're as much a fraud as Dollmaker Shean!" another villager had yelled, a cry followed by echoes of agreement that'd quickly mounted into hateful accusations of treachery and deceit.

Until that moment, a small part of Shean hadn't quite believed Ikiisa's story of being driven out of so many towns and cities. Watching the ire of Web turn from her to Ikiisa, though, Shean's doubts had fled. She'd opened her mouth to protest, to insist that the villagers were mistaken in putting the blame on anyone but herself. Ikiisa had beaten her to it.

"No!"

Ikiisa's voice had rung out loud and harsh and silencing, a startled hush falling over Web. Into which Ikiisa had yelled.

"Do you know why my dolls failed? It's because I've had to repair them so many times, they couldn't endure the Shod! If all of you hadn't spent so much time destroying my dolls, they would've been able to do the work I made them to do!" She'd stomped her foot, shout reaching a fevered pitch. "This is *not* my fault!"

Thinking about the stunned looks on the villagers' faces after that declaration still made Shean smile.

"Dollmaker Shean?" Dola said, pulling Shean back to the present.

"Yes?" she said, setting her spoon aside and reaching for the teacup. She took a sip of the liquid within, an herbal mix that was biting and sharp on her tongue.

Dola shifted on her knees, fidgeting with her hands and looking at the ground. "Are you really leaving tomorrow?" she asked, voice soft.

Shean set the teacup down. "I am."

"Do you have to?" Dola looked up, brow pinched. "No one's mad at you anymore. They can't be, not after how much you've helped rebuild our houses and with cleaning up the Veil, and giving us all those dolls to harvest silk with."

Shean doubted there were no lingering hard feelings among the villagers of Web toward her. People had been injured, lives had been disrupted, nightmares had been ignited. Their village had been ruined and their livelihoods threatened; realities that couldn't be ignored, no matter how quickly she'd helped restore Web back to a semblance of livability.

It was nice of Dola to believe as much, though. Shean smiled as she picked up her spoon again, taking another bite of rice and honey and egg. She chewed and swallowed before answering.

"I know. And I appreciate that. But I can't stay. I have people I . . . need to see."

Not that I want *to see them*, she added to herself, suppressing a grimace. The thought of facing Nock and Licensor Maton made her stomach braid into knots, a trepidation almost enough to sap away her appetite. But not quite—she finished scooping up the insides of her bowl, making short work of the remaining rice and draining the teacup in three swift gulps. She arranged the dirty dishes on the tray so they wouldn't tip over when picked up, nudging the platter toward Dola and twisting to reach for the mannequin awaiting her attention. When she turned back to her work desk she expected the tray to be gone, Dola standing to leave the way she always did after bringing food.

But the tray was still on the desk. Dola sat with shoulders hunched, fists pressed to the tops of her knees and eyes downcast in a way Shean recognized as reluctant.

"Dola? Is something wrong?"

Dola hesitated, then nodded. She slipped a hand into the front of her tunic, pulling out a journal bound shut by cords. Shean recognized the notebook at once—the one Dola used to practice writing the Breath Mark in. The one she'd almost gotten herself killed for during the attack, and the one Silver had . . .

Dola untied the cords of the notebook, holding the journal out when she finished. Shean took it.

"It's for you," Dola said, staring at the ground.

"Me?"

"Yes."

Curious, Shean opened the journal, flipping through its pages. The first few were covered in deliberate, neat handwriting that wrote out what Shean was expecting—letter drills and Breath Mark diagrams. A few pages into the notebook, though, a different handwriting started peppering Dola's practice. This script was scrawling and thin, more like slanted scratches than properly formed letters. Legible, but barely.

Shean frowned as she thumbed through pages filled with this

writing, pausing on a sketch of the village called Web from before the Shod attack, careful and well-made depictions of houses and the village square surrounded by little notes mentioning materials and heights. More scenery was sketched on the next few pages—drawings of different parts of the forest called Deep, a lovely two-page spread showcasing the Veil just as it'd been the night Shean had first seen it, spiderweb constructions floating about, spiders leaping beneath a moonless sky. Shockingly, there was even a drawing of the Shod attack Shean had seen on her way to Web, the sketch of dead monsters sprawled across a pottery-strewn, blood-stained road realistic and detailed enough to make her shiver.

"Did you draw these?" Shean asked, looking up at Dola. The girl shook her head, eyes still locked on the ground. "Who did, then?"

Dola opened her mouth, hesitated. Struggled for a moment, then said, "There's more. I . . . I'll tell you when you finish looking."

Shean wanted to argue, but Dola looked distressed enough, and her curiosity was piqued enough, that she didn't, relenting and turning back to the notebook, flipping to the next page. After the landscape folios came what looked like profiles for the villagers of Web, from Ilo to Lenna to everyone in between. A person's name was written at the top of their page, a drawing of them sketched out beneath that title, and a list was dictated under each sketch that contained information like age and eye color and habits, the occasional question scratched off to the side ("Why does he close his eyes when he sneezes?", "Unresolved childhood trauma?", "Fleas?"). Even Dola had a page dedicated to her, though her profile had no list, only sketches with little notes labeling them—pictures of her sitting or standing or looking through this very notebook, rendered in such fine detail Shean caught her breath with appreciation.

Then Shean flipped to a page with her name scrawled at its top. Beneath it was a list:

Confident, lacking self-awareness.

Argumentative—unafraid of confrontation.

Hard worker.

Dedicated.

Organized.

Driven.

Focused.

Refuses to admit when she's wrong—never believes she's wrong?

Has the potential to do great things, currently falling short.

There was a sketch on this page, too, beneath that last, hurtful line of the list. A portrait of Shean, facing toward whoever was looking down at the paper. She was laughing, head tilted a bit to the side, a hand up to hold the hair back from her face.

Shean looked at Dola, fingers squeezing the edges of the journal. "What *is* this?"

This timc, Dola gave her an answer. "Silver's research," she said.

Shean flinched at the name, pain driving through her chest. She took a deep breath, setting the notebook in her lap. "Silver?"

"Yes." Dola pushed a hand back through her hair, rubbing her knuckles over one of her eyes and sighing a delicate, soft sigh. "I-I know you probably don't believe me, but he *did* talk to me. And he could write. And draw. When we met, that first night you were in Web, he asked me for a notebook. I asked him what he was going to put in it and he told me 'research.' I wasn't sure what he meant; I . . . I'm still not sure. But he asked me to keep his notes secret until he said it was okay to show you." Dola looked down at her hands. Her bottom lip wobbled. "I'm sorry I didn't give them to you sooner. I should have. I felt guilty. Because it . . . it's my fault he died."

Shean
Confident, lacking self-awareness.
Argumentative – unafraid of confrontation.
Hard worker.
Dedicated.
Organized.
Driven.
Focused. Refuses to admit when she's wrong – never believes she's wrong?
Has the potential to do great things, currently falling short.

Her voice cracked. But she didn't cry, which was impressive—every time Dola had brought up Silver before now had turned into a wet experience ending in Shean patting the girl's back while she sobbed herself to the brink of exhaustion. This time Dola bent forward instead of weeping, pressing her hands flat to the ground and bowing so low her forehead touched the floor.

"I'm sorry," she said again. "I'm sorry."

"That's all right. I understand. And I believe you," Shean said, and she really did. She thought of Silver's shout, that single *"No!"* that'd escaped him in the moment before his death. She'd *heard* him speak—and it wasn't difficult to believe he could write and draw as well. For all she knew, some of her other dolls could speak and write and draw, too.

Leaving that theory to be explored at another time, she looked down at the journal. "Thank you for giving this to me," she said, tracing a finger around the lines of writing as she spoke, rereading the list about her. She grimaced at the lack of tact in the words, but found it hard to disagree with any of the observations. As she read something gnawed at her, though, something that had nothing to do with the words themselves. There was something about the lines of Silver's writing. Something familiar . . .

Shean sat up straight, eyes wide. She twisted and reached for the small bag Lenna had sewn for her, made from the scraps of the Gleam dress found littered around Web in the aftermath of the Shod attack. The purse was just within arm's reach and she picked it up, tugging open its top and pulling out Nock's license. Flipping it facedown, she held the license next to the writing in the notebook, looking from the question scrawled on the card's back to Silver's writing on the page.

"It matches," Dola said. She'd lifted herself from her bow and was leaning forward, staring at the card. "Silver wrote this?"

Shean felt a lump in the back of her throat, struggling for a moment before she managed to swallow. She thought back to that day on the road, when they'd seen remnants of a Shod attack, how Silver had riffled through the dead Shod as if inspecting them, her pride refusing to let her ask what he was doing while another dollmaker was watching them, and his morbid curiosity ultimately, easily, dismissed as nothing but another one of his oddities.

That had been the first time Silver had ever seen the Shod. Was that when he'd first suspected? Was that when he'd started to think about the Breath Mark and the Shod as connected in some way?

As if in response, a softer, shorter memory came to mind—Silver holding Nock's license out to her that first morning they'd spent in Web, her scolding him for taking the card without permission and putting it back into the pocket of the Gleam dress without a second look. Silver holding his finger up to his smiling lips. Winking at her.

"Yes," she said, answering Dola as much as herself. She lifted the license, holding it against her chest. "Silver wrote this." She closed her eyes for a moment. When she opened them she replaced Nock's license in the Gleam purse before gently closing the notebook, picking it up and turning to Dola.

"I want you to have this," she said, holding the notebook out. Dola's eyes widened.

"Really?"

"Yes." Shean smiled. "Thank you for showing it to me. I'm glad I know what Silver wrote for me. But his notes mean more to you than they do to me."

"But—"

Shean interrupted the protest by shoving the journal at Dola, not in the mood for an argument—and worried she'd change her mind if she hesitated. She let go too fast, before Dola had a firm grip, and the notebook fell to the ground between them, springing open with a rustle. Something slid out from the back of the book, long and rectangular and made from paper. Shean picked it up, turning it around to find it sealed with a dollmaker's lock.

"This is . . ." Shean said, trailing off in amazement.

Nock's letter. She'd forgotten about it.

Staring down at the dollmaker's lock, the pad of her thumb pressing against Nock's seal, Shean remembered trying to pry the letter open. Just a couple months ago she'd stood in Lintok's stable, so desperate to know what Nock really thought of her, tugging and clawing at his letter as if knowing its contents was a matter of life or death. Now the sight of the letter, the feel of its weight in her hand, filled her with foreboding. She could only imagine what Nock had written to Ikiisa about her, words of warning and caution, words of despair. Shean felt the compulsion to rip the letter up. To find a fire and throw it into the flames.

But this letter wasn't hers. It wasn't hers to dispose of.

"Dollmaker Shean?" Dola said, voice anxious. "What's wrong? What is that?"

"A letter," Shean said, pushing herself to her feet. Doing so made her left leg feel tight—the injuries the Shod had inflicted on her were all but healed, even her ankle close to recovered, but the scars forming in loops around her leg were taut and hard to get used to. She gave Dola a smile when the girl leapt to her feet, face concerned.

"I'm fine," she said, holding up the letter. "I just need to deliver this."

"To who?"

"Ikiisa."

"Oh." Dola's eyes shone with curiosity. "Can I come with you?"

Shean imagined having an audience while Ikiisa read Nock's letter, and shook her head. "This is something Ikiisa and I need to discuss alone."

Dola deflated, eyes dropping to the ground. "Oh."

"I'm sorry."

"That's okay," Dola said, shifting her weight from foot to foot in a disappointed shuffle that negated her nonchalant words. "Gran needs me to help her soon, anyway."

Shean eyed the girl for a moment, then decided to relent. At least a little.

"Ikiisa is probably in Web," she said. "Let's walk over together."

Dola's face lifted, brightening. "Okay!"

"Don't forget this," Shean said, bending to pick up Silver's notebook. She pressed it into Dola's hands.

Dola's fingers curled over the journal. She stared at it for a moment, then looked up, face anxious. "You're sure?"

Shean rested a hand atop Dola's head, smiling. "Very. Now, let's go."

AS EXPECTED, THEY FOUND IKIISA IN WEB, GUIDING HER DOLLS IN HELPING SEVeral villagers weave their houses back together. All parties were doing a good job—when Shean stepped onto the cobbles of the town she could almost believe she was in the Web she'd arrived in weeks ago, complete with houses bundled in orbs of twig that made the midday air smell fresh and clean. Of the twenty-three houses that'd been destroyed, thirteen had been replaced so far. The last ten were in various states of construction.

Even given the help they were receiving from Ikiisa's dolls, Shean was impressed with the productivity of the villagers of Web. When Pearl had been decimated in the Red Tide, it'd taken over five years for reconstruction to be complete. Of course, Pearl was a hundred times the size of Web, and the people of Pearl hadn't had dolls to put to work rebuilding their homes. But, still. There were few people in the world, Shean suspected, with a work ethic as strict and consistent as those in Web—from dawn to dusk they toiled to restore their homes, and still somehow found time to weave the silk that'd ensure their future survival. And Ikiisa was just as impressive as her employers; she'd made a good hundred dolls to Shean's forty in the past weeks, all of them as strange and effective as their predecessors.

Dola parted from Shean at the edge of the village with a word of goodbye, running to where Lenna was supervising the replacement of the Spider Mother statue in the center of the town square. Shean watched her go, returning the wave Lenna gave her a moment later. Then she headed toward Ikiisa. She came up behind the woman, touching her on the shoulder.

Ikiisa jumped, turning with an owlish blink of surprise. Then she smiled.

"Shean! Is something wrong?"

"Not exactly." She glanced at the villagers helping Ikiisa with her work. They were staring at her, but turned away when she looked at them. It was either kind or naïve of Dola, to interpret such coldness as forgiveness.

Not that Shean deserved anything better.

"Are you busy?" she asked.

Ikiisa glanced at the villagers. "I can take a break," she said, whistling at her dolls before turning and walking away, gesturing for Shean to follow. Her dolls whistled return notes as Shean passed, a cheerful melody of confirmation following her out of Web.

“Have you seen Roque today?” Ikiisa asked as they walked, heading back toward her house.

Shean shook her head. “Why? Do you need him for something?”

“Not really,” Ikiisa said. She laughed, sliding a hand back through her hair and making the fine brown strands flip around her cheeks. “I’m just worried he’ll disappear one day without telling anyone.”

Shean could see that happening. Roque had decided to remain in Web after the Shod attack, but not to help with the reconstruction of the village. He’d occasionally eat meals with her and Ikiisa (during which he said little), then he’d excuse himself and walk into the forest called Deep. Sometimes he’d be gone for days at a time, off exploring, Shean supposed, though she couldn’t imagine what held such interest for him in the woods.

It was a bit disappointing to Shean, that even after a month she didn’t know more about Roque than what she’d known before coming to Web. The ease of their conversations remained, but he never shared stories of his home or even spoke of his work to her. He was like a ghost drifting on the borders of Web, saying little and, by and large, ignored by the villagers, who, Shean suspected, would’ve been reluctant to accept his help in repairing their homes even if he’d offered it.

A few days ago, after sharing a dinner of stewed dandelion stems, he’d seemed about to say something to Shean, something more than pleasantries, hesitating and looking at her the way Nock did when something was on his mind. But in the end he’d said nothing of substance, bidding her good night and disappearing into the trees. That was the closest they’d come in weeks to a real conversation.

If he wanted to remain silent, it wasn’t Shean’s place to question him. She owed him that much—not only had he alerted Web of the Shod attack and kept the villagers safe during said attack, but a week after the attack Roque had emerged from the forest with

Lintok in tow, the elk dirty and thinner, but otherwise fine. Shean had wept with relief, thanking Roque over and over again as she'd clung to Lintok's dusty neck.

She'd cried a lot over the last few weeks. More than she had in all the years of her life before coming to Web. She wasn't sure if she liked that or not.

"I wonder how long he'll end up staying," Ikiisa said, her wistful tone poking at Shean's thoughts.

Shean shrugged. "As long as he wants to."

"You're probably right."

They reached Ikiisa's house, then, and Shean sat down on the step leading up to the door. Ikiisa joined her.

"What was it you wanted to talk about?" she asked.

Shean fingered the letter in her hands. "I have something from Nock." She held the letter up, looking past Ikiisa rather than at her. "My master. He met you during the Red Tide."

Ikiisa nodded. "I remember him. He's a kind man."

Shean swallowed a lump in her throat, remembering the last time she'd spoken to Nock. How she'd bullied him.

"He is." Before she could change her mind, she handed the letter to Ikiisa. "He wanted me to give this to you when I reached Web."

Ikiisa eyed the letter, gaze curious. "What is it?"

"A letter of introduction."

"Oh." Ikiisa flipped the letter over, inspecting its dollmaker's lock for a moment, then twisting it. It came away easily, and Shean felt heat in her face, remembering how she'd pulled at the lock until her fingertips went numb.

Ikiisa unfolded the letter and Shean's embarrassment chilled. She wanted to run. She wanted to hide, to cover her ears and shut her eyes so she'd never hear or see what Nock thought of her.

Ikiisa startled, eyebrows lifting. She lowered the letter, looking at Shean.

"This isn't for me," she said.

"Yes it is. Nock told me to give it to you."

Ikiisa shook her head, forcing the letter into Shean's hands with a smile. "It's addressed to *you*."

Shean looked down at the letter. Sure enough, her name was at its top. A cold, nervous sweat trickling down her spine, she read.

Shean,

Do you remember Master Yenru's design competition? You were eight (or was it nine?) at the time you entered. Far too young, but you begged me so fiercely (and tearfully) that I found I couldn't deny you.

Apprentices from all nine of the far shore cities came to compete, and you were excited to meet others training toward the same goals you had. You insisted you be allowed to ride Lintok to the city called Drift by yourself, without any help, and by the time we arrived you were bursting with anticipation, refusing to wait for me as I stabled the elk, racing ahead to Master Yenru's house.

I didn't see much of you during the competition itself—you were busy talking with the other apprentices. At the awards ceremony held at sunset that day, you were announced the winner. I'd never seen you beam so brightly. I lost track of you in a flock of apprentices, and an even larger herd of masters come to congratulate me on my excellent student. We didn't see one another again until we were heading back to Pearl. I found you waiting for me at the stables. You were crying.

*Do you remember that? Do you remember what you told me? I'm sure you do—you said the apprentices who'd been so nice to you all day, so complimentary of your skill, had cornered you after the award announcement. How, rather than congratulate you, they'd expressed a bitter, petty lack of surprise at your success. You were, after all, the ward of Master Nock, a dear friend to Master Yenru. And you were, after all, an orphan of the Red Tide—of **course** you won.*

*You were distraught, thinking your success built upon a foundation of circumstance rather than skill. I told you those apprentices were giving in to envy and jealousy, but you wouldn't hear a word—you vowed to prove to everyone that your dolls won because they were the **best** dolls. That you were the **best** dollmaker on the far shore.*

*This is what I **should** have told you that night:*

Those apprentices were in the wrong, yes. But you don't need to prove yourself to them. There is no one, in fact, that you must impress.

You wish to be a guard dollmaker. I'm confident you've many, valid reasons to desire what is, truly, an admirable goal. But I fear that you wish to make guard dolls because you feel you've been told you cannot; because you feel the way you did all those years ago, when your peers diminished your accomplishments to satisfy their pride.

Licensor Maton is not like those apprentices. Pretending that to be the case is foolishness. And if there is one thing I've learned from dollmaking, it's that you can't control the impact your dolls will have on the world around them—when I was young, my own master encouraged me to yearn for neither a guard license nor that of an artisan. Of course I had childish hopes and dreams, wishes. But I did my best to heed her advice, and by the time I was given my license I was neither particularly relieved nor disappointed by the result.

I wish I'd urged you with the same wisdom of spirit possessed by my master.

Shean, I believe that you can be anything you want to be, achieve anything you set your mind to. I'd be a fool not to. But I fear that I've done you a disservice by never teaching you the value of introspection, of soul-searching and meditation, of listening to the voices of others only insofar as they help you come to understand and appreciate who you are. There comes a time when all other voices must be blocked from your mind, a time when you must turn inward and ask yourself who <u>*you*</u> *are, what* <u>*you*</u> *want, and how* <u>*you*</u> *can best achieve those goals. No one can do that for you. I should've told you that years ago.*

Forgive me. And, please, I beg you—choose to listen to yourself. Choose to see your dolls for the good they can do, and let them do that good. If you do so, I believe you'll find the peace you've searched for since the Shod took that which was precious to you.

Yours,
Nock

Shean dropped the letter. It fluttered to her knees, then to the ground.

So that . . . that was what Nock thought of her. This was how he really felt; that she could do anything, be anything. That it was his fault, not hers, that she'd been blind to the nature of her dolls.

He might not feel so generous, once word reached him of what she'd done to Web.

Shean closed her eyes, pressing her face into her hands.

"Shean?" Ikiisa said, voice concerned.

Shean shook her head, forcing herself to look up. She picked up the letter, holding it in one hand while using the other to rub a sleeve over her eyes, smearing tears across her cheeks.

"I've let him down," Shean said, voice hoarse. "He . . . he's going to *hate* me." Ikiisa patted her shoulder.

"I doubt that," she said. Shean looked up to find her smiling. "The best teachers forgive their students' most idiotic mistakes. Nock is a good teacher, isn't he?"

Shean nodded.

"Then there's nothing to worry about." Ikiisa's smile softened. "Master Nock reminds me of my master. I'm sure everything will be fine."

Shean wasn't sure. But she decided not to argue, folding Nock's letter before her tears could smear his words. She tucked the letter into the front of her tunic, where it would be safe, rubbed her eyes again, then said, "Even if he's not angry, that doesn't solve anything."

"What do you mean?" Ikiisa asked.

"Assuming I can even get a license after all this," Shean said, waving a hand to indicate Web, "I still don't want to be an artisan." She slumped, elbows resting on her knees and head bowing. The words were ones she'd been thinking for weeks now. Saying them out loud made them all the more depressing. "I can't see myself being content making art—I keep telling myself I'll *have* to be content, but . . ." She trailed off, looking down at her hands, thinking of Nock's words.

Ask yourself who <u>you</u> are, what <u>you</u> want, and how <u>you</u> can best achieve those goals.

"I want to face the Shod," she said. "Even after all of this, I still want to protect people from the Shod. Somehow."

"You *have*," Ikiisa said. "What you discovered about the Breath Mark is going to change everything about how we handle Shod—it's going to make fighting them so much easier!"

"But you'll still be the one who actually *fights* them," Shean said. "The country called One still needs guard dolls; writing the Breath Mark on the Shod doesn't kill them. It just slows them down." She sighed, resting her chin in her hands. "I want to be a part of *ending* this, a part of not just *slowing* the Shod, but *stopping* them. For good. And that isn't what an artisan does."

"They do in a way," Ikiisa said, voice contemplative.

Shean side-eyed her, voice wry when she asked, "How?"

"Toy dolls keep away nightmares, and that's what the Shod are, aren't they?" Ikiisa lifted a hand, waving it as she said, "Master Coen told me once that the most dangerous part of the Shod's existence is how they occupy people's minds, driving out good thoughts with bad, frightened ones. Toy dolls distract from the darkness; they fill people's lives with beauty and companionship."

The words made Shean feel sick with resignation.

"I know," she said. "But I still . . . I still want . . . not *more* than that, but something else. Something different."

"Like what?"

"I don't know."

Shean reached back to undo the cord holding her hair in a tail behind her head, a style she'd taken to as the length of her hair had grown increasingly irritating during days spent immobile while healing, sitting at her work desk for hours on end. One could only flip one's hair over one's shoulders so many times before the urge to simply cut it all off became more than tempting.

Knowing she'd regret such a decision later, though, she'd settled for tying it back.

Now she felt an odd comfort at the sensation of hair falling onto her shoulders, draping the sides of her neck. A pressure lifted from her head with her hair freed and she sighed, rubbing her hands up and down her face with a vigor that hurt.

"Isn't there another option?" she said when her hands dropped. She looked at Ikiisa. "A third path? A manner of dollmaker that's neither artisan nor warrior?" She leaned forward. "You said there was, didn't you? Back in the hideout, when we were sheltering from the Shod. So tell me—what else can I do?"

"I did say that," Ikiisa said, slowly. Her voice was reluctant. "My master used to say dolls do whatever they're meant to do, and the distinction of artisan or guard is an oversimplified binary."

"So what's the other option? What's the in-between path of being a dollmaker?"

Ikiisa looked down. "I don't know," she said. She was quiet for a moment. Then she cleared her throat, clasping her hands together in front of her and fidgeting a moment before, in a reluctant voice, adding, "Have . . . have you tried asking?"

"Asking?" Shean echoed, puzzled.

"Your, um, dolls," Ikiisa said, voice small with embarrassment, and eyes remaining glued on her shoes.

Shean sat up straighter, eyes widening. "That's right. You asked your dolls what they were meant to do, didn't you?"

Ikiisa blushed, but nodded. "I know it's strange. But maybe you should try that. See what they tell you."

Shean stood. "I will."

Ikiisa looked up at her, surprise bright across her face. "You will?"

Shean smiled. "Why not? Who knows what they're made to do

better than my own dolls?" She snorted, folding her arms and rolling her eyes skyward. "In theory, anyway—your dolls are special. Maybe mine won't be able to tell me anything useful."

Ikiisa leapt to her feet, returning Shean's smile with a blinding grin. "I'm sure they will! Wait here!"

She spun and ran into her house, leaving before Shean could ask where she was going or what she was doing. A moment later she returned, one of Shean's dolls in tow.

It was one of the dolls she'd made for the villagers of Web—a stocky piece dressed in scrap fabric stitched into a semblance of a dress that fell to round, wood-grained knees. The doll's face was highlighted by eyes carved from a darker wood than what Shean used for the rest of the build, serious, ponderous eyes that lifted to Shean when Ikiisa came to a stop in front of her, the doll's hand in Ikiisa's, its bald, lacquered head bright in the sunlight.

This was the first time Shean had seen one of the dolls she'd made for Web since giving them to the villagers—she hadn't even named this one before it'd been whisked away to work. All the dolls she'd provided practically lived in the Veil now, tending the remaining silk spiders and working to rebuild the clearing while providing fresh silk for the villagers to weave with. Staring down at the doll in front of her, Shean wondered what it was doing here instead.

"I borrowed her from the Veil today to help clean up some of the lingering mess in my house," Ikiisa said, guessing at Shean's thoughts and answering them.

"Oh," Shean said. She made herself blink, breaking the staring contest she'd been having with her doll and pushing through the uncanny sensation of feeling awkward around one of her own creations. She gave the doll a strained smile. "That makes this easier."

Ikiisa nodded enthusiastically, leading the doll down the steps of her house while Shean sat back down, putting her close to eye level with the doll when Ikiisa let go of it and it stood directly in front of Shean. Ikiisa joined her on the steps of the house, eagerly fidgeting as she waited for Shean to ask the question.

With a jolt, Shean realized she was nervous. No, more than that—she was *scared*. Frightened as she gazed at her doll because what if it said yes? That it *was* meant to be a piece of art after all, making Shean, in turn, an artisan? Every part of Shean groaned in resistance to that idea, aversion so fierce she found herself wondering if this was a mistake. If it'd be best if she didn't know—best if she didn't ask, if the answer she received was something that'd only dishearten her.

But she couldn't keep going like this. Wondering what she was meant to do, who she was, what her fate was now that she knew, in no uncertain terms, that she would *never* be a guard dollmaker.

Clarity was needed. Clarity was *necessary*. So Shean took a bracing breath, looked her doll in the eyes, and forced herself to ask.

"Are you art?" Shean pressed a hand to her own chest, fingers shaking against her sternum. "Am I an artisan?"

Her doll shook its head. Immediately, without a hint of hesitation. Relief flooded Shean, making her shoulders sag as tension left them. She shared a happy look with Ikiisa, then turned back to the doll. "Are you a guard doll after all, then? Are you meant to fight the Shod?"

Her doll shook its head again. Immediately, without a hint of hesitation.

Shean's relief curdled to exasperation, the violent glimmer of hope that'd struck up inside of her smothered with a twinge and ache. She flung her hands up, next words perplexed bordering on despairingly bewildered. "Then what *are* you meant to do?"

The doll folded its arms, shrugged. The edge of its mouth lifted in a small smile that made Shean think of a different doll, a white-haired doll with a fondness for winking. Arms dropping, she shook her head in despair, but found herself smiling, too.

She also found herself crying. Again.

"Shean?" Ikiisa said. She rested a hand on Shean's shoulder, expression concerned when, wiping tears from her vision, Shean looked at her. "Are you okay?"

"Not really," she said, a hiccupping chuckle escaping her. "But I think I will be."

Ikiisa looked unconvinced by that, but gave her an uncertain smile and nod anyway, patting her shoulder in a reassuring gesture. Letting out a shaky breath, Shean turned back to her doll, who was still smiling at her, a smug look on its face.

Not art. Not guards. Through tears that felt half happy and half frustrated, Shean thought maybe, just maybe, her dolls were just as confused as she was.

And maybe, for whatever strange reason, that was a comforting thought.

Resting her elbow on her knee and her cheek in her hand, Shean shook her head again, felt her smile widen as tears dripped off the edge of her chin. "I'll keep asking," she said, voice hoarse from the crying, exhausted from the confusion. Determined. "However many times I have to, for as long as it takes. Until I figure out what you—*we*—are meant to do."

In response her doll gave a solemn nod, rewarding Shean's statement with a double thumbs-up of clear, pleased approval. Which made Shean laugh.

"Excuse me," Roque said. Shean jumped, so hard she fell off the step she sat on. Ikiisa let out a yelp, hand flying to clutch at her chest as she rocked backward. The doll yawned.

Picking herself up from the ground, Shean turned to find the man standing off to the side, out of sight for anyone sitting on the front steps of Ikiisa's house. As always he had his travel bag slung over his shoulder, a demure look on his face, and he spoke in a voice of strict politeness when he bowed his head in apology. "Forgive me. I didn't mean to interrupt."

Shean had a hard time believing that. She shook her head, letting out a strained bark of laughter and pushing the hair out of her face. "No need to apologize. We were just talking ourselves in circles."

"I see." Roque studied Shean's face for a moment, glancing at her doll before his eyes slid to Ikiisa. Then he straightened, smiling a slight, friendly smile as his gaze returned to Shean. "In that case, may I have a private word with you?"

Shean glanced at Ikiisa, who stood. "We need to get back to work, anyway," she said, grabbing the doll's hand as she spoke. She patted Shean's shoulder. "We can talk more later."

Shean nodded and Ikiisa turned, her and the doll leaving with a farewell wave.

"Shall we?" Roque said. Shean rubbed lingering tears off her face and nodded.

"Yes."

ROQUE LED SHEAN INTO IKIISA'S HOUSE, TO THE ROOM HE WAS, ALLEGEDLY, staying in. When he opened the door it was to a bed that looked suspiciously unused, with a window opened to let the light of the noon sun spill across the floor. Two kneeling cushions were waiting, Roque gesturing for Shean to take the one nearest the window. She sat, watching him settle across from her, pulling off his travel bag and setting it to the side, his hand resting atop it in a gesture she'd once thought protective and, now, struck her as reassuring. Like he needed to touch the bag to know it was still there.

"I've heard you plan to leave Web tomorrow," Roque said, wasting no time with pleasantries.

"I do. I have one more doll I need to finish tonight, and then I'll be leaving."

"The villagers are satisfied with your work?"

"Yes. I've made all the dolls they requested, and extra. I told Lenna I mean to leave tomorrow, and she didn't object."

Roque nodded. "Then I'll leave tomorrow as well."

Shean felt a small rush, a ridiculous increase to her heart's speed that she tried to ignore. "You want to travel together?"

Roque shook his head. "No. But the reason I've been staying in Web is you."

"Me?" Shean felt heat in her face, a delighted little clench in her stomach.

"Yes," Roque said, and though his voice was pleasant, it wasn't the voice of a man declaring affection so much as fact. He didn't smile as he continued, gaze serious as he held hers. "I suspected when we met in the city called Ports, and was convinced when we met again in Web. After the Shod attack I'd made up my mind, but I didn't want to rush you. And besides, I had plenty to do in the forest called Deep."

Shean frowned, lost. "I don't understand. What're you talking about?"

Roque leaned forward. "Shean, do you know why you defeated the Shod?"

The question was surprising, not only because it was unexpected, but because Roque had said so little to Shean these past weeks about the attack, she'd started to believe he had no interest in hearing any more than what she'd already told him and Ikiisa after they'd found her in the wreckage of Web. For a moment she was so taken aback she said nothing, only breaking her silence when Roque gave her a questioning look. "I . . . Yes," she said, tugging at the end of her left sleeve, fingering the fabric as the slight flutter of nerves she felt whenever she talked about the attack batted against her ribs. "I wrote the Breath Mark on them. That made them fall apart."

Roque nodded. "Yes. But *why*?"

Shean had thought about that a lot. Why *had* the Breath Mark worked like a weapon on the Shod? The writing on Nock's license—Silver—had wondered what would happen if the Mark was put on the Shod, but he hadn't left any explanation as to the reasoning behind that theory. And he wasn't around, now, to offer any clarifications as to why it affected the monsters the way it did.

At the time, while the Shod had been attacking her and right after she'd finished putting the Breath Mark on them, Shean had thought, she'd been all but *convinced*, that the monsters were dolls. Twisted, somehow, corrupted and made into fiends seeking repair and peace. Afterward, once she'd had time to calm down enough for the rational part of her to speak up, she'd realized that was impossible. Ridiculous, even.

But she couldn't stop remembering the Shod that'd reminded her of her brother's doll. She couldn't shake how the Cry of the Shod sounded like the wail of lost children, searching for their families. Couldn't dispel her memory of the Red Tide, what she *knew*, now, she'd heard the Shod say to her.

Please, please, please. Save me.

"I don't know," Shean said. Roque's eyebrows raised.

"You don't?" he said, and she could tell he didn't believe her. She swallowed, looking down. She picked at the frayed embroidery of the kneeling cushion she sat on. With Roque staring at her so intensely, though, she could only hesitate for a moment.

"I thought . . . I thought, for a moment, that they, the Shod, I mean, might . . . might be . . ." Her voice diminished to a whisper. "Dolls." Shean looked up. "But that's ridiculous!" she said, quickly. "The Shod aren't dolls. They *can't* be."

"Why not?" Roque asked. Shean was shocked to see he didn't look the least bit surprised by her absurd theory. If anything, he looked pleased.

"Because Shod are Shod. And dolls fight Shod," Shean said. "They can't be the same thing."

Roque smiled. He leaned forward, tapping the ground between them, a soft rap to punctuate his words. "What happens to dolls when their dollmakers die?"

"They're buried with their makers," Shean said, confused by the question.

Roque nodded. "Yes."

"And?" Shean said, feeling a prick of impatience. What was he getting at?

Roque straightened, tucking a strand of copper hair back from his eyes. "Before the attack on Web, I was looking through Deep for the Shod. I ran into one of your dolls. We searched together, and came upon someplace called the Dollmaker's Graveyard."

Shean stiffened, appalled. "You went to the *Graveyard*?"

"Yes."

"It's forbidden! Only those carrying fallen dollmakers to their final resting places are allowed in the Graveyard!"

"We arrived by accident, I assure you. And by equal happenstance we witnessed something strange." He continued, explaining the dolls crawling from their grave, the Shod amassed on the edge of the Graveyard. How Shean's dolls had stood there staring at the Shod as if in a trance, unmoving even when he ordered them to run.

Shean listened with mounting alarm, then sickened horror. When he finished she had to brace her hands against the ground, leaning on them for support.

"By the First Dollmaker," she said, arms and voice shaking. "They really *are* dolls." All of a sudden her personal struggles, her pain over not knowing what sort of dollmaker she was, felt so petty and time-wasting. Small and insignificant in the face of this shift in her reality. She squeezed her eyes shut, the tremors in her words swapping out for an agonized crack as she said, "But *why*? Why here? Why Web?"

"You told me that after the Red Tide the Shod all but disappeared," Roque said, the grim tone of his voice far too calm for the subject at hand. "If a large enough number of them were destroyed in the Tide, I think we can assume they retreated to lick their wounds. As it appears dolls become Shod once a dollmaker has died, it makes sense they'd fall back to a graveyard to regroup."

Shean shook her head. She didn't want to believe what he was saying. She wanted him to be lying.

But something told her, something sad and sick and scared, that he wasn't.

"No," she said, a whisper.

"You say it's forbidden to visit the Dollmaker's Graveyard,"

Roque said. She looked up at him, and his gaze was so intense she flinched. "Is that true of all graveyards for dollmakers?" he asked.

"Yes," Shean said.

"Is it also common to place such graveyards far away from populated areas?"

"Y-yes."

"Have you ever wondered why you bury dead dollmakers so far from cities? Why you can't return to pay your respects to the dead?"

Had she? Really? No. Because . . . because she'd never *wanted* to come back to her family's graves, never desired to relive the trauma of burying them. And, besides, some things had always been the way they were, were never going to change and therefore were pointless to question. Some things just *were*.

"It's . . . it's what the First Dollmaker decreed," Shean said, the excuse a weak approximation of her actual feelings, which were far too big at the moment to articulate. "It's tradition."

"Tradition is wisdom clouded by habit," Roque said, and he sounded like he knew exactly what he was talking about. "In the case of dollmaker burials, that wisdom is the Shod."

He was probably right. Intolerably, horribly correct. Shean shook her head. "This is . . . The Shod are . . ." She sat up, wrapping her arms around herself as a chill swept through her. "This is terrible. Shod can only be killed by dolls—how can they *be* dolls?"

"They aren't. They *were*."

Shean looked up at Roque, arms dropping. A dreadful thought entered her, voiced before she could repress it. "But this means when we make dolls we're really making . . . We have to stop." She clutched the side of her head, tight enough to hurt. "But if we don't make dolls, we'll have nothing to fight the Shod with—even using the Breath Mark on the Shod isn't enough. It doesn't kill them. A doll has to do that." She shook her head once, eyes squeezed shut. "We *can't* stop making dolls, because they're *still* the only thing that can permanently stop the Shod. But when we make dolls, we're also making *Shod*?" Her voice raised to a wail and she shook her head again and again, so hard her ears rang. "This . . . this can't be true!"

A rustle and flap. Shean opened her eyes to find Roque sliding an opened book toward her, twice the size of Dola's journal with off-white pages covered in writing. Through a mist of tears, she looked over symbols she couldn't understand, lines and dots and swirls written in a way that denoted language, but not one she knew.

In the center of the pages Roque displayed to her were two designs she *did* understand, at least to a minor degree: large, bold shapes composed of lines curved and straightened at very deliberate spots, triangles drawn in carefully designated places around the lines. The designs looked similar to the Breath Mark.

"What are these?" Shean asked, voice thick with distress and confusion, reaching out and touching the edge of one page. The paper was softer than she expected.

"Marks," Roque said.

Shean looked up at him. "Like the Breath Mark?"

He nodded. "Yes. But for different things."

"What sorts of things?" Shean asked.

Roque waved a hand through the air. "Anything. For warmth and cold, for pain. For destruction." He touched a finger to his face, tracing one of the white lines decorating his jawline. "There are even Marks that make wounds heal as if they never were."

Shean touched her leg, feeling the ridges of damage under the fabric of the trousers she wore. For a moment her alarm around the origins of the Shod diminished, replaced by more selfish concerns. "If that's true, why didn't you heal me?"

"I only use Marks in emergencies," Roque said, voice matter-of-fact and bluntly unapologetic. "Your wounds weren't life-threatening. Nor were they going to cripple you."

Shean resented that—if what Roque claimed was true, he was hoarding Marks that could do many people much good. *If* his words were true. She looked back down at his book, at his Marks, deciding she was done being distracted. "What does this have to do with the Shod?" she asked.

"I'll explain that in a moment. But before I do, I need you to understand that the Breath Mark is not the only Mark."

Shean sat back, arms folded. "Can you prove that to me?"

Roque cocked his head to the side. "You don't believe me?"

Shean shrugged. "What you're saying is strange."

Roque considered her for a moment. "I suppose this is an emergency, then." His eyes gleamed in a way Shean would've thought playful, if she didn't know better. "You mustn't blame me for the consequences, though."

With that he pulled his book back toward himself, flipping through a few pages before pausing. He read for a moment, then closed the book, reaching into his travel bag and pulling out a stick of lead. He drew on the floor in front of his kneeling cushion, making no protest when Shean leaned forward to watch.

The Mark he drew was simple—a triangle with lines slashing through two of its sides. When he finished drawing and sat back, the floorboards creaked. Then they strained, bursting open to allow a slender stalk to shoot up, growing thicker as it rose, developing a bud that uncurled into a flower with delicate, lacy white petals and a shockingly yellow center. Shean sat back with a gasp, inhaling the sugary perfume of the bloom.

"A Flower Mark," Roque said. He reached out, fingering one of the petals, rubbing it as if it were the ear of a hound pup. "Specifically, the Mountain Crest Flower Mark." He bent forward, using his sleeve to rub away the Mark he'd just drawn, erasing all traces of the symbol. When he straightened he put away his stick of lead, explaining. "Even with the Mark visibly erased, this Mountain Crest will continue to bloom in this room. Forever." His face sobered as he stared at the flower. "It won't die."

Shean was shaking. She wrapped her arms around herself but the tremors continued. It was all she could do to keep her voice steady as she said, "Why are you showing me this?"

Roque looked up from the flower, face returning to its normal, pleasant expression. "Because, as I've said, it's important you understand that there're more Marks in the world than the Breath Mark."

"Why?"

"Because I've been making up my mind whether or not I should trust you. And I've decided to." He closed his Mark book, returning it to his travel bag. "You used the Breath Mark to fight the Shod. Even without knowing that the Shod are what they are, you found their undoing."

Shean shook her head. "What I did slowed them down, but, as I've said, it didn't *kill* them—a doll was *still* the only way to destroy them completely."

"But what you did *changed* them. Changed them in a way I've never seen." Roque folded his hands in his lap, fingers laced. "I'm not saying you're the first to ever realize what the Shod are, or even the first to attempt to use the Breath Mark on them—from what you've told me, whoever set your traditions knew perfectly well what the Shod really are."

That was a good point. The First Dollmaker, he was the one who'd penned the law forbidding visits to dollmaker graveyards.

How much had he known about what the Shod really were? How many of his edicts and laws had to do with that knowledge? The thought was troubling. It made Shean feel like the ground under her feet, the "truth" she'd relied on her entire life, was, if not crumbling, then shifting. Taking on new angles and layers and weight.

"But you *are* the first dollmaker I've met to put such knowledge into practice," Roque continued, voice reaching Shean through her worrying realizations.

She shook her head. "You're wrong."

Roque's eyebrows arched. "Am I?"

"Yes," Shean said, hands curling into fists that pressed to her knees. "Because *I* didn't think of putting the Breath Mark on the Shod." She told him about Nock's license, about Silver's notebook pages. When she finished, a smile split his face.

"Even better," he said.

Shean let out an exasperated noise. "How so?"

"You're telling me that one of your dolls, based on what limited knowledge he had of the Shod, thought up the idea of using the Breath Mark on the monsters. And that that same doll kept records, detailed records, of every person in Web." Roque chuckled, pushing a hand back through his hair as his smile turned wry. "I've been wondering why your dolls wouldn't run from the Shod, or fight them—I think I understand, now. They were *studying* the Shod. They wanted to understand them, and help you understand them, too."

The implications of that theory gave Shean pause. Could . . . could that be true? It was clear to her, now, that her dolls weren't guard dolls *or* artisan dolls. But could the answer to their purpose really be this . . . simple? She thought of all the times she'd seen Silver imitate her, other people. The way he'd caught on so quickly with how to silk spiders.

"Research"—Dola had said that was what Silver had called his notes. Might her dolls be capable of "researching" the Shod, and finding ways to kill them that way? A thrill of excitement trilled through Shean at the possibility.

Then she shook her head, feeling ridiculous. And manipulated. Even if what Roque was saying was right, he was only saying what he was saying to point her in some direction he wanted her pointed—knowing that, she dropped a fist into the ground in front of her, making the flower between her and Roque shiver and bob. "No!" she said, as firmly as she could manage. She glared at Roque. "Even if everything you're saying is true, I still don't understand any of this! Why are you telling me these things? What do you *want* from me?"

"Communication," Roque said, and he said it so simply, with such open frankness, Shean's frustration deflated. She sat back as Roque continued, voice tired. "There's one thing you must understand about me, Dollmaker Shean; my goal and purpose in life is to find a way to break the Marks."

"Break them?"

Roque nodded. "As things are, once a Mark is used it can't be unused—once you make a doll and give it the Breath Mark, it can't be returned to a mannequin, can it?"

Shean shook her head. "But a doll *can* be destroyed," she said.

"What I speak of is more permanent than death—it's erasure. Undoing. I don't want to simply find a way to kill that which is created by Marks, I wish to find a way to make it so Marks can no longer be used." Roque leaned forward, eyes lowering to the ground. "I've searched for a Mark to undo Marks, a Mark to render all other Marks useless. But I fear that's a false hope—that no such Mark exists. Even so, I *must* find a way to break Marks. Even if that very act feels, and so often *is*, one way or another, impossible."

He looked up at Shean. "Take your dolls and the Shod, for example. Given what I now know of the Shod, the easiest way to drive the monsters to extinction would be to stop making dolls. But, as you've said, you can't do that or you'll have nothing to stop the Shod with. You could try to destroy every Shod in existence, then destroy what dolls remain and outlaw the practice of making them. But that in itself is an impossible task."

He was right. Everything Roque said was true, and Shean hated it. She swallowed, mouth chalky and dry with the understanding that her world was a loop. An inescapable cycle started by the First Dollmaker and perpetuated by every apprentice who made a doll today. By every doll she herself had ever made.

No one would believe her if she told them that. Even if they did, they'd say what Roque was saying now—that to outlaw the making of dolls was an invitation to the Shod to kill them all. Nothing could stop a Shod but dolls, not arrows or fire or acid. And not the Breath Mark, either.

Shean stood. Paced across the room for several minutes. Stopped when the movement did nothing to spur a solution inside of her head.

"What do we do?" she said, voice thin. "What *can* we do?"

"Dolls are given life by the Breath Mark. But so are the Shod," Roque said. "The solution, as I've said, is to erase the Breath Mark."

Shean turned to face him, arms lifting in an imploring gesture. "What if even that doesn't work? What if we find a way to 'erase' the Mark like you say, but it only affects dolls?"

"That's unlikely. I've always known the Shod are moved by some Mark, and now it's clear that Mark is the Breath Mark. The same Mark, fueling two different entities—both doll and Shod will fall if their Mark is taken from them."

He spoke with a confidence Shean couldn't share. But he also, clearly, knew more about Marks than she did. She deferred to that knowledge, returning to her kneeling cushion and folding her hands in her lap.

"You want me to help you find a way to erase the Breath Mark," she said. "Permanently." Her hands shook as she said the word, her fingers lacing in an attempt to still their own trembling. "You want help erasing the Breath Mark not just from dolls, but from existence. Making it vanish. Forever."

As she spoke, Shean tried to imagine a world without dolls. A world where she couldn't make dolls. Tears pricked her eyes.

"There's no need to be distressed," Roque said, voice gentle. "As of yet, I've no idea how to undo *any* Mark, let alone the Breath Mark. For all my searching, I've yet to find anything that comes even close to Mark-Breaking." He gave her a kind smile. "And, no. I'm not asking, nor do I expect, you to take up my mantle. As I said earlier, what I want from you is communication."

"Explain what that means," Shean said. "Please."

"I'm going to leave the country called One. Soon. When I do, I'd ask you stay in touch with me. Continue your life in whatever manner you choose, but update me if you—or another, dollmaker or otherwise—ever figure out how to stop the Shod for good. Inform me if the Shod are ever, truly, defeated. That's all."

That was all, was it? That was all, after Shean found herself knowing what the Shod were, what her dolls *would* be, what ruin her country was facing. And how deeply, truly that ruin was their own fault.

Eyes squeezing shut, Shean said, "Why are you telling me this?" She was unable to keep an edge of despair from her voice. "Why are you asking this of *me*?"

"I've told you. I've decided to trust you."

Shean shook her head, opening her eyes and pressing the heel of her palm to her forehead, which was throbbing. "No. I mean . . . you and Ikiisa are friends. Why aren't you asking for *her* help?"

Roque's eyes cleared with understanding. "Ah. Yes, Ikiisa is my friend—she saved me from the Shod once, many years ago. And I'm grateful to her. But Ikiisa is not so interested in finding a way to eliminate the Shod as she is in finding a place where she can protect people from the Shod. *You* want the Shod to disappear."

"Yes," Shean said, agreeing without a thought.

"Even if making the Shod disappear means your dolls will disappear with them," Roque said.

Now Shean hesitated, wanting to say he was wrong. But she couldn't.

"Yes," she whispered.

"That," Roque said, "along with how you used the Breath Mark on the Shod, is the difference between the two of you. I think no less of Ikiisa for that difference; she's like most of the dollmakers I've met. You, though, can choose to be different."

Ask yourself who you are, Nock had written. *What you want, and how you can best achieve those goals.*

What I want. How I can achieve those goals.

"I want to end the Shod," Shean said, and the words weren't anything new or different; this was a statement she'd said many times, her goal ever since the Red Tide. Yet she felt the phrase in a strange way, a firmer, fuller way than ever before. With a conviction that, though it had flagged only minutes ago upon confirming the origins of the Shod, returned to her now full force. And unyielding. She met Roque's gaze, jaw set. "That's what I have, and will always, choose."

Roque smiled. "Good. Then I ask for your help, Shean of Pearl.

There are Marks, thousands of them, scattered across this world, and I intend to search through them until I find one, some combination of several, or some other means that will lead to success in destroying them all. Searching for a way to purge the Marks from existence is a vast task, and I can't be everywhere at once—your willingness to keep me informed of the changes to the Breath Mark of the country called One will be greatly appreciated."

Shean winced at the word "purge," conviction not weakening so much as shuddering. "Without our dolls, we . . . we'll lose something," she said, unable to stop the words.

"I'm aware," Roque said. "And I apologize—sometimes I get carried away in my feelings, and forget that mine aren't the only emotions to take into consideration." He rubbed the back of his neck, eyes moving from Shean to stare into the distance. "I intend to find a way to break the Marks—that will never change. But when I succeed, I'll then have before me the moral quandary of which Marks, if any, *should* be broken." His gaze slid back to hers, voice taking on a deceptively light air. "If someone could find a way to ensure dolls won't become Shod upon their masters' deaths, though, destroying the Breath Mark completely would be unnecessary."

That sounded like a challenge. An impossible task.

But, also, an exciting one. A way she, Dollmaker Shean of Pearl, could help the country called One in their battle against the Shod. A way she and her dolls—be they art or weapons or something else entirely—could help her people.

"I'll do it," she said. "I'll find a way."

Roque's eyes gleamed. "I don't doubt it."

Shean lifted her chin, shoulders straight. For the first time in weeks she felt a glimmer of former confidence, a hint of that pride that'd driven her to all sorts of ruin in Web. Tempered, now, with experience, and no small amount of shame. But still strong enough to carry her onward.

"I'll keep in contact with you, Roque," she said. "I'll do what I can to protect my people, in whatever way I and my dolls can. But you have to promise me something in return—if you *do* find a way to break Marks, and if you discover that way before I find a way to keep dolls from turning into Shod, you have to bring that way to One. You have to give us that knowledge, so we can decide for ourselves whether or not we wish to destroy the Shod at the cost of our dolls." She gave him a hard look. "That decision is *not*, and never will be, yours."

Roque leaned forward, pushing down the flower growing from the floorboards between them, bending the delicate thing's stalk and making it bow low for Shean. He smiled.

"It's a deal."

THE NEXT MORNING WAS TINGED IN AMBER. AUTUMN WAS STEALING THE LEAVES of the forest, russeting their green and covering the ground in a thin layer of copper. The wind blowing through the village was cool, making the tips of Shean's nose and ears throb with chill as she saddled Lintok.

She'd decided to leave Web at dawn, a bit too early for most villagers to be up now that the silking of spiders had, by and large, become the pastime of dolls. When she finished with Lintok, checked on the doll tucked into her saddle bags, and headed toward the road through the forest called Deep, though, a small crowd was waiting for her: Roque, Lenna, Dola, Bobble the doll. And, of course, Ikiisa.

Shean stopped in front of Lenna first. It was hard to meet the older woman's eyes, but she forced herself to.

"I'm sorry," she said. "For everything."

Lenna smiled. "We appreciate the dolls you've given us. We won't be holding a grudge."

The words answered a question Shean hadn't dared ask. Blinking back tears, she bowed her head. "Thank you."

Lenna pressed a hand to her shoulder. "Live well," she said.

"I'll try."

"Good."

A hand slipped into Shean's, small and cold. She looked at Dola, who was doing nothing to hold back her own tears.

"I-I'm sorry about S-Silver," she said, damp face growing red splotches of distress as she spoke.

Shean squeezed Dola's hand. "I'm glad he saved you. That's all that matters."

They were words she should've said sooner, but she was glad she was saying them now. Dola's lips trembled into a smile.

"Thank you for making him," Dola said, voice thick. She swallowed, glanced at Lenna, who nodded. Dola took a deep breath, looked back at Shean, and launched into a characteristic outpouring of words: "I-I'll come visit you someday! I'm going to become a dollmaker that makes dolls as good as your dolls, and then I'll come and show you my dolls!"

"We'll both come," Ikiisa said, stepping forward and taking Dola's other hand. She smiled at the girl, and it was the most genuine smile Shean had ever seen. "I'll want to see the look on Dollmaker Shean's face when she sees how brilliant my apprentice is."

"Apprentice?" Shean echoed. Dola nodded, beaming.

"As soon as I turn thirteen and pass the Breath Mark exams!" she said.

"That's right," Ikiisa said, laughing.

Shean looked from Ikiisa to Dola, smile flagging. She glanced at Roque, their conversation from yesterday like a wall between them and the rest of the world. Shean wondered if Roque always felt this . . . queasy. Did he understand how her happiness for Ikiisa and Dola was tempered with fear of yet another dollmaker making more dolls that would, someday, become Shod?

He did. He had to. But none of that mattered because Shean was going to find a way to end the Shod. She was going to find a way for Dola to make dolls that never turned into demons.

Telling herself that, firmly, Shean widened her smile.

"Congratulations," she said, releasing Dola's hand and giving her a bow of one apprentice dollmaker to another, her arms straight at her sides. "You'll make a splendid dollmaker."

"I have to pass the Breath Mark exams first," Dola said, blushing.

"You will," Shean said.

Something bumped against her legs as she spoke. She looked down to find Bobble headbutting her. Smiling, she crouched in front of the doll. She cupped its lumpy head in her hands and kissed it between its misshapen eyes. "Thank you," she told it. Then she stood, resting her hands on Ikiisa's shoulders, fingers gripping tight. *"Thank you."*

Ikiisa's eyes were bright. She let go of Dola, stepping forward and wrapping her arms around Shean. It was an embrace Shean returned, chest tight. They both had to wipe at their eyes when they broke apart.

"Well," Shean said, stepping back and taking Lintok's reins in a hand. "Take care of yourself."

Ikiisa smiled. "I will," she said, and looking at her standing there,

Lenna and Dola next to her, a village she'd helped rebuild behind her, Shean believed her.

"Goodbye, Dollmaker Ikiisa."

"Goodbye, Dollmaker Shean."

Roque cleared his throat.

Ikiisa startled, glancing at him. Then she let out a short, revelatory noise, the fist of one hand coming down on the palm of the other. "Oh! Shean, I've something for you." She stepped forward, removing something from her pocket, holding it out. Shean recognized the pendant they'd used to call Roque.

"Roque asked me to give this to you," Ikiisa said.

"But that's Ikiisa's!" Shean protested, looking at Roque. His eyebrows raised.

"She was borrowing it," he said. "Now you need it."

"Can't you make me another one?" she asked.

"No," Roque said. He stepped up to her, voice lowering to a murmur only she could hear. "This stone has a Summon Mark. It's the only way for you to keep in touch with me, and the risk of one falling into unfriendly hands is terrifying. I make as few of these pendants as possible."

"But—"

"It's all right," Ikiisa interrupted. Before Shean could further protest Ikiisa stepped forward, forcing Roque to move aside as she slid the necklace over Shean's head, stepping back when she finished.

"You don't mind?" Shean asked, fingers closing around the pendant.

"No," Ikiisa said. "I don't need it anymore."

"You're sure?"

Ikiisa glanced at Dola. She smiled. "I'm sure."

Shean felt a lump in her throat, and she wasn't sure if she felt like crying or smiling or both. More than anything, she felt relieved. Like Ikiisa's insistence on her taking this necklace was a promise between them. A promise that all would be well, now. For both of them.

"Even without that stone, you can always consider me an ally and friend," Roque said, bowing as he spoke. "I hope we meet again, Ikiisa of Web." Ikiisa bowed back.

"To you the same," she said, smile widening. She looked at Shean. "And to you."

"I don't deserve that," Shean said, the lump in her throat growing, making her voice crack with a gratitude that warmed every inch of her.

"Of course you do. You saved Web."

"Only after allowing the Shod to destroy it."

"A wrong for a right, then," Ikiisa said.

"But—"

"No arguing!"

Before Shean could say another word Ikiisa turned, taking Dola's hand and grabbing ahold of Lenna's arm. She propelled the villagers of Web back toward their home, Bobble trotting at their heels as Ikiisa called at Shean and Roque over her shoulder.

"Take care! Both of you! And thank you!"

Then the dollmaker of Web was gone, vanished into her village. Shean dropped the hand she'd reached out after Ikiisa, closing her mouth against whatever final words she might've said. She smiled.

"Shall we go?" Roque said.

In response, Shean turned her back to Web. She inhaled the scents of the forest called Deep.

And took a step forward.

THEY'D ONLY BEEN WALKING FOR A FEW MINUTES WHEN ROQUE STOPPED.

"Our paths split here," he said.

"Oh," Shean said, disappointed but not surprised. After all, Roquc *had* said that, despite the fact that he was leaving Web with her, they weren't going to be traveling together. Even so, she'd hoped they would. At least for a while.

A false hope, evidently.

Roque stepped forward, tapping the pendant hanging from her neck. "If you ever need to tell me something, address this stone by my name, then speak. If you need help, I'll try to come."

Shean nodded, distracted from his words by his closeness. For the first time she noticed there was frost in his hair, tiny clear crystals of ice giving the impression of his head being decorated with a subtle scatter of diamonds. The crystals caught the sunrise dappling through the leaves over their heads, flashing with a promise of imminent melting.

Frost. Shean had to suppress a giggle, gripping Lintok's reins hard with the strain. Had Roque stayed outside all night, long enough to gather frost like a blade of grass? That wouldn't be a surprise, but, really. *Frost.*

"Shean?" Roque said, head tipping to the side. "Is something wrong?"

Shean shook her head, smiling. Keenly feeling the absurdity of his hair being dotted in ice like that, she found the courage to say something she'd wanted to say to him for a long time.

"Before you go, may I ask you something?"

"Of course."

"When we met, you told me a story about someone called the Mountain Queen. And her king. A man who the people of the country called Steep believe still lives, and will return to identify their next queen."

"I did."

Shean gazed into Roque's storm-cloud eyes. "Are you that king?"

Roque smiled, and for a moment Shean thought for sure he would confirm her guess. But all he said was, "I'm glad I met you, Shean. It takes a burden from my mind, knowing you're here in One."

Then he turned and walked away, stepping off the path and into the forest called Deep. Shean watched him go, biting back a shout of protest at his evasion, and then hesitating as a desire struck her. A silly, wonderful desire.

A desire she'd regret allowing to go unfulfilled.

"Roque! Wait!"

He paused, turning back to her. Before she could change her mind, she dropped Lintok's reins, strode up to him, grabbed him by the sides of the neck, and kissed him.

Shean had kissed, and been kissed, by plenty of people. Silly people at silly feast parties, even sillier people at the wild, sensory-overwhelming festivals of Pearl, lips and teeth finding hers amidst confusions of paper streamers and pearl beads thrown from high windows, showers of decadence falling on their heads to mark the arrival of each new year, season, wedding, the anniversary of the First Dollmaker's first victory over the Shod, and so many other things. Sometimes she saw the faces of the people she kissed. Sometimes she saw the masks they wore, barriers removed in her search for willing mouths. And sometimes she saw nothing at all.

This was the first time she'd ever wanted to see who she kissed. The first time she'd ever *wanted* to kiss someone, for that matter—

not because all those around her were kissing or because she was bored, but because she felt Roque slipping, receding like a tide. In moments he'd be gone. And before that she wanted to taste him.

He tasted of travel. Of dirt and leaves and rain, his skin giving off the fragrance of a map held to her nose, musty and aged and covered in ink that illustrated entire dimensions beyond her reach. When she stepped back his eyes were wide, his lips remaining parted for a moment before he closed them.

Shean felt a spike of satisfaction. So Roque *could* be surprised.

She smiled. "A blessing for your journey," she said. Then, before he could run away, she placed her hands on either side of his face, standing on tiptoe to kiss his forehead and whispering. "May you find what you're searching for."

Recovering, Roque took her hands, lowering and holding them in his own. For one anxious, almost-regretful moment, she worried he was angry with her. Then he leaned forward to kiss her forehead, returning her smile.

"And may you find what you desire as well," he said.

"Visit me," Shean said. Something she'd meant to say as a question, but which came out as a demand. A plea.

Roque's smile softened, and, for the first time, he looked at Shean the way she wished he would—with eyes warm with affection.

"I will."

Then he let go of Shean and was gone, faded into the trees before she could take another breath. She stood for a moment and listened to his absence, filled by birdsong and leaves rustling and the trickle of a stream winding through the loam nearby.

A temporary quiet. One she knew would, someday, be broken by his voice once more.

Smiling to herself, Shean turned, returning to the road. Lintok was waiting for her, grazing on bits of grass poking from between the cobbles. He looked up at her arrival, bumping her shoulder with his muzzle in that familiar, affectionate way of his. Patting his neck, she pulled herself into his saddle. Her leg pressed against one of her saddle bags, and she could feel the shape of the doll within the satchel. Comforted by that, she picked up Lintok's reins.

"All right," Shean said, taking a deep breath and releasing it in a rush. She widened her smile, flicking the reins against Lintok's neck. "Let's go."

SHEAN'S FIST LINGERED IN LICENSOR MATON'S FACE IN THE FORM OF A NOW-crooked nose. Aside from filling Shean with guilt, the change to the licensor's features made her look worn. And tired.

"Shean of Pearl," Maton said, sounding just as she looked. They sat across from one another in the audience room of the licensor's house, the space hastily lit by two glow lanterns when Shean had, unexpected and unannounced, arrived on the doorstep. She counted herself lucky that Maton hadn't turned her away, though that might've been preferable to the way the licensor was looking at her—with obvious, curt dislike.

"Have you come to apologize for your actions?" Maton asked.

Shean bowed, pressing her forehead to the ground.

"Yes. Please forgive me."

Maton was quiet. Shean's back started to ache. She didn't dare lift herself from her bow, though, remaining bent low as she awaited forgiveness. Or a lack thereof.

"First you reject the license I give you," Maton said, voice hard. "Then you go off and illegally challenge a licensed guard for her employment. You allow an entire village to be overrun with Shod, jeopardizing a priceless field of silk spiders in the process. The damage you've caused is more than substantial, and the fact that no human life was lost is nothing short of *miraculous*."

Shean hunched forward, wincing. She was surprised, but knew she shouldn't be—of course word of her escapades had preceded her to the village called Twig, home of the Licensing Guild. The trip from Web to Twig was over three weeks long, during which the autumn caravans would've come and gone from Web. By now, the whole country probably knew of what'd happened. Including Nock.

Shean decided not to think about that.

"I'm aware of my mistakes," she said instead. "I apologize."

"Apologize," Maton echoed, slowly, as if she were tasting the word, rolling it around in her mouth to savor its flavor before swallowing. She sighed. "Lift your head, Shean."

With relief Shean obeyed, wincing as she unfolded her travel-sore body and straightened, resting her hands in her lap and meeting Maton's gaze. The licensor's eyes were thoughtful, her head cocked as she contemplated Shean.

"What you've done is unacceptable."

"Yes."

"Apprentices have done far less and been denied a license for life."

"I understand."

Maton folded her arms. "What makes *you* different?"

Shean felt the weight of Roque's pendant around her neck. She could feel his words, his secrets, budding at the back of her throat, pushing forward as a means of salvation, a way to show Maton that she, Shean, was special. That she, Shean, was an exception.

She ignored such thoughts. They were cowardly. And stupid.

Instead she rested her hand on the saddlebag set on the ground beside her and said, "I'm not different."

Maton's eyebrows raised. "Oh?"

Shean lowered her head, gaze fixing on the ground. "I've broken many of the First Dollmaker's edicts, and I'm unfit to hold a license."

"If you know that, why have you come to me?"

"Because you deserve an apology. And because I have a request."

"What request?" Maton said, voice suspicious.

Shean bowed again, prostrating herself and speaking clearly, lest her voice be muffled by the floor. "If I can't work as a dollmaker, please allow me a provisional license!"

"Provisional license?" Maton echoed, voice surprised. "To what end?"

Shean squeezed her eyes shut, desperation and fear of denial strangling her as she said, "I wish to continue making dolls for my own use and purpose. I swear not to attempt to make a profit from my work, either as works of art or guards."

Quiet, long and thoughtful. Then a command:

"Sit up."

Shean obeyed. Maton pulled at the collar of her tunic, rubbing at the gold embroidery in the red fabric, vibrant colors that made the pallor of her face even worse.

"You seem . . . different," Maton said after a moment. "Older than I remember."

Shean wasn't sure if that was meant as a compliment or not. She decided to stay silent.

Maton dropped her hand from her collar, fingers lacing in her lap. "Yesterday I received an interesting letter. It was from one Master Ikiisa, who, if I recall correctly, is a war hero of the Red

Tide, as well as the dollmaker of Web you recently attempted to displace. It arrived with a most . . . peculiar doll. Do you know what it said?"

Shean shook her head, surprised—she hadn't told anyone in Web that she meant to come to Twig. Not even Roque.

"That you are the most skilled dollmaker Master Ikiisa has ever met. And that it would be a great loss to the entire country if you were to be denied a license."

Shean smiled.

"I'm not sure I agree," Maton said, voice dry. "But it says something, that the dollmaker of the village you destroyed is willing to vouch for you." Maton rested her hands on her knees, eyes narrowing. She stared at Shean for long, uncomfortable moments. "Tell me, Shean. If I were to give you a license, what would you do with it?"

The question gave Shean a spark of hope. She didn't hesitate to answer.

"As a dollmaker, I wish to make dolls and employ them in the best way they can be employed, to be the most helpful to the world as they can be. I want to use them to help those who need help."

"And who might those people be?"

"Everyone."

Maton's lips quirked. "Aren't we ambitious. What makes you think your influence can reach so far?"

Shean took a steadying breath; here came the part she was most apprehensive about. The part where she uttered truth that either made her sound enlightened or insane. Drawing her shoulders back and leveling her gaze with Maton's, she folded her hands in her lap to hide their trembling and spoke in a steady voice. "Because I've learned things about the Shod. Things that change everything we thought we knew about dollmaking."

Maton eyed her, a wary glint in her eyes. But, also, curiosity.

"What sort of things?" she asked, voice level.

Shean explained. About the nature of the Shod, the truth behind the graveyards of dollmakers. About the second, powerful use for the Breath Mark.

When she finished, all traces of eagerness had faded from Maton, leaving her pale and tight-lipped. Her shoulders were so stiff they looked about to snap. "What you say has serious implications," she said.

"I know," Shean said. "But it's true."

"Dollmaker Ikiisa can confirm that?"

"Yes."

Maton let out a noise, not really a sigh, but not really a whine, either. A fraying, creaking noise, like strained rope. She closed her eyes, pinching the bridge of her nose and shaking her head. Slowly. "If what you say is true, if the Breath Mark can be used in such a way . . ." Maton lowered her hand, forcing her eyes open with clear effort and giving Shean an apprehensive look. "I *will* have to confirm your words with Ikiisa. And speak to the guild masters." She grimaced. "Assuming I can convince them that what I say is not some ill-advised prank."

"You believe me?" Shean said, voice tentative, edged in the surprised amazement of being taken seriously.

Maton stared at her, long and hard, brow furrowed. "In defiance of the entirety of my sense of logic and wisdom, yes, Shean of Pearl. I do."

"Why?" Shean asked, blurting the question in a wave of relief and wonder.

Maton's grimace deepened. "Because you are not the first to ascertain the true nature of the Shod."

"I'm not?" Shean said, at first shocked, then distracted by the thought of what Roque had said to her before, about the First Dollmaker's edicts seeming to mask the true nature of the Shod. Shean's chest tightened, and she wasn't sure what she felt (disbelief, pain, burning inquisitiveness?) at the idea that he was correct.

The fact that the Shod were the dolls of the dead was known . . . by whom? And how many? Did Nock know? Ikiisa? Ilo or Lenna or even Dola?

"Who else—?" Shean started.

Maton cut her off with a shake of the head, lifting a hand in a halting gesture. "It's not something I'm allowed to discuss with you. Not like this. I *can* tell you that you're the first dollmaker foolhardy enough to attempt to write a Breath Mark on a Shod."

Shean shook her head, ignoring the slight note of praise in Maton's voice. "But if it's known that the Shod are dolls, why are they buried with us? Why aren't the dolls of dead dollmakers destroyed before they become Shod?"

Maton gave her a withering look, all admiration fading from her eyes. "Do you honestly believe that hasn't been tried? That no other dollmaker has ever thought to destroy the creations of their dead peers before the transformation?"

Shean's face grew hot, but she didn't back down, hands curling on her lap as she held Maton's chastising gaze. "You'd have me believe dolls can't be prevented from becoming Shod, even if you destroy them? Even if you burn them to ashes?"

Maton shuddered, closing her eyes. "Have you ever heard of the Ash Shod?"

A prickle swept through Shean—of course she had. Who *hadn't* heard of the Shod that rose to prominence some decades ago, wraithlike terrors that swept into cities and towns like buzzing, rattling clouds of smoke and lashing wind, devastating in their speed and strength, almost impossible for even dolls to kill? In truth, Shean had always thought such Shod mythical, stories made up to scare those who heard them.

Now, looking at Maton's drawn expression, Shean realized the stories were true. And, with a shiver, she understood why.

"Fine," she said, wetting her lips, which felt very dry. "You can't stop dolls from becoming Shod. And we need dolls to fight the Shod, so we can't stop making them. But even if destroying dolls doesn't prevent them from being reborn as Shod, why aren't guard dolls posted around dollmaker graveyards? Why do we allow the Shod to emerge and move beyond the bounds of their birthplaces?"

"Because the Shod are at their most aggressive, and dangerous, when they first emerge," Maton said, voice tired. "Newborn Shod are all but undefeatable; they only weaken, slightly, when they have to travel to find prey. Which is why dollmaker graveyards are, traditionally, arranged far from any large cities or towns." Maton eyed Shean, brow bunching. "Surely you noticed the Shod you faced in the village called Web were far stronger than any Shod that attack closer to the coastline."

Shean *hadn't* noticed that. How could she, when the Shod of Web were the first Shod, outside of the Red Tide, she'd ever faced? The first Shod she'd ever attempted to fight?

"How do you know all this?" Shean asked, a deep, consuming hunger stretching wide inside of her, ravenous and greedy for further revelation. More knowledge. More truth. "Who's studied the Shod enough to tell you these things?"

"As I've said, I'm not at liberty to discuss such matters," Maton said, voice crisp and final. "All that aside," she said, changing the subject before Shean could protest, "given what you achieved in

Web, and despite the trouble you've caused, I admit that I see potential in your dolls. And their maker. Do you have a doll with you?"

Shean had come into this meeting hoping for that question; a reality that made her push aside the appetite she felt at hearing so many previously unknown details about Shod and what dollmaking society knew about them—such were realities to be mulled over (thoroughly, obsessively, frantically) at a later time. For now, she focused on the task at hand and sat up straighter. "Yes."

"May I see it?"

Shean nodded, turning to open the saddlebag at her side. Once she unlaced the pack's straps, one of the last dolls she'd made in Web emerged, stepping out to stand beside her.

With this doll, Shean had decided *not* to make something as realistic as possible, nor as refined as her previous work. Rather, she'd aimed to create something ethereal, something as delicate as she desired, with no regard for whether or not the result was strong enough to face the Shod. By Shean's estimations, she'd succeeded; only about a foot tall, the doll was studded with the glass of broken windows, naked but for leaves painted over a sloped chest and long legs, with a diadem of jewel beads ringing a bald head. The Breath Mark was painted on the back of one long, pointed ear, the other decorated in lines of ink that resembled wafting smoke. Carved from the wood of what'd remained of Web's houses, this was a doll lovely and eldritch, a far cry from Silver's humanlike beauty.

She was the most fragile doll Shean had ever created. And the loveliest.

Maton was impressed. She tried not to show it, but the emotion was obvious on her face, the way she pursed her lips against a smile. "Does it have a name?" she asked.

"Alloy," Shean said. Alloy looked up at her as she spoke, face stony except for one eye, which winked. Shean returned the wink, smiling. "Her name is Alloy."

"Very well," Maton said. She shifted, pulling her branding pipes from a pocket. She smiled, the expression softening her face. A little. "For your discovery concerning the Breath Mark in the village called Web, I will re-grant you your license, Shean of Pearl. You'll make a wonderful artisan."

"No," Shean said.

Maton's smile vanished. "No?"

Shean flinched at the warning packed into that single word. She swallowed, ducking her head. "Forgive me. That was rude."

"You have an objection. *Again*." Maton's voice had a suffering edge. "What is it?"

"I appreciate, and am flattered, that you're willing to forgive my mistakes and award me another license. But I don't wish to be an artisan."

"You *still* want to be a guard dollmaker?" Maton said, exasperated.

Shean shook her head. "No. I don't wish to be either an artisan *or* a guard dollmaker."

Then Shean hesitated. She hadn't planned on this—she'd meant to convince Maton to give her a provisional license and go on her way, to do and live as she wished without any more authorization than what a provisional license granted her. Now that Maton was trying to fully license her, though—to say nothing of all they'd spoken of concerning the Shod—that didn't feel like it was enough. The licensor deserved some sort of explanation for why Shean was rejecting her for a second time. Some clarification concerning just what Shean had decided she wanted to do with her life.

"When I was in Web," Shean said, "I asked my dolls what they were made to do."

Maton's eyes widened, slightly. A flicker of surprise that was, quickly, masked. "Did you?" she asked, voice oddly careful. "And what did they say?"

"That they are neither guard dolls *or* pieces of art."

Maton lifted an eyebrow in a delicate, skeptical arch. She looked from Shean to Alloy, addressing the doll. "Is this true?"

Alloy nodded. Then she stifled a yawn behind a hand.

True shock crossed Maton's features—shock she failed to hide, the color draining from her face as she stared at Alloy for long, wide-eyed moments. When she finally turned back to Shean she shook her head, apparently at a loss for words until, finally, she managed to speak, voice strained. "This is . . . unheard of."

"I was confused, too, when I asked," Shean said. "At first."

Maton pulled a hand back through her hair, expression growing weary and making her look older than she'd appeared a heartbeat ago. "Suggesting you've come to some conclusion as to the purpose of your dolls yourself," she said, the statement punctuated with a tired sigh.

Shean shook her head. "Not *all* by myself. I had a talk with a . . . friend of mine back in Web. Something he said about his interactions with my dolls got me thinking." Shean turned to Alloy, who was inspecting her left foot at the moment, leg lifted and bent and heel clasped in a steady hand. "Alloy, are you meant to research the Shod?" Shean asked. "Is *that* what you're made for?"

Putting her foot down, Alloy gave a so-so gesture with her right hand. Then she shrugged. And, finally, nodded.

It was the same response Alloy had given Shean a few days ago, when she'd written the Breath Mark on the doll and brought her to life. That first time, Shean had laughed at the response, a short burst of mirth in response to both the confirmation and stubborn ambiguity of Alloy's reply. In the present she held back another chuckle, smiling instead and performing an exasperated, but affectionate, shake of her head. Turning back to Maton, Shean said, "Not exactly solid confirmation, but I think that response is enough to work with. For now."

Maton gazed at her for a moment, expression schooled into a subdued mask that was hard to read. Then, softly, she said, "What are you requesting, Shean?"

"That, as I asked, I be given a provisional license. That I be allowed to continue making my dolls with the intent of using them as research tools to further study the Shod in some way—if we can come to better understand the nature of the Shod, we can better understand a way to fight them. And *that's* what I want to use my dolls to do."

The words felt good. This was the first time Shean had verbally articulated her plans (vague and uncertain as they still were), and she straightened with each assertion, sitting tall as warmth spread from her chest to every inch of her. The soothing comfort of feeling that, finally, she had an idea of what she was meant to do.

Finally, she'd found the path she'd always been meant to find.

Maton's eyes narrowed, and Shean's tentative contentment shied back from the look, a creep of worry entering her. But all the licensor said was, "I see. An admirable goal."

The words weren't an outright refusal. Bolstered by that, Shean said, "Just think about the potential—with my training as a dollmaker, and with the help of my dolls, I could accomplish things no other dollmaker has! Not through fighting or art, but *learning*!" She leaned forward, caught in a rush of passion. Alloy mimicked her with a deadpan expression that made her miniature tilt peculiarly elegant. "When you think about it, *not* having dollmakers dedicated to researching the Shod is a missed opportunity—who knows the Shod better than those who create tools to fight them? Those who, even if they don't know it, are the actual *source* of the Shod? Dolls become Shod, and who knows dolls better than dollmakers? And yet, what dollmaker has ever thought to spend their lives studying the secrets of the Shod? Is there a single dollmaker who's *ever* dedicated *all* of themselves to research?"

Maton frowned. "Yes."

"Oh," Shean said, taken aback. "Who?"

"The First Dollmaker."

"Oh," Shean said again, suddenly afraid everything she'd just said was striking Maton as arrogant. Her face burned.

The licensor's frown deepened. But she didn't look angry. "That's truly what you wish to do as a dollmaker?" she asked. She glanced at Alloy. "Research? That's what you're made to do?"

Alloy repeated her so-so, shrug, nod combination. Shean nodded.

Maton shook her head, an edge of vexation entering her voice. "Even so, I fail to see how dolls can help *anyone* with research, given how little they can communicate with their makers—they can follow your orders, but there's a limit to how useful orders can be when it comes to gathering intelligence on the Shod."

"I believe my dolls are different in that regard as well," Shean said. "At least one of them has learned to write."

Maton laughed a short, barking laugh. "That's impossi—"

"And talk," Alloy said, voice surprisingly deep and carrying for someone who looked like her. She said the words with crisp clarity—no one would ever guess they were the only words she knew how to say.

For now.

Maton blanched, eyes bugging. Shean bit her tongue to stop a laugh as the licensor stared at Alloy, looked at Shean. Looked back at Alloy.

"How did you do that?" Maton asked.

"Do what?" Shean asked.

Maton shook her head. "What indeed." She pursed her lips, eyed Alloy with a mixture of caution, fascination, and unease. The doll was studying her fingers with a lazy interest that did a good job of making even Shean question if she'd really spoken.

Eventually Maton shook her head, sighing. "Fine. Fine! If I'm being honest, Shean of Pearl, I think I'd agree to anything at this point, if it meant being rid of you."

Shean smiled. "I understand."

Maton snorted. "I'm sure you do. There is, of course, no license for what you propose. The only option, really, is a provisional license. Which, as you've acknowledged, doesn't grant you the right to use your dolls for profit in any way." She folded her arms, fixing Shean in a stern gaze. "That said, there *is* a way for you to do as you wish *and* find a way to avoid destitution."

"Really?"

"Yes. By joining the Research Guild."

"The Research Guild?" Shean echoed, surprised. She frowned, recalling in a vivid flash the last time she'd seen researchers, that group of scholars back in the city called Ports who'd tailed her for a time, clearly intrigued by Silver. Embarrassment pricked her as she recalled how thoroughly she'd ignored and disdained those men and women, mentally sneering at anyone who chose to *study* dolls and the Shod, rather than *making* dolls to *fight* the Shod.

The irony of her thinking that way in the not-so-distant past wasn't lost on her.

"Has . . . Do dollmakers ever join that guild?" she asked, voice a little strained.

"No," Maton said. "But I doubt you'd be rejected if you requested consideration." The licensor sighed. "To be frank, the Research Guild has been petitioning the Licensing Guild for a dollmaker liaison for years. But the cost of giving them a guard dollmaker to work with is too high, and no artisan dollmaker has yet been convinced to dedicate their time—or even a *portion* of their time—to academics. You would be their first dollmaking member. They'd be grateful to have you and your dolls." Maton paused for a moment. Then, voice thoughtful, she said, "And, if your work with the Research Guild goes well enough, the Licensing Guild *might* consider the possibility of allowing you to head a new dollmaking school dedicated to research. Perhaps Master Nock would be willing to allow you to inherit his school, even, and rededicate it for that purpose."

A place in a guild that would support her efforts, the potential to, one day, take over her and Nock's beloved home and revitalize it, starting her own school dedicated to a whole new form of dollmaking . . .

"I . . . I can do that? Really?" Shean asked, voice close to breathless with longing, with the aching pleasure of realizing her new goals might, in fact, be realistic.

"Yes," Maton said, voice grim. Shean wondered if the tone was because the licensor was reluctant to grant a dollmaker to the Research Guild, or if she simply disliked the idea of doing Shean a favor. "You can."

Tears filled Shean's eyes, her next breath catching in a happy little gasp. "Thank you," she said.

Maton's expression softened. A little. "There is some paperwork that'll need to be filled out," she said. "But, in the meantime, I'll grant your provisional license—that'll give you access to sanctioned dollmaker records in any part of One, and permission to interview dollmakers who've had direct conflicts with the Shod." Maton's face, and tone, hardened again. "You are *not* to go Shod hunting; that is illegal, no matter what manner of dollmaker you are. Is that understood?"

"Yes," Shean said, wondering how fine a line there was between Shod hunting and Shod observation. She had a feeling she'd find out soon.

"Good," Maton said, lifting one of her branding pipes. From another pocket she produced a blank license card. She began the process of burning the proper seals and phrases into the card, speaking between puffs on her pipes.

"For the time being, return to Master Nock in the city called Pearl. I'll contact the Research Guild's leaders and tell them of your licensing, and of your desire to join them—they'll contact you directly from there. Once you're accepted into the Guild, feel free to tell them about your discovery concerning the Breath Mark—I'll warn them beforehand that their top Shod specialists will have something to discuss with you. Until then, you mustn't speak of what happened in Web, or about what you now know about the Shod, to anyone." Maton lifted her gaze from the license forming in her hands, fixing Shean in a stern, unforgiving stare. "Publicizing that information would undoubtedly cause a mass panic. So you *must* hold your silence. Is that understood?"

Shean nodded, feeling like her chest was about to burst, a part of her unable to believe this meeting had gone so well. That everything she now felt she was meant to do with her life was, possibly, in reach.

"Understood," she said. "I'll do what you say," she added, when Maton gave her another, pointed look.

"See that you do." Maton pulled the pipe from her mouth, shaking her head and heaving an exasperated sigh. "Things are so *simple* with most dollmakers. Artisan. Guard." She pressed the end of her brand into Shean's license, looking up through the resulting billow of smoke and sizzle of wood. "You're truly neither, are you?"

Alloy yawned, crossing her arms and leaning against Shean's knee, a bored expression on her beautiful face. Shean looked at her doll. Smiled.

"No," she said. "I'm not."

NOCK'S BREATH MISTED THE AIR AS HE OPENED THE DOOR TO HIS HOUSE, FACE searing in the cold of morning and his winter coat failing to shield him from a shiver as he gazed across his school. It was early enough that the city called Pearl had yet to officially awaken, the rush of the ocean nearby all he could hear as he faced a new day. Another, quiet, day.

He still wasn't used to the quiet. His school had been largely empty for years, true, but Shean had a way of filling spaces, of making even the most desolate of places feel bursting with life and sound and excitement—good or ill—when she was around. In her absence Nock's home had taken on a somberness he'd never experienced and didn't like. Even when he sighed against the stillness, it held, his quiet exhalation followed by the equally weak creak of the door closing behind him, his footsteps dull thumps along the porch and down onto the cobbles of the main courtyard.

Feeling achy from the cold, he crossed to the building that'd once served as his students' writing hall, where he now kept his records tracking where his dolls were employed, as well as his financial statements. He'd been putting off updating those archives for weeks, but with the first snow of winter due any day now, accounting season was on the horizon and a member of the Ledger Guild could show up on his doorstep at any moment. He couldn't put off getting his affairs for the year in order any longer.

He hadn't thought, had never imagined, Shean would still be gone by accounting season. He was starting to believe—starting to fear—that she was never coming back. As he climbed the stairs and approached the door of the writing hall, he slipped a hand into the pocket of his coat, fingers curling around the letter he'd received some time ago, from an acquaintance further up the far shore. A recounting of a story spreading out from the village called Web, the tale carried by the autumn caravans that'd performed their seasonal pass through the forest called Deep some weeks ago. An account of a violent Shod attack resulting in Web's near annihilation, the story detailing actions of a far shore dollmaker named Shean, who had, the rumors went, caused said attack.

Your Shean? his acquaintance had written at the bottom of the letter.

Nock sighed, pausing in front of the door of the writing hall and staring down for a moment.

His Shean. His lost, misguided Shean.

He didn't know if the story was true. He didn't know where Shean was now.

All Nock knew was that he wanted her to come home.

A tug on his leg drew his attention to the side, where a doll had appeared with uncanny silence. One of Shean's dolls, left behind and—if its extreme attentiveness to him over the last few months was anything to go by—ordered by its mistress to look after him.

Carved from a red wood that gave it an almost ruby appearance, the doll wore purple robes and stood a little over a foot tall, long blond hair tied into a fashionable chignon at the back of its head and eyes mosaicked together from pieces of moonstone, emerald, and onyx. Expressive eyes that gave Nock an expressive look as the doll tugged on his pants leg again, features imploring when the doll pointed at the door in front of them.

"You're right," Nock murmured, uncurling his hand from the letter in his pocket. "We should go inside."

The doll nodded and Nock slid the door open, allowing the doll to scramble inside ahead of him and pausing a moment to remove his shoes. A fire had already been lit in the writing hall, rosy warmth leaching the chill from his face as he closed the door and moved to the work desk he'd arranged for himself in one corner of the hall, close to the bookshelves lined against the walls. Sitting down on the kneeling cushion in front of the desk, he let Shean's doll take his coat from him, finding a writing pen and his ledger book set out and waiting.

Doing his best to put aside the near-constant worry he existed under these days, Nock began writing, asking Shean's doll to pull this and that record from the bookshelves as he went. He was about a third of the way through the work, enough time passing to make his hips and back start to feel sore from sitting, when he heard the clack of hooves outside. At the *shunk-thunk-shunk* he looked up and stood, a faint spark of hope rising in him, like it always did whenever he had a visitor these days. The blaze died quickly, though—that had to be the representative of the Ledger Guild he was expecting, come to give him a sour look when he begged an extension on reporting his records. A glower that would become all the darker when the time came for Nock to explain that not only was he late in his accountings this year, but he'd also misplaced his license, an identifier that was pivotal to the filing process.

Bracing himself for an unpleasant conversation, Nock took his coat from Shean's doll when it held the garment up to him, shrugging the clothing back on as he walked across the writing hall. Slipping on his shoes, he opened the door, a gust of wintry air bursting into his face, making his eyes water.

A great black elk stood in front of Nock, like an ink stain splashed across the cold grays of his school's courtyard. A woman wearing a thick travel coat and winter skirt was dismounting from its saddle, her long hair whipping in the wind and her booted feet thumping to the cobbles the moment Nock opened the door.

Letting go of Lintok, Shean looked at Nock. And immediately fell to her knees, hands flattening to the ground as she bowed, forehead pressed to her knuckles.

"I'm sorry!" she said, voice shattering the quiet that'd fallen over Nock's world, striking like a lightning-fringed thunderclap. "I've already been to the village called Twig, I've spoken to Maton—I apologized for my actions toward her. I've also apologized to the villagers of Web; I made dolls for them to compensate for the damage my idiocy and bullheadedness caused them and their village." She sat up enough to reach for one of the pockets of her jacket, head remaining bowed as she pulled something out—Nock's license, held toward him in a trembling hand. "I'm sorry for not only disobeying your request to go and speak to Ikiisa, but for tak—stealing this as well." Her shoulders hunched as she tipped forward even further, her whole body taut as a bowstring. "I'll face any punishment you see fit for me, Master Nock. Please forgive me!"

Nock felt several things, still standing in the doorway of the writing hall, staring at his final student as her words rang in his ears, the reality of her arrival taking a slow, sun-dawning moment to wash through him.

Relief. Anger. Curiosity and accusation and anxiety.

But, most of all, joy.

Nock stepped forward. Walked to Shean. Knees protesting, he crouched, taking her shoulder, his grip tight in the thick fabric of her coat. She straightened when he touched her, looking up. When their eyes met, he wrapped her in his arms, pulling her close.

"Welcome home," he said, voice cracking as the tears welling in his eyes began to fall, leaking down the lines of his face like the first rain after a long, blistering summer.

ACKNOWLEDGMENTS

For me, the hardest part of writing is figuring out where to start. So I'll just start.

One of the most astonishing things that has ever happened to me was finding publishing professionals who not only liked my writing but believed in it enough to want to publish it. My agent, Matt Bialer, and his assistant, Bailey Tamayo, were some of the first of these mythic individuals, and they have all my heartfelt gratitude for the continual, never-failing support, belief, and enthusiasm. My gratitude also to my editor, David Pomerico, who embraced *The Dollmakers* in all its strangeness with eagerness and affection, helping me polish it to a luster as brilliant as one might find in a jewel sewn on a certain decadent dress. I can't even begin to express how much that means to me.

Many thanks to the whole team at Harper Voyager. Without you, *The Dollmakers* would never have managed to make it here, into the hands of readers. Thank you, thank you, thank you—I'd go on, but doubling this book's page count with several hundred pages of "thank you" would just make your lives harder.

Ash Mackenzie illustrated the stunning cover, an honest-to-goodness dream come true—thank you, Ash, for bringing Shean, Ikiisa, and the dolls of Web to such vivid, atmospheric life. And much gratitude to Richard L. Aquan, who was the art director for the cover.

A special thank-you as well to Deandra Scicluna, who designed the Breath Mark and provided two absolutely gorgeous interior art pieces for the book (featured on the title page and right after these acknowledgments), and Conor Nolan, who illustrated Silver's sketches, bringing Shean's journey to further, delightful life.

My journey to this point has been a long, sometimes arduous, one, and I've been blessed to have many friends along the way to encourage, listen, and sometimes forcibly drag and/or carry me forward.

First off, thank you, Brie, for believing in me from the start, reading every crappy and hopefully-not-as-crappy piece of writing I've put in your hands and encouraging me forward all the way. Being a writer can be a lonely thing, but less so when you have a friend to tell you not to quit.

Thanks to Maia Christensen and Natalie Teela for the moral support and listening ears through the ups and downs of publishing, for the sympathy and encouragement and Ghibli/bread parties.

Huge, years-spanning thank-yous to my writing groups (past and present) for all the feedback, pep talks, and writerly debates over the years. To be more specific, nods of appreciation to Leah Welker, Michela Hunter, Adam McLain, Kiri Case, Jarom Harrison, Courtney Archer, Jeremiah Scanlan, Liz Blodgett, Mari Harrison, Bob Connick, Kellyn Neumann, Kathleen Dorsey Sanderson, Mem Grange, that one guy, Emily Shaw-Higham, Octavia Escamilla, Hayley Lazo, Lex Willhite, Michael Bateman, and Anna Earley.

Emily Sanderson, Maia Christensen, Forrest Burton, K. Bosgra, Jennifer Neal, and Joe Blodgett beta-read *The Dollmakers* for me, all of their feedback invaluable. And I want to give a special thanks and notice to Michael Bateman, who helped me correctly format *The Dollmakers* when it was my MFA thesis project—without that help I wouldn't have graduated.

And, speaking of my MFA, thank you to John Bennion, Chris Crowe, and Billy Hall for not only letting me write a fantasy novel as my thesis, but encouraging me to do so. Particular thanks to John and Chris for giving me feedback and advice on *The Dollmakers* and so, so many other projects over the years, for teaching wonderful classes I count myself lucky to have taken, and for helping me soldier on when the dread of potential failure crept up on me.

Thank you to Jeanne Cavelos for accepting me into the Odyssey Writing Workshop in 2019, and for all the mentorship, advice, and support offered both during the workshop and in the years since. Thanks as well to my Odyssey cohort—I am immeasurably grateful to have met you all, and there's no doubt in my mind that *The Dollmakers* wouldn't exist without that summer we spent together.

Thank you to my coworkers for the moral and emotional support; I'd list you all by name, but we are now legion enough to make that impractical. Just know you're the best Dougs I could ever ask to know, and I'm grateful to count myself among your ranks. Special thanks to Octavia Escamilla, Katy W. Ives, Kara Stewart, you-know-who-you-are, Jeremy Palmer, Kellyn Neumann, Taylor Hatch, and Makena. Thank you all for cheering me on.

As a college student, I was frantic. And at times neurotic; I was determined beyond a sense of reason to publish, to be an author, to have the accolade of a physical book in my hands that I had written. I had many friends and professors who helped me stay in one piece through all of this—I've mentioned some already. But I've yet to properly thank one person who indulged my writing madness with infinite patience, who was always there to give me an encouraging word when I was nearing despair, who answered every question I threw at him (often many times over), and who paved the way for me to spend time writing even after graduation came and the "real world" set in around me—my mentor and friend, Brandon Sanderson. Thank you, Brandon. For everything you've taught me, for reminding me to be optimistic as well as gracious and kind, and for always believing in me. Often when I don't believe in myself.

Isaac Stewart drew the map for this book. That astonishing beauty is just the tip of the iceberg of how much he's done for me as I've worked toward publication—thank you, Isaac, for listening to me worry and brainstorm and wonder, for offering sound advice that has more than once saved me from spiraling into dark, possibly bottomless, holes of fretfulness and overblown fears. Thank you for talking about art with me, and sharing your own words and stories with me. Thank you, too, for reminding me to hope.

As mentioned in the dedication to this book, my parents never once told me I couldn't be a writer, or to think of something more "practical" to aim toward when considering my future. I was raised to believe I could do anything I set my mind to, even if that "doing" included perceived failures and the discovery that I do not, in fact, possess every talent known to mankind. "Doing" doesn't always mean succeeding. But the only true failure is never trying in the first place.

Thank you, Mom and Dad, for teaching me that. I can scarcely imagine what my life would look like if you never had. And thank you to my siblings, Ben and Lauren, for supporting me, too.

Lastly, thank you for reading this book. Whatever dreams you have, whatever you're fighting for or toward or away from, don't give up. Remember: it's only when we stop trying that we fail.

ABOUT THE AUTHOR

Lynn Buchanan is a fantasy writer based in the foothills of some impressive, chilly mountains in Utah. She's a 2019 graduate of the Odyssey Writing Workshop and holds an MFA in fiction from Brigham Young University, where she taught creative writing. When she isn't writing about monster-fighting dolls, moody painters, and mummified arms used as dancing props, she enjoys playing the oboe, buying houseplants, and watching Ghibli films.